What readers are say...
original

The 50...

'A highly original take on the serial killer novel . . . Tightly wound, with electrifying pace and fantastically written characters . . . Throwing in enough twists and turns to leave you off-kilter throughout'   Luca Veste

'Thrilling, compulsive and difficult to put down . . . You should not presume to think you know what is going on until you have read to the very last page'   *Guardian*

'Mosby has packed a complex, sometimes bewildering plot with brilliant ideas. His book is fiercely original, truly intriguing. This is speculative fiction at its reckless best'   *Literary Review*

'Mosby writes with confidence and originality, and displays an impressive feel for horror'   *The Times*

'A terrific thriller that is cerebral, pacy, intelligent and compelling'   *Huddersfield Daily Examiner*

'Mosby steers clear of genre formulae in this flawless thriller'   *London Lite*

'It's been a long time since a book gave me actual chills . . . Loved it from start to finish'

'Within 24 hours I had read the complete book, it kept me hooked'

Steve Mosby was born in Leeds in 1976. He studied Philosophy at Leeds University, worked in the Sociology department there, and now writes full time. He is the author of ten psychological thrillers which have been widely translated. In 2012, he won the CWA Dagger in the Library for his body of work, and his novel *Black Flowers* was shortlisted for the Theakston Old Peculier Crime Novel of the Year. He lives in Leeds with his wife and son.

www.theleftroom.co.uk
🐦 @stevemosby
🆕 /theleftroom

Also by Steve Mosby

You Can Run
I Know Who Did It
The Nightmare Place
Dark Room
Black Flowers
Still Bleeding
Cry For Help
The 50/50 Killer
The Cutting Crew
The Third Person

THE 50/50 KILLER

STEVE MOSBY

ORION

First published in Great Britain in 2007 by Orion
This paperback edition published in 2019 by Orion Books,
Carmelite House, 50 Victoria Embankment
London EC4Y 0DZ

An Hachette UK company

1 3 5 7 9 10 8 6 4 2

A CIP catalogue record for this book
is available from the British Library.

ISBN 978 1 4091 8873 5

Typeset by Deltatype Ltd, Birkenhead, Merseyside

Printed in Great Britain by CPI Group (UK) Ltd
Croydon, CR0 4YY

www.orionbooks.co.uk

For Lynn.

ACKNOWLEDGEMENTS

Thanks, as always, go to my agent, Carolyn Whitaker, and all the fine people at Orion who have helped with this book and the others, especially Jon Wood and Genevieve Pegg.

In addition, a few other people have contributed greatly, and so huge thanks are due to James Kennedy, for permission to use his poem, and Gary Li, for helpful advice along the way.

More personal thanks for general support and friendship go to: the writers John Connor and Simon Logan; J and Ang, Neil and Helen, Keleigh and Rich, Ben and Megan, Till and Bex, Cass and Mark, Gillian and Roger, Katrina, Emma Lindley, Marie, Debbie, Sarah, Nic, Jodie, Emma and Zoe, Jess, Carolyn, Julie, Louise, Beccy Ship and Paula, Liz and Ben, Colin, Fiona and everyone else in the Sociology Department at Leeds. And, as always, thanks to Mum, Dad, John and Roy.

Most of all, a massive thanks to Lynn: without you, it wouldn't have been possible. And so this story of dark love is dedicated to you – but with the plain, old-fashioned, soppy kind instead. Now and always.

PROLOGUE

'We don't have to go,' she said. 'Not if you don't want to.'

John Mercer stared at himself in the mirror and didn't reply. He just watched his wife's hands reaching round him, pulling his tie together. She was looking after him, as she always did. He lifted his chin a little to help her with the knot. She did it loose to begin with, then tightened it gently.

'People would understand.'

He wished that was true. On the surface, people might sympathise, but deep down they would recognise it for what it was: a dereliction of duty. He could easily imagine the talk in the canteen. People would remark upon his absence and say that he must be taking it hard, and what they'd really be thinking was that, no matter how he was feeling, he should have turned up for the funeral: bitten down and taken responsibility. It was the least he could do. And they'd be right. It would be unforgivable not to attend. But he had no idea how he was going to cope.

Eileen tucked the stray end of his tie between the buttons of his shirt. She smoothed it all down.

'We don't have to go, John.'

'You don't understand.'

The air in the bedroom appeared steely blue in the morning light. In the mirror, his skin was white and slack, his face almost lifeless. His body, well, she still had to stretch a little in order to reach round it, but he didn't feel as sturdy as he'd been once. Things were heavier to pick up than they should be. He got tired too quickly. Right now, his face was frozen somewhere between sadness and emptiness, his arms hanging there. Somewhere along the line, he'd grown old. It felt like a fairly recent development.

Eileen said, 'I do understand that you're not well.'

'I'm fine.'

But he wasn't. Whenever he thought about standing there in front of all those people, something began turning inside his heart, winding it

I

up, tighter and tighter. When he thought about it too much, it became hard to breathe.

Behind him, Eileen sighed. Then she hugged him round the top of his arms, her cheek against his back.

He felt relief. When she held him it allowed him to be simply this man, here and now, and to forget all the duties and responsibilities, all the things that weighed on him. He reached up slowly and covered one of her hands with his. She had small, warm hands.

They stood like that for a time, man and wife embracing, and he watched himself in the mirror. Despite the comforting pressure of her, he was still a statue, cast at a moment of blankness. He could see occasional flickers of emotion in his eyes, but it was like being in a plane, catching patches of ground through the cloud. There was nowhere safe for his mind to land. And yet you couldn't stay in the air for ever.

He gave Eileen's hand a final squeeze and then broke the embrace.

'I need to go and practise the tribute.'

Funerals were sad for a hundred reasons, but what struck him most was the number of people who attended. The dead would surely be surprised by how popular they had been and how many lives they'd touched without realising. Death had a way of summoning those with even a passing acquaintance with the deceased. People always came.

At police funerals, the effect was increased. Mercer looked around. Most of the department was here, including officers who had never worked with Andrew, probably never even known him. A feeling of responsibility and family had brought them. Each and every one of them had paid their respects to Andrew's family as they entered, then taken their seats on the right-hand side of the chapel, the side reserved for colleagues. Most were wearing their uniforms.

Mercer was sitting at the front on that side, the other members of his team beside him. Eileen was seated back on the left, and he kept glancing behind, hoping to catch sight of her. Every time he saw her, his panic eased a little and he settled back in the pew. Increasingly, he was desperate to be with her, but he belonged here, with Pete, Simon and Greg.

The four of them sat in silence; the coffin at the front of the chapel held the fifth. Mercer stared at it. Surely it was too small to contain the man who had worked for him – *with* him – for so many years? Death reduced everyone. It was another sadness of funerals. Even a religious ceremony, deep down, felt utterly godless.

He cocked his head slightly and listened to the hum of subdued conversations, the shuffling of bodies making their way to seats. Every now and then, there was a flurry of deep, echoing coughs, like birds caught in the rafters.

Eventually, the officiant walked across and stood at the lectern at the front of the chapel. Everyone fell silent. The man spoke through a microphone that amplified his voice, but only slightly.

'We are gathered here today to pay tribute to the life and memory of Andrew Dyson, who died on the fifteenth of December, taken from us in the course of his duty. Andrew did not have a firm religious belief, and so a religious funeral service was not thought to be appropriate. I am an officiant, accredited by the Humanist Association, present today to conduct a non-religious ceremony.'

He looked up towards the back of the chapel, his face bathed in amber light.

'The world is a community, and Andrew has been part of it with us,' he said. 'In everyday life, it is easy to forget. We conduct our own business. But in fact, we are all involved and affected by the life and death of each and every one of us.'

Mercer glanced across to the left and saw Andrew's wife. She was sitting between their two young daughters, holding their hands tightly, being strong for them. When he had gone to her with the news that her husband was dead, she had cried long and hard, but she had also been capable and practical. He sat with her all that evening, and that was when she'd asked him if he would read a tribute to Andrew today. Unable to refuse, he'd felt the panic stirring even then. He was now head of this side of the chapel, just as she was of hers, but he had none of her resolve.

'The comfort of having a friend or a valued colleague may be taken away – but not the comfort of having had one. In important ways we have lost what we had, but we must not only reflect upon losing our friends, but also appreciate the benefit of their having once been ours.'

The officiant looked down at his notes and then back up.

'The fact of death cannot be cancelled or reversed,' he said. 'But it can be transformed by our continuing and enduring love for those who have left us, and for each other.'

It was at that point that Mercer began to realise that something was wrong. It announced itself as a ringing in his ears, and as he stared at the officiant everything around the man became starry and distant. The hackles on his neck began to rise. His heartbeat was quickening.

Something was wrong.

'The final parting of death is bound to bring sorrow and shock,' the

3

man said. 'Those who feel deeply will necessarily grieve deeply. No religion or thought process ever practised can prevent this natural human reaction.'

Mercer turned in the pew and scanned the people crowded behind. A sea of bodies and heads. At the back of the chapel, the door was open. Even more people were standing beyond.

'But whatever relationships death breaks in upon, and whatever our personal beliefs, we can at least be certain that those we have lost are now at peace.'

He tried to pick out faces. Despite the sheer number of people, he couldn't see anybody he knew. A few of the heads were turning his way, though.

Eyes began to flick in his direction.

The officiant had fallen silent. Mercer looked back to see he had moved to one side of the lectern and was now looking down at him expectantly.

He had missed his cue. A few polite coughs echoed around the chapel as he stood and walked across. The papers he had prepared were already there. He picked them up, his hands trembling, and leaned towards the microphone.

'My name is John Mercer,' he said. 'I am saddened, but also honoured, to be speaking here today. Honoured to have known Andrew Dyson, both as a friend and as a colleague.'

He could hear himself saying the words, but they sounded as if they were coming from someone else. Cold sweat was beading all over him. Suddenly, he felt as thin and weak as an old man. His heartbeat seemed hard enough to break through his chest.

'I worked with – I had the pleasure of working with Andrew for ten years.'

He swallowed.

In the pew, the rest of his team were looking at him, concerned. Pete, his second-in-command, was frowning. He unfolded his arms, as though about to get up and come across to him. Mercer shook his head: *I'm okay.*

But he wasn't. It was hot in here and yet he was shivering. His legs—

'Throughout that time ...'

Eileen. He looked towards the back of the chapel, seeking her out. He knew roughly where she was, but now that he needed her he couldn't find where she was sitting.

4

As he glanced from face to face, the panic rising with each that wasn't hers, he carried on speaking.

'Throughout that time, he was one of the most professional officers I have ever worked with.'

Something caught his eye and then was gone. He searched for it.

'I hope it can bring some comfort to—'

But then he saw it again, and the words disappeared. One face among all the others, watching him inquisitively.

It was Robert Parker, wasn't it? Parker, who had murdered five young boys in a city south of here? The last time Mercer had seen him had been in a well-lit room. Parker, dressed in orange, had been lighting a cigarette awkwardly with his cuffed hands. Several months later, he had died at the hands of another inmate.

'Some comfort to Andrew's wife and children.'

He faltered.

It couldn't be Parker. But then he noticed the man sitting two rows behind him. Slicked-back hair on top of a round, childish face.

Sam Phillips. Mercer had consulted on that one, and had only ever seen photographs of the man himself. But he'd inspected the rusted-iron equipment Phillips had constructed in the room below his detached house. He couldn't be here, either. He was in prison, hundreds of miles away.

Parker and Phillips rose to their feet.

'No,' Mercer said.

Quickly, he looked around – here and there – and saw that more men were standing up in the crowd. His gaze moved to each in turn, his breath shortening with every familiar face.

Charlies Yi, who had broken into the home of three women and left their bodies chained to radiators.

Jacob Barrett, the quarry murderer.

'No.'

Craig Harris, who had taken whole families, one at a time.

And one final figure, standing alone at the back of the chapel. Mercer couldn't see him properly; he was covered in shadow. But he could tell the man's head was the wrong shape. There were horns, too ...

As one, the men began to make their way left and right, squeezing past people's knees, moving towards the central aisle. Each and every one of them was staring at him.

His heart dropped away inside. There was no tension any more; there was nothing. He didn't exist. All there was, all he could feel, was panic.

'No.'

Pete was there beside him. He put his hand on Mercer's arm—

'It's okay, John.'

—but Mercer twisted and threw it off, staring at him.

'Can't you see them?' He pointed down the aisle.

Pete was always a little hangdog, a little put-upon, but his face now was more full of sadness than Mercer had ever seen. He couldn't meet his boss's eyes, faced down instead, his jaw flexing at the corners.

'John.' He spoke quietly. 'Please come and sit down.'

'No, you don't understand.'

He looked down the aisle. The men were moving very slowly, like dead men would walk. All looking at him with empty eyes.

Pete put his hand on his arm again. 'John, it's me – it's Pete.'

'You don't understand.'

'I do.' Pete put his arm around him. 'I do understand.'

Mercer hesitated, lost for a moment, then hugged him, beginning to cry.

Pete held him and whispered, 'It's okay. Let's go.'

Pete led him down the aisle. Mercer tried to keep his eyes closed. When he opened them, even for a second, he saw pale faces close to his own, watching him pass. He allowed Pete to lead him, Greg and Simon falling in behind. Halfway down the aisle, he felt Eileen touch his arm on the other side. People moved out of the way for them.

And like that, huddled together for protection, they walked out into the light.

TWO YEARS LATER

PART ONE

One of the first things you learn is that an important element when beginning an investigation is to keep an open mind. And, to an extent, that's true.

For example, you should never assume anything when you arrive on a scene, no matter how obvious or clear-cut it may seem. Every unattended death should be considered (and investigated as) murder until it has been definitely established otherwise. Your first job is to assess the evidence available to you and make deductions purely on the basis of that. The facts must always determine the direction of the case, and you must allow them to lead you where they inevitably go.

That much is true; but, as any experienced officer will tell you, there is always room for instinct. As the years pass, you develop a finely tuned inner voice that you learn to listen to even when others cannot hear it. And, within reason, there is no harm in following this voice where it takes you.

From *Damage Done*, by John Mercer

People rarely go into their attics. Kevin Simpson was no different.

He'd been up once when he first moved in – put his head and shoulders through the dusty hole, shone a torch around, and had the usual notions of doing something with the space while knowing deep down that he never would. Then he'd retreated down the precarious ladder and largely forgotten about it.

If he'd gone up there today – four years after that brief initial exploration – he would have found the devil, crouching in the corner, bathed in grey-blue light.

The devil was almost entirely still, focused on the small monitor in front of it, listening to the feed from the surveillance equipment in the house below through an earpiece. Simpson wouldn't have been sure what he was seeing at first, and he would probably have thought that it wasn't real, that the devil was just an incongruous statue, squatting motionless on its haunches. As the light flickered across the implacable face, it might have looked a little like a dead man in a dark room with the television still on.

But Kevin Simpson, like most people, rarely went into the attic. The devil had spent days up there without being disturbed. It had slept directly over him, keeping its food in one bag, its waste in another. It had spied on him.

This day, it had spent its time watching and listening to the couple moving around the house below, unaware of its presence high above. The girl had arrived at quarter past nine in the morning. They'd drunk coffee and eaten together. They'd talked. The girl had eventually left at four fifteen.

Everything they said and did, the devil heard and saw.

When the girl had gone, it waited.

And waited.

Now, finally, it unfolded itself from the corner, the light off the monitor casting elongated spider shadows from its limbs. The most important items – the rope, the lighter fluid – were secreted downstairs in Simpson's spare room. But it took the hammer with it as it crawled nimbly along the beams to reach the trapdoor.

The latch and the mechanism on the steel steps had been oiled one day

10

while Simpson was at work. They opened without a sound, and a wedge of light from the hallway below appeared in the attic, illuminating the grey, curling cobwebs in the rafters overhead.

And the devil descended.

There wasn't a moment when Kevin Simpson woke up; his return to the world was more a gradual hardening of awareness. He kept his eyes shut throughout. It seemed sensible, although his thoughts weren't together enough for him to be sure why.

Even without his consent, the sensations around him grew stronger.

The wet slop of heat all over his body.

A dull pressure encasing him.

The chill of air on his face ... but he could also feel sweat beading on his forehead and the sides of his nose. The temperature: it was like being in the sauna at the Leisure Club.

Water was rushing and splashing. Hot, churning bubbles were bustling around his toes.

I'm in my bath.

Immediately, he hated himself: *if I don't think it, it won't be true.*

But there was no taking it back, and Kevin reluctantly became aware of other sensations. The world, though still out of sight, appeared around him. He could tell he was lying down, could tell he was naked and submerged in water. The hard porcelain at the back of his neck; the bath tight against his arms.

An awful, throbbing pain in his shoulder ...

That was when he remembered the intruder. There had been a man in his room, the man had attacked him, and—

Panic reared up and he tried to thrash, but there was rope binding his arms to his sides, and his feet were locked together, too. Water sloshed up his nose. He tried to cough but couldn't – Jesus, there was something over his mouth as well. The panic became a shrill ringing in his heart. Desperately, he blew out through his nose and then sucked air back in. Bitter, salty liquid in his mouth. He swallowed quickly, trying not to be sick.

'Keep calm, or you'll drown yourself.'

At that, Kevin held completely still. He kept his eyes closed, too.

A burglar.

If Kevin didn't think about how he'd been sitting there after she'd left, trying to write an email to her, he could convince himself that was it – he'd disturbed a burglar. Never mind that he'd turned round and seen the man standing in the doorway behind him, or that the man was wearing a devil mask and carrying a hammer. The man was only after money, and he had been forced to tie him up. Soon he would take Kevin's things and leave.

He heard a screech as the taps were turned off, then nothing but the hushed noise of the water in the pipes. It sounded as though the veins of the house were boiling behind the plaster.

'Open your eyes.'

He didn't want to, but did it anyway. The bathroom was filled with steam. He could see the greasy, wet sweep of it across the mirrors on the cabinet doors. It was on his forehead, too, trickling down his temples.

The man was sitting on the closed toilet beside the bath. He was wearing that same hideous mask: pink, rubbery skin; clumps of black hair stuck at the chin and tufting the head; horns made of what looked like old bones.

The devil. Kevin just stared at him.

'That's better,' the man said, nodding.

Kevin realised he was lying tied up in a bath of hot water, at the mercy of this terrible stranger. This stranger, wearing *that* mask.

A mistake, he thought. It has to be a mistake.

The man reached down between his feet and picked up a hammer. Kevin felt his panic growing stronger, but this time he kept as still as possible.

Don't drown.

'I'm sorry about this.' The man stared at the weapon curiously, as though he wasn't sure what damage could have been done by it. 'It's possible you'll come out of this alive, and if that's the case I'm sorry I had to hurt you. It was necessary.'

Possible. Necessary.

'Nod if you understand.'

Kevin nodded as best he could. A mistake, he kept repeating to himself. If the stranger would only remove the gag and let him speak, he'd be able to explain.

The man put the hammer down.

'I know who you were emailing,' he said. 'I've been watching you both for a long time.'

Oh, Jesus.

'And I've read all the other emails you've written to each other. I have all your passwords. I had keys cut from moulds I took of all your locks. See?'

The man held up an enormous bunch of keys and shook them. Kevin's eyes flicked from one to another, but they were flashing too quickly and he couldn't make out which of them might be his. Not all of them, certainly. It didn't matter. He nodded anyway.

The man put the keys on the floor.

'Sometimes I come into your house when you're not here. I go through your things. I read your letters. I sleep in your attic. I follow you to and from work.'

Not a mistake, then. Kevin stared at the man and thought back desperately, trying to remember seeing anything, anyone suspicious. There was nothing. You simply walked along, didn't you? Never paid much attention to the people around and about. A clever person could follow you easily.

'You've never seen me,' the man said. 'I'm very careful. But I've seen you. I've been watching you all day. Both of you.'

Kevin nodded carefully. Sweat ran down his forehead into his eye, and he blinked it away. The water lapped at the sides of the bath.

The man in the devil mask reached down to the floor and picked something else up. A red and yellow tin.

Lighter fluid.

Kevin's stomach went cold and dead and hard. He tried to recoil but couldn't move. Instead, he was aware that he had wet himself.

The stranger clasped his hands together, holding the tin between them. It was the kind you might squirt onto an outdoor barbecue to make the flames roar. The man was pointing it vaguely in Kevin's direction. He inclined his head and – despite the mask – somehow he looked thoughtful.

'We're going to play a game about love,' he said.

3 DECEMBER   **7.23 A.M.**
EIGHT MINUTES AFTER DAWN

It was enough.

Simpson's body was still twitching in the water, but he had ceased any kind of struggle. Through the smoke in the room, the devil could see that most of Simpson's hair was gone and that the skin on his sightless face had scorched and burst. He didn't appear able to breathe any more. If he wasn't dead yet, he would be soon. These things were always a matter of degree.

The devil turned off the digital recorder and checked the display.

Eight minutes and fifteen seconds of audio. It would need only a fraction of that.

The bathroom stank, and the devil was glad to move back out onto the landing and shut the door on the mess within. Overhead, the wires hung down from the smoke-detector it had broken before ending the game, so that the air would remain unalarmed by Simpson's passing.

There were a few more things to do before the devil could leave. On the few occasions it had left Simpson alone, it had removed all traces of its surveillance equipment from the house. That didn't really matter at this stage, of course, but the activity had helped to keep it occupied while it waited for Simpson to regain consciousness. It had also checked his computer for emails. It wondered what the girl who had been here yesterday was doing right now.

Sleeping, probably, oblivious of what she had done.

That wouldn't last.

There were still a couple of items to collect. It headed downstairs, putting the digital recorder in the pocket of the overalls as it went.

It would need the recording when it came time to make the phone call.

3 DECEMBER   **8.40 A.M.**
22 HOURS, 40 MINUTES UNTIL DAWN

Mark

Given how much I missed her, I guess it was strange I hardly ever dreamed about Lise. There had probably been only a handful of occasions in going on six months, and even then I didn't dream *about* her exactly. She was always conspicuous by her absence. Just as she was when I was awake.

The dream that morning was no different. I was sitting on the beach in my shorts, staring out towards the horizon. My skin was wet and peppered with sand, and I was shivering. The sea in front was calm and serene, the waves rolling slowly in, the water gently unravelling. Curls thinned out, stretching up the shore, before retreating with a quiet hiss. Above me, the sky was blue and blurry, whitening until it met the flat sea in the distance. A strange grammar of birds formed italic sentences against it.

That was all.

Harmless on the surface, but as I woke up it left me feeling crushed; there was a physical sensation of despair pressing down on me. For a moment, I didn't recognise the almost empty room around me. What ...? Then I remembered the move across country. The flat, the job. I began to rub the sleep from my face, and my hand came away sweaty.

Christ, Lise, I thought.

You pick your days to visit.

And then I paused, because something was wrong. It only took a second to place it. There was music playing in my new bedroom. That was wrong because I had dim memories of different music playing earlier on, before I'd drifted back into the dream. I rolled my head sideways and glanced at the radio alarm.

'Shit,' I said. It wasn't quite enough. 'And fuck.'

I should have been fresh out of the shower and powering up the coffee machine over an hour ago. I closed my eyes.

You really pick your days to visit.

A lesser man might have jumped up immediately, expanding on the whole 'shit and fuck' subject matter at a louder volume, but some things are more important than being late. And so, instead, I lay there for a few more seconds, breathing deeply and clinging to the dream as it faded from me. The heavy feeling of despair remained, and it wasn't great, but sometimes despair is better than nothing. Sometimes it's the right thing to feel.

You pick your days to visit, I thought.

But you're always welcome.

And then, finally, I scrambled out of bed and into the corridor, trying to remember where on earth the bathroom was in my new flat.

At nine thirty, exactly half an hour late for my first day, I drove into a car-park of crackling gravel and chain-link fences.

Weather-wise, it was a miserable, shitty morning – and therefore an appropriate backdrop for my current frustration. The sky was filled with dirty smears of cloud, like snow after a day of slushy footprints, and it couldn't decide whether to rain properly or not, so it just occasionally darkened and spat. The grass verges dotted around the car-park were churned to mud. On the way over here I'd listened to the local radio, and the weather forecaster had cheerily explained there was good news and bad news. The rain would stop by late morning. But he promised snow for later.

At the far end of the lot, the police reception building sat squat and

15

low. There was a network of buildings behind it, connected by beige concrete walkways, and what little glass there was reflected the dark sky and gave away nothing. A month ago, when I came for my interview, I'd thought that the department looked more of a place to commit a crime than report one. It was like an abandoned mental hospital.

I killed the car's engine, and the rain created a more intimate patter on the roof. It settled on the windscreen, gradually blurring the view.

Late on my first day. I couldn't have been any more unprofessional if I'd turned up in a fucking clown suit. My right index finger tapped absently on my left elbow for a moment, but there was nothing I could do, and so instead of dwelling, I gathered myself together, then got out and made my way across the tarmac towards the entrance.

The reception area was typical of its kind: black ceiling above, fuzzy carpet below, and pale breeze-block walls keeping order in between. There were pamphlets tacked to noticeboards – *Protect your bicycle!* – and a row of orange plastic seats in a small waiting area where nobody was waiting. From outside it looked like a mental hospital; from within, a leisure centre.

The reception desk was opposite the door. There were two reasonably attractive girls sitting behind it, and the one on the left smiled at me as I approached, so I smiled back. She had light brown hair tied back in a neat ponytail, and sparse makeup that she'd applied well. The other girl was busy on her headset, taking calls.

'Hi, there. I'm Detective Mark Nelson. I'm the new member of John Mercer's team.'

'Ah yes.'

She reached to one side and came back with a clipboard.

'Mercer's new lackey. We've been expecting you.'

'Traffic was bad,' I lied.

'I wouldn't worry.' She passed me the clipboard. 'You need to sign some things for me.'

My name was printed at various points on the sheet, and I worked my way down, putting my signature next to each. The girl studied me the whole time.

'This is your first assignment, isn't it?' she said.

I smiled without looking up. 'Word travels fast.'

'Are you surprised?'

'Not really, no.'

I genuinely wasn't, because there was bound to have been speculation about anyone John Mercer appointed to his team, never mind me. Partly

16

it was down to his status, which was as close to celebrity as a working cop generally got. Apart from being a well-known, well-respected police officer inside his regular working hours here, he was also sought after for lectures and talks, consultancies, articles, papers, even occasional television appearances.

More notoriously, he'd written a book about his experiences catching killers – but hadn't had the decency to retire first. Instead, he'd written about the overwork and stress that had led to a breakdown two years before. It was a brutally honest piece of writing, but it certainly hadn't won him any friends. And in the harsh world of police work, many said his breakdown hadn't done so, either. But Mercer wasn't one to care much for the opinions of others. Since returning to work a little under a year ago, he'd appointed a number of more, shall we say, seasoned officers – all of whom had failed to live up to his infamous standards.

When you considered all that, it was probably inevitable that anybody who got the job would be eyed with an odd mixture of extreme resentment and abject pity.

With me, I knew there'd be added interest. Both those emotions would be blown up a hundred times over. In terms of traditional experience, Mercer was taking a chance at entirely the other end of the spectrum with me: this was indeed my first assignment. All of which meant that, yes, I wasn't surprised the girl on reception had heard of me. In fact, she very probably knew more about me right now than I did.

'Your first post,' she said, shaking her head in mock sympathy, 'and you got Mercer. Some people are just born unlucky.'

'Ah, but this is what I wanted.'

'Well, give it a week.' She smiled, but I couldn't tell if she was joking. 'Anyway, look up there and say hello to the camera.'

There was a black ball hanging from the ceiling. I faced up, noting the red light on the side.

Flash.

Say hello to the camera.

That photograph shows me for what I was at the time: a man in his late twenties, of above-average height and with an athletic build reduced to slim by a new suit he isn't used to wearing. Brown hair, cut short and neat. Average looks, if we're honest. Not a great photograph, either, but cameras and I have never really got on. They generally seem to catch me halfway between two different expressions. In that picture, I look pretty confident and full of resolve, and yet you can tell there's a bit of nerves there. In person, one on one, I could hide it better. But that camera caught me out.

The file the photograph is attached to gives potted details of my history. My name, Mark Nelson. My age, twenty-eight. At that point, I had officially, if unsuccessfully, been a detective for half an hour.

My background. I was an interview man by trade – my area of expertise was talking to suspects, victims, witnesses, handling door-to-doors. Putting people at ease and picking apart the seams of their secrets. I completed a PhD in psychology before I joined the police, part of which had involved interviewing a handful of serial offenders. That had sparked an interest, and I guess I'd always thought I'd end up working in behavioural psychology. Like in the films. Only it didn't happen that way. Instead, undramatic as it might be, I discovered I had more of an aptitude for interviews – not something I'd imagined specialising in, but life throws you these curveballs and sometimes you catch them.

The file would tell you that I'd graduated from the academy five years ago and spent the intervening years as part of the grunt pool, pulled into service here and there by the detective teams who handle the cases. It's not great fun but it's what you do, and while that was going on I was also attending every relevant training course that came along, collecting whatever experience and minor positions of authority I could. Punching my clock, basically, but always with an eye on promotion. Eventually, anyway.

It was two months since I'd found out Mercer had a gap for a door-to-door man, and when I read the ad I'd thought, why not? What was there to lose? I could go for the interview, let my record speak for itself, argue my case as best I could in person. Aim for the stars, as they say, and settle for less.

Weird as it sounds, I didn't expect to get the job. And so when I received the appointment letter – a month ago – I'd literally jumped around our old flat like a kid. The application and interview had never quite left my mind, but even so, I'd been telling myself that there was no chance – and, obviously, that I didn't care anyway. But at that moment, equally obviously, I'd realised how much I did.

That evening, I'd sat down and reread Mercer's book from cover to cover, and the excitement had become slowly tainted by nerves and self-doubt. Mercer was a legend, after all; how was I going to measure up? More to the point, what if I didn't? In response, I'd remembered what Lise had always said about having more confidence in myself, about not worrying so much about life and simply going for it instead. I'd looked around that rattly apartment, the one in which, as in my occasional dreams, she was so conspicuous by her absence, and I'd managed to grow some determination from the seeds of our old conversations.

But still, given Mercer's reputation, it was only natural that a little of that fear had remained. When I look at that photograph now, I see a hint of it emerging from below the confidence and I can tell I was nervous about what my first day would bring.

And back then, I really had no idea.

Fifth office down the corridor, I stopped and checked the plaque. Then I took a deep breath and opened the door.

There was nobody there.

The room was silent apart from the whirring of computers on standby. Given the time, I suspected the team might be out, but even so, what an incredible first impression I'd made.

I blew out heavily.

Say sorry, and try not to make the same mistake again. That's that.

I closed the door and switched on the light. It hummed and flickered before coming on, and the resulting glow hardly seemed worth the effort. It was the kind of wan, sickly efficient light you'd find in any old office, although what lay below was hardly the grandest of assignments. Five old desks, covered with too much paper for any team of five people to process; a few monitors and bulky hard drives; tangles of wires; old files stacked beside weathered chairs.

There was a triangular silver nameplate on each desk, and I quickly found mine. It would have been better if it had been empty and clear, but of course it wasn't. Among the dust and paperclips, there were several crammed files that would take days to work through. There was also a pile of CDs wrapped in a rubber band with a Post-it note attached, marked for my attention. I picked it up and then put it down again. Ongoing files – cases heading for court. Jesus. The morning felt even more insurmountable than before. Weeks of playing catch-up would have to be crammed into hours.

I glared at all the paperwork for a moment, attempting to let it know that I was in charge and would unquestionably conquer it. It didn't look particularly intimidated.

One back from mine, I found Mercer's desk.

'Holy shit.'

I didn't know whether I was surprised or if, on some level, this was exactly what I'd been expecting, but whichever, there was literally no clear surface space to work on. The piles of paper that covered it didn't look as though any single sheet in them belonged with the next. I glanced down and saw similar stacks resting under the desk. The red indicator on the answerphone showed he had a full fifteen messages.

So this was my new boss: the famous Detective Sergeant John Mercer. His workspace was a jumble of either genius or madness. I couldn't tell which, but I had a feeling that if he was suddenly hit by a truck about fifty ongoing case files would probably need starting again from scratch. Nobody was going to inherit this and hope to make sense of it.

I looked at the wall behind the desk. There was a black-and-white photocopied picture tacked to it, showing Mercer and the mayor. He'd received a civic award earlier that year for services to the community. In the top corner, he'd written '*ha! ha! ha!*' in black biro, as though the award was more embarrassing than anything else. *See what I have to put up with?* But the picture was there on the wall, and the more I looked at it, the more I thought his expression was at odds with the sentiment scribbled at the top. He hadn't been back in work long at that point, if I remembered right, and there was something sad about him around the eyes and mouth. The mayor was putting a medal round his neck. To me, Mercer seemed worried that the weight of it might be too much for him to carry.

Obviously, I'd met him at the interview, and I remembered him as being more than slightly distracted. He'd been interested in the interviews I'd done up at the Niceday Institute – especially Jacob Barrett, one of the men he'd put away – but other than that he'd left most of the questions to his team.

I was still looking at the photograph, puzzling at the contrasts within it, when the phone on Mercer's desk started ringing. I stared down for a second, feeling strangely caught out.

Get yourself together, Mark, I thought, and I answered it on the third ring.

'Detective Sergeant Mercer's office. Mark Nelson speaking.'

'Hello, Detective Nelson.' The woman's voice was relaxed and warm, and she sounded slightly amused. 'I'm Eileen Mercer. I don't believe I've spoken to you before. You must be my husband's new servant?'

She didn't actually laugh, but accented the last word enough to let me know she wasn't serious.

I smiled. 'That's exactly what it says on my new card.'

This time she did laugh. 'I'll bet. Is my husband there?'

'No, I'm sorry, he's not.' I glanced around the office as though he might materialise. 'Nobody is.'

'Nobody at all?'

'Just me.'

'This is your first day, isn't it?'

'Yes.'

'I thought so. John told me about you. He said he was very impressed with your CV and he was looking forward to working with you.'

'He did?'

'Absolutely.' She didn't seem to realise she'd told me something astonishing, but added: 'I'll say that to you because I'm sure he won't. How are you finding it so far?'

'Not good.' I slid into Mercer's seat. 'I was late. To be honest, I don't even know where everyone is at the moment.'

'That was going to be my next question.'

'I'm sorry.'

'Oh no, no, don't be. Poor you. For what it's worth, I'm sure they'll understand. The roads are a nightmare at the moment. My husband got lost at the weekend, so don't let him give you any grief.'

'Okay.'

'You're new to the city, I'm guessing?'

'Yes,' I said. 'I moved over from the coast a couple of days ago. But I still can't believe I've turned up late.'

'Can I call you Mark?'

'Of course.'

'How old are you, Mark?'

'I'm twenty-eight.'

'So young. I tell you what, Mark. You sound very nice, and I know how intimidating my husband can seem – to other people, anyway. So what I suggest is this. If you do me a favour, I'll make sure John goes easy on you. He does listen to me.'

'That's nice of you,' I said. 'But I'll do the favour regardless.'

'Well, the favour's easy. I want you to tell my husband I phoned. And tell him: "Don't forget."'

'"Don't forget,"' I repeated.

'That's right. It won't please him much, I imagine. And don't ask him what it means.' Her voice dropped to a stage whisper. 'It'll just annoy him.'

'I think I can manage that.'

'That's good—'

Another shrill tone interrupted us. I swivelled on the chair and looked at my desk. My phone was flashing.

21

'Er …'

Eileen Mercer saved me any embarrassment. 'That'll be one of the gang, Mark. You have to go.'

'I hope so.'

'Remember the message and have a good day. I'm sure I'll talk to you again.'

'Okay. Take care.'

'You too.'

I hung up and scrambled over to my desk, thinking: Don't forget, don't forget. If I didn't remember to pass on the message, the sheer irony would kill me before Mercer did.

'Detective Nelson.'

'Mark? Pete.'

Pete Dwyer was Mercer's second-in-command. At the interview, it had been him who asked most of the questions, looking slightly baffled and annoyed by all the paperwork throughout. He was an amiable bear of a man, constantly either frowning or thinking about it, but he'd done his best to put me at ease, and I'd mentally thanked him for it.

'Hi Pete. I'm—'

'Don't worry about it. We need you out here in the field. You got a pen?'

'Uh-huh.'

He explained the situation briefly. We had a dead body out in the suburbs. Suspicious circumstances. Simon Duncan, who was the forensics expert on Mercer's team, was working with scene-of-crime officers right now, so official judgments were being reserved, but it was almost certainly a homicide. They needed me to get the door-to-doors started with the neighbours – probably about half an hour ago.

'Right,' I said, scribbling furiously. 'Where am I heading?'

3 DECEMBER   **10.10 A.M.**
21 HOURS, 10 MINUTES UNTIL DAWN

Eileen

After talking to Mark Nelson, Eileen found herself wandering through the house from room to room. It felt like she was waiting for something to happen, and was reluctant to do anything else until it had. In the meantime, she couldn't settle.

Which was strange. Her schedule was free for the day, and although her sister sometimes called round she never turned up unannounced. There were no pressing tasks, no appointments; her calendar was clear. But still, when she heard the knock at the door, the sudden, apparently unexpected noise seemed to resolve something.

It had been this way since before the weekend; she'd been suffering from a sense of unease ever since the dream on Friday night.

Eileen had gone over it in her head upon waking, and then talked about it with John a little later. The dream had been brief and uneventful, consisting of her walking around the house and noticing that things had changed and items were missing. In the way of dreams, her mind conjured up a flash of complicated back-story to explain it all, but all she remembered was that John had left her. It was his possessions that were gone. Books leaned at angles on the shelves, supporting each other. Pictures had been taken down from the walls, leaving pale stamps on the paint. Her clothes, hanging in their shared wardrobe, formed a multi-coloured barcode.

'I hope you're not planning on running off,' she'd told John over breakfast.

Her tone had made it clear she wasn't serious, but even so she'd been waiting for an answer. Eileen often talked about dreams when they bothered her. Sometimes she even made the contents up, so that she could discuss any issues they were having in a more circumspect way. John didn't know that, but they had been married for a long time, and he understood her well enough to know she was asking for reassurance, which he generally gave. After over thirty years together, it would have been odd if he couldn't read between her lines.

'I'm too old to run,' he'd said.

'Is that the only reason?'

He'd thought about it. 'Too tired, as well.'

'That's all right, then.'

But reading between the lines went both ways, and Eileen had noticed that his first response had been play, his second more considered. There were a hundred other reasons John would never leave her, of course, but he'd known she'd take those as givens. Instead, he'd raised something else. Too tired.

She'd watched him all weekend, thinking that tired didn't cover it. Tired was a problem that sleep could solve, whereas over the past few weeks John had looked as though he slept fine, but woke up every morning a little bit more depleted than the night before. Too lost was a more accurate reason. In order to run away, after all, you needed a direction to start off in.

And so, after talking to Nelson, Eileen wandered the house, wondering if it was this new detective's appointment that was concerning her husband. 'He reminds me of me,' John had said, sounding unsure whether that was a good or a bad thing. Maybe it was that, playing on his mind. Perhaps it was just replacing Andrew. Or it could be nothing in particular. The last two years had been full of good and bad times, and she hadn't been able to pin them all down. Sometimes, he'd barely had the energy to get out of bed; other times, he'd been the same as before his breakdown. But whatever it was now, it was *something*, and she wished he would *talk* to her about it, the way—

Knock, knock, knock, knock, knock.

She stopped. There was somebody at the side door, at the extension she reserved for her clients. She didn't need to check her diary to know she hadn't forgotten an appointment. It was Thursday, a day off. Her private working week had finished yesterday.

'Just a moment.'

Eileen gave herself a cursory glance in the glass front of one of the kitchen cabinets. She had a tendency to slob a bit when there was nobody to see, and while she wasn't vain it was important that her clients were met with a professional façade. Because of the nature of counselling, it was necessary that personal information flowed only one way. She looked slightly messy – jeans and a blouse – but her hair was okay. No face mask, at least.

Knock, knock, knock.

'I *said*, just a moment.'

But the knocking continued regardless. Eileen made her way through, halfway between concerned and annoyed. Reaching the door, she buried the second emotion as deeply as she could. Even more than a face mask, obvious irritation had no business being seen on a counsellor.

Before she opened up, she checked through the fish-eye lens.

James Reardon was on her doorstep.

He had one hand in his pocket, and was jigging impatiently on the spot: looking down the drive anxiously, as though watching for someone.

Eileen reached out to unhook the security chain, but then hesitated. She had been counselling Reardon on and off for over a year now, and he was one of her few private clients with a criminal record and a propensity for violence. In her clinical work she was accustomed to that, but by necessity that work was always done in safer surroundings. None of those people would she ever have allowed into her home, even if any of them had been free to visit.

In James Reardon's case, however, she knew that both problems were largely down to his domestic situation and alcohol. He had always been quiet, polite and respectful in their sessions. Reardon was a confused and angry young man, but he was also intelligent and seemed genuinely interested in the process: determined to engage. She had often seen him agitated by what they talked about and had never felt in any danger. But she'd never seen him like this.

Eileen opened the door, but kept the chain on. Reardon's attention snapped to where she was standing.

'Eileen.'

'Hello, James,' she said carefully. 'I'm sorry, I don't think we have an appointment today.'

'I know. I'm sorry.' He looked away again, and then back to her. His face was scared, plaintive. 'I just wanted to tell you that I'm sorry.'

'Sorry for what, James?'

'I've tried my best, I really have. Over the last year, it's been so hard.'

'I know it has.'

'But you've really helped me, honestly. You've been the only person who's been there for me.'

She kept her expression neutral, but what he said was twisting their relationship a little. Under normal circumstances, she might have tactfully corrected him. He paid her to be there for him, but it was a specific type of support, involving nothing more difficult than listening. She allowed him the space to understand the fragments of his life, one small piece at a time. She certainly wasn't his friend.

'You've been helping yourself,' Eileen told him.

He shook his head: that doesn't matter.

'I just want you to know that I *have* tried hard. I don't want you to think I've let you down.'

Eileen frowned. 'James, what's wrong?'

'You've got to remember, whatever I end up doing, it's all for Karli.'

That set alarm bells ringing. Karli, Reardon's baby daughter, had been the product of a brief reconciliation with his ex-wife, Amanda. As Eileen understood it, that relationship had been volatile from the start, but their two children had created a knot that stopped it unravelling smoothly. Even now, Reardon maintained that Amanda was an unsuitable mother, but the court had sided with her, ultimately granting a restraining order against James and refusing him access to his children.

It wasn't Eileen's place to be judgmental about this. Her job demanded that she remain impartial, allowing him to come to his own conclusions about his behaviour. James was undoubtedly a danger to his ex-wife, but it had also been clear from the beginning that he cared deeply for his children. In seeking a counsellor in the first place, his motivation had been to acquire a level of understanding and control that might allow him to return as a presence in their lives.

His success at session level varied immensely. Sometimes he seemed consumed by hate and rage. On other occasions he was introspective and seemed to be doing well. Overall, Eileen thought, he'd been making progress. And now this.

'James, what have you done?'

'Whatever you hear about me, I'm doing it for her.'

He looked at her, pleading, and then down the drive again.

Making a decision, Eileen unhooked the security chain.

'Why don't you come in for a minute?' she said. 'We can talk about this.'

He was already backing down the step, shaking his head. 'No, I shouldn't have come.'

She stepped outside. 'But you're here now. Why don't you come inside?'

'I'm sorry.'

'James—'

But he turned and ran. She stepped down onto the drive and called after him again, but he ignored her, reaching the street and disappearing. Eileen looked down at her feet. Slippers. She couldn't have caught up with him in running shoes.

Whatever you hear about me, I'm doing it for her.

The cold rain started tapping on her blouse. She shivered, rubbing her arms, but stayed outside for a moment, staring down the empty drive.

James, she thought, *what have you done?*

3 DECEMBER   **10.20 A.M.**
21 HOURS UNTIL DAWN

Mark

Disobeying a number of somewhat minor traffic laws, I made the crime scene in good time. The street turned out to be a cul-de-sac, ending fifty metres from the main road in a bulb of tarmac. In between, two rows of drab grey semis faced each other across a short, narrow road. Realistically, there wasn't room for proper pavements or grass verges, but the council had squeezed them in anyway. The rest of the street was filled with police.

Vans and cars were lined up down one side of the road. A small group of officers in black rainslicks were waiting by one – on the balls of their feet; their hands in their pockets – while a few others were talking casually to the neighbours, who were understandably braving the weather, standing out in their gardens and wondering what the hell was going on. One of the subtle jobs those officers would be doing was keeping them all separate: preserving the integrity of witness statements in much the same way as the yellow tape across the road preserved the integrity of the scene itself. I was pleased to see it. If they'd not been doing so, I'd have had to tell them to.

I drove up to the yellow cordon, which wavered as the rain tapped on it, and a policeman jogged up to meet me. I wound down the window and showed him my badge; he took it off me and stared at it for a few seconds. There was a small, unobtrusive camera clipped to his raincoat, which I knew was recording an image of me.

'Detective Nelson,' I prompted him. 'I'm with Mercer's team.'

The policeman passed my badge back. 'He's inside.'

I parked up, set my face in a professional grimace and made my way up to the house. Two crime-scene techs were working in the garden, and an officer was guarding the front door. More cameras. I showed my badge again.

'Sir.'

The officer on the door fitted me with a camera of my own. It would take intermittent pictures and record audio, both of which were transmitted on a coded frequency to equipment in one of the vans outside. This enormous scramble of information – hours of footage from one crime scene alone – would be filed, and then filtered into meaningful fragments of data.

The officer led me into the hall.

'Most of your team's upstairs. But Detective Duncan is through in the kitchen: you need to see him first of all.'

'Thanks.'

I moved through. The living room was on the right-hand side of the hallway. I glanced in and saw more techs on their knees, working carefully along the skirting boards. A camera flashed, and I looked away again and carried on. A little past the living room, stairs led up, again to the right, and then the hallway finished at an open door straight ahead. The room beyond was decorated in fleshy tones – red carpet, cream walls, dark crimson curtains hanging either side of bleary patio doors. More people were working quietly in here. The bulb in the ceiling was unshaded and too bright, giving everyone a harsh, half-shadowed face. More camera flashes: sharp and vivid. Fresh crime scenes are always like this: the weirdest party you've never been to.

I found Simon Duncan in the kitchen, which was separated from the back room by a pair of wooden saloon doors. The fittings in there were pale, clean and expensive, lit by a row of stripbulbs in the ceiling. Simon emerged from the kitchen, slapping off a pair of white gloves, and gave me his smile first, his strong hand second.

'Nelson, yes?' His voice was relaxed and quick: bursts of conversation that challenged you to keep up and get the joke. 'If I remember rightly, that is. Mark Nelson?'

He was taller than I remembered, with a climber's rangy build and tan, and was bald apart from curls of greying hair above his ears, mirrored by similar whorls on the back of his hands. At the interview, he'd twiddled a pen the whole time, asking only one question and that so quickly I almost missed it. He'd interjected on two other occasions with fast comments, each of them signposted by an arched eyebrow and a wry smile. He was reasonably well known in the academy himself: an intellectual troublemaker.

'That's right,' I said. 'Nice to see you again.'

'Got here eventually, eh?'

'The traffic.'

He wasn't bothered; he squeezed past me and we moved back into the hallway.

'The victim's in the bathroom, but there's been activity all over the house. Looks like our subject held him for quite a long time before killing him.'

'Definitely a homicide, then?' I said.

Simon raised that eyebrow of his. 'Pete didn't tell you?'

'We only spoke for a minute.'

'Well, they'll fill you in. Let's just say you're in for an interesting first day at work. Follow me and we'll have a look at the body.'

'Right.'

Before I could ask anything else, he was disappearing up the narrow stairs to the first floor, and I had to move quickly to keep up. I had a feeling I'd be doing a lot of that today.

We stopped on the dark landing. The carpet up here was red, the same as downstairs, and the curtains on the single small window were closed. As I breathed in, I caught the smell of it in the air: hideous and strong. The air was greasy with it, and I felt myself grimacing. Simon nodded towards the bathroom door.

'In here. Are you ready?'

This was a test of sorts, I supposed. But I'd seen bodies before, and I forced myself to put the grimace away.

'Sure.'

We moved into the bathroom – as much as we could, anyway – and that terrible smell increased. Petrol, smoke, meat.

Jesus.

The room itself was small – economical and well decorated. There was a shower cubicle to the left of the door, and the entire room was only twice the width of that, maybe three times as long. There was the toilet and, opposite that, a sink and a mirrored cabinet on the wall. Finally, at the far end beneath the window, there was the bath, running the width of the room. On the window sill above, there were enough gels and foams to fill a men's magazine special supplement, while a silver, executive-style waterproof radio was stuck to the tiles above the taps.

Two other people were in the bathroom and both of them looked up as we entered. One turned back to his work straight away, and Simon introduced me to the one who didn't.

'Mark, this is Chris Dale. He works for the Medical Examiner's Office and he's taken charge of our corpse. Chris, Mark Nelson.'

Dale was younger than I'd have expected for an ME, but then he probably thought the same about me.

'Good to meet you.'

'Likewise.'

Simon nodded towards the end of the room. 'And obviously our victim is the one in the bath.'

I looked between the two men. The bathwater was stained red. You couldn't make out much below the surface, beyond that the man lying there was naked and had rope tied round him. The lower half of his body was obscured, although the backs of his hands broke the surface, forming still, pale islands. Some of the fingers appeared to be missing, and at least one of those still there had been bent right back. At the far end of the bath, his head was visible. It was craning back, staring eyelessly up at the ceiling. The face was burned beyond recognition. The blackened skin had split and peeled away, and where the hair had survived at all it was matted and scorched. His head looked smaller than it should have done, like a pot left in a fire, reduced by the heat.

Keep calm.

'The water's cold,' Dale noted for my benefit. 'Judging by his skin, the hands, it looks as though he was tied up in here for most of the night.'

'Okay.' My voice didn't sound right.

'Given the body's ambient temperature in relation to the water, I'd estimate a time of death between three and four hours ago. Somewhere around seven o'clock this morning, give or take.'

I didn't reply this time, just blew out, wanting to go back into the hallway and close the door on this. But even as I was staring at the victim and feeling that odd crime-scene emotion – a mixture of revulsion, fear, pity and fascination – my training was taking over, turning the death into a puzzle and beginning to work out the blanks.

The victim had been tied up in the bath all night, but he was only killed this morning. That raised questions, and when we found the answers we'd be closer to solving the puzzle. Already I was thinking of robbery, possibly some kind of extortion: something on that level.

'What was done to him?'

Dale looked over at the dead man.

'Preliminary, this. He has the clear injuries to his hands there, and that's repeated over most of his body: he has a substantial number of shallow cuts, a few deeper ones. As to his face and head, I'd guess he was doused with lighter fluid and set on fire.'

'Okay.'

'He has obvious internal injuries to the mouth and throat, indicating that he ingested the lighter fluid as well. Despite all the obvious external injuries, I imagine the official cause of death will turn out to be asphyxia.'

A moment of silence panned out. I stared at the victim's ruined face, unable to imagine what it must have been like to die in such a manner. Instead, I experienced a shiver of something that was part horror, part grief. A sensation of profound sorrow, both that someone had to go through this and that someone could actually carry the act out.

'Are you all right?' Simon said.

'I'm fine. Just thinking.'

'Good. Come on through – the rest of the team are in the spare room. John's been waiting to hand out assignments.'

I followed Simon out of the bathroom, grateful to be back on the landing, and we walked into the spare room at the far end. It smelled of vomit, and I quickly noted the source. There was a stain soaked into the carpet – spatters of blood on the wall, too. Crime-scene techs were attending to both; the man on his knees by the vomit looked as though he'd prefer to be downstairs checking the skirting boards with everyone else.

The rest of my team were in the opposite corner, circled round a computer table. The monitor was open on an email package, and Mercer and Pete Dwyer were standing on either side of the team's final member, Greg Martin, who was sitting down, facing the bright screen. Greg was younger than the others, not much older than me, I thought, and was the team's IT expert. His jet-black hair and sideburns were cropped to the same neat length, and the glasses he wore looked fashionable and expensive. In fact, he was one of the trendiest geeks you were likely to encounter, and I imagined his collection of bathroom potions would probably rival the one belonging to our victim. But at the interview – borderline arrogance aside – he'd seemed relatively friendly.

'Mark is here,' Simon announced.

Mercer held up a finger without looking in our direction.

'One minute.'

Greg clicked something and the screen changed. The hard drive below was whirring away to itself, like a happy cat that didn't know its owner was dead. Additional fluorescent cables ran up from the hard drive, connecting it to the police laptop that Greg was working on.

I looked around the room, and saw a photographer standing a little away from us, angled back, concentrating on the wall behind the door. As the camera flashed, I took a step closer and looked at his subject.

Immediately, my skin began to crawl.

Somebody had drawn in black marker pen on the wall. It was an utterly alien design – an enormous spider web, perhaps, or some kind of dreamcatcher – and it disturbed me for reasons I couldn't put into words. Whatever it meant, I only needed to look at it for a moment to know the person behind it was unlikely to be the dead man in the bathtub.

Those thoughts of robbery or extortion ... seeing this design kicked the legs out from under them. What had been done here had been motivated by something else entirely.

Let's just say you're in for an interesting first day at work.

The camera flashed again.

Over by the computer, Greg and Mercer were ignoring us. Greg was clicking on different onscreen folders while Mercer directed the pointer, checking through the dead man's files. Pete, however, moved over to talk to me. He looked grateful to escape. His hair was messy, and the reason became clear as he ran his hand through it again, disrupting it even further. I'd seen men look more worn out, but rarely this early in the day.

'Have you seen the body?' he said.

'Just now, yeah.'

He blew out heavily, and then gestured behind him.

'Well, what we're thinking is the victim was working here at the computer, where he was surprised and attacked by an intruder, probably yesterday evening. The victim appears to have been subdued after a small struggle and then spent the night tied up in the bath. Clear evidence of torture. This morning, he gets burned alive. No sign of a break-in.'

'Do we have an ID on the victim?'

'Not concrete. There'll be a formal identification later, but for now we're assuming it's the house's owner, Kevin James Simpson.'

Pete went through the facts of the case as it stood, using his big fingers to indicate each point, one by one. Kevin Simpson was thirty years old, and had been resident at this address since he bought the house four years ago. He owned a low-level IT company, CCL, which provided business solutions: mainly database and website packages. The way Pete said it, I didn't think he held those areas of expertise in especially high regard.

'CCL called us this morning.'

The company had received an anonymous phone call a little after eight o'clock. It had featured a short recording of terrible screaming, and then the distraught woman on the switchboard had been given Simpson's name and address. CCL didn't tape incoming calls, but Greg's IT team had already checked Simpson's home phone account. The call had been made from here, downstairs in the lounge.

According to the medical examiner, then, there had been a period of up to an hour after Simpson had been murdered before the killer made his phone call. More questions. As well as waiting so long to kill his victim in the first place, what had the killer spent his time doing afterwards?

'Simpson lived alone?' I asked.

Pete nodded.

'We don't know about girlfriends yet. We're checking through his backlog of conquests, as far as we can. Accessing his emails.'

'Right.' I nodded at the spider web on the wall. 'What about that?'

Pete looked at it, and the weariness in his face deepened. He was obviously troubled by the web and unsure how to address it. But he was saved by an interruption: on the other side of the room, Mercer and Greg had reached a hiatus in whatever they were looking at, and Mercer walked over to us. I forgot the artwork for a moment.

'Mark.' He gave the briefest of smiles as he shook my hand, but was clearly too distracted to mean it. 'Good to see you again.'

'You too.'

Actually, I thought, it was strange to see him, rather than good. As Mercer's hand returned to his side, it occurred to me that – disregarding the picture at the back of his book – I'd only ever seen him either sitting down or from a distance, and I was struck now by how small he seemed in the flesh, standing in front of me. He was only average height, for one thing. For another, although his build might have been broad and strong when he was younger, it now appeared slightly wasted and crumpled, like a shirt he'd lost too much weight to carry off. He looked a lot older than I'd been expecting. As men age, it's not the wear in the face that gives it away so much as an increasingly visible weakness in the body. John Mercer seemed to be on the cusp of that, and it was startling. He was only in his early fifties, but an extra fifteen years were hanging off him, making him slump.

'You remember Greg?' he said.

'Sure.' I nodded hello.

Greg raised his hand in greeting, but he was preoccupied and deep in thought; he was using his heels to circle the office chair back and forth, probably in serious breach of some crime-scene rule. In fact, everyone was distracted. I was clearly missing something, and I had the feeling it centred on the spider-web design the killer had painted on Kevin Simpson's wall.

'Right,' Mercer said. 'Assignments. Pete's talked you through the basics here, am I right?'

'The basics, yeah.' I paused briefly, and then nodded at the design. 'But not that.'

Mercer glanced across. He seemed almost to be noticing it for the first time.

'Ah, yes,' he said. 'We were just talking about that before you arrived.'

I expected some kind of explanation, but instead there was only an uncomfortable silence. Mercer himself wasn't troubled by it – he simply stared at the spider web. I watched his gaze trace the lines, moving here and there. It was as though he'd been hypnotised by it. Then, the camera flashed again, and Mercer blinked. His attention returned to me, and then moved to his watch.

'Okay, good,' he said. 'Let's get moving on this. We'll have the first briefing at two o'clock, so make sure you're all either back at the office by then or have access to a terminal. Simon, I need as much in the way of forensics as possible. Greg, you're working the computer and the phone records. Pete, CCL.'

'Yep.'

Mercer looked across at him. 'You know where you're going?'

Pete, hands still thrust in his pockets, gave his boss a look. 'Yes.'

'Okay. Everyone who's going, get gone. Mark, hang on for a second.'

Pete and Simon headed out of the room. Mercer moved a little closer to me.

'Door-to-doors,' he said. 'You've got three additional men allocated from the pool. They're waiting downstairs for you.'

'Right.'

'We need every house canvassed. Make a note of anywhere there's no answer and we'll follow them up. In the first instance, we want general opinions on Simpson. Information on friends, girlfriends. Activity in the street.'

It was obvious stuff: 'Yes, sir.'

'Sounds of commotion,' he continued, ignoring me. 'Any previous incidents that might be relevant, however tenuous.'

As he went on, I grew slightly irritated. It wasn't so much what he was saying as the way he was doing it: his attention elsewhere; his gaze directed at the wall behind more often than at me. I found myself simply nodding, wanting to head downstairs and get on with it. Mercer knew all about my record, and according to his wife he'd been impressed, and yet he still felt the need to talk me through things I would have done anyway. Perhaps if he'd explained about the spider web, this wouldn't have been necessary, and—

His wife, I remembered. Hold that thought.

'Any unusual vehicles,' Mercer finished, pointedly. 'And visitors, especially women.'

'Yes, sir.'

'Is there anything else?'

'Your wife phoned. Just before I left the office.'

His expression went blank.

'She said to remind you, "Don't forget". She said you'd know what it meant.'

'Okay. Thanks for that.'

I turned to go.

'One more thing,' he said. 'Remind your team that everyone needs to have their cameras on. Everything needs to be recorded. All the time.'

Standard procedure, which I would have done without thinking.

'Yes, sir.'

The irritation must have been audible in my voice, because he frowned. I was expecting a rebuke, but he didn't seem able to concentrate long enough to make one. The spider web was calling to him again, and he returned to it. But the frown remained.

'Okay,' he said absently.

I was dismissed. I headed downstairs and then outside, grimacing up at the rain.

Stupid, maybe, but I couldn't hide my disappointment – you build these things up into something they're not. In the weeks leading up to today, I'd imagined my first meeting with John Mercer a hundred times, and each time it had felt far more triumphant, more of a vindication of all my hard work, than what had just occurred upstairs. In reality, I felt excluded, and more than a little patronised. Not exactly the fucking Kodak moment I'd been hoping for.

It's just his way, I reminded myself. It wasn't as though he wasn't famous for being difficult to work for.

It made me remember what the girl at reception had told me: *Give it a week.* I would; of course I would. At least then maybe I'd have proven myself enough to be treated like the rest of the team, or as though I knew what the fuck I was doing.

I shook my head, smiling at my own belligerence, then put the emotion away and walked out through the gate and over to the van, where my new interview team was waiting.

3 DECEMBER   **11.55 A.M.**
19 HOURS, 25 MINUTES UNTIL DAWN

Jodie

Jodie walked quickly across the office and perched on the edge of the desk. Michaela started from her work, looking surprised, as though her friend didn't do this every day and had somehow appeared there by magic.

'Okay.' Jodie leaned down and tapped her pen on the pad of yellow Post-it notes where she'd already written down the other orders. 'What are you having? Knock me out.'

This was Jodie's lunch-hour ritual every weekday. It took twenty minutes to walk to Theo's, where she collected sandwiches for the other five temps in the office, and twenty minutes walking slowly back again.

She saw it as an act of solidarity among the troops. They were all in the same boat, after all, data-monkeys for the insurance firm, spending every morning and afternoon punching in figures from invoices. It was a thankless task, setting down in stone the details of money lost. The company didn't like to pay out, so the account inputters were kept in a dusty old room near the top of the building – a dirty secret hidden away from the proper employees, the ones who actually made money rather than just recorded it leaving. The computers in the office were ancient: sticky and patchy from spilled coffee and old labels that had been torn off. The desks were antiques. The lights fizzed and flickered, as though their real purpose in life was attracting and killing insects. No radiators, no daylight. You punched in and punched out. Jodie thought of it as a digital sweatshop. When she couldn't avoid thinking about it, anyway.

Most of the other temps were rolling stock – students who would be gone in a few weeks, replaced by others who wouldn't stay much longer – but Michaela had been working with her for over a year, and she counted her as a friend. It made her feel even worse for lying about where she'd been yesterday.

Michaela gestured for the pad. 'I'll go today.'

'Uh-uh.' Jodie moved it back. 'What do you want?'

'You're not well. I'm happy to go.'

'I'm fine, honestly. It was just a pissy little migraine. All gone now. See?'

Jodie waggled her head from side to side.

See? No permanent damage.

The older girl grinned, and Jodie felt better.

When she'd arrived at work this morning, the first thing Michaela had done was come over and give her a hug, which was the kind of person she was. Later, at coffee break, she'd told Jodie she hoped Scott had been looking after her. Jodie had wanted to burst out crying. The whole universe seemed to be aligning to make her feel guilty, and it really didn't need to.

When she'd got back from Kevin's house yesterday, she'd done her best to act normal – throwing her bag on the chair, and then herself down on the settee next to Scott. All the way home, she'd been trying to convince herself it was just a huge mistake; she'd put it behind her, forget about it, move on. But Scott had known something was wrong. In the end, she'd

36

had to go through to the bedroom and lie down. She needed to keep away from him to avoid blurting it out.

Sleeping on it had helped a little, and she woke up with a fresh sense of resolve. There were problems. She needed to let the dust in her head settle, and then she and Scott had to think and talk carefully about what was going wrong between them. Their relationship was heading off at a bad angle, and a bit of adjustment was required. There'd probably be a few more wobbles along the way, but wasn't it the same for everyone when a relationship went long-term? They'd sort it. Before long they'd be back on track, and it was worth the effort.

In the meantime, she had to keep in mind that lying to Scott had been bad, but telling the truth would be worse. But it was difficult, and she wanted to be on her own for a while. She'd been looking forward to the peace and quiet since that first guilty hug when she'd arrived.

'I don't mind going today,' Michaela said.

'No, seriously.' Jodie thought: *Bless you.* 'I'd like to go. The fresh air will blow away any remaining migraine devils.' She made her index fingers into little horns and glared menacingly.

Michaela smiled again. 'Idiot.'

'Yeah, yeah. Come on, I haven't got all day. What do you want?'

'I'll try what you normally have. It always looks nice.'

'Duck in hoisin.' Jodie nodded and wrote it down. 'Excellent choice.'

'Do you want some company?' Michaela turned in her seat. 'I could walk with you.'

Jodie gave her a smile.

'You're okay, sweets.' She clicked off the pen, tore the Post-it note from the pad and folded it. 'I'm going to listen to some music and not think about stuff. But thank you.'

She headed down to the lobby in one of the back lifts.

Floor Ten. First, she got the iRiver out of her handbag. It was forty gigs of hard-drive space, currently holding over five thousand songs. Black and silver casing. As with every hi-tech gadget she laid her eyes on, Jodie loved it. The unit clipped onto the belt of her jeans; the remote control onto the hem of her jacket; and the headphones hung snugly in her ears. She pressed the [on] button on the remote, heard a faint beep and waited for the digital library to assemble itself.

Floor Six. The lift didn't provide the best lighting for checking your appearance in the mirror, but she did it anyway. There were mixed results. Sometimes she thought she was pretty, but today she just thought that she'd do. Thin, dark-brown hair, tied back – a wedge had come loose, though. She undid the scrunchy and held it in her mouth, bunching her hair up and retying it. Then she checked her makeup, which was minimal at the best of times.

Floor Two. The overhead lights made her skin look amber. She pulled a couple of wide-eyed funny faces at herself as the lift clicked down to Ground Floor. Then she smiled at her reflection. Not like a friend, exactly, but sort of.

You're not the worst person in the world. You're just human.

The doors *tinged*, opening onto a back corridor near the lobby. As she stepped out, she felt a vibration in her handbag, and she stopped between a radiator and a fire-extinguisher to retrieve her phone.

Quick, quick, quick.

The display read [1 message received] and she clicked green until it appeared. It was from Scott. She'd been waiting for this all morning, but instead of reading it, she pressed red to cancel and went to [create message]. Her phone stored a text message once you started to write it, and she'd composed a message to him earlier on. It was a general 'how are you, hope your day's going okay, I love you' kind of message. It appeared in the display now and she pressed [send], imagining Scott receiving it at home, imagining they'd texted each other at the same time.

She clicked through and read his message. It was pretty much the same thing he wrote every day, and more or less the same as she'd written to him. She smiled at the number of kisses he'd put at the end, felt a little sad, then locked her phone and put it back in her handbag.

On a normal day, she might have written him another text immediately – one of their 'what a coincidence, texting at the same time, great minds think alike' messages. But she couldn't bring herself to do it. The little bit of fake magic she'd injected felt even more like cheating than it usually did.

Instead, she pressed [play] on the remote and headed towards the main lobby.

By the time Jodie stepped out onto the busy street, the music in her ears was crunchingly loud, and a couple of people glanced at her, obviously wondering what on earth she thought she was doing to her hearing. She ignored them and looked above her, annoyed by the weather, put her hood up, then made her way left. The familiar route out of the centre, back towards the suburbs. Business as usual.

It was a miserable lunchtime. The sky was like something that might form over an industrial factory, too grey even to make out the clouds. As she moved out of the centre, the trees were shuffling in discomfort, twitching at the touch of the rain. The people on the streets hustled around her, shoulders huddled, faces full of pain: all moving more quickly than they would if it was sunny. A miserable day; let's get it over with.

For Jodie, trapped in that office, most days were miserable, and it was another reason for her lunchtime ritual. She'd learned over the years that music was the best way of separating yourself from everything, of carving a little '*you*' space. If you turned the volume up high, you didn't need to think about anything except the song in your ears. The disappointing real world faded out around you. The rain didn't matter, your shitty morning at your even shittier work didn't matter; even the drab fucking city you lived in wasn't so bad. Altruism aside, this was the main reason Jodie volunteered for the sandwich run. It gave her an opportunity to assert some control over her life by absconding from it.

The music changed at random to a song she didn't like: some hideous ballad that must have crept on as a result of her collector mentality. She clicked the remote, skipping it. A heavier song came on. Better.

But it was proving harder than normal to escape into her head. Whatever she tried to think about, her mind kept returning to Kevin and Scott, and what she'd risked losing because of her stupid, *stupid* actions yesterday.

Jodie skipped another song, then another.

A few moments later, still trying to find a track she wanted to listen to, she reached the edge of the waste ground. From the sky, she imagined, it would look like an ulcer on the land, pale and ridged and unappealing, nestled against the mouth of the main road. It was mostly old gravel, dotted here and there with clusters of bushes and trees. Around Valentine's Day, travellers came, bringing a fair with them. The rest of the year, people parked and brought their dogs.

The road skirted it, but that way took longer: it was quicker and easier to cut across. Scott would be worried if he knew she went this way every day, but even with nobody around you were still close enough to the road to feel safe. And, as she'd already established, what he didn't know wouldn't hurt him.

Jodie moved round the old, rusted barrier and set off. In the distance, she could see a council estate of square grey houses; behind them there were the woods, and then the haze of the mountains. Like the rest of the city, the estate looked sodden and frozen. Once she was on the waste ground, the day seemed even more grim than before. The ground was grey in the cold. It was a wind-trap here, too. The air was icy and painful. It kept surprising her from the side.

She was halfway across, taking a path between old, skeletal bushes, when she heard it – something in the music that shouldn't have been there. It was a real-world noise, like a siren; an ambulance or a police car in the distance.

She clicked [pause] on the remote control. The music disappeared but the sound remained.

A baby crying.

Jodie stopped walking, more alarmed by it than the sound perhaps warranted. She looked around, but there was nobody ahead of her, nobody behind. Suddenly, the cars on the road sounded a long way away, and where she was standing the only noises were the baby crying and the creeping patter of the rain.

Her skin prickled. It was coming from the right, she thought, on the other side of the bushes. But there were no adult voices to go with it. No sound of activity. Apart from the bushes moving in the wind, the waste ground was still and desolate.

The rain picked up a little and the baby began screaming. It was like an alarm going off, and it set light to some instinct deep inside her. She found herself pulled a step closer to the bushes.

'Hello?'

Nobody replied.

Jodie blinked rain out of her eyes and took another step. She wanted to investigate but something held her back. What if she made her way through and found the baby with its mother? People didn't appreciate you nosing like that: it implied they were bad parents. So she hesitated for a second, but then the screaming became more high-pitched, like a car engine changing up a gear, and she thought, Fuck you if you're there, you *are* a bad parent, and she began to push her way between the bushes.

'Hello?' she called again. 'Ouch. Hello?'

Still no answer.

It was muddy here, and the sharp branches poked at her, catching on the cable of her headphones. But it took only a couple of seconds to break through. There was a gap between the bushes and it was there, resting in the mud like an abandoned picnic basket, that she found the source of the cries. The baby was bundled up in a pink blanket, lying on its back and screaming in anguish. Its face looked like a small, red rose.

'Oh, God,' Jodie said. 'You poor thing.'

Quickly, she detached her iRiver and stuffed it into her coat pocket. The situation was unreal: she wanted to pinch herself. This was something that happened in movies or newspapers, and yet here it was, happening to her. Some awful person had abandoned this child out in the cold and the rain. Jodie had never thought of herself as the maternal type – never got on with the babies she'd met – but now, without hesitation, she stooped to pick it up.

As she did, she felt a vibration against her hip. The phone in her handbag. Another text.

Not now, Scott, she thought, glancing down at her side.

Out of the corner of her eye, she saw a man in the bushes to the right. He'd been standing completely still, but now he was moving towards her. Jodie's first thought was Oh, it's the father, but then she caught sight of his face and the mental signals changed, confused. He was wearing a pink devil mask: big eyes, strands of lank black hair. It shocked her into a single moment of stillness, and that was all it took.

The man was holding a bottle of gardening spray. It sloshed as he raised his hand, then hissed as the mist clouded into her face. Her nose and mouth wrenched themselves closed; her eyes shut tight. Ammonia. Everything was burning. She was on her knees, coughing, her hands fluttering against the mud. And then he kicked her in the head and she was on her side, stunned by the ferocity of it. She managed to open her eyes – and then suddenly she was looking at the sky. Watching the rain materialise above her, without any real comprehension, as the grey sky sparkled and went white.

3 DECEMBER   **1.55 P.M.**
17 HOURS, 25 MINUTES UNTIL DAWN

Mark

It felt strange to take full charge of my own team, no matter how small. The main reason was that I was painfully aware the grapevine would have been in full swing, and that the three officers appointed to me would know this was my first assignment. The reality of that hit me as I approached the van where they were waiting, and I encountered a bundle of nerves like a tripwire across the path. I took a deep breath and stepped over it. All I had to do was be myself and play it by ear. Myself ought to be good enough, after all.

Fortunately, the three officers – Davy, Ross and Bellerby – seemed determined to behave well. They listened attentively as I outlined the case and indicated the areas we needed to concentrate on, and then split the four of us into two pairs to tackle opposite sides of the street. I also told them that any suggestions they had would be welcome, a comment I'd appreciated hearing in the past. I figured it would sugar the pill before I finished up by repeating Mercer's instructions.

'Make sure your cameras are on at all times.'

They looked at me like I was stupid.

'I know it's obvious,' I said, 'and I know it's standard. But it's also Mercer's specific orders.'

They glanced at each other, but did their best to hide it. Once again, I realised there was a lot going on here that I was too new to be included in. This time, I didn't mind. Whatever the reason, at least they understood it wasn't me who was being a dick.

'Let's get on with it.'

The door-to-doors went as well as could be expected. Everyone was shaken by what had happened, and they were all keen to help in any way they could. Murder isn't common, after all: most people's experience of it is confined to films or reports on the news, not having it occur next door. Simpson's death had given his neighbours a stark and shocking reminder that it happened in the real world, too, and consequently of their own vulnerability. Identifying a reason why he had been singled out would help to dislocate them from the horror, and yet none of them had a single suggestion why someone might do this to him. For all they knew, his death could easily have been theirs instead. It was a frightening idea to deal with, and I wished I could have reassured them for certain that it wasn't true.

We canvassed the entire street, missing two houses where nobody was home, and in those cases we left messages and flagged them for follow-up. But nobody could recall any altercations: no fights or confrontations, no public bust-ups. Simpson had seemed a nice enough guy, they said. None of them knew if he was seeing anyone. They noticed different girls occasionally, but not recently. The whole time, they looked desperate to find something else to say, and I did my best not to look desperate to hear it.

It wasn't all bad news. We ended up with two separate witnesses recalling a white van in the street the day before. The first sighting was just after midday, at which point it had been parked further down the road; the second was around eight o'clock in the evening, when it had been outside Simpson's house. Neither witness saw the occupant arrive or drive away, and we had no number plate or make to go on, nor any specific markings. But it was something.

At number fifteen, the house opposite Kevin Simpson's, we got more. The occupant, Yvonne Gregory, was brief but specific. Yvonne was retired and had been at home yesterday afternoon, watching television. During an ad break, around quarter to five, she had gone through to the kitchen to make a cup of tea. From there, she had a clear view of Simpson's house through the window. I knew this because I went in to check, leaning on either side of the sink as she told me about the girl.

'She was leaving his house.' Yvonne gestured across the road. 'I remember that she turned back and waved to him from the end of the path.'

'What did she look like?' I asked.

'Oh, she had brown hair, to here.' Yvonne chopped her hand at about shoulder length. 'She had a raincoat on, and a handbag, I think. And headphones, too.'

'How old was she?'

'She was quite young. Perhaps your age, Detective.'

I saw that she was joking with me. I smiled.

'Have you ever seen her before?'

'No, no.'

'Is there anything else you can remember?'

Yvonne thought about it for a moment.

'She looked a little upset, I thought. Well, not upset, exactly. More as though there was something bothering her, if you see what I mean. She looked troubled.'

Doesn't everyone? I thought.

So we came away with a basic description of a vehicle, and also of a girl who'd been at Kevin Simpson's house, probably shortly before he was attacked. None of it would stop the case in its tracks, but nevertheless I was pleased, and as I made my way back to the department to file the reports and attend the briefing, I felt a lot more positive. Even the irritation from Mercer's over-specific instructions had faded. Obviously, I wasn't just going to slot into the team right away: I needed to prove myself first, and the morning's interviews were a first step in the right direction.

But it turned out that my report would have to wait for a while. When I arrived at the office, the rest of the team were already focused on something. A digital recording was being played and something close to Hell was unfolding in the air.

'Are you listening to me? We're going to play a game about love.'

The voice on the recording sounded strange. It was mostly dead and flat, but there were also curious lifts in it, as though the man was talking to himself rather than his victim, occasionally asking himself rhetorical questions.

'It's about you and Jodie and Scott,' the man said.

Mercer clicked his fingers: remember those names. Then he returned to the position I'd walked in on: elbows on the desk, fingers steepled, staring intently into space, index fingers tapping his lips. He seemed calm, but there was an edge to the rest of us. Simon was very still; Greg had his head on one side, listening professionally to the recording; Pete had his eyes closed. For me, each sentence felt like a jab in the chest.

'I watched you today,' the man said. 'With her. And I've read all your emails. I know what was happening here. And we both know where she is now, don't we? Back home with her boyfriend.'

Jodie, I thought. Shoulder-length brown hair. About my age.

'How do you think she's feeling now?' the man said. 'Do you think she feels guilty about lying to Scott and spending the day with you?'

In reply, there was only the urgent rush of hot water in the house's pipes, and then a quiet slosh from the bath. Simpson didn't answer out loud. In my mind's eye, I saw him there in the bath, a gag wrapped round his pale face.

'Is she pleased she's home?' the voice carried on. 'Or does she wish she was still here with you? Is she even now writing an email to you, the way you were to her?'

Mercer looked across: 'Greg?'

Greg shook his head. 'No old emails from or to "Jodie". No "Scott". Nothing in his Contacts folder, either. The killer must have cleared everything out.'

Mercer frowned. Beneath the desk, his foot was tapping impatiently.

The voice said: 'You think you love her.'

Nothing.

'Don't you.'

Still no reply; not even a slosh of water. When the man spoke next, he sounded disappointed not to have received at least some kind of response.

'Well, we're going to find out. The rules of the game are very simple, but you won't have much input. If Jodie emails you before dawn, I'll stop hurting you and I'll let you go. But if she doesn't ...'

There was a slight pause, followed by a creak. I got the impression the man was turning to pick something up.

'… I'll pour this down your throat and over your face, and I'll set fire to you. Nod if you understand.'

There was another pause.

'I said, "Nod if you understand."'

Simpson began thrashing in the bath water, slapping around everywhere. I couldn't see it, but somehow I knew that the killer had squirted lighter fluid at him, reinforcing the point.

'That's good.'

Another creak.

'Try to keep calm. We have so much to talk about.'

The recording continued for a moment, then cut off.

Greg turned to me.

'My IT team have been working on Simpson's computer,' he explained. 'They found two new audio files saved on the desktop. That was the first.'

'Play the second,' Mercer said quietly.

We all looked at him. His head had slipped down so that his hands obscured his face. His foot had stopped tapping. There was nothing to be impatient about here. He knew what was likely to be on the second file – we all did – but at the same time we needed to be sure. CCL hadn't recorded the phone call they received this morning, the one filled with terrible screaming, but we were probably about to hear it for ourselves. It wasn't anything to relish.

'Okay.'

Greg double-clicked, and it began.

'I'm sorry,' the voice said. 'I hope you understand now how stupid you were. How little she deserved everything you invested in her.'

He paused.

'Do you understand?'

There was frantic noise then: desperate splashing and muffled cries.

'If it's any consolation, Jodie and Scott are one of my couples. I will be visiting them later, and they'll have their own game to play. But ours is finished.'

My heart was beating too quickly for comfort. My hand began rubbing my chin, while all around me the office was receding.

'Picture her in your head now. Imagine her sleeping peacefully in her boyfriend's arms.'

More noise from the bath.

45

'Shhhhh,' the man whispered.

He must have taken Simpson's gag off, because now – finally – we heard his voice. It was shrill and full of panic. He was pleading and begging for his life, but speaking so quickly that it was impossible to make out the words. Almost immediately, they were cut off, replaced by a terrible choking as the liquid was squirted into his face, his mouth. The recording was full of coughing and hacking breath.

It hurt me in the heart to hear it. Nothing could have prepared me for this; there was almost a spiritual pain to listening. A complicity; a frustration.

I closed my eyes when I heard the scrape of a lighter.

Perhaps I expected a *whumph* of some kind, but there was nothing like that. You could only detect the moment Simpson was set on fire by the way he began screaming – and even then, most of the sound was lost. He was gargling with flame: able to vocalise his panic and shock only with a thin, breathless whine. I imagined his throat contracting. The unbearable burning, crumpling his lungs like tissue paper. It was the most awful thing I'd ever heard.

Knowing how it would end, I wanted Simpson to die quickly. But he didn't, because it was out of his control; his body refused to give up, fighting against an oblivion that must surely have been welcome. His murder seemed to go on for ever.

And all the time there was another, quieter sound in the background. It was an inhuman hissing, and it took me a moment to work out where it was coming from. It was the killer.

A shiver ran through me.

While his victim was dying in agony, this man was standing above him, watching it, taping it, his mouth open, teeth slightly apart, sucking in the smoke and smell of it.

It was as though he was drawing Kevin Simpson's soul in through his teeth, piece by piece.

I opened my eyes and looked at the team. We could all hear it, and on every face I saw a reflection of my own feelings: disbelief and horror. Every face except Mercer's. I couldn't see his because he was staring at the desk. His hands were clasped in front of him, almost in prayer.

The noise continued, slowly abating, and then the recording mercifully cut off. When it did, the silence in the office felt tainted. Nobody said anything for a moment; nobody even moved. Then Mercer leaned slowly back and rubbed his face, looking like a man who had just woken up.

'Everybody take five,' he said.

46

I went out front, into the ice of the afternoon air. The temperature was a slap in the face, which I needed. The rain had stopped, but the sky remained thick with dark-grey cloud and the wind, when it came, was freezing. A crisps packet went skittering across the tarmac. The forecast had been snow, and it didn't feel far off. Even in my coat, I was trembling – but that was also down to the poison of unused adrenalin. I felt like I could run for ever. I wished I could.

Dying is one of the great taboos. I'd seen my share of bodies before, and those had been horrible enough. But bad as that could be, it was only ever the end result. You felt sadness and grief, of course, but by that point you were looking at something that was already dead, and that's a world away from being forced to hear or see it happen: to experience the terrible process by which a living human being, no different from yourself, is deadened and ruined, reduced one spark at a time to an empty shell.

Inevitably, it made me think about Lise. But I didn't want to do that, and I couldn't afford to, not right now. It was hard enough to deal with the end result – that she was dead and gone – without plunging my imagination into the deeper horrors of what it must have been like for her. What she might have been thinking as her life disappeared.

I shook my head, turning my thoughts back to Kevin Simpson instead.

Five minutes?

I could take five fucking years and that recording would stay with me.

But five minutes would have to do.

Back in the office, everyone still looked grim, but also professionally determined. Each of us had put his feelings about the recording away, perhaps to examine later, perhaps to forget for ever. Once again, Mercer seemed detached from it. He was staring into space when I went in, giving the appearance of feeling nothing. No doubt it was down to his experience, and I wondered whether I'd ever be capable of doing that: of abstracting myself from the situation and seeing it solely as a puzzle to be solved. It seemed heartless, but I didn't doubt that in reality he felt what had happened every bit as keenly as the rest of us. This was simply his way of dealing with it – by concentrating on solving the crime and catching the man responsible.

Greg started off: 'Like I said, we've got no Jodie, not Scott—'

'But the killer mentioned emails,' Mercer interrupted, 'so they must exist.'

47

'Yes, and if he deleted them it might be possible to recover them. But it depends how thorough he's been. We'll try, but we shouldn't count on finding them through the computer.'

Mercer frowned. 'It seems clear from the recording that this Jodie, whoever she may be, was having an affair with Simpson. If we can't find her and her boyfriend in time, our subject will. That's if he hasn't already.'

'We've got a description,' I said.

He turned round immediately. 'Tell me.'

I explained about Yvonne Gregory, relating the details she'd given me of the girl leaving Simpson's house – Jodie, presumably. Late twenties, brown hair, bag, headphones. Obviously, it wasn't specific enough to be very useful, and I was aware of that as I spoke. After listening to the recording, I didn't feel so triumphant any more. I finished up by describing the white van, and at that point Mercer nodded, as though he'd been expecting it. He cut me off before I could finish.

'CCTV?' he said, directing the question to Greg.

'The nearest is on the main road.' He took a deep breath. 'It doesn't capture Simpson's street, but I guess we'll be able to check traffic.'

'Well, that's your priority, then. Find us any white vans there between eight and nine this morning. Check yesterday afternoon, four thirty to five thirty, see if we can find this girl. And we have to find this girl.'

Greg didn't say anything.

'What are you thinking?' Mercer asked him.

Greg was rotating his chair, using his heels, as he had been at Simpson's house that morning. He looked preoccupied.

'I guess I'm still not convinced,' he said.

Mercer spread his hands, as though this should all be obvious and he couldn't understand why it wasn't. It certainly wasn't obvious to me, but of course there was a context to the day's events I wasn't included in.

'We have the signature,' Mercer said. 'We have a white van at the scene. We have the game. We have torture. And, despite how it seemed to begin with, we have a second victim.'

'I'm not saying there aren't compelling similarities.'

'So what are you saying?'

Greg sighed, and I was surprised by what seemed to be open rebellion. Mercer was in charge here, and I'd have expected Greg just to do as he was told. He clearly had doubts about continuing, but after a moment he decided: fuck it.

'I'm saying that at the end of the day white vans are very common.

48

Girls are very common. The signature's compelling, like I said, and yes, there's the mention of the game. But otherwise the scene is different.' He counted on his fingers. 'The killer held him in the bath. The girl walked out of there yesterday afternoon and wasn't an active part of the game ...' He ran out of things to count and leaned back. 'It's totally different.'

'Of course it's different. It's been two years.'

'I know it's been two years.'

'Well, he's been planning. It shouldn't surprise us – surprise you, I mean – that he's changed. It's our job to understand why and how he's changed.'

Greg looked sulky, as though he wanted to disagree more but couldn't. I noticed that Pete was eyeing him carefully.

But Mercer wasn't going to let Greg off the hook that easily. 'Well?'

Greg looked up at him. My surprise increased. There was a pointed meaning in his expression. I didn't know what it was, or what lay behind it, but I knew it wasn't good.

'Maybe it's not that I'm not convinced,' he said. 'There's just something about this that's making me uneasy. Sir.'

They looked at each other for a moment, and the atmosphere in the office hardened into something awkward and sharp. Nobody said anything, and I decided it might be a convenient and possibly even helpful moment to butt in. Gently.

'Can I ask ... ?'

'Yes. Of course.' Mercer turned to me, face full of stone. 'The situation is this. I believe that this murder is connected to an earlier case. There are a large number of similarities, many of them conclusive. On the other hand, Greg is quite right to point out that there are also some small differences. I believe this particular killer has slightly altered his MO.'

'Right,' I said. 'So—'

'As soon as the briefing's over, you'll have a chance to read the file. You can catch up on the details then.'

'Okay.'

It felt ridiculously uncomfortable in here. At least Greg had stopped looking at Mercer now, but even with his attention directed at the floor his expression remained the same. I could practically feel the carpet wilting.

'Pete?' Mercer said. 'Simon? Anything you want to add?'

He seemed to be speaking mainly to Pete, his second-in-command, but Pete looked unhappy at the attention, reluctant to offer his support either way.

What was being left unsaid here?

Simon saved everyone from more embarrassment.

'Whatever the case, we carry on in the same way, surely?' His voice was quick, matter-of-fact. 'We follow up the van, the girl. So it doesn't matter, does it, and we can simply see what further evidence arrives.' He paused, and to me his next sentence seemed loaded. 'Make a decision then.'

Pete nodded, said nothing.

Greg shrugged, satisfied but feigning uninterest.

'I agree,' Mercer said. 'That's how we'll proceed. Mark will spend the afternoon reading the file. Let's divide what the rest of us need to do.'

So I was going to be playing catch-up. That was all right. In the light of the disagreement, I was curious to see what I would make of the file – see if it shed any light on what was happening among the team. In the meantime, I listened carefully as they received their assignments.

As well as continuing the computer work, Greg's IT team would review the CCTV footage. Simon would follow through the forensics. Pete would handle a small press briefing in half an hour, during which Simpson's name would be released to the media and a request for acquaintances called Jodie or Scott to come forward would be made. Then he would chase up Simpson's exes and see if any of them matched the girl's description, just in case Jodie wasn't the girl's real name.

'We *have* to find this couple before dawn,' he pressed.

When the briefing was finished, everyone gathered their things together. Greg seemed eager to get out of there; Simon was making a phone call, indifferent to the tension; while Pete moved slowly. I heard him sigh quietly as he picked up his papers.

Mercer passed across a note with a case number and log-in code, and I decided to put everything else out of my head for now. There was work to be done. I turned to the computer and typed in the details. The screen froze while it loaded, and then a few seconds later the file title appeared at the top.

```
Case file no A6267
50/50 Killer
```

Scott

```
Number 273. We text each other at the same time.
```

Scott sat back, rolling the scrollbar with the mouse to check he hadn't already included it. Ridiculous if he hadn't ... but no, it wasn't there. How could he have forgotten that one?

He reached the top of the list.

```
Five Hundred Reasons Why I Love You.
```

He scrolled back to the end and typed: `Number 274.`

And then paused, his fingers hovering over the keyboard. After a moment, he grimaced, considering the flashing cursor.

After he'd cracked the two hundred mark, it had become a lot harder – that was when it started drying up. New reasons did keep occurring to him, but it was usually because Jodie had said or done something that caught his attention, like with the crossed texts earlier. It didn't matter, he supposed – as long as it kept happening. And it did. Even with things as difficult between them as they'd been recently, he still found himself noticing details about her that he loved, and returning to his list to add them as soon as he could. It made him happy. At the same time, it made him sad.

Now his mind was blank, and the next one wouldn't come. He needed reminders.

Leave it for now.

Scott pressed [ctrl-s] to save the document and then alt-tabbed from the Word file back to his art software. The current view showed three different pictures of his face. He should have been working on these anyway.

The pieces he was concentrating on recently, they all consisted of either seven or nine paintings of an object or a person. The first in the series was always photo-realistic, although usually done in strange colours. The face on the left of the screen, for example, had been painted in shades of green and yellow, but other than that it could have been a photograph. When the first painting was finished, he scanned it into the computer and manipulated it with the software: blurring it slightly, perhaps, or hardening the edges of the colours so that the whole picture became blockier. Then he printed it and painted a copy of the image. That was the second piece in the series. And so on. It was an iterative process. He ended up with a row of small canvases showing an image slowly disintegrating, reducing itself to the bare components of colours and shapes.

Somewhere along that line, the viewer lost track of what the object was. The last painting in this series of self-portraits would be four rectangles of orange and green, dividing the final canvas slightly off centre, like a stained-glass window. Only three images in, the picture on the right of the screen had become alien. It was recognisably human, but Scott couldn't see much of himself in it any more.

Artwork. There was theory and intent behind what he did, but his degree was far enough in the past for him to have relaxed on that front. A younger version of him might have sniffed at it, but he painted this way because it interested him and, all else aside, the results looked good.

Other people were starting to agree. A small gallery in town had taken some of his single pieces, sold a couple – it wasn't much money, but it was something. They'd phoned a fortnight ago, interested in showing more of his work, so he'd taken this week off to get a few more together. When he got the call, he'd been enthusiastic, but then disappointed by Jodie's reaction. She was pleased, or she said she was, but it was shot through with the same lack of enthusiasm – indifference, almost – that permeated the rest of their lives.

Last night, for example. She'd come home from work and flopped on the settee. He'd asked what was wrong and she'd said nothing. But he wasn't the type to let things like that go, so it had turned into an argument, and eventually she'd gone and flopped in the bedroom instead. It often happened. Their flat was well-decorated, clean and spacious, but sometimes when he watched her mentally pacing the place, it was as though she needed to find an undiscovered room or go insane.

The feeling was contagious. They hadn't been happy for months, and although his instinct was to do something to make it right, he had no idea how. Her refusal to talk about whatever was bothering her created a knot of frustration inside him, and sometimes it grew so hard it hurt him to swallow.

He looked at the face on the screen. Perhaps it was down to the photograph he'd started with or the choice of colours, but the one thing you could say for sure was that it was sad. So maybe not so alien after all.

He alt-tabbed back to the list and scrolled up to find it.

```
Number 87. Even though it's stupid, you support
my painting.
```

The first bit of that was something like his standard self-deprecation; if you put yourself down first, it reduced the risk of getting hurt. In the early years of their relationship, Jodie would have told him off for that, especially about his art, but now ... he wondered how she would react. Maybe Number 87 wasn't even true any more.

Scott felt it more than ever, but it was as much a part of their general unhappiness as anything else. It was okay to have dreams when you were younger, but at some point they needed to be abandoned, didn't they? His paintings wouldn't buy them out of here; the menial work they did to make a living wouldn't; and so if nothing changed then this was it. They would carry on in exactly the same way for the rest of their lives, and at the moment that was impossible.

He scrolled back down.

```
Number 274 ...
```

It was the last one on the page. If he could at least get this one, he'd have three full sheets of reasons.

His mobile phone was on the table beside the keyboard. He picked it up, reading again the text she'd sent him earlier:

```
hi again gorgeous, boring day here, hows
painting goin? cant wait to c u later.
sorry for how ive been. Love u w all my
heart. x x x x x
```

Scott put the phone aside, smiling. That was all it took. One message, or a short conversation, in which she talked to him the way she used to, and everything was wiped clean.

Of course, it was a transitory feeling, and the concern would build up again – but everything in life was one foot in front of the other. As long as they both held on, they could weather this and, instead of driving them further apart, perhaps facing this problem together would eventually bring them even closer.

Number 274.

Despite everything, he typed, you don't give up on me.

He'd started the list at the beginning of the year.

They'd just moved into this flat, and had begun to realise how lively their new neighbourhood was going to be. In their short tenancy, they'd already seen a midday car-jacking, listened to a minor stabbing in the alley behind, and been evacuated due to a bomb scare in the charity shop up the road. It was the best area they could afford to rent in, and the flat was nice enough, but neither of them felt safe, happy or remotely at home.

There were still boxes everywhere: some half emptied, others parcel-taped shut, as though if they didn't unpack it meant they weren't really staying. They'd taken out the kitchen stuff and put away a few clothes, but their only genuine concessions to making this home were the stereo and the TV, which had both been set up on the first night.

They were sitting in the front room watching television. Jodie couldn't stand to miss the soaps, while Scott could take them or leave them – mainly leave them. Either despite that or because of it, her devotion was about to become Number 56.

Before that, though, the situation got to him.

'This is shit.'

Jodie looked at him, then rested her head on his shoulder.

'Yeah,' she said. 'But we'll survive.'

He put his arm round her. 'You think?'

They'd been taking turns: one of them moaning, the other being optimistic. It was an unspoken agreement. If both of them went down at the same time there'd be nobody left to pull them out.

'Yeah,' she said. 'Because I love you.'

He touched her hair gently. It was dark and straight and thin; she didn't like it, but he did. Touch her hair and you touched her head straight away. It made her seem more fragile than she actually was.

'But I love you more,' he said.

She tapped his chest. 'No, you don't.'

'Yeah, I do.'

This, one of their regular games, would become Number 5.

'Prove it.'

'Prove it? There are a hundred reasons why I love you.'

She shifted to look at him. 'Go on, then.'

'What?'

'One hundred reasons.' She was warming to it. 'Let's have them.'

'Hmmm.'

'You see? All talk.'

'No.' Scott stood up. 'I was thinking where I could find a pen and paper.'

Actually, he was thinking: shit. But he was also thinking that here was an opportunity to do something good: something that might inject a little light into the situation. So he went through to the hallway and rummaged in a couple of boxes, returning a minute later with a notepad and a pen.

Jodie was wearing a bemused smile. But it was a happy one, too.

'You don't really have to, you know.'

Scott pressed his finger to his lips as he sat down next to her. 'Shhh. Watch your soap, woman.'

'Okay.'

She turned her attention back to the television, and he sat next to her and started writing. Line after line. Occasionally she craned to look, and he had to tilt the page to hide it from her.

'Ah-ah.'

'Let me see!'

'Not yet.'

A hundred reasons. When he started, he had no idea how difficult it was going to be or whether he'd make it. But he could feel Jodie beside him, smiling quietly, trying not to show how pleased she was. It was the happiest he could remember her being for ages, and it was more than enough to keep him going: scribbling down one after another. Hold that smile.

A few minutes later, the credits rolled on the television.

He flipped the page, carried on writing.

Now, nearly a year later, Scott minimised the Word document and headed into one of the spare rooms. One of the benefits of such a cheap area was that they'd managed to find a place with three bedrooms. Of the two they didn't sleep in, one belonged principally to Scott. He kept his painting equipment at one end, his weights at the other.

Stretching his neck from side to side, he set up the barbell on the bench and put some loud music on the small stereo.

Weights were a hangover from his teenage years, when he'd been skinny and a little physically aimless. He'd picked them up when he was fifteen and, to his own surprise as much as anyone else's, he'd kept with them until now, at twenty-eight, they were a regular part of his life. He lifted three times a week, for at least an hour each time, and when he missed more than one session in a row he got anxious and thought less of himself. He knew it was stupid, but he felt it anyway. Apart from that, it gave him the chance to switch off for a while. It was an escape – or was meant to be in this case.

He warmed up by bench-pressing a lowly thirty kilos before stacking the ends of the barbell with extra weights and taking it up to ninety. Then he lay down and took a careful grip, adjusted his hands slightly, breathed in and out. The heavier weights were always a shock to the system to begin with.

He lifted it, exhaled, lowered it, lifted it.

`Number 8,` he thought. `The way your hair feels.`

Lifted the weight. Again. Already, his chest muscles were beginning to burn.

Again.

`Number 34. You can be really girly sometimes.`

'Fuck off!' She'd given him a light punch before turning the page.

`Number 35. All right, you're not` *`that`* `girly.`

'Very clever. I take it back.'

Scott got to fifteen reps with the barbell and then forced himself to do just one more, raising the weight a fraction at a time, his arms shivering with effort.

The weight clanked down on the struts.

He sat up, breathed out.

`Number 89,` he thought, calming down. `When I wake up in the morning and you're looking at me.`

She'd kept smiling as she read the list. There was a quiet happiness that seemed to be mostly inside her, but he could see it on her face, too, and it pleased him more than he could tell her. The sensation it created threatened to burst something inside him. That smile, on that single occasion – he'd immediately marked it down in his head as Number 101.

'I really, *really* love you,' she'd told him.

'I love you, too.'

He'd been flushed with success. It had turned out to be much easier than he'd thought; in fact, as he'd closed in on Number 100 there had been more reasons in the front of his mind, and even more – he was sure – ready to rise up and take their place. He could have kept going all night. That, coupled with wanting to keep her smile from fading, had led to what happened next.

'It was easy. I could have got five hundred.'

'Bollocks.'

'Right – give me that here.'

She'd pulled the notepad out of reach. 'Don't be silly. You'll be here all night.'

'Okay. But I won't forget. Perhaps it'll be a Christmas present.'

'That might be more acceptable.' She put it down on the settee beside her and patted it safe. 'But you'll have to start again from scratch, because I'm keeping this.'

'No problem.'

That was what he'd said, feeling relieved if he was honest. But determined, too. Christmas had been more than eleven months away so there was plenty of time to work on the other four hundred reasons. He'd even had crazy ideas of reaching a thousand. Except that now, with Christmas only three weeks away, it didn't seem like 'no problem' any more. He wasn't even going to finish what he'd promised.

Scott took the weight down to forty kilos and began to do overhead presses with it from behind his neck.

One, two, three.

Would three hundred reasons do? She was expecting five, so what did it say if he ended up giving her less?

I don't love you as much as I thought?

But then again, he could be too hard on himself. How many people could come up with three hundred reasons, let alone five? How many would even try? So it did say other things, too.

He grimaced from the strain of the weight, but kept going anyway. Nine, ten ...

Three hundred reasons said: I'm doing the best I can.

It said: I realise not everything's perfect, least of all me, but I'm still trying. Because I so desperately don't want to lose you.

Clank.

For the next three-quarters of an hour, he worked through the rest of his usual sets: upright and bent-over rowing; bicep curls; tricep extensions. He finished off with a hundred sit-ups, his feet lodged under the barbell on the floor. When he was finished, he stood up, drank the rest of the water and turned off the music.

Part of the music continued.

Scott stood still for a second, listening. It wasn't part of the music. It was another sound, which had been there all along, only now he could hear it better. He frowned and walked towards the door. His first thought was that Jodie had come home early for some reason and was watching the television. He opened the door and called out.

'Jodie?'

Yes, it was the television.

Scott stepped into the corridor.

The front door was closed. Momentarily, he felt a flash of disappointment that she'd come in and not said hello, but it was replaced almost immediately by concern. If she was back early, perhaps something was wrong. He headed towards the front room, calling again, 'Jodie?'

He pushed the door open slowly, unease keeping him a little way back from it. It creaked. Came to a halt.

The television was on in the far corner, but there was no sign of Jodie. He walked across into the middle of the room.

Too late, Scott thought about the doorway into the kitchen, off the right-hand side of the lounge. He saw movement out of the corner of his eye, felt motion towards him, and he flinched sideways from it – but again, too late.

It was as though he'd walked into a lamp-post: a sickening collision. Suddenly he was looking at the ceiling.

Fuck!

And then the devil leaned in from above.

PART TWO

As an investigation progresses – and in general in this line of work – it always helps to remember a difficult but necessary truth: there are no such things as good and evil. Your opinion may differ, but in my experience thinking like that won't help you sleep any easier at night, and it certainly won't help you catch the people who commit serious crimes.

Labelling someone 'evil' is too convenient. The hideous effect these people can have on the lives of others is such that they shouldn't be swept under the carpet so easily. In reality, they are cogs in the mechanism of society that have slipped from their axes. The machinery that churns out useful, caring citizens like you and me went awry as they passed through it. They have been manufactured into the 'monsters' we see, and we owe it to their victims, and the victims of others like them, to attempt to understand the flaw in the process that has created them.

In police work, there is no God, no Devil, no Good and no Evil. There are no monsters. There are just damaged people.

The people we seek, like everyone else in the world, stand at the focal point of the damage done to them and the damage they do.

From *Damage Done*, by John Mercer

Mark

It was over six years since I'd driven up the long, curling road to the Niceday Institute in order to interview Jacob Barrett.

It had been summer, and a hot and oppressive one. I'd had my shirt sleeves rolled up, the window rolled down, and the whole way up I'd admired the acres of woodland on either side of the driveway: listening to birdsong from the trees to begin with; then, as I drew nearer the main building, to the fizz and buzz and crack of a groundsman at work with his strimmer. The hospital gave an illusion of peace and contentment that was a stark contrast to the people who were kept there. In reality, the place was run like a barracks.

I was still a student, working on my thesis, and I was nervous. I was about to come face to face with that most reviled, feared and least encountered member of society, the serial murderer, for the first time in my life. Naturally, I was on edge, but I needn't have been. The experience was strangely anti-climactic. It turned out that Jacob Barrett was only a man.

Because I'd read about him, his crimes hung around him like a dark halo, but without that foreknowledge I'm sure I would have found him dull. He was a bore: self-obsessed and arrogant, while having nothing to back up those convictions. He peppered his speech with comments like 'Now, I'm not a smart guy, but ...' and there was never any need for the 'but'. He could barely read or write, and he gave off sly so obviously you could smell it. His body was fat, rolls of it pushing at his tight blue shirt, and the skin on his face was mottled round beady eyes, which blinked too hard and too often, as though the light was bothering him.

His forearms were brawny, though. That was how he did it. Jacob wasn't a charmer; he was all about force. He slumped through the whole interview, with his arms folded in front of him, strangler's hands resting across thick, flabby biceps, revelling in the attention he was receiving. He liked to scare people and give off an aura of danger, despite his incarceration; he liked to imagine you were in awe of him. So he didn't like me much because I wasn't scared or in awe of him, and I didn't want to hear him boast about his crimes so much as I wanted to talk about his childhood.

Behind those blinking eyes, I knew, there was no emotional connection with other people. As he had passed through adolescence, the acceptable spectrum of sexual desires had finished up trodden and smeared. A well-adjusted adult wants to give and receive pleasure to and from another consenting adult, but Jacob's fixations were different. People were simply objects to him. They were there to be posed as his misdirected drive required them to be. He was sexually malformed, and over the years he had learned to hide it, faking normality well enough to get by.

How did he become that way? That was why I was there at Niceday. My doctorate involved an attempt to chart the grey area between the child he'd been and the adult he now was. Ultimately, the day formed a small, inconclusive part of a forgettable thesis, although the experience stayed with me a lot longer. I went home that night and was very quiet. Lise did her best to prod me out of my unease, but I couldn't articulate it back then. I'd probably have trouble even now.

One thing could be said for sure about Jacob's past: nobody abducts a girl from the side of the road and strangles her in a quarry on his first time out. Like anything you do in life, murder takes practice. And that was how he ended up being caught. John Mercer had surmised correctly that the quarry murderer must have worked up to his first known crime. He guessed that the killer had probably picked up hitchhikers before, for example, bringing his secret fantasies into reality one trembling step at a time. So the police had worked in reverse: records of attempted abductions and assaults were checked; reports of suspicious behaviour investigated. They used the relative sophistication of the killer's behaviour in the present to speculate on the mistakes he must have made in the past and learned to avoid.

The same is generally true of any sexually oriented killer. It's likely he'll be caught on an initial step of his journey, the way an artist probably gains a pile of rejection letters before selling his first work. For a killer, there might be a history of minor sexual assaults, or other activities that would have brought him to the attention of the police – things that halted him slightly, and then allowed him to go on later, a little wiser as to what had tripped him. That was how Jacob Barrett had been caught. He didn't rise out of Hell fully formed, because nobody does. It's too easy to think like that.

Yet the file in front of me now was a stark challenge to that principle.

The first murders attributed to the man who became known as the 50/50 Killer were so elaborate, and committed with such assuredness, that everyone assumed he must have practised and refined his technique beforehand. However, despite a background investigation that spread nationwide, nothing remotely similar was ever uncovered. He really did seem to have come out of nowhere.

His first known victims were Bernard and Carol Litherland. I scanned the details. They were both in their seventies, married for nearly fifty years, and had lived in the same house for the last thirty. They had two children, both of whom now had families of their own. The Litherlands were considerate neighbours, quiet but still active in the local community, and pleasant and agreeable in conversation.

A neighbour discovered their bodies the morning after their murder, concerned that the front door had been left ajar. There was a photograph in the file of the house. It looked grey and ominous, the door, an opening to Hell that drew you in the more you stared.

I read the post-mortem report quickly, reducing the extensive injuries to facts on a page.

The Litherlands had been handcuffed to the bedposts by their hands and feet. Carol Litherland had been burned with an iron. She had also been cut and stabbed. There were fifty-six separate injuries, including blinding in one eye, and a wound to her throat which had finally killed her. Her husband had also been tortured, receiving burns and cuts to his legs, arms, chest and head. He had been blinded in one eye as well, but had died of a heart attack, probably brought on by shock.

Steeling myself, I began to click through the photographs of the crime scene, referring back to the report as I went. The bodies on the bed, illuminated by police cameras, were hideous things, their pale hands protruding from the cuffs on the headboard, fingers splayed and still. Their tattered faces were turned away from each other, resting upon crimson pillows.

I moved quickly through close-ups of their wounds, pausing on a photograph of the wall above the headboard.

Immediately, the events of the day made more sense.

The Litherlands' killer had finger-painted a large pattern on the wall, almost identical to the one found in Kevin Simpson's study. Again, it was like a dreamcatcher or a spider's web, but distinct from either. The lines of the webbing were smeared and broken. Whatever it was supposed to represent, the report revealed it had been drawn in the Litherlands' blood.

From the beginning, it was clear that the murder of the Litherlands wasn't a burglary gone wrong. When the killer had finished with them, he had cleaned the house, and exited when the street was empty. No prints were found at the scene. Not a shred of forensic information had been left behind that would help catch him. Nothing appeared to have been taken.

The investigation started nowhere and didn't progress much beyond, and as time went on the number of officers assigned to it dwindled. At that point, the case belonged to Detective Sergeant Geoff Hunter and his team. Mercer didn't own it for another five months, when the next two victims were discovered and the police began to understand a little better what they were dealing with.

After finishing the first section of the file, I clicked back to the photograph of the spider web design on the Litherlands' wall, maximising the window so that the image filled the computer screen.

Then I leaned back, considering it.

As Mercer had said, it was too similar to the design today for it to be a coincidence. The same killer was surely responsible for both. So I wondered again about Greg's initial reticence – and also the less vocal reluctance of the rest of the team. Where could that be coming from? Certainly there were differences – some aspects of the older crimes seemed to be missing from the current one – but what had been found was conclusive enough, and I couldn't understand what was bothering everyone so deeply.

Maybe it's not that I'm not convinced. There's just something about this that's making me uneasy.

I frowned, remembering Greg's words. Then I returned to the file.

At the second crime scene, the 50/50 Killer had closed the front door upon exiting the house, and this became the first real insight into his methods and motives. The Litherlands' door had been left open because they had both died. But one of his second pair of victims was still alive and able to attract attention. The 50/50 Killer wanted his victims to be found.

The Roseneils, twenty-three-year-old newly-weds, had been restrained in the same way as the Litherlands. Daniel Roseneil was gagged during the ordeal and passed out at some point, through pain or terror or both. Upon regaining consciousness, he found the killer gone and his wife lying dead beside him. The killer had removed his gag but left him tied to the bed. Daniel screamed for over an hour before the neighbours broke in.

The Roseneil murder was assigned to Mercer's team before it had been officially tied to the previous case. Under different circumstances, Hunter would have handled both, but Mercer recognised something in the crimes he couldn't shake off, and he petitioned for and won the whole case. I could imagine that wouldn't have gone down too well. But whatever the internal ramifications, from that point on the hunt for the 50/50 Killer belonged to our team.

Again, I skimmed the details.

Julie Roseneil's body displayed similar injuries to Carol Litherland's, in both number and intensity. Extensive cuts and burning; disfigurement of the breasts and genitals; mutilation of the face and head. Like Carol's, Julie's throat had been cut. Daniel Roseneil had been tortured as Bernard Litherland had, but in the end the killer had left him alive.

I clicked through the scene-of-crime photographs, attempting without success to maintain some distance from what I saw. I noted that a similar pattern to the first one had been painted on the wall above the Roseneils' bed. Half dreamcatcher, half occult symbol, the webbing smeared by those little cross-checks.

This was the 50/50 Killer's signature, then, present but subtly different at each of the crime scenes. None of the patterns had ever been identified from books, but it was clearly meaningful and important to him. Whatever his motivations for the murders, these designs played a key role in the underlying pathology.

The photographs concluded with a black-and-white picture from the Roseneils' wedding, taken four months before the attack. They were both standing. Their bodies were facing away from the camera but they had turned back slightly to smile for it, hands held between them. It was hideous in comparison to the other pictures: the ones taken afterwards. They seemed so young and happy; their grip on each other's hands looked good and strong. And then Daniel had regained consciousness to find his dead wife beside him.

There was interview footage in the online file. It was in black-and-white, like the wedding photograph, but that was the only similarity. In these images, Daniel Roseneil's face was bruised and downturned, his body language one big flinch. He didn't look at the camera once. The video reminded me of the Gulf War clips of captured US soldiers forced to make statements, only this was infinitely worse, the injuries far more extensive and disfiguring. Text in the corner of the screen stated that the interview was conducted by Detective Andrew Dyson.

I put in the headphones attached to the monitor.

Dyson: 'Daniel, could you tell us what you remember about the night?'

Daniel Roseneil was looking down and to the left. His features were swollen and ruined. As he spoke, his lips clicked, sticking together slightly.

Roseneil: 'There was a man in the bedroom. I don't know what time it was. I woke up and he had a knife at my throat.'

Dyson: 'Did he say anything?'

Roseneil: 'He was whispering. I think he was reassuring me. But I can't remember exactly what he said.'

Dyson: 'That's fine. Can you remember what happened next?'

Roseneil: 'He had handcuffs. He made me tie Julie up, her hands and her feet. Then he tied me up as well.'

Dyson: 'Then what did he do?'

No response.

Dyson changed tack: 'What did he look like?'

Roseneil: 'He was the Devil.'

A pause.

Dyson: 'The Devil?'

It turned out that the intruder had been wearing a pink rubber demon mask, secured with elastic round his head.

Throughout the ordeal, the man had been calm and controlled. Daniel had kept looking for a moment when he could *do* something to stop what was happening, but the opportunity never came. From the moment Daniel awoke, he was going to end up either cuffed to the bedposts or with his throat cut. The intruder didn't slip up once.

Roseneil: 'A game. He said we were going to play a game.'

Dyson: 'What kind of game? It's okay, Daniel. Take your time.'

Roseneil: 'A game about … love. He was going to hurt one of us. He said … he said I had to choose who it was.'

Dyson: 'It's okay.'

Roseneil: 'One of us was going to die and I had to choose. He said I could change my mind, all the way until dawn.'

Dyson: 'Can you remember what happened after that?'

Roseneil (determined): 'I chose me.'

From that point on, his recollections of what had happened became disjointed.

It was understandable. There were flashes and impressions, but the actual memories of being burned or cut were buried too deep. He simply couldn't remember, and any attempt to probe in that direction resulted in a partial shutdown. He didn't recall Julie being tortured, either, or acknowledge the fact that, at some point, he had probably changed his decision, the pain finally becoming too much. When her name was mentioned, he turned further away from the camera, as though even attempting to retrieve that memory was a step too far.

Dyson backed off, and I approved.

They turned the clock back a little. The killer had talked to him a lot. The exact words were lost, but he knew the man had been calm, almost friendly, acting as if he'd known the couple for years. Daniel recalled thinking *How did he know that?* But not what had been said to prompt it.

All this had gone into the notes to follow up – *'Possible acquaintance?'* – but although the subsequent investigation was exhaustive, nobody with any connection to the Roseneils seemed good for it. The team worked that angle hard and got nowhere. For his part, Daniel was convinced he'd never met the man before.

I minimised the interview window and clicked through the file. Simon and Greg had worked up a possible solution to how the killer knew so much about the Roseneils. Just as with the Litherlands, the killer had left the scene as clean as possible, but there was certain activity that he couldn't hide. From dust residues, it looked as though the plug sockets and light fittings had been interfered with and, once again, there was no sign of forced entry. There was also evidence that the killer had spent a certain amount of time in the attic. Initially confusing, those discoveries began to make sense in the light of what Daniel half remembered.

I read through the IT report.

Greg had listed examples of the type of surveillance devices he suspected were being used: microphones and cameras that could be hidden in sockets or left secreted around the house; devices that could intercept emails and passwords; moulds and kits that could be used to model locks and keys. It was frightening how easy it was to acquire them.

The theory was that the killer had gained access to the house long before the murder, and had been watching and studying his victims for some time. Recording their conversations. Spending nights above them in the attic. Living with them, to an extent – perhaps even for many months. He learned their secrets and their lies, and he used his knowledge to hurt them emotionally in addition to inflicting physical pain.

All of it was part of his 'game'. He tortured people to make them abandon the person they loved.

I closed my eyes. Horrific as the murders were, I found I was thinking at least as much about the survivors. About the choice they'd had to make.

I'd die for you, I couldn't live without you – people say those things all the time, but they almost never have to deliver on them. The victims the 50/50 Killer left behind had to face the reality of failing to live up to their words. Despite what they'd told their partners, they hadn't loved them enough, and so now that person was dead. They had chosen themselves.

I opened the photograph of Daniel and Julie Roseneil again, the one from their wedding day. They looked so happy and unaware, the picture full of possibility and promise. It was a reminder that you never know what lies ahead. Most days everything is fine and normal, and then one day it isn't. By its very nature, you don't see it coming. The terrible things that happen in life hit you like a truck out of a side road.

And then back to Daniel Roseneil in the interview footage, with his ruined face and his ruined life. Out of nowhere, his wife was dead and he was alone, and in some ways he was responsible for that. Unhelpful as it was for the investigation, I didn't blame him at all for not remembering what had happened that night. I didn't blame any of them.

There had been two further attacks, both taking place during the following year. The third victims were Dean Carter and Jenny Tomlinson, a couple in their late twenties, and at this scene the killer had reversed his scenario, allowing Jenny to choose who would be tortured and killed. She was badly hurt but survived the night; her boyfriend died in her place. Seven months after that, the 50/50 Killer targeted his fourth victims. Nigel Clark was given the choice. He was hurt so badly that he would never walk again, while Sheila, his wife of over twenty years, was killed.

In each case, the killer's technique was impeccable. There was no sign of forced entry. No useful forensic evidence was ever left behind.

I didn't need to see the photographs of these last murders. Instead, with time pressing, I returned to the main menu and opened two overall summaries. The first dealt with witness impressions; the second was a psychological profile.

In the first, the 50/50 Killer had been reduced to a list of basic attributes. He was white, slightly taller than average, slim but athletic, calm and polite, articulate. He had dark-brown hair. While carrying out the attacks, he didn't seem to enjoy what he was doing – but nor did he find it difficult. The torture was mechanical, done without emotion or pleasure.

It wasn't what we'd expect from this type of killer. In cases like this, the victim is generally an object to fulfil a fantasy or a need. But although sexual assault was involved in the 50/50 Killer's crimes, it seemed to be more part of the tools he worked with – a way to terrorise and hurt – than an end in itself. He appeared calm and dispassionate, mutilating people

67

before killing them and then leaving them alone when they were dead: when the game was over. Any enjoyment he gained from the process was kept well below the surface.

And yet, remembering that terrible hissing sound he'd made, it was clear he was getting something from it.

I turned to the psychological profile, ready to approach any concrete claims with hefty scepticism. But I was surprised. There were more question-marks here – more readily acknowledged guesswork – than anything else. Specifically, there was a reluctance to address the exact nature of the killer's pathology. Why did he do this to people? He used torture and pain to manipulate them, forcing them to betray their partners. What was he getting out of it? Each speculation met a contradiction. The report confined itself largely to more general assumptions, instead, and I settled into the familiarity of these.

He was likely to be over twenty-five years old, because the sophistication of the crimes suggested an older, more experienced offender. He would certainly be of above-average intelligence, but would lack anything that a normal person would think of as an emotional life. Given the cost of the surveillance equipment, he probably had money, and he was mobile but not transient. A white van, never identified, had been seen in the vicinity of two of the scenes, and the equipment he used would certainly be easier to transport and monitor from a van. Plus, a tradesman parked up was less likely to arouse suspicion.

Both his financial stability and his age made it likely he functioned adequately in society – that like Jacob Barrett he was successful at masking his true nature. But any relationships he held down would be a front. His real life happened in other people's homes at night, and the pursuit of that would be constantly occupying him behind the façade. Friends and acquaintances would be casual at best, and were likely to have worries or concerns about him. It was suggested that he might be fascinated by weapons, and might own or have read books on torture, police techniques and the military.

And so on.

I couldn't find anything I disagreed with, but none of it was written with anything like the usual confidence. There was something about this man and his crimes that precluded definite statements. Nothing could be taken for granted, and perhaps at the heart of it lay the devil mask he wore. Nobody would say it, but the ease with which he operated, the methods he used, the carnage and ruin he left behind ... Well, it was stupid, but you couldn't help but think.

'He was the Devil,' Daniel Roseneil had said.

And of course he wasn't. There was no such thing. But nevertheless everything in the profile read as guesswork. Tentative ideas that circled a black hole, afraid to touch.

Jodie

The path through the woods was scattered with the remnants of autumn: a mush of dirty red leaves with dark-brown mud pushing up in between. Her shoes sank into it, making her balance uneven. The ground either sucked at her or else slid beneath her feet, but she moved as quickly as possible, keeping just behind Scott, her hands out to catch him in case he should slip.

Jodie had never thought of herself as practical or sensible, and she was surprised by how calm she felt. Despite the man with the knife, and despite the fact that her hands were cuffed in front of her.

A voice in her head kept telling her what to do, and at the moment it was instructing her to concentrate on her footing, to remember every detail she possibly could and, most of all, to look after Scott. His hands were cuffed as well, but the man had also put a black bag over his head, so he couldn't see the slippery ground they were walking on. The bag seemed to have taken away his resolve and strength. He was subdued: a man stumbling to his own execution.

He needs you, the voice kept saying. *Look after him. One thing at a time.*

The voice was reassuring and sensible, and so she encouraged it and clung to the advice it offered. If it went silent there would be space for panic to rise in its place; if it kept talking, she wouldn't have to think about what was happening to them, she could reduce it to instants and obstacles, and occupy herself with taking care of one problem after another.

One thing at a time.

Observe. Remember the route. Look after Scott.

She glanced to her right and saw a thick black tree trunk sprouting out of a ridge of earth. The ground was sodden, like potters' clay. Elephantine roots spread down to the path, while thin branches hung down from

69

above like old hair. She would remember that tree. Newer leaves on the ground seemed to point to it. Bright red darts.

If necessary, the voice cautioned, *you should pretend you remember nothing*.

This practical, reasonable voice hadn't been there to begin with. At first, there had been only fear and panic. After the attack on the waste ground, she'd come properly awake lying on hard, ridged metal, breathing in the pungent stink of diesel. Her body was cramped, twisted; her wrists and shoulder hurt; the side of her head felt like it was expanding and contracting.

She had opened her eyes to see rust and rope, and it all juddered as the road passing beneath them jolted the van's suspension.

This isn't an ambulance.

She had been dimly aware there had been an accident, so it would make sense for her to be in an ambulance. Her memory returned slowly, drawing increasingly black lines beneath the underlying impression that something was terribly, terribly wrong. The baby. The man in the devil mask.

Then she had seen the drawing on the side of the van, painted on the white metal inside, and she had started to panic. Rape, she thought. Torture. And worse. Her mind ran a sieve into the depths of her imagination and dredged up horrors she was shocked she could even think of.

There was a gag tied round her head, so she couldn't call out, but she leaned back a little and could see the roof of the van, and then the top of the seats at the front. She made out the back of the driver's head, and a topsy-turvy city-scape of sky through the windscreen, which bounced around as they drove. She could still hear the baby crying, too. The upside-down man turned his head, reached out to the passenger seat and told the child something soothing.

At that moment, the panic had threatened to overwhelm her. It felt like she might have gone mad for a few minutes.

But that section of time wasn't important any more, and as the voice instructed she put it out of her mind. What mattered was negotiating the landscape: the precarious ground, the soft mud and leaves that slipped under her feet. Trees thrust out on either side like black antlers, jutting against each other, one ridge of wet earth fighting another for supremacy.

The land went up steeply, then went down. For long stretches, it was practically a mudslide. In the gaps between the trees, there was more mud, and more trees, further away. Above it all, the mountains in the distance.

It was freezing – so, so cold. She could hardly feel her face any more. In an attempt to generate some heat, she tensed and untensed her muscles. It must be worse for Scott. He was an odd sight, dressed in tracksuit bottoms, white T-shirt and his bulky coat, staggering along in front. She reached out and touched his shoulder, hoping he understood: I love you. But the coat was smooth and cold. He probably couldn't even feel her.

Jodie took her bunched hands away, but left them close.

She thought back, remembering the van stopping, and how she had been sure it meant something awful was about to happen. Instead, she was left on her own for a time. The next thing she'd known, the double doors at her feet opened and early evening light streamed into the van.

'Get inside.' The man's voice was quiet and reasonable, almost mannered. 'Lie down. If you run or fight, I'll drive away and hurt her.'

Jodie looked up carefully and saw Scott clambering into the van, his hands cuffed in front of him like hers, a grim expression on his face. She was surprised and confused. The van tilted and rocked as he moved, lying down awkwardly beside her. The man outside was a brief silhouette against the sky, then he slammed the doors shut.

'It'll be okay,' Scott whispered. His voice was so serious that she knew he was terrified. 'I'll get us out of this.'

After a few moments, the engine rumbled into life, and they were on the move again. Jodie glanced up at the driver's head, and then at Scott. Unable to reply because of the gag, she rolled over – one and a half turns – bringing her back against his front in the way they slept sometimes. She felt the bundle of his tied hands pressing into her but nevertheless was comforted by his warmth. He kissed her head through her hair, tensed himself against her. They were in it together, and they would get out of it together.

That was when the voice had first appeared. She remembered being quite calm. Now that Scott was here, it felt as though she understood her predicament better, and that allowed her to relax into it, accept its parameters. Fighting wasn't an option, and escape was unlikely. Observation, then, was key. Her thoughts had moved on to what it might mean that she and Scott were in this together. Most importantly, it implied that what was happening wasn't random; the man in the devil mask had a plan and he was following it. Successfully, too. She didn't know what his intentions were, but it was obvious he knew exactly what he was doing.

No plan is perfect, the voice had told her. *No plan is continuous.*

There would be links between the stages – spaces and gaps where he relied on luck more than at other times. If they were clever, and if the luck went their way instead, they might be able to exploit that. Their lives might be saved or lost in the possibilities offered by a small number of intervals.

It had summoned up reserves of anger and determination inside her.

You will get out of this alive.

Yet so far there had been nothing. His plan had ticked successfully along from one point to the next. There had been one more stop, when the man took the baby out of the van. After another short journey, he'd parked. When he opened the van doors they had found themselves on a road by the edge of the woods.

'If you run,' he said, 'I'll kill the one who runs slowest.'

It had been almost surreal. He was standing there in the early-evening light on what was normally a busy road, wearing a devil mask and holding a knife with a long, cruelly thin blade. Their hands were bound in front of them. The scene was unequivocal. And yet no cars had passed them the whole time.

'We're going in there.' He'd gestured at the path into the woods, and she had thought: Possibilities. He couldn't control them both for ever. There would be some kind of chance; there had to be. But then he had put the bag over Scott's head and made him go first, walking a little behind the pair of them. There had been no opportunities at all. There had been nothing.

In front of her, Scott stumbled, tripped. She had enough time to see it happening, but not to stop it: as she reached out – 'Careful!' – his feet went from under him and he fell hard. Mud and leaves scattered out in front.

'Shit.'

A rock went off to the right, clattering down the slope. It rolled quickly, hit a tree with a sound like a gunshot, and then came to rest further down against a row of old stones. There were a lot of those in the woods, jutting out of the ground like giant half-buried jawbones. Old structures, mostly demolished.

She crouched down beside Scott.

'Are you okay, baby? Are you hurt?'

He shook his head as best he could, but didn't say anything. She heard that he was crying.

'Come on, sweetheart. We'll be okay.'

She helped him to his feet, fighting back the urge to join him in tears.

There was no place for that at the moment. Only one of them should cry at a time. Feeling desperate and panicked and scared was acceptable, as long as one of them remained strong for the other. That could be her for now; she could do that.

As they struggled up, the man didn't help them: he just stood back and watched from behind that inscrutable *fucking* mask. One hand held the knife; the other hung onto the shoulder strap of the bag he'd brought with him. For a while, she had wondered what might be in that bag. The voice had told her to stop.

'Be careful,' he said. 'And be quiet. There are people in these woods who will hurt you for a lot longer than I will.'

Jodie brushed at the mud on Scott's coat, but it didn't work: it smeared down the sleeve and made her hands dirty.

The man was right, of course, and he didn't need to remind her – there were so many stories about this place. It was dangerous territory and by her best estimation they were now a long way off the map. Her brain teased her with images. The two of them tied to trees. Blood in the dirt. Their bodies, brown and dry as rope by spring.

Even if there were bad people here, the man didn't seem too concerned. But then he had the face of a devil, and he was carrying a knife and God only knew what else. He moved like he belonged in these woods. She certainly couldn't imagine anyone or anything more frightening was moving around out here.

He gestured with the knife: keep moving.

They set off again.

You aren't frightened, the voice told Jodie, but this time it was wrong. She was frightened – and not just of the man and his knife and whatever he had in the bag. She could make as many observations as she wanted, but the truth was they were heading straight into the heart of these woods, to a place this man had chosen. He knew the paths; he knew the dangers and pitfalls they had to avoid; he was at home here. Whereas Jodie had never felt so utterly isolated, so far away from anything she knew.

Her mind worked itself around the voice and, rather than listening to its attempts at comforting her, she thought about myths and fairy-tales. About stories of travellers who took forbidden routes and found themselves facing monsters and doorways to death. She thought about the River Styx, with its creaking, skeletal ferryman who took passengers across to the afterlife. About Dante wandering where he shouldn't and discovering the circles of Hell.

That was exactly it, Jodie realised. The Devil was taking them into Hell. And – despite Scott's quiet tears up ahead; despite everything she'd told herself – she allowed herself to cry.

3 DECEMBER   5.30 P.M.
13 HOURS, 50 MINUTES UNTIL DAWN

Mark

One of the many problems with the 50/50 file was the sheer size of the thing. There were summaries, but I was forcing myself to read it from the beginning, so that the facts and theories I learned would have context and make sense. In effect, I wanted to approach it as the rest of the team had. But it was a big file and it was taking time. The text was difficult to read, the photographs hard to look at.

I had to keep taking short breaks, usually via the canteen to pick up coffee for me and Mercer. I was on my way back, carrying two plastic cups, when I felt my mobile buzz in my pocket.

'Shit.'

I put the cups down on the floor and fished out my phone to read the text. It was from my parents.

```
Hi Mark. Thinking of you. Hope your
first day has been good. Hope you're
well. We worry. Ring us when you have
chance. Love m&d xx
```

I checked my watch, surprised to see that my first day was officially over – although of course it wasn't. The investigation had 'all-nighter' stamped right the way through it.

I wondered whether I should text back. My parents always worried. They hadn't wanted me to be a policeman in the first place, and even though I was nearly thirty they were still concerned that something was going to happen to me. Since Lise died it had become worse, and I'd had to stop returning their calls sometimes, simply because I couldn't take it. And now I'd moved across country ... I guess it was only natural they were worried, and on some level I appreciated it, but the fact remained I couldn't handle it well. I needed to be on my own. It felt like they *wanted* me to grieve and break down, and were worried something was

74

wrong when I didn't, but the truth was that I just had my own way of dealing with things. Talking about what happened wasn't part of that, not yet.

I decided not to reply. Instead, I slipped my phone back into my pocket and returned to the office, putting Mercer's coffee on the desk beside him, then resuming my position at the computer.

'Thanks.'

He didn't look up when he said it, but that was okay.

As I struggled in the glue of the file, Mercer was performing a similar task with the ongoing operation. The rest of the team were either out in the field or working from offices in other parts of the building, and since the briefing it had just been the two of us here. Conversation hadn't flowed, but we were both busy. Members of the team logged in as necessary to bring reports and updates, and when he wasn't discussing things with them Mercer maintained the same pose: head bowed, poring over paperwork, co-ordinating everything from the confines of his own head. When he wasn't making calls, he was taking them; when he wasn't doing that, he was reading through piles of documents or chasing others. He didn't get up from his seat, but every time I looked at him I saw a flurry of internal activity.

Among it all, there were regular phone calls to his superior, Detective Inspector Alan White, informing him of developments as they occurred. Mercer always seemed eager to get rid of him. I didn't know whether he disliked having to answer to someone else about his own case, but whatever the explanation he constantly downplayed its importance – to the degree that I began to really notice it. Not once did he refer to the 50/50 Killer. Instead, he focused on the minutiae of the case, and I thought it was strange, given his insistence on how obvious the connection was.

What little progress there was came in dribs and drabs. Simon phoned in from the crime lab. Two sets of prints had been found in the house. One belonged to Kevin Simpson; the other was unknown. Although it was possible the killer had left us a gift, it was more likely the second prints belonged to Jodie. And we were no closer to discovering who she was.

Pete had been talking to Simpson's ex-girlfriends, sending a report in after each. I watched a little blankly as one after another was crossed off the list of possibles. My own door-to-door team were similarly prolific; the results equally unhelpful. Previous gaps in the record had been filled and the interviews had moved on to the surrounding streets, but no new leads had emerged as a result.

I watched Mercer the whole time, quietly astonished by the way he was handling things. He seemed to hold everything in his head at once, staring intently at the screen during each report, nodding to himself. His expression occasionally became blank and faraway as he slotted each new fact into place. For me, it was hard enough playing catch-up on the file, never mind how it was continuing to grow. At least I had a framework to rethink the crime scene at Kevin Simpson's house. Although the signature and the game were key, Greg was right that the scene this morning was different. Whoever this Jodie was, she hadn't been involved in the same way previous victims were.

It's been two years. He's been planning.

I wondered at the picture Mercer was working with, but for now that was his concern. Our job was to gather the small amounts of evidence that were available; his was to make sense of them.

And so it continued.

A little before six, Greg videophoned with an IT report. There was bad news. If there had been any reference to Jodie or Scott on Simpson's PC, whether in email, contacts or a random document, the killer had erased it. As Greg had told us earlier, we wouldn't find their identities from the computer.

'However, we do have a major victory,' he said.

His tone was a little off, but Mercer had no time for the sarcasm.

'Go on.'

Greg sent the clips through. There were six: grainy CCTV stills of the main road near Simpson's house. Six different white vans. You couldn't read the number plates in these images but IT had enhanced them and managed to secure identification of all six.

'These were all taken this morning, around the time the killer would have been leaving.' Greg was absently scratching his sideburns. 'It goes without saying, there are a lot of white vans around at that time of day.'

'But you said it anyway, Greg. Well done. Names and addresses?'

'On their way over now.'

Mercer turned to me: 'Your door-to-door team?'

'Still working the streets around Simpson's house. With ever-decreasing returns.'

'Pull them and get them on this instead. Greg's right that it's probably nothing, but you never know.'

'Okay.'

'Full video and audio.'

There it was again. I found myself gritting my teeth, then told myself it was just his way and contacted my team, setting about the transfer of the names and addresses I needed them to investigate. I deliberately repeated Mercer's instructions – a little archly myself – but his attention was elsewhere: he was dialling a number, presumably to let White know about this latest development.

His expression was unreadable. Looking at him, I thought, was like trying to watch a battleground from above the clouds.

After talking to the door team, I returned my attention to the file. There was a large section towards the end I'd yet to read, and it was about to provide me with more insight into the day's events than was entirely comfortable. This part was about Detective Andrew Dyson.

A father of two, Dyson had been working on Mercer's team for over ten years. I had listened to him interviewing Daniel Roseneil, who had told him all about the Devil. A year after, Dyson met that Devil in the flesh, in the process becoming the last known victim of the 50/50 Killer.

Now, two years later, I was sitting at what had once been his desk, watching footage from the day it occurred.

The film had been taken by a CCTV camera on a lamp-post in a quiet suburban street. It was angled badly but gave a reasonable view of the road. Perhaps fifty metres from the lens, I saw Dyson. He had parked outside an ordinary semi-detached house and was walking up to the front door. The clock in the corner of the screen said it was two thirteen in the afternoon.

These were Dyson's final moments: the last time he'd been seen alive. In this case, the seeing had been done by a digital storage unit, which was colder and more clinical than an actual witness, and made him seem even more vulnerable. On screen, he was already a lonely figure: his hands in his pockets, coat pulled tight round him against the cold. I wanted to reach out and warn him, but I was watching a ghost and all I could do was reach out for coffee. And watch as the last moments of his finished history repeated themselves.

It had been three months since the Clarks were attacked, and in that time the investigation had hit a wall. There was so little in the way of forensic evidence to go on, and the handful of leads had petered out or been exhausted. Mercer's resources were being steadily depleted; his men allocated to newer, more pressing assignments. For now, the team itself wasn't giving up – or at least Mercer wasn't. They were going over every fact they had: reinterviewing friends, family and neighbours; chasing the edges of gaps and gaining extra detail where they could.

I knew what it was like to be involved in the late stages of an investigation that was going nowhere: there was an inevitability to it. You knew you'd failed, but you kept going anyway, hoping for some kind of break. But never this kind.

The house Dyson was visiting was as flat and square as the pale red bricks it was made from; it looked like it had been built as a bodyguard for the more expensive properties in the distance. There was a long, straight driveway down one side, ending in a dark garage. Two bins, a black one for rubbish, a green for recycling. The garden out front was generally neat, but it had been left untended through the winter months. I could see the bushes trembling slightly in the wind. Behind all this, the sky was dark grey and mottled. Ominous. Along with the space between properties, the sky made the entire street look like a row of drab gravestones, frozen and weathered away in some cliff-top cemetery.

Dyson had rung the bell. Now, he was shuffling in the cold. He seemed too small, dwarfed by the house, as though it might swallow him whole.

Come on, come on, I thought.

He rubbed his hands together.

It's freezing out here.

He glanced up and down the street before leaning on the doorbell again.

The surveillance equipment the killer used was expensive and specialised, but there were at least two shops in the city that sold it, along with numerous sites where it could be bought online. By their very nature, the places that did stock it weren't keen on co-operating with the police, but under pressure they had. Lists of security experts, jealous husbands and assorted oddballs had been checked, the suspects on each list eliminated one by one.

That day, Dyson was going over old ground, revisiting the home of Frank Walker, a man who'd bought a couple of listening devices a few years before. He'd already been interviewed without any problem: no flags, no concerns. This visit was just a formality, so the day should have been a non-event. Dyson had no reason to think he might be in any danger. The file speculated this was why he hadn't turned on his recording equipment yet.

When I came to that, I forced myself to reread it. But there it was: one single lapse in concentration, brought on presumably by boredom or repetition. A lack of alertness. If he'd been more on guard, perhaps things might have turned out differently. The audio of his attack would have been relayed from the clip at his belt to the receiver in the car, and from there to the department. He might have lived.

I glanced across at Mercer. He was buried in the reports and didn't notice me looking, but I saw him in a slightly new light. Earlier, I'd resented his insistence on full video, full audio in the interviews. In a way I still did, but at least now I understood the reasons behind it.

On the computer screen, the clock in the corner ticked away the seconds. A full fifteen elapsed before Dyson reached out and pushed the door. It must have been slightly ajar because it opened inwards at the pressure. He leaned inside, his hand on the doorframe. I imagined him shouting,

'*Hello? It's the police.*

Anyone in?'

He hovered for a moment, and I felt my heart flutter. This was the moment. The exact truth about what happened after this would remain lost to us until we caught the man who'd lived there, the man who had been hiding within. Even then we might never know why Dyson decided to go inside. One theory was that he must have seen something in the kitchen that disturbed him enough to enter; another, that he heard a noise – a fake call for help, perhaps. Whatever the explanation, within seconds of opening the door he had entered the kitchen and disappeared.

The next camera to record him would belong to a crime-scene technician.

I kept watching, anyway. Whoever had compiled the footage had included an extra ten seconds at the end showing nothing but the still house and its quivering garden. It was possibly out of respect, but I found myself thinking about what was happening inside, out of sight, and I was glad when it cut off.

Returning to the main report, I read that Dyson's body had been found three hours later, after he'd failed to check in and not responded to calls. It was all too easy to imagine the unanswered crackle echoing around the empty living room they eventually found him in; his location had been traced from the car parked outside.

The house belonging to 'Frank Walker' turned out to be empty. The floorboards and walls were bare, and there was nothing in the way of furniture apart from a desk by the phone line and a mattress upstairs. Even though the place had been rented by Walker for several years, it was obvious that nobody had lived there for any length of time. Frank Walker was a fiction, a cleverly engineered fraud with an elaborate but false history laid out behind him, as empty and hollow as the house itself.

The 50/50 Killer had invented him as a ghost identity. Both the name and the accommodation were just bolt-holes to him.

I pictured the killer flitting between the nests he'd made throughout the city, shedding identities the way a spider discards its skin. The house in the film was a little pocket of rank air, bubbled up to the surface of our world. It had been discovered, so he had moved on to another.

Nests. It made him seem even more of a monster.

Andrew Dyson was found lying on the floor in the living room, curled on his side, hugging the puncture wounds in his stomach. The killer had calmly attacked him with two long, thin-bladed knives, stabbing him six times: methodical and calculated. The cuts were clean and deep, in two bunches: front and side. There were no further injuries. Dyson had died slowly, of shock and blood loss, while his murderer moved around the house and cleaned any remaining evidence carefully away, room by room.

By the time the police arrived, he was long gone: disappeared out the back, apparently on foot. No vehicle had ever been registered to him. Nobody knew him. His bank account contained several thousand pounds, but the transactions were muddied and impossible to trace. No further attempt at withdrawal was ever made. He dumped the money as easily as the identity.

Frank Walker simply vanished, leaving Dyson's corpse behind: one last victim, like a husk in a web.

There was more to the file after that but, like the CCTV footage, it carried on for a few faltering moments that were ultimately unnecessary. Greg had completed a full dissection of the Frank Walker identity, exploring all the possible leads before coming to a halt at each dead end. Walker's house was stripped down practically to its foundations, but proved as clean of forensic evidence as any of the killer's primary crime scenes. His neighbours were all interviewed. None of them had ever seen him.

Nothing came of any of it.

As I finished, though, I found I was more concerned by what wasn't in the file. The team had maintained authority for the investigation after Dyson's death, but John Mercer's name was almost immediately con-spicuous by its absence. The case had been placed back under the overall control of Detective Sergeant Geoff Hunter.

I broke off from the file and looked over at Mercer.

He was still in that familiar pose: elbows on the desk, fingers now splayed over his downturned face, lifting his hair up at the front. Still deeply involved in the papers and reports he was wrestling with.

I watched him as subtly as I could, thinking about the book he'd written – the one I'd reread when I'd got the news of my appointment.

In the early sections, he discussed several of the team's high-profile cases in detail, including two that remained unsolved, but the 50/50 Killer wasn't one of them. In the chapters at the end, where he detailed his breakdown, he'd written about being overloaded with work and about the pressures that came from sharing your headspace with one killer after another. The implication was that it had been the general stress of the job that had sent him over the edge for a time. There was no mention of Dyson's murder. Looking at it now, though, the chronology fitted; it couldn't be a coincidence. He had pushed his team hard, one of them had died, and shortly afterwards he had ended up in hospital. And not just any investigation, but this one –

Mercer was looking at me.

I turned back to the screen.

'What?'

'Nothing, sir.'

But he was still looking at me and I felt my skin growing hot. I glanced back. His expression was blank, but I imagined he was reading my thoughts and knew full well that I was intruding in an area of his life that was none of my business. A look of realisation appeared on his face.

'It's nearly seven o'clock, isn't it?'

'Oh,' I said. 'Yes. But that's okay.'

He leaned back. 'No. It's been a long day. I'm sorry, it's just one of those things. We're going to be here a lot longer. Is that a problem?'

'It goes with the territory,' I said.

'Yes, but you've not eaten.' He glanced at his watch. 'Take half an hour.'

I was about to protest, but then I realised I was starving. And exhausted. More than anything, I wanted to get out of this office and away from things for a while.

'Go on,' he said. 'I'll hold the fort here.'

'Yes, sir.'

'Besides, I have to ring my wife. There's a canteen down the hall. You can get something there.'

I made my way to the door, pausing when I realised what he'd told me about the canteen. I glanced at his desk. The cup of coffee I'd brought him was sitting on the corner, empty. It seemed to have escaped his mind that I'd been to the canteen a few times already.

'Can I get you a coffee?' I said.

'No, thanks.' He had already returned his concentration to the files on the desk in front of him, making notes and swapping his attention back and forth between them.

He said, 'Not this time.'

Eileen

Three little words that sent her heart fluttering: 'I'm working late.'

In the study, on the phone, Eileen was playing with the cable. She was looping it round her finger, releasing it, beginning again. She forced herself to stop.

'You will take care of yourself, won't you?'

On the other end of the line, John said nothing. Over the years she'd become used to deciphering these silences, and she had no trouble picturing him. He would be sitting at that desk, staring at something in front of him. Concentrating. Not wanting rid of her exactly, but unable to focus completely on the conversation. It always took a moment for the question to jostle its way through everything else in his head. In the background, she could hear him typing.

'Of course I will.'

As though it was obvious.

When John had first told her he was thinking of returning to work, Eileen had experienced a number of different emotions, the first of which had been sheer disbelief. He'd been in his dressing-gown at the time, half collapsed on the settee in the front room. Even walking from room to room seemed hard for him; he moved slowly, like an invalid. And so she hadn't taken him seriously.

When it became clear that on some level he meant it, the disbelief had shifted swiftly into an almost righteous anger. She'd shouted at him: what in hell did he think he was doing? Not just to himself, if he wasn't bothered enough about that, but to *her*? She'd reminded him of the care he'd needed, and which she'd patiently given, and of the sacrifices she'd had to make. She'd spelled out the worry that had felt like it might destroy her, too.

When her husband had broken, Eileen felt her entire life hold its breath while she picked up his pieces and pressed them together, holding

82

them in place and praying they would stick. He had no right to risk putting her through that again. He owed her better, she told him. They were supposed to be a partnership.

Stung by this, he'd taken her words on board. And yet, over time, Eileen had found herself relenting. She looked at him, day after day, and knew that mentally and emotionally he was withering in front of her. There was a helplessness about both of them during this period. John was dead-eyed, drained of energy: hollowed out more with every passing day. He wasn't growing healthier, or even staying the same, but visibly sinking. And she didn't know how to help him.

So after a time she'd suggested – tentatively – he might return to work. But not like before; that was the deal. He must *never* do that to her, she'd insisted, and he'd agreed that he wouldn't. There would be no more living inside case files at the expense of his life with her; no more working through the night. His job had to remain a job, locked up and left behind at the end of each working day. He would ring her at intervals. That was the promise he had to make.

As far as she could tell, he'd stuck to it, and over the past couple of months he'd seemed better. It was only in the last week or so that she'd started to become concerned again. The worry had returned.

Now, those three little words. 'I'm working late.'

'Isn't there anyone else who can take over?' she repeated. 'You sound tired.'

'I'm fine.'

She was looping the cable again.

'Right, well, I'll go, then, shall I?'

'I'm sorry, it's not that.' His voice sounded far away. She imagined him squinting at the screen while he talked to her. 'I'm just … This is busy here, that's all.'

She wanted to scream, 'Come home!'

Instead, she took a deep breath and made sure he heard it.

'Okay, John. I'll let you go. I love you.'

'I love you, too.'

But there was no sign in his voice that he was even thinking about the words, never mind feeling them. They were only what was required at the end of their conversations, the way a sentence always needed a full-stop.

Not fair to think like that. He does love you. He's just distracted.

In the old days, that would have been fine. But no, it was still okay. This was an over-reaction – she just hadn't been prepared for the slice of

83

panic that had gone through her. Eileen put the phone down and stood there, breathing deeply, bringing it all back under control.

After all, she had company.

Geoff Hunter was still in the front room where she had left him, but in her absence he'd stood up and helped himself to a look around. He was a tall, slouching man, given to standing with his hands deep in his pockets, chin tucked in, looking down at people as though they were small, badly-behaved children. The posture made the ends of his trousers lift up slightly, revealing an inch of black sock above his polished shoes. As Eileen walked back in, she despised him afresh.

'It's good of you,' she lied, 'coming down here yourself.'

Hunter didn't respond. He was preoccupied with a photograph on the mantelpiece. It was her and John on their wedding day. The photographer had been crammed into the front passenger side, taking the picture backwards, between the seats. They were in the centre of the frame, leaning towards each other, smiling and happy.

Hunter could easily have sent a junior officer to interview her, and if he had this might all have been finished by now, but she thought he wouldn't have missed this opportunity for the world. For him, entering this room full of John's private, personal items was like gaining access to a rival's diary. He was standing there quite brazenly leafing through the entries, searching for signs of weakness.

'Professional courtesy,' he told her absently.

'Well, you must be very busy.'

'We always look after our own.'

Eileen suppressed the enormous swell of anger she felt at that, at the implicit reduction of her to John's property. She wanted to tell him that her husband didn't belong to them at all. His life was here with her, not padding around with some kind of gang.

She said, 'I know you do.'

He finally stopped inspecting the photograph and turned to face her.

'Was that John?'

'Yes.'

'Did you tell him I was here?'

'No. It's nothing to do with him, is it?'

Hunter inclined his head, not so sure, but let the matter drop.

'How is he? John, I mean. We work together, but I haven't seen all that much of him since he came back.'

Eileen felt herself tensing. 'He's fine.'

84

Hunter checked his watch. 'I didn't think he usually stayed this late any more?'

'He does sometimes.'

That was several lies in under a minute.

Hunter was about the same age as her husband, and she knew there was some one-way resentment between them. Hunter might be posing as a friend, but in reality he was more like a jackal, sniffing casually for blood. It was astonishing how quickly John's colleagues could get her hackles rising, even the ones who supposedly cared about him. Since his breakdown, she was always on the offensive, and it had got to the point now where she avoided seeing any of them unless she had to. They were all the same deep down. Either they took a perverse delight in his weakness, or else they tried to reassure her, which was even worse. They were talking about a man she'd known and loved for longer than some of them had been alive.

'Shall we talk about James Reardon now? You said you were busy.'

'Yes, we should.'

Hunter walked over to the settee and sat down on the middle seat. Eileen remained standing, watching him. He produced a tape-recorder from his coat pocket and placed it beside him, then rested his elbows on his knees, cupping his hands in front of him. His trousers, she noted, were now riding two inches high.

'Detective Sergeant Geoff Hunter,' he told the tape-recorder, 'interviewing Eileen Mercer in relation to the assault on Colin Barnes and the abduction of Karli Reardon. For information, Eileen is the wife of Detective Sergeant John Mercer. Eileen, can you indicate your consent to be interviewed at this time?'

Irritated by his manner, she simply nodded.

'Out loud, please.'

'Yes.'

'For the record, Eileen has reported that the suspect, James Reardon, came to her house this morning in a state of some agitation. Eileen, what time would this have been?'

'About ten.'

'And you're his ... counsellor? Is that right?'

Hunter injected the word with a drop of venom. It was interesting, she thought, how quickly his true colours emerged. Perhaps it was because this tape would go on file, and so he was playing to a crowd.

She nodded.

'Out loud, please,' he repeated.

'I have been involved in counselling sessions with him, yes.'

'For how long?'

'Just over a year.'

'That's a long time. So ... what sort of things have you discussed?'

'That would be confidential,' she said. 'And irrelevant.'

'Did you talk about his terrible upbringing?'

Eileen folded her arms.

'Or perhaps,' Hunter continued, 'he complained about how hard his life has been?'

'Are you enjoying this for some strange reason, Detective?'

'I'm sorry, I guess I'm just struggling with the whole notion.' He leaned back and then sounded more serious. 'How did James Reardon seem? What was his manner?'

'He was agitated. Apologetic.'

'For what?'

'For letting me down. He wouldn't say why.'

'But now you know.'

'Yes,' she said. 'Now I know.'

Reardon had left Eileen with a feeling of disquiet that she was unsure how to act upon. His words and behaviour were troubling, and she knew what he was capable of. She'd considered calling the police, but finally discounted the idea, albeit with a few reservations.

Reardon had not told her he'd committed a crime – or even that he intended to – and as a client he was entitled to speak to her in confidence, a principle she'd decided held true even though he'd turned up unannounced. There would be consequences to violating that. Given his record, and her connection with John, the police would likely have come down hard on him, and any trust they'd established would immediately have been destroyed. Perhaps for no reason. So: no police. Instead, throughout the day she'd tried without success to contact Reardon himself.

It wasn't her habit to watch television during the day, so she didn't catch the news until the six o'clock report. It was only a small item – part of the local news at the end of the broadcast – but she heard Reardon's name and listened carefully, her heart slowly collapsing. *Oh, James.* At that point she'd had no choice. No reservations, either.

Hunter said, 'And now you're aware that, just before James Reardon visited you, he stalked and assaulted the man currently dating his ex-wife?'

'I'm aware of that.'

'The man in question, Colin Barnes, has identified Reardon as his assailant. Barnes had Reardon's youngest daughter in a pushchair at the time. That child is now missing.'

Karli Reardon, yes. All this had been on the news.

If Hunter was right about the timing – and she was sure he was – James Reardon had already abducted his daughter when he came and spoke to her. Eileen had been his last port of call before going on the run.

Whatever you hear about me, I'm doing it for her.

Hunter reached into his pocket again, this time producing a photograph, which he held out to her. She resisted for a moment, knowing the crass point he was attempting to score, but then took it anyway.

'This is Amanda Reardon,' he said. 'The picture was probably taken around the same time her ex-husband approached you to talk about all those problems he has.'

Eileen studied the woman's face, taking in the swellings and the single cut, the look of abject defeat and humiliation. Hunter must have known about the counselling she did with offenders. If he expected the face of a victim to shock or shame her, he should have known better. Impassive and unaffected, she handed the picture back to him.

'Did he talk to you about how he felt when he did that?'

Yes, he had.

'I'm afraid I don't see the relevance to your investigation.'

'Personally, I'm surprised he came to a female counsellor. Aren't you? I mean, he obviously has, shall we say, strong feelings towards women.'

They had talked about that, too. People like Hunter, Eileen thought, always saw things in black and white. What James Reardon had done to his ex-wife was hideous and inexcusable, but Eileen also knew that he was no blanket misogynist. Hunter simply wanted a Bad Man to blame; he wanted his villains in black hats, his heroes in white, whereas in real life people were too complicated to fall into their roles so easily and comfortably.

'I'm afraid,' she repeated, 'I don't see the relevance to your investigation.'

'You don't?' Hunter leaned forwards, bored of taunting her. 'Well, let's finish up. Why didn't you call the police this morning? You could have saved a lot of people a lot of trouble.'

'I didn't know he was going to commit a crime.'

'He already had.'

'So how could I have saved anyone anything?'

There was a beat of silence, and Eileen felt a small, petty thrill. But this entire conversation was absurd. She unfolded her arms.

'Let me make myself clear, Detective Sergeant Hunter. No matter what you think, I am not on James Reardon's *side* in this. I am not protecting him; I do not condone his actions. But it's not my job to judge him. It's my job simply to listen, and hopefully to help him understand why he's done these things.'

'Understand.' Hunter nodded. 'I like that.'

'That's right. You probably find it uncomfortable to think of things in these terms, Detective, but despite what James Reardon's done, he's still a person.'

Hunter glanced at the tape-recorder.

'For the record,' he said, 'the witness seems slightly hostile.'

Annoyed with herself, she turned away and walked across to the mantelpiece. Behind her, Hunter stood up, preparing to leave.

'Well, that's where we differ, Eileen. To me, he's just a target. *My* job – if you're interested – is to find his daughter and arrest him before he hurts her or anyone else.'

'He wouldn't hurt her.'

Hunter laughed.

'You know that, do you? You know about the circumstances in which he attacked his ex-wife, that she was in her car at the time? That he smashed the window with a hammer, dragged Amanda out of the car, and beat her by the side of the road?'

'You're enjoying telling me that too much.'

Hunter, for all the play of his taunts, sounded genuinely angry.

'Karli was there, of course, strapped in the passenger side. His baby, covered in broken glass, screaming, while he's kicking her mother around outside the car. *That's* how much he loves that child, Mrs Mercer. That's how much she means to him.'

Eileen pushed the emotions away and turned round. 'Is there anything else, Detective?'

'Yes. Did he say where he was going?'

'No.'

'Nothing at all?'

'No.'

'Then I guess we're done.' Hunter clicked off the tape and then nodded to himself. 'Thanks for your time. I'll see myself out.'

'Yes, you will.'

She watched him go, resisting the urge to slam the living-room door behind him. Instead, she remained where she was, listening as the front door opened and closed, then watched through the nets as he passed the window and walked off down the path.

When he was gone, she turned to the wedding photograph on the mantelpiece, in which she and John had been frozen in one black-and-white moment of time, so many years before. They were young there. John had aged so much, especially recently. All that was left of the man in the frame was his eyes and something in his smile. But these days he hardly smiled at all, and his eyes, when he looked at her, often seemed to be gazing all the way through.

I love you, too.

Very quickly, Eileen walked out of the room.

They were partners, and she needed to be strong. He would be all right, and he'd be home soon. There was nothing to worry about.

And she was damned if she was going to break down and cry in front of him. Not even in a photograph.

---

3 DECEMBER   **7.15 P.M.**
12 HOURS, 5 MINUTES UNTIL DAWN

Mark

In keeping with the style and décor of the department, the canteen was old and half shut-down. It was a large, drab room filled with fixed-in for-mica booths that looked as though they'd been ripped out of a truck-stop and given the most cursory of wipe-downs in transit. On the far side, shutters were closed against the night. The bulbs in the ceiling produced a constant nasal buzz.

I went over to the counter. There were roasting dishes full of curry that looked like turf, and sausages that were mostly burned skin, so despite my hunger I just picked up the first couple of sandwiches I saw and took them to the till.

'That's two thirty.'

'And another coffee, please.'

'Two eighty, then.'

I sorted through my pocket change absently, still thinking about Mercer and the 50/50 case file. The timing of the two events – Dyson's death and Mercer's breakdown – was too close for it to be coincidental. It didn't matter what he did or didn't say in his book: that was a book, after all; a single snapshot he wanted the world to see.

89

To me, this connection made sense: I could hardly imagine what it must have been like. Bad enough to be supporting the weight of such a terrible investigation, feeling both professional and personal pressures to stop this man hurting anyone else. But then, while pushing your team, to have one of them die at his hands ... Christ, it would be too much for anyone. So I thought I understood a little better what had been going on today: Mercer's determination and distraction; the team's unease. It all seemed a lot clearer now.

'Two eighty,' the counter-girl repeated.

'Sorry.'

I gave her the correct change, then located Pete, Greg and Simon in the corner of the room. Pete raised his hand; I nodded and made my way over. At the same time, I clocked their body language and thought I saw a conversation being hushed and finished. I was nervous as hell. With what I'd learned, they seemed more like a small, self-contained gang than ever. Although I belonged with them, I knew I didn't really, not yet. Not in terms of all this shit, anyway.

'Hi, there.'

Simon was arranging forkfuls of salad on a large plate, while, opposite him, Greg had an early evening fry-up of eggs, bacon and chips. Pete was holding one sandwich, while the empty packets on the table indicated he'd devoured another already. Without saying anything, he moved a couple of trays over to give me some table-space.

'Thanks.' I squeezed in beside them. 'So what have I missed?'

Greg nodded across at Pete. 'I'm just complaining. Pete's spent the afternoon talking to beautiful women.'

Pete shrugged self-deprecatingly.

'And it's not even my day off, you know.'

I smiled. Pete was wearing a thick wedding band. Earlier on, I'd noticed the passport photo tacked to his desk divider: two young girls crammed into a picture-booth.

'Talking to Simpson's ex-girlfriends?' I said.

Pete nodded. 'Not as enjoyable as Greg might imagine. Obviously, none of them were exactly pleased to hear the news. And they all gave pretty much the same impression of him.'

'What?'

'Too much of a lad to go out with – ever again – but basically a nice guy. The last girl said he was a disaster in a relationship, and a cheating bastard, but they'd been good friends since they broke up. Said he was like a lost little boy.' Pete blew on his coffee. 'Go figure.'

'Which is typical,' Greg said. 'Here we have more evidence that women love a bastard, and I can't even get a date.'

'Strange when you put it like that, yeah. Anyway, none of them is this "Jodie". We've accounted for all their whereabouts.'

'Right.'

It was predictable, but still disappointing.

'We do have six white vans, though,' Greg offered sarcastically. 'Surely that's the break we've been looking for?'

Simon arched an eyebrow at him. As he did, I realised I'd caught a glimpse of the conversation they'd been having before I arrived.

'What you mean,' Pete said quickly, 'is that you have nothing constructive to say.'

'Well …'

'The killer drives a white van, yeah? The CCTV has given us leads to follow up on white vans. And that's it. Let's see if anything comes of them.'

'I'll bet you a thousand pounds we get nothing.'

'Let's just keep the whole fucking thing positive. Okay?'

Greg conceded the point with a shrug. If I hadn't been there, maybe he'd have carried it on – but then maybe Pete wouldn't have shut him up so quickly either. I wondered; the tensions were difficult to read. But whatever, we ate quietly for a moment. When I was halfway through my sandwich, Greg broke the silence, changing the subject to the more comfortable one of me. Comfortable for everyone else, anyway.

'So,' he said, 'how was the move?'

'Fine.' I nodded. 'Not much of a move, in all honesty. It's kind of depressing when you find your whole life fits into one car-load.'

'You've got to be ruthless.'

'That's what I figured.'

In fact, I'd spent my month's notice sieving my property and working out what I was going to keep, what I was going to throw. It had been an agonising process. There was so much I wanted to hold on to for sentimental reasons. I kept imagining what Lise would have said and done. I told myself that if she'd still been around to look after me, she'd have binned it all herself to stop me moping. 'Everything important enough to keep,' she'd have told me, 'is stuff you don't need to pack. It'll turn up wherever you are by default. So get rid of all this pointless crap.'

But even though I knew that would have been her attitude, I couldn't summon it up myself. When I could bear to picture her in my head, I found that she wasn't saying anything at all to me. I couldn't read the expression on her face or imagine what she'd be thinking.

In the end, I'd sorted the stuff I needed to bring from the stuff I didn't. The latter items were now in storage in my parents' garage.

Greg smiled. 'You're not married, I guess?'

I picked up my coffee and blew on it gently. I didn't want to talk about this, and there were things I could say to move the conversation on, but for some reason it would have hurt not to be honest.

'I was engaged,' I said, 'but not any more.'

'Ouch. I've been there. Well, I wasn't engaged, but we were living together. Sometimes these things don't work out.'

'She died,' I said.

'Oh, shit. I'm sorry.'

'It's okay. It was a while ago now.'

One thing I'd found whenever I told anybody for the first time was that – bizarrely – it was me who felt the need to reassure them. 'It's okay,' I'd tell them, when of course it wasn't. In the same way, six short months turned into 'a while ago'. And the other thing I'd found was that reassuring people generally led to more questions.

'What happened?'

'Greg.' Pete warned him off with both words and eyes.

'It's okay.' I put my coffee down, then got through it quickly. 'We were on holiday, camping. This beach campsite. We went swimming. Just messing about, really, but we drifted out of our depth, and didn't realise the current was so strong. We called for help, but there wasn't anybody on the beach. So we just had to swim for it. And basically, I made it to shore and she didn't. There was nothing anyone could have done.'

'Christ. I'm sorry.'

'Forget about it.' Carefully, I picked up my coffee again and blew on it. 'So what about you guys? All attached?'

'Married and happy,' Pete held up his hand, showing me the thick gold band. 'And Simon has a woman in every port.'

'Oh yeah?' I couldn't resist raising an eyebrow at him.

Simon waved it away. 'An exaggeration.'

'I'm *far* too single,' Greg said. 'They should have sent me to interview Simpson's ex-girlfriends. The opportunity was wasted on Pete.'

'Well, they looked like they had taste, so the opportunity would have been wasted on you, too.'

'You're not funny.' Greg pointed a chip at him. 'At least not in the way you think.'

I smiled. The atmosphere improved slightly, and we chatted a little more while finishing our food. The whole time, I was weighing and judging the way the three of them interacted. Despite the vague animosity of the day, there was the easy banter between them that comes from working with people for a long time. I recognised and appreciated the rhythms, but I also knew better than to try to emulate them. Things had relaxed, but we weren't there yet.

Nevertheless, they did their best to include me. Simon asked where I was living, so I told them about the small flat the department had found for me until I could scope out somewhere better. We talked about where I'd worked before, some of the cases I'd handled.

'Nothing like this, I bet,' Greg said.

'No. It's been an intense first day.'

'Busy so far. And there's still a way to go yet.'

'My empty flat isn't exactly calling me.'

Greg laughed without humour. 'Fuck me, mine is.'

'How's the afternoon gone?' Pete asked me.

'Well, I've worked through the file. As best I can, anyway.' I paused, but then decided it needed to be said: 'For what it's worth, I'm sorry about what happened.'

Greg dipped his last chip into a pool of ketchup and stirred it around; Simon nodded, serious for once. For a moment, I thought I'd misjudged it and spoken out of place. Pete leaned back, looking over at the window, as though there was something interesting to see there rather than just flat, pale shutters.

Pressed too hard, I told myself.

Then Pete sighed.

'It hit us all hard,' he said. 'Some of us more than others, obviously. It's a difficult thing, losing a colleague. And Andy was much more than that.'

I nodded, catching the subtle reference to Mercer. 'Obviously', Pete had just said, and 'some of us more than others'. It was tacit confirmation, beyond the timings in the file, that this case had contributed to Mercer's breakdown, if not caused it outright.

'Of course,' I said.

Greg and Simon were silent, deferring to Pete. I could guess what this was about: whether I was going to be included in whatever was on their minds. Pete was still looking away, tapping his finger on the table. After a moment, he came to a decision and turned back to me, and I knew that I was.

'What do you make of him so far?' he said.

'Mercer?'

'Yeah. What's your opinion of him?'

I paused. The question was so loaded that I let it hang for a moment, considering what to say. A divide of some kind clearly existed between Mercer and his team, but it was also obvious that they'd worked with him long enough to have developed a complicated dynamic. There were things he'd said and done today that had pissed me off, probably them, too, but over time you can develop a weird kind of affection for those sorts of eccentricities. It would be a mistake to say anything negative about him. And perhaps strangely, I found I didn't want to, anyway.

'He's not what I expected,' I said. 'I mean, his reputation precedes him a bit. And so I guess he's a lot more … human than I was expecting.'

Pete nodded, but it wasn't quite what he'd been after.

'Does he seem fragile? It's okay. Be honest.'

I frowned. 'Be honest,' Pete had said. Did Mercer seem fragile? My impressions of him today were of a man surrounded by paper files, taking the full heft of the investigation on his shoulders, thinking it all through at once. Intense and full of concentration – and, being honest, not much different from many other team leaders I'd met.

But then I remembered my first encounter with him at Simpson's house – when I'd noticed how old he seemed. And yes, he was far from the superman his reputation implied. He had the look of a man who'd lost weight and could be pushed over more easily than he used to. There was certainly an air of vulnerability about him.

'A little, maybe,' I said.

'Do you remember how he was at the interview?'

'He was a bit distracted.'

That was a charitable understatement, and we all knew it. Mercer had barely spoken to me, except when we'd briefly discussed my encounter with Jacob Barrett. The rest of the time he'd been content to sit back and let the others ask whatever questions they wanted. As though he was just waiting for it to be over.

'Distracted,' Pete agreed. 'He's been that way for a while. Since he's come back to work, he's basically been pottering around. Nine to five, not taking on anything too heavy. Not engaging.'

It was a sensitive issue, but we were having the conversation so I decided to bring it out into the open.

'Since the breakdown?'

'Yes.' Pete looked down, nodded once. 'Since the breakdown. He's been taking things easier. Doing the bare minimum.'

'Treading water,' Greg said.

'Exactly. But today he's been totally different. More like how he was in the old days. Committed. Absorbed.'

He glanced at his watch.

'I mean, it's half past seven. He's not been in the office this late for two years.'

'So you're worried?'

'Not just about that,' Greg said. 'It's this case. He shouldn't be on it.'

'We talked about that,' Pete snapped. His voice was too loud, too harsh. He toned it down, turning back to me. 'We talked about that – before John came back to work. If the case went live again, we knew he'd want to be involved, and we decided if that happened we'd play it by ear. Problem is, I guess, we're listening to different music.'

I looked at Greg, who shrugged, making no attempt at an apology.

'My objections are pretty clear. It was always going to be Pete's call.'

'It's a shit day for you to have started,' Pete said. 'I'm sorry about that. I don't know where we're going with this at the moment.'

'How do you think he's coping so far?' I said.

'I don't know. When he first came back, there's no way I'd have let him take this on again. But ... he seems okay to me. Part of me is pleased to see him so engaged. Back to his normal self, I guess. The other part of me is just worried.'

I breathed out heavily. Before I could say anything, Greg interrupted.

'For fuck's sake, Pete. He needs to know the rest of it.'

I looked from one to the other.

'Needs to know what?'

'Have you seen that the cases aren't connected?' Greg asked me. 'Officially, I mean. On the computer system.'

I hadn't. 'No. But I did notice he didn't mention it in his reports to DI White.'

Greg nodded. 'Exactly. Deniability.'

'I don't understand.'

Pete leaned forwards, taking over. 'Greg means all that stuff he was arguing with John about earlier. He was doing it to give him at least some level of deniability.'

'No, I was giving *us* deniability.'

'Whatever.'

I shook my head. 'Deniability of what?'

'Deniability of the cases being connected,' Pete said. 'This investigation doesn't belong to John. On paper, it's Geoff Hunter's. And given the history here, there's no way White would allow John anywhere near it if he knew. Not a chance. When he finds out ... Well.'

'Deniability,' Greg repeated.

I sat back in my chair and folded my arms, processing what I'd been told.

From the moment I'd read about Andrew Dyson's death, I supposed I'd been expecting something like this. The first time Mercer had confronted this case, it had ended in the murder of a colleague and his subsequent breakdown. It was only natural that the team were concerned. They had to balance their loyalties and friendship to their boss with their worries about what facing this investigation for a second time might do to his state of mind. It was good they felt able to include me in that. What I hadn't thought about was the professional repercussions of that choice – our responsibility to the department as a whole. Now, I was included in that as well, and I had to consider my position carefully. Deniability was one thing; misconduct was another.

But for now, at least, there was going to be no question where my loyalties would lie.

'Obviously, I'll follow your lead.'

'Okay,' Pete said. 'Basically, our job is the same as it's always been. We're here to support him. One way or another, that's what we're going to do. We're going to hope we can find these two people before dawn.'

'Jodie and Scott,' I said.

'Yes. Because Christ knows what it will do to him if we can't.'

We sat in silence for a moment longer, then Pete pushed his tray back and got to his feet. He looked tired.

'Right,' he said, 'come on. Hard job done. Let's get back to the easy stuff.'

We all stood up, and as we did I heard a beeping. Pete took his pager off his belt, frowned at it for a second.

'One of the vans.' He inclined his head slightly, then glanced at me. 'Your door team's got something. A thousand pounds, wasn't it, Greg? You'll be wanting your chequebook.'

Scott

It was an old building, and the space he was in was very confined. The walls to either side were made from big stone slabs, laid out in uneven rows, as though whoever had built it had done so with whatever rocks were close to hand. The place must have been abandoned for years, left to generations of spiders and ants. Season after season of dead leaves had blown in and rotted away to dust on the flagstones. The cobwebs on the ceiling were either thin and grey or else hanging down like dirty string.

Scott had no idea what this place had been used for in its lifetime. Perhaps it had been an outhouse or a storeroom. Which would be fitting, as it was now being used to store him.

If he leaned to either side, he could touch the wall with his shoulder, and despite the spiders, which were big and brown and ugly, he kept doing so. That and stretching his head to one side: trying to relieve the tension and cramp building in his neck and the muscles of his back.

He was sitting on something, he couldn't see what. His hands were cuffed, his forearms resting on his thighs. The man in the devil mask had tied rope round all four limbs at once, lashing him into place.

His nose was running; he kept having to sniff. It was partly a result of the cold and partly because he kept crying. He couldn't help it. Before today he'd thought of himself as strong and capable, but now he knew different. He was no hero; not as calm and collected as people seemed to feel in the movies.

This couldn't be happening.

There had been anger to begin with, but not any more. Determined to free himself – to get to her – he had fought against his constraints as hard as he could, gritted his teeth and stretched as much as he could bear, but they were too well placed. The rage and hatred had swiftly given way to frustration.

He was held firmly in place, utterly powerless.

Panic and fear had set in; he had cried. It disgusted him, but he was so scared. He was at the mercy of the man in the devil mask and right now, his heart fluttering so quickly, he wanted to say the right thing, do whatever it took to get himself out of here.

He would do anything.

In front of him, the walls and ceiling continued for about two metres.

Then there was an open doorway through which he could see the woods. The building was in a rough clearing.

Out of sight, the man must have built a fire. Orange light flickered and danced on the ground, and he could hear the burning wood crackling and snapping. There was only a little heat from it, but when the wind shifted, smoke drifted across the doorway, full of softly illuminated texture.

It had also started to snow. The light from the flames turned it into yellow blossom. It was already forming a thick carpet.

He shivered, trembled. It was partly the cold and, again, partly not.

Jodie, he thought. He couldn't bear the thought of what might be happening to her.

The man appeared in the doorway.

Scott stopped thinking and tried to shuffle backwards. But there was nowhere to go. The man bent down and moved into the outhouse, kneeling down in front. Practically a silhouette, although the firelight gleamed off the edges of the mask, highlighting its crimson, beetle-like ridges.

The man leaned his elbows on Scott's knees and held two items up between them.

In one hand, he had sheets of paper, stapled together.

In the other, a screwdriver.

'Shhhh,' he said.

Scott realised his breath was so quick that he could hear it coming out of him: bursts of breathlessness. He did his best to calm down and stop. He must do anything this man wanted.

'We're just going to talk a while,' the man said. 'You see what I have here? Before we left your house, do you remember what I did?'

Scott couldn't remember, although he desperately wished that he could.

'No.'

'I was on your computer.' He emphasised the sheets of paper slightly and seemed to be studying them intently. 'I printed these. "Five Hundred Reasons Why I Love You", it says. But there's only two hundred and seventy four here. Why's that?'

The fire popped. Other than that, the world outside the storeroom was silent and still. For some reason, it felt important not to disturb that.

'I've not finished yet,' he whispered.

'It was going to be a Christmas present?'

'Yes.'

'That's funny. A Christmas present for her. This.' The man shook the papers. 'This is a plaster for a gunshot wound. Do you understand?'

'Yes.'

'No, you don't. But you will.'

'Why are you doing this?'

Scott's voice broke slightly, and his vision blurred. Damn it. He didn't want to cry in front of this man. He sniffed hard. The tears came regardless, and through them he saw the man watching him, pitiless, as though he was a specimen under a microscope. When he spoke, it was like the answer should have been obvious.

'Because you have something I want, Scott.'

He knows my name.

The man held the papers out in front of him.

'All this belongs to me now. It's a burden for you, and I'm going to take it away. You should thank me.'

Scott didn't understand. He sniffed again, said nothing.

'I imagine it was all done fairly randomly, but the first reason you've put down is interesting. Can you remember what it is? Think hard, now.'

He remembered. Of course he did.

His voice came out thick: 'Something about how we met.'

'That's right.' The man nodded. '"Number One", it says. "We were so lucky to find each other."'

Scott took deep breaths and made an effort to stop crying.

'What does that mean?' the man said. 'I want you to tell me about it.'

'About how we met?'

'Yes.' He leaned a little closer and the light wormed around the contours of his mask. 'Tell me about how lucky it was.'

The message appeared on the screen without fanfare or warning. If he'd been typing his essay rather than surfing the internet, a pressed key would have instantly dismissed the small window and that would have been that. It would have flashed up, disappeared, and their lives would have been very different.

They'd talked about that and laughed, looking into each other's eyes. 'Can you imagine how terrible it would have been if ... ?' Later, he read somewhere that it was a standard early stage of a relationship, the 'I might have never met you' conversations.

At university, Scott often got network messages from his friends. You could access a list of usernames that showed who was logged on, and then click on someone you knew and send them a message. This time he didn't recognise the sender.

99

```
isz5jlm: [Hi - how are you?]
```

'isz' signified the department – computer studies – although he had no idea where the abbreviation for it came from. '5' meant the year of university entry was 1995: the same year as him. And 'jlm' were the person's initials.

He stared at it for a couple of seconds, trawling through his mental list of friends, and then the circle of acquaintances that surrounded them. Maybe it was somebody he'd met at a party. JLM, JLM ... If it was, he couldn't remember.

He frowned, and clicked on the cross in the corner of the window, closing it down. Then he turned his attention back to the web.

Twenty seconds later another message appeared.

```
isz5jlm: [Ooops - sorry!]
```

And that was all.

At least the second message made it clear: the first had been a mistake. Scott felt strangely disappointed.

Seconds of inactivity passed. Moments of time, he thought later, where the wonderful life he would have was hanging in the balance without him even realising.

He opened up the list of logged-on users for his network. There were about two hundred and fifty, but they were arranged in alphabetical order so it was easy to scroll down to the iszs. There were several. isz5jlm was the last on the list.

He deliberated over it some more, and then thought, *Why not*? Double-clicking on the name brought up a small dialogue box. He typed:

```
[Am fine thanks. Hope you are too. But who are
you?]
```

The mouse-pointer hovered. Perhaps he should just forget about it, he thought. It was clearly a mistake, and there wasn't anything to gain by pursuing it. At worst, the person might ignore it, making him feel stupid.

But hell, if that was the worst then – once again – why not?

He pressed [send].

The snow outside was coming down much harder now and Scott's breath clouded in the air as he spoke, billowing around the man in front of him.

'We just started emailing each other,' he said. 'We didn't meet for about a month and a half.'

'So it was an accident?'

Scott nodded, but the man was looking at the papers and ignored him.

'The odds against that happening must be astronomical,' he said. 'But everybody feels the same way. People look into each other's eyes and talk about what might have happened if ... How things could be different. Did you ever do that?'

Scott found the smallest trace of rebellion.

'No.'

'I think you did. People always start by telling each other they're soul mates, that they couldn't be happier, they were meant to be together.' The man looked at him curiously. 'Is that what you believe?'

'Yes.'

'That's good.'

Suddenly, the pressure on Scott's knees increased, and then lifted altogether as the man stood up and went back outside.

Gone.

For a moment, he could have been entirely alone in the woods. The snow beyond the entrance was peaceful and silent; the fire beyond, burning away happily. It was almost serene. But the man's footprints were there on the ground in the snow. He had been here. He would come back soon.

Scott tested his bindings again, but they were as tight as ever. All he could do was twist and stretch as much as they'd allow, trying to ease the cramp in his muscles. Everything was becoming solid.

A minute passed. Then another.

The footprints outside were almost invisible now. Already becoming lost among the white all around them.

Perhaps he really *had* gone.

But then, footsteps.

The man moved back into the outhouse and crouched down where he'd been before: a huge presence, filling the world. The pressure on Scott's knees returned. The man was still holding the papers and the screwdriver, but this time he had brought something else.

Not an item so much as a smell. A sensation of heat.

He heard the man breathing out through his nostrils, sighing.

'Like I said, you have something I want.'

Scott nodded quickly. He'd identified the source of the smell and the heat – both came from the screwdriver the man was holding. He knew what had happened. The point of it had been heated in the fire.

The man held the screwdriver up between them and Scott thought he could see the steam curling off it.

No, no, no, no, no, no.

'And you're going to give it to me. Do you understand?'

He put the papers down and reached out to Scott's face. Scott whipped his head round, but the man caught him: grabbed a fistful of his hair at the back. Held his head steady. God, the man was so strong. His voice fell over itself, it ran from him so quick:

'Don't, please don't, don't—'

'Do you love her?'

Scott wasn't breathing right. It was too short, too fast, all in the nose. There was electricity running through him, building up as his body insisted that he needed *to get away*. But he couldn't move, and it built up and up—

He was screaming in terror and *panic*.

'Do you love her?'

'Yes!'

The man nodded.

'That's what I want,' he said.

And then put the screwdriver into Scott's eye.

3 DECEMBER   **9.30 P.M.**
9 HOURS, 50 MINUTES UNTIL DAWN

Mark

In a quiet, sleepy street, an enormous police presence acts as an alarm call. Lights flash across windows; fists bang on doors; and people look up from the television and wonder what the hell's happened. Everybody feels afraid.

I stood at the top of Carl Farmer's steps and looked down at the scene before me. We'd sealed off the housing complex at the entrance from the main road, and the vehicles inside the cordon – four vans, three cars – were illuminating everything with steady sweeps of blue. There were lights on in every house, and most of the residents were out at the top of their steps. I could hear the scratchy noise from police radios, the echo of quiet voices.

Earlier in the evening, before we left the department, it had started to snow. There was a soft layer of it on the ground here, blackened in places by the slush of footprints and the cut of tyres. It was still falling, descending heavily from the sky. Thick and heavy and slow, filling the ice-cold night air as far as the eye could see, blurring into the night. It caught the streetlights and formed amber static across the street.

The four vans below were lit up from within by white monitors, the light obscured by the huddle of rain-slickered bodies waiting by the open doors. I spotted my door-to-door team and checked my watch. Half past nine: I'd been at work for twelve hours. It was tempting to go and grab another coffee, but there'd be time for that before we started the interviews.

The interviews ...

I looked around the street and sighed. We were in one of the nicer areas of the city. I'd driven through on the way here, and most of the houses were large and expensive, occupied by middle-aged families or older couples. Normally, for an interview man, that would have been encouraging, but Carl Farmer's house was in one of the newer developments that backed onto the canal. Although they were in the heart of the district, these areas were an entirely different proposition.

Small streets led off the main road into enclaves of six or seven houses. The buildings were all the same: light-brown brick, complemented by dark-brown wooden steps, sills and garage doors. The kitchen worktops, cupboards and cabinets – all the same. A single blueprint had been taken and used like a cookie-cutter, again and again, to create nice houses someone could choose off a peg if they didn't want to think too hard; which meant they were aimed at young professionals. There didn't appear to be any feeling of community here, and I imagined that nobody was likely to know their neighbours very well. My gut instinct was that the door-to-doors were going to be a nightmare.

Taking a last breath of cold air, I turned my back on the flashing lights, and made my way into the kitchen.

There were two crime-scene techs there, gamely working their way over everything from one wall to the other. The evidence so far suggested that, like the house Andrew Dyson had been killed in, this place had been another nest for our killer. Even so, the man who called himself Carl Farmer had rented it for almost a year and it seemed inconceivable that he'd left no evidence behind.

'Anything so far?' I asked one of the techs.

'Just the obvious.'

He nodded at the kitchen counter, which I'd seen when I arrived. And of course, earlier this evening, the officers chasing up the owners of the white vans caught on CCTV had arrived and seen it, too.

There were none of the usual gadgets or equipment you'd expect: no toaster, kettle or sandwich-maker; no crumbs or stains to suggest a meal had ever been prepared here. But it wasn't entirely bare. A single piece of evidence had been placed opposite the front door, ready for the officers who arrived, and the front door had been left slightly ajar, so that anyone who came up the steps would see it straight away.

It was propped against the wall at the back of the counter. Dark, bushy eyebrows. Jet-black goatee. Plastic piercings through pink skin the colour of sunburn.

I stared down at its cut-out eyes, my thoughts still on the conversation in the canteen. For one thing, our deniability was now pretty much shot. More importantly, I couldn't imagine what it must have been like for Mercer to enter the house and see this.

The devil mask that Carl Farmer had left for us.

The front room.

Or at least what would have passed for it in an ordinary house.

The furnishings were basic and had obviously come with the rent: a white leather suite, a simple wooden table and chair; an old coffee table, which had been pushed out of the way against a wall. The other rooms were bare and unused. Farmer appeared to have operated out of this one, and there was no indication of where he might have slept, if he had slept here at all. His only remaining possession here, the mask aside, was a laptop, left open and running on the table in the corner.

The room was busier now than it had presumably ever been during his tenancy. Two IT techies were working at the computer, while Simon was liaising with another two scene-of-crime officers. Mercer was standing in the centre of the room, arms folded, staring at the wall. Greg and Pete were slightly to one side of him, talking the scene over. Every now and then, Pete glanced at Mercer and looked concerned.

I walked across to join them.

'How much does it cost to rent a place like this?' I said.

'A fair whack.' The snow had wetted Pete's hair, making him look more dishevelled than ever. He seemed tired, as well, but he still reeled off the facts and figures without referring to notes. 'Seven fifty a month.

I've spoken to the rep at the rental agency. He wasn't best pleased to be disturbed at this hour.'

Greg nodded at the wall Mercer was staring at so intently.

'He's going to be even less pleased when he sees what Farmer's done to the place.'

One of the SOCOs appeared behind us. 'Excuse me, can I get a picture of that, please?'

We edged aside while he prepared the camera.

In the middle of the wall, the man known as Carl Farmer had written the following:

> *In the space between the days*
> *you lost the melancholy shepherd of the stars.*
> *The moon is gone and the wolves of space move in*
> *grow bold*
> *and pick his flock off one by one.*

Around that short poem, the white wall had been covered in the type of spider-web drawing found at each of the 50/50 Killer's crime scenes. They were drawn in black marker rather than blood, but the similarities were unavoidable. Some had been scribbled out; others had been smudged and redrawn. On some of them, there were the same little crossings and cuts made across the strands.

We'd already identified one of them as the image left at Kevin Simpson's house. It had been drawn more definitely here than many around it. Most of the others gave the impression of idle jottings, as though he'd been drafting patterns and seeing what looked right before settling on a final design. The effect was eerie. The webs surrounding the poem looked like strange, spiral galaxies around a dead sun.

I wondered what it all meant – not the meaning behind the symbols so much as the scene as a whole. By leaving the devil mask where it would be seen, he was taunting us. Or challenging us, perhaps. Certainly not indifferent to us, anyway. And now this wall here. Was it the same? If it was a display he'd intended us to see, what was the message? It was strange to think that, when I imagined him here, drawing on the wall, the man I saw in my head was very probably imagining me back.

The photographer moved on. Pete put his hands in his pockets and sniffed.

'The agent's on his way down here now, anyway.'

'What do we know about Farmer so far?' I said.

Pete deferred this one to Greg.

'He's thirty-one years old,' Greg said. 'Unmarried. No kids that we know of. No criminal record. On paper he works for a plumbing company, although I think we're going to find that's a front. All of it, probably. The guys at the section are going through the details, but so far it looks the same set-up as the Frank Walker ID he used. Just another paper trip.'

Pete glanced around the room, as though the place was derelict and he expected the ceiling to collapse. Then he took up the thread.

'The agent says Farmer paid a year's rent up front, including the deposit, which is a total of over nine grand. We'd all agree that's a hell of a lot of disposable income.'

'So whatever he does, he's well paid,' Greg suggested.

'Independently wealthy,' Mercer told us.

I turned to look at him. He was still studying the patterns on the wall: immersed in them, even, as though they were a language he might decipher if he stared hard enough.

'You think?' Greg said.

Mercer gestured at the wall. 'Look at this. It seems to me that he's gone through different drafts, practising until he's happy. The patterns may look random to us, but there's real method to it. It's important to him. And I can't see him holding down the level of job he'd require for the amount of money he seems to have.'

Greg seemed to want to disagree, but he didn't.

'You can see him standing here,' Mercer said quietly, mostly to himself. 'He must have been totally absorbed in this. Making it perfect. This is full-time. This right here is his job.'

'The surveillance equipment as well,' I realised.

Mercer looked at me. 'What do you mean?'

'Well, he watches his victims, maybe for months. He wouldn't have time to immerse himself like that if he was holding down a career.'

Mercer stared at me for a moment, not blinking, then turned back to the wall, nodding slowly. Clearly, we had only half his attention. He was concentrating on the designs, trying to capture an elusive thought. Had I helped or hindered that? I left him to it.

'What about the poem?' I said.

Greg sniffed dismissively. 'We've done a preliminary online search and can't find it. That doesn't mean it's not there, but my guess would be that Farmer wrote it. Or whatever his real name is.'

I thought he was probably right. For one thing – and more explicitly than the devil mask on the counter – the poem seemed to be addressed to us: 'In the space between the days, *you* lost the melancholy shepherd of the stars'. Also, the theme appeared to fit with what he did, what he wore. There was an obvious religious element to the poem. But how much of it – if any – we could take at face value was another question. As was what it meant to the 50/50 Killer. Did he see himself as a wolf of space, picking 'us' off one by one?

I opened my mouth to say something along those lines, but Pete nudged me and I stopped.

Mercer was still staring at the wall, but his expression had altered. Where before he'd been half with us, he was now wholly absent, wrapped up in what he was seeing. I watched his gaze flicking between the different designs. Here, there. His expression altered again, and it reminded me of the sun coming up. A level of understanding was dawning in him, his face brightening as he allowed it time to rise over the horizon at its own pace. He was on the verge of—

'Sir?'

One of Greg's IT people broke the spell, calling from the other side of the room. Pete tensed slightly and he glared at the techie. Mercer's face froze. Then he gave a rueful shake of his head, filing the half-formed insight away.

The techie, holding out a piece of paper, was oblivious of the atmosphere he'd punctured.

'Sir, you need to see this.'

Pete walked across, took the paper from him and brought it back, passed it to Mercer.

It was a printout from Vehicle Licensing. Initially, we'd only got the addresses for the owners of the six white vans, but the IT people had now downloaded the full licence for Carl Farmer. He'd updated it within the last five years, so had one of the new licences that included the driver's photograph. The IT people had isolated it and blown it up to fill the A4 sheet.

At last, we had a face.

Carl Farmer glared emptily out of the page. He had a thin face, and skin that looked rough: leathered and hard, as though it had been bruised over and over, healing badly each time. His brown hair had been frozen by the camera in a messy, dark swirl. The expression was blank and dead. His eyes, more than anything – they were like hands pressed flat against you, pushing you away.

Mercer stared intently at the photograph, as he had at the designs on the wall. Seeing more than was there. All day I'd noticed how closely he paid attention to every detail of the case, but here in the killer's nest he seemed to have gone up a level. He looked as though he was receiving partial information on a wavelength the rest of us couldn't get. Trying to keep calm, listening carefully, but I thought there was also an air of controlled panic about him.

We're going to hope we can find these two people before dawn. Because Christ knows what it will do to him if we can't.

'Let's remember this probably isn't him,' Greg cautioned.

Mercer didn't look up. 'You don't think?'

'This could be anybody. He's been too careful before.'

'He's still being careful, Greg, still very capable and controlled. But he's been planning this for two years. Perhaps it's what he's being careful about that's changed.'

Greg turned away. 'It'd be a schoolboy error. This isn't him.'

Mercer continued to stare at the photo, but after a second he inclined his head.

'Maybe you're right. But we'll find out one way or another. At the very least, it's someone.' He passed it to me. 'So let's see if Farmer's neighbours have any idea who.'

My shoes crunched and packed the snow as I walked down and across to my team. They were bundled up in black coats and gloves, their faces pink in the cold. Ross passed me a polystyrene cup, its contents steaming.

'Coffee, sir?'

'Thanks.' I blew on it gently.

They already had copies of Farmer's picture, which had come through to the computer in the van. I told them we needed to get impressions of the man, information about his appearance and his manner, last sightings, known associates.

'He's lived in this place for nearly a year,' I said. 'In all that time, someone must have known him or talked to him. Someone must at least have seen him.'

I looked at the ring of houses round the cul-de-sac. The buildings were obscured by the falling snow, which seemed to be getting heavier.

'Someone must know him,' I repeated.

There were sixteen houses and flats and, despite my initial reservations, I thought that made good odds that someone would be able to tell us something about Carl Farmer. But at house after house we got the same response. It wasn't just that Farmer's neighbours had never seen him or spoken to him; they didn't even know his name. His van was sometimes seen outside, sometimes not; the curtains were opened or they were closed; windows lit up and then went dark again. He had done enough to make sure he didn't stand out.

My first impressions had been depressingly on-target. The people who lived here were young, well-heeled professionals, who just wanted somewhere neat and clean to spend the few hours they weren't in the office. The end of the day came along, and these people were like files returning to separate drawers in a cabinet. The 50/50 Killer couldn't have picked a better place in which to make a nest.

The sixth house that Ross and I went to was opposite Farmer's. At the top of the steps, the door into the bright kitchen was open and a girl was standing outside. We walked up to meet her, pressing footprints into the thickening snow.

She was wrapped in a big black coat, leaning against the back banister: little more than a mass of tied-back, pale dreadlocks, bowed over the mug of coffee she was cupping in her hands. She gave us a brief smile as we stopped in front of her. My immediate thought was that she was far too young to be able to afford a place like this, and I was in the wrong profession.

'Hi, there.' I showed her my badge. 'I'm Detective Nelson. This is Officer Ross. We're sorry to bother you and I hope we don't use up too much of your time.'

'It's fine.'

'Can I take your name, please?'

'Megan Cook.'

'Nice to meet you, Megan. Like I said, this won't take long. We're trying to find out a little bit about the man who lived opposite you.'

She sipped her drink and I caught a waft of it. Not coffee, hot chocolate.

'I don't think I'll be able to tell you anything, to be honest.'

'Well, we've interviewed a lot of your neighbours. Nobody seems to know much.'

'Nobody would. I think I've spoken to about three of my neighbours the whole time I've lived here. It's that kind of street.'

'I got that impression, yeah. So you don't know Mr Farmer?'

'Is that his name? No, I'm sorry. I never met him.'

'You've never had any contact with him at all?'

'I saw him this morning.' She wrinkled up her nose. 'I guess that doesn't really count.'

'No, I'll take that.' My stomach fluttered a little, but I did my best to keep my tone even. 'Where did you see him and at what sort of time?'

She gestured across the street with her mug.

'Over there. He came and parked by his house. I'm not sure what time. Probably about eleven? Something like that.'

'Okay.'

Not exact, but good enough. I did the maths in my head. Farmer had made the phone call to CCL just after eight o'clock, and presumably left Kevin Simpson's house immediately afterwards. Three hours later he was parked outside his own home, or one of them, anyway. What had he done in the interim?

'Did you see him arrive?' I asked.

'Yeah. I was on the phone by the front window.'

Megan told us that she was a self-employed web-developer and did most of her work from home, a file that never left the drawer. The fact she'd been on the phone was especially useful: we could check the records and pin down the time she'd been at the window.

'And you've never seen him before today?' I said.

'I don't think so. Seen his van a few times. I guess that's why I noticed him this morning. *That's* what he looks like. You know? Like, wow, I've seen my neighbour.'

I handed her the photograph from Vehicle Licensing.

'Yeah,' she said, looking it over, 'this is him.'

The fluttering in my stomach grew stronger. Without admitting it, I'd shared Greg's doubts about whether the photo was genuine. But now we had a positive on it. Just one, of course, and I wanted more, but unless Megan was lying it was strong support that this really was our guy. And I didn't think she was lying.

I took the photograph back. 'What was he doing when you saw him?'

'He parked and sat for a second. Then he went inside for a bit.'

'How long?'

'Not long. I was only on the phone for a minute, and I saw him come out, so it can't have been long. He came out and drove off again.'

So he must have already cleared the house out by then. Why had he come back? I couldn't be sure, but I could make a guess. He'd returned to leave us the devil mask.

'What has he done?' Megan asked.

'I'm afraid I can't go into that.'

'I mean,' she said, 'should I be worried?'

But I didn't reply. I was preoccupied by thoughts of what the 50/50

Killer *had* done, and what was happening here.

He'd held Kevin Simpson hostage overnight, tortured him and then killed him at dawn, leaving his usual signature: but beyond that, his actions were different from before. The nature of the game had changed. He'd made a phone call and he'd left us the recording. A message had been left for us here, where he'd known we'd follow. And there was the uncharacteristic lack of care, too: the fact we had his face. He'd never allowed himself to be seen before.

Yet Mercer was right that there was a similar degree of control. He'd come back here, for example, when the hunt was already on. It was unlikely but possible that we could have arrived here and caught him.

It seemed strange for him to be so precise about things like that, only to make the mistake of being seen. To me, it lent weight to Mercer's assessment of the situation: that our killer was still being careful, but what he was being careful about had changed: 'He's been planning this for two years.' That was fine – but if he was being as cautious as he wanted to be, it implied that concealing his identity was no longer a priority.

Why?

Megan was looking at me curiously, and I realised I'd gone away and done a Mercer for a moment. Gathering myself together, I tried to give a reassuring answer.

'No,' I said. 'He won't be coming back here.'

It was all I could say. Even that, I didn't feel I knew for sure.

Back at the van, I rubbed my hands and touched them to my cheeks. They were numb and frozen. All I could feel in my fingers and face was the coldness of my skin: dull pressure without sensation. I'd decided to leave Ross to do the last couple of interviews. I needed to get Megan Cook's statement on file and let Mercer know about the photograph.

I unhooked my recording equipment and handed it to the guy on plug-in duties inside the van. As the data was transferred, I glanced towards the entrance to the street and noticed that the media had gathered beyond the cordon. There were vans, groups of reporters, big bulky cameras balanced on shoulders. A moment later I saw Pete making his way back through the cordon, hands thrust into his pockets.

The snow was still heavy and his hair looked soaked, but he seemed troubled by more than just the weather. Snow was snow, and he had more important things to worry about. I figured he'd spent a good few minutes lying to reporters, which was never much fun. They could smell it, and always held it against you.

He headed back to Farmer's house. I looked across. Mercer was standing outside at the top of the steps, a dark shape leaning on the banister staring away from the cordoned-off street below.

From that distance, with his back to me, he became a figure open to interpretation.

Perhaps he was unconcerned with the snow falling all around him. Maybe he was lost in thought and watching the night. But then again, it was possible he was simply exhausted: leaning on the rail for support. I had no way of knowing. Was his indifference to the snow a gesture of strength or surrender?

He didn't appear to acknowledge Pete when he reached him, but Pete stood beside him anyway, leaning on the banister and staring out into the night along with him, sharing the view. They stood in silence, two black figures, slightly apart in the snow.

Our job is to support him.

'Finish that up for me,' I told the officers behind me.

And then, carrying the photograph, I walked over to the house.

3 DECEMBER
8 HOURS, 40 MINUTES UNTIL DAWN

10.40 P.M.

Jodie

The first thing Jodie had done when he left her alone was follow the advice of the voice in her head and take a full inventory of the situation. Where she was, and what she had that might help her get somewhere else.

The 'where' was easy enough, provided she wasn't too specific. The man in the devil mask had made them walk deep into the woods, eventually bringing them to a location he'd obviously had in mind from the beginning. There was a clearing in the trees where he'd already built a large fire. Chunky logs were piled up, and he'd balanced a large rusty sheet of metal on top of four stone columns to keep the fuel dry. There were a number of old stone structures at the periphery of the clearing, most of them broken down to their foundations.

All except two, in fact.

The man instructed Scott to wait by the side of the unlit fire. He did as he was told – just stood there, his head bowed, his body still. With a single gesture of the knife, Jodie was ushered across to one of the stone buildings. She followed the order, and had to duck to get inside.

It was an old storeroom, barely wide enough for her to move into. At the back, there were slabs of granite stacked on top of one another, covered in moss and cobwebs. The walls were like that, too – threaded through with green veins, covered with the grey, dusty hair.

She paused, but the man prodded her forwards. She understood what he wanted.

Sit down. She did.

The man was framed in the doorway for a moment, then he swung the wooden door closed and the room collapsed into total darkness. She felt a section of her heart sink away into it. A second later, there was a click of metal as the door was locked.

Just like that. No more words or threats. Nothing.

Alone in pitch darkness.

With nothing left to observe, the voice was at a loss as to what advice it could offer her, and for a short time she began to panic – really panic, the darkness around her filling with small curls of light – before the calm attempted to reassert itself.

Where are you?

What do you know?

The questions were insistent, and after a time she tried to answer them.

Two, maybe three, miles into the woods, handcuffed in the freezing cold in some old building. A place you stored things until you needed them. The man had built the fire in advance, so they were obviously being held here for some purpose.

The bag, too. He had brought things with him in that bag.

Stick to what you know for sure, the voice suggested.

Not long after the door closed, a flickering yellow outline had appeared around the edge: the man had lit the fire. He must have had petrol or lighter fluid with him, because it went up quickly. She could hear it crackling, the wood beginning to blister and pop. Almost immediately, she smelled the charcoal aroma of the smoke.

But not the heat, she thought. Or at least, not enough.

Ignore that. What have you got on you?

Her bag was gone, of course – her mobile phone with it. The man wasn't that stupid. So what else?

It was difficult to search her pockets in the cramped space, especially with her hands still cuffed in front of her, but she did what she could. She bent double and patted down her trousers. House keys; small change.

Possibilities there? She had attended a self-defence course at university, and some of the more unlikely suggestions came back to her now. You could throw a handful of coins into an attacker's face. Bunch your keys between your fingers, create a spiked fist. It was pretty desperate stuff. But still, a small advantage was still an advantage. Don't discount anything.

Next, her coat. There were a couple of old receipts in the outside pockets, which even the self-defence instructor would probably concede were useless. The iRiver in the inside pocket. At least she had that. An electronics expert would probably take it apart and find a way to make it broadcast a distress message, but she couldn't think of any use at all for it. From the instructions, she had a vague memory that it could receive radio, but she'd never used it for that and didn't know how.

Perhaps they would be on the news.

It was dark outside, which meant that she'd been missing for some time. What would have happened when she didn't return to work that afternoon? Probably nothing. It was too much to hope that search teams were combing the woods for them. Michaela would have reminded her bosses that she hadn't been well, so the most they would have done was call her mobile, which was lost, or else her home number, where there was nobody to answer. Maybe someone had seen or heard something at the flat when the man attacked Scott?

But even if they'd been reported missing, the police would have no idea where to look.

They were on their own out here. At this man's mercy.

Time passed.

As it went on, Jodie couldn't help thinking about Kevin. The guilt and despair were too much, but still, she couldn't stop. How could she have done that to Scott? To them both? She thought about all the ways she had let him down, in fact, and about how she might now never have the chance to explain.

The voice advised her not to.

Then Scott began screaming.

Jodie had been sitting in the semi-darkness, blanking her mind, but when she heard that she lurched back to the present and her heart started hammering in her chest.

It was an awful sound, the worst thing in the world, and more than ever before she wanted to go to him, help him, make the man stop whatever he was doing.

Calm down.

The screaming carried on.

She wanted to throw herself against the stone walls until they broke down, kick the door until it splintered. Instead, she sat there, trembling and terrified, and then started to cry with frustration and fear, punching her thighs over and over.

She was tied up in the woods around a campfire. A monster out of her nightmares was torturing Scott – hurting him for fun. They had been reduced from people to playthings. She— they were going to die out here. Suffer beyond anything they'd ever felt before, and then die.

It continued for a long time, and Jodie sat, rocking gently, trying not to listen. Sometimes it went quiet, but then she could hear the man talking gently to Scott and Scott talking back, and there was something conspiratorial – something horribly intimate – about it. Sometimes she could hear him sobbing. But the screaming was worst: it broke her heart. He sounded like an animal.

It was too much. She kicked the door, but it was solid despite its age and didn't move, didn't break. She worked her fingers into the bright gaps between the wood and the stone and shook it. Nothing. There was a small hole on the edge of the frame near the top where she could insert her whole finger and try to pull. It all did nothing.

She pressed her eye to the hole instead. She could see the fire burning, the flames licking at the underside of the metal. It was snowing – the air was thick with silent flurries and the ground was covered.

Nothing else for a time.

But she kept looking. After a while, the man in the devil mask walked across to the fire from the other side of the camp. He was carrying a screwdriver. She couldn't breathe.

He crouched down by one of the stone columns and began heating the end in the flames. Turning it round casually, snow falling all around him.

Something on the point caught fire, burning briefly.

Jodie sat down again. She couldn't bear this.

There was no option but to hear, though. Not unless she miraculously managed to shut down entirely.

Do not shy away from this.

The voice didn't sound sure of itself any more. But it reiterated its point.

Do not shy away. Remember this. Use it when it comes to it.

So Jodie listened to her boyfriend's screams, his crying. She gritted her teeth and she tried her best to use what she heard to weld some resolve in her heart. The man who was doing this would pay for each and every second of it.

No matter what, she wouldn't allow it to happen to her.

You are going to get out of this. And if you get the chance, you're going to hurt him for what he's done.

At some point, the sounds stopped. All she could hear was the fire. She waited, but the next scream didn't come. No more quiet conversation. No crying. Just the crack and spit of flames feeding on wood. She held her breath, counting slowly to ten and then twenty. Over and over again. Nothing.

Was Scott dead?

Everything went a little hazy then. She remembered waking up with him this morning, a lifetime ago. It seemed incomprehensible that he might be gone. If she hadn't been sitting already, she'd have fallen. As it was, she sagged and went weak, and the stars in her vision returned. She was going to faint – she wanted to, in fact, wanted to faint, and then wake up when all this was done, or else not wake up at all.

Pay attention!

No. She'd run out of patience with the voice. Until now, she'd done everything it wanted; and it had helped her as much as it was ever going to. She had her keys to punch with, her change to throw. She knew roughly where she was. She'd tried being calm, but now Scott was dead. She wasn't going to listen to the voice any more.

Jodie fumbled awkwardly at the inside pocket of her coat, pulling out the threads of the headphone cables. She might not be going to faint, but she could certainly find another way to shut the voice away. Shut everything away for a while.

Her hands were shaking with the fear and the cold.

First one ear; then the other.

She clicked the button to turn the player on and waited for the library to assemble itself. Seconds passed.

Finally, a beep.

Another click on the button. Faint music entered her ears – the track she'd been listening to on the waste ground, picking up where it left off – and the volume steadily increased. Up and up, overtaking the crackling of the fire, filling her head, drowning out her thoughts.

She closed her eyes and emptied her head of thought.

A few minutes later, when she felt a waft of air on her face as the door to her cell was opened, she kept them closed. She blocked out what he said to her, and she thought about nothing at all.

PART THREE

It's a paradox, but often you find that an investigation can become clouded by the facts. The more you uncover, the harder it sometimes is to understand how it all fits together. As a team leader, you're constantly receiving updates about the case, and one of the most difficult skills to learn is the ability to sort what's important from what should, for the moment, be held to one side. As developments occur, often unexpectedly, and evidence accumulates, it can become a classic case of 'not being able to see the wood for the trees'.

So when in charge of an investigation it is usually necessary, every now and then, to take a step back. Although the specific facts – and the hard evidence that supports them – are always cornerstones of the case, nevertheless it is easy to become overwhelmed and then to feel lost among the detail. When that happens, the only solution is to extract yourself a little. You take a step away from the facts, and move to a distance from where you can see the whole picture developing at once.

From *Damage Done*, by John Mercer

Mark

Nearly one in the morning. It was still snowing and the roads were solid
with it – a time to drive carefully, you would have thought, especially
after such a long day. But Greg had only one hand on the wheel. With
the other, he was counting off symptoms and trauma, and he kept glancing at me to make sure he had my full attention. He certainly had.

'Hypothermia,' he said. 'Frostbite, shock, God only knows what else.
I mean, look at this fucking weather.'

I nodded, peering through the windscreen. The snow was unfolding
out of the sky: quiet, relentless and heavy. The van's wipers kept squeak-
ing across, clearing it away, but a dozen handfuls of wet, white kisses were
thrown onto the glass after each swipe. Despite the heaters being on full
blast, my hands still felt numb from being out and about around Carl
Farmer's house.

We were in one van, Mercer and Pete in a second, Simon in a third.
The others were slightly in front, and we were all heading for the hospital.
The haze of this long day had erased much of the pre-first-day research I'd
done on the city's geography, but I thought we'd be there soon. Assuming
we didn't crash, of course.

The report had come through after I'd finished filing the door-to-door
reports. A couple of hours earlier, a half-naked man had run out of the
woods at the north of the city, onto the ring road, where he'd nearly been
hit by a car. The vehicle's occupants, Neil and Helen Berry, had stopped
just in time, and then called the police. The man claimed that he and
his girlfriend had been kidnapped and held hostage in the woods, and
that his girlfriend was still in there. The report also mentioned he had a
number of injuries.

The details were interesting, but – even given the killer had changed
his MO – holding people in the woods was a huge deviation from the
previous crimes. But the report also gave the man's name. It was Scott
Banks. His girlfriend was Jodie McNeice.

The names were enough. Within ten minutes of the report coming
through, we were on our way.

On our way to interview him.

Greg said, 'The doctors aren't going to let us talk to him tonight.'

'They might.'

It would depend on what kind of condition he was in, and from the initial report we simply didn't know. Given how cold I felt – and I'd been wrapped up for the evening – Greg was probably right about the hypothermia and frostbite. If Scott Banks had been out in this weather for any length of time, he was going to be in trouble. And if his other injuries were serious the doctors weren't going to let us anywhere near him for the time being.

But at the same time, Mercer wasn't likely to be easily dissuaded. At Farmer's house, I think we'd all felt a little aimless: unsure of where to go next. We had until dawn to find the killer's next victims, but no indication of where to start looking. For once, Mercer looked as up in the air as the rest of us. When I'd told him about the confirmation on the photograph, he listened but was obviously distracted by other concerns. People's lives were at stake, after all. So he was impatient, waiting for something to happen, and frustrated at not knowing where to move in the meantime. When this report had come through it was obvious he'd been hoping for it, or something similar. Immediately he was galvanised again: back on track. I didn't envy anyone who attempted to tell him 'No' right now.

'You've interviewed victims before, right?' Greg said.

'Sure.'

Never anyone in quite this situation, admittedly, but I had some experience with trauma victims; I knew what I was doing.

'Nervous about it?'

'Not really,' I said. 'I'm looking forward to it.'

That was true in a way. On a purely practical level, I knew it was a real chance – both to use my skills and to make an impact on the investigation. But I also felt a lot more nervous than I was prepared to admit. Remembering the footage of Daniel Roseneil, it wasn't going to be an easy or pleasant experience, but talking to victims never is. There was more to it than that. Despite my tiredness, I was on edge.

I glanced at my watch. Greg saw me looking.

'I'm exhausted,' he said.

'Me too.'

A minute later, he pulled left, following Pete and Simon into the car-park at the front of Accident and Emergency. It was a large expanse of tarmac with Reception at the far end, the lights inside so bright they hurt my eyes. The ground was solid with snow in places, cut to slush in others by the loops of tyre tracks. Pete and Simon took their vans all the way across to the side of the ambulance bay. Greg followed, parked up beside them, and we all got out.

A couple of paramedics in green overalls were smoking by the entrance. We nodded to them as we went past; they nodded back, unfazed by the sight of five police officers arriving at this time of night.

In Reception, to the left of the sliding doors, there were rows of orange-peel plastic chairs screwed onto metal frames, separated into bunches by vending machines and cheap metal tables. About half the seats were occupied. There were two teenagers standing rocked back on their heels in front of a third, who was seated and dazed, holding his bloody forehead. An older man in denim sat imperiously against the far wall, arms folded high up on his chest, underlining a face gone crimson from years of alcohol. A few chairs along, there was a couple on either side of a small, teary child, who was holding her arm out like it was a dead bird she'd found in the garden. A drunk was slumped in the corner. A thin old woman sat in a wheelchair, skin the colour of vinegar. Three younger couples were dotted among the rest, the men all looking flushed with drink.

The police department this morning – I remembered thinking it looked like a doctor's waiting room. Now, I was walking through a hospital reception area which looked like a holding bay. As we crossed to the main desk I could feel everyone checking us out.

An electronic screen above it displayed red digital messages to the people waiting. *You will not be seen in the order you arrived ... It is not first come first served ... Average current waiting time: 2 hours.* Behind the desk, it looked and sounded like any other office: filled with the quiet sounds of phones ringing and fingers typing, the buzz and hum of computer equipment. The counter was wide and deep. A young nurse was sitting behind it. She looked up and smiled. Mercer leaned on the counter and didn't attempt to smile in return.

'Detective Sergeant John Mercer,' he said. 'We're here to see a Doctor Li? About Scott Banks.'

'One moment.'

She picked up the phone and dialled through. The drunk lads behind us, oblivious or indifferent to our presence, started mock fighting with each other, reliving whatever skirmish had landed them here. One of them was doing upper cuts in the air. He seemed quite proud of whatever it was he'd done to someone else, and I found it slightly soul-destroying.

'Head down to the left there,' the nurse told us, leaning over to point the way along the corridor. 'Waiting Room Eleven.'

'Thanks.'

We headed down. Waiting Room Eleven was a small, cramped consultation room, barely big enough for the five of us. There was nothing to sit on apart from a waist-high bed, the old blankets covered with a stripe of tissue paper feeding out of a holder on the wall. Across from it, there was a trolley containing basic equipment: bandages, needles, thermometers. In the corner, a tall, flexible lamp. None of it inspired confidence. The room felt like it had been assembled on the fly at a disaster zone.

The far wall was just a half-drawn curtain across a larger area where people were bustling around. I could hear casual talk and footfalls; the clank of metal on metal; the sound of water running.

We waited. Mercer checked his watch twice.

'Where is he?'

'Probably saving someone's life,' Greg suggested.

Mercer peered through the curtains.

'Excuse me?' he called out. 'Doctor Li? Yes? No?'

No, apparently. He leaned back in and we waited a minute longer. I wanted the doctor to show up as well – to get this over with, one way or another. At least then I'd know where we stood and what I had to do.

Eventually, Doctor Li arrived through the curtains, drawing them roughly shut behind him. He had closely shaved black hair and was short and solid, his white coat stretched across a broad back. He didn't look like he took much shit, outside or inside the hospital, and his expression indicated he was both expecting and prepared for a difficult conversation. So that was the way it would be. Clearly, I wasn't going to be interviewing anyone here tonight without a battle; equally clearly, there would be one.

Li produced a pen and a clipboard and perched on the edge of the bed.

'Sorry to keep you. Busy night.'

'Okay.' Mercer hid his impatience and showed Li his badge instead. 'We're here about the young man who was hit by a car on the ring road.'

'Scott Banks. He wasn't hit by a car but he looks like he was.'

'Tell us about him.'

'I don't know much. From his records, we've seen him a couple of times before, but never anything serious. We've got basic information in the file – home address, and so on.'

'That would be useful.'

'I've told Reception they can give it to you.'

'He claims he was held captive in the woods?'

'Yes. Although he's very unclear about a lot of what's happened to him.'

He ran through the details.

Banks could remember being at home that afternoon, and that something had happened to him there – an attack of some kind. From that point, his memory became disjointed. He recalled being in a van, with his hands tied in front of him. A man in a devil mask, who had been hurting him. His girlfriend, Jodie, screaming. Most recently, himself running through the freezing woods, lost and frightened.

There was no string of sense to thread these memories on, but it was familiar and it was sufficient. Scott and Jodie. A man in a devil mask.

I needed to think carefully about how I was going to handle the interview, assuming I could get one. If Banks's memories were disjointed, like Daniel Roseneil's, there were good, painful reasons for that. I would have to be careful when questioning him.

'Okay,' Mercer said. 'Simon, do you want to grab that address from Reception and get going?'

Simon leaned away from the wall. 'But I've already left.'

Mercer turned back to Li. 'We'll need to speak to Banks as soon as possible.'

Li shook his head. 'I'm afraid he's in no condition to be interviewed. He's not long come out of emergency surgery and he needs to rest. He does want to help, but every time he tries, the block comes down' – he ran his hand down in front of his face – 'and then he can't remember. Mentally and physically, talking about his ordeal is simply too much for him at the moment.'

Li weighted his last comment with authority, throwing down the diagnosis as a gauntlet. I expected Mercer to contest it. Instead, he nodded and moved on.

'Emergency surgery? What are we looking at here? What's been done to him?'

Li inclined his head slightly. 'The surgery was for his eye. We couldn't save it, but we had to clean out the wound to prevent infection. In answer to your question, it looks like a hot piece of metal was used on him.'

Christ, I thought.

Mercer simply nodded again. 'Probably a screwdriver,' he said. 'That's what the man who did it has used in the past.'

He let that sink in for a second. Then: 'What else?'

Li looked uncomfortable. 'He's been hurt very badly. There are a large number of cuts and burns to his chest, arms and face.'

'Injuries consistent with torture?'

'I wouldn't be familiar. But I imagine so.'

'Severe torture by an unknown subject.'

Li thought about it, choosing his words carefully. 'The injuries are obviously consistent with infliction of pain and disfigurement, rather than an attempt to subdue or incapacitate. Yes.'

'Only blinded in one eye, though,' Mercer said. 'Do you know why?'

It was a rhetorical question because, of course, Li didn't.

'It was so that Banks could watch his girlfriend being tortured when the man was finished with him.'

Li paled. I felt myself doing the same, but for different reasons: as far as I could remember, that particular insight hadn't been in the file. I glanced at Pete. He wasn't giving much away, but I could tell by his face that he'd clocked it, too. I supposed it was obvious with hindsight. The killer's game contained as many reversals as the participants could bear. The impetus for those changes was being forced to witness the suffering of the person they loved. The victims had never been blinded in both eyes, never punctured in both eardrums. They had always been able to see and hear.

Victims. I cursed myself. It was so easy to forget that we were talking about a human being here. A man like me. When Li said Scott Banks had been blinded, it meant that someone had held his head still and stuck something hot and sharp into his eye. I could barely imagine the panic, the fear, the pain caused by that. It seemed unendurable.

'What else?' Mercer prompted.

Li cleared his throat. 'Three broken fingers.'

'Go on.'

'The soles of his feet. They've also been severely burned. Bear in mind that he then ran through the woods, in this weather. So there's hypothermia and frostbite as well.'

Mercer nodded.

'Have you ever encountered this before, Doctor?'

'I don't really see the point in that question.'

'You don't see the point.' Mercer looked up. 'Well, there is a point. Three people with similar injuries have passed through your hospital. Two men, one woman. Did you encounter them?'

Li blinked. 'No.'

'You're sure?'

'I'm sure I'd remember.'

'I'm quite sure you would. We've been following the individual who carried out this attack for quite some time now, so we're familiar with the effect his crimes can have, even on seasoned professionals.'

'Detective—'

Mercer held up his hand. 'When Scott Banks talks about his girlfriend being in danger, he's quite right. As we speak, the man will be hurting Jodie McNeice in exactly the same way. The best result we'll get tonight is that you see injuries like Scott's again. If you don't see them, it's because Jodie has been hurt so badly that she's died.'

Li started to say something, but then turned to look at the curtain, frowning.

Mercer let the silence pan out for a moment. Then he gestured at me: 'This is my colleague Detective Nelson. Mark?'

'Pleased to meet you,' I said.

Li glanced at me with an expression somewhere between annoyance and frustration. He certainly wasn't pleased to meet me in return. I wasn't hurt.

'Detective Nelson is the man who needs to interview Scott Banks,' Mercer said. 'Is there any advice you could offer about how he should approach it? What he should expect?'

Despite the noise of the activity behind the curtain – the beeps of machinery, the bustle of rushing bodies – it seemed very quiet in the room. After a moment, Li rested the clipboard on his lap, rubbed the bridge of his nose, and sighed.

'Okay,' he said. 'Let's cut the crap. For whatever record there is, I do not want this patient to be interviewed at this time. It is not in his interests, and I have a duty of care towards him. He needs rest; he needs privacy; he needs time to recover.'

'Noted.' I recognised Mercer's tone of voice. The matter had been settled, and his attention was shifting to the next obstacle to be considered. He actually waved Scott Banks's comfort away. 'He can have all that tomorrow. Hopefully Jodie can as well.'

'That's the deciding factor in me allowing you to interview him.' Li paused so that Mercer could note the wording. But he was disappointed. 'As long as my objection is recorded.'

'It is. You have security guards here?'

'Yes.'

'Could you arrange for one to stand outside Banks's room, please? It's unlikely he's currently in danger, but we need to be sure.'

'Of course.'

'Okay.' Mercer stood up. 'What we're also going to need is a room. I think some of us, at least, will be here most of the night, so it would be handy to have a place to set up shop and work.'

It wasn't exactly a question, but Li nodded. 'I'll see what I can do.'

'Thank you, Doctor.'

'I'll be back shortly.'

He opened the curtains and stepped out of the waiting room. When he was gone, Mercer closed the curtains and turned to us.

'Okay,' he said. 'Thoughts?'

My first thought was how tired he suddenly looked. He'd put on a good show for Doctor Li, but the last few hours seemed to have worn him down. Partly it was the overhead light in this room – paling and waxing his skin; making dark sockets of his eyes – but it wasn't just that. His body had the slump of exhaustion; his expression seemed too heavy. He wasn't moving much, either, unless he had to.

But then we all probably looked the same.

Pete was leaning against the wall and staring at his feet. Without looking up, he spoke slowly.

'He's totally changed his MO.'

Mercer nodded. 'Taking the couple out into the woods, rather than holding them in their home. Yes. He's altered the form of the game. And we've just reached the next stage. What's new about this part? Come on, Pete, don't fall asleep on me. Talk us through what's happened.'

Slowly, Pete leaned away from the wall and sat down on the bed. He looked at the floor and began rubbing his big hands, as though washing them with the warm, sickly air.

'Banks is abducted at his house,' he said. 'Presumably, he's taken somewhere in the woods, along with his girlfriend. He's subjected to a period of torture. He runs through the woods, gets to the road.'

'Succinct.' Mercer stared down at the top of his deputy's head. 'Okay. Banks has been tortured, so there's at least some correlation between this crime and the previous ones. If we assume the killer's playing his usual game, Banks is with us ahead of time, isn't he? It's not dawn yet. And I think there are two possible explanations for that. Greg?'

Greg shrugged. 'He escaped?'

'Look lively, Greg. That's one. Mark?'

'The killer let him go,' I said.

'Exactly. The game played out and Scott Banks chose to abandon his

girlfriend. Which means we have until dawn to stop her being mur
dered.'

There was a moment of silence while we all considered this. It didn'
make sense. Pete broke the quiet without looking up, his voice slow and
weary.

'John, she's dead already.'

'No, she's not.'

'He's killed her.' Pete spread his palms on either side. 'Whatever's happened, he's smart and he's going to have counted on Scott Banks getting
out of the woods. He's not going to wait around for us. The game's over
He finished it early. He killed the girl and he's long gone.'

'No.' Mercer shook his head confidently. 'It's not.'

'So you think he's just there, then? Waiting for us?'

'Not exactly. But he's been planning this for two years, Pete. He's not
concerned about hiding his identity from us any more. And he left us
the recording of Simpson's murder – he explicitly said "dawn". The game
he's playing has changed, but not the time limit on it. So we have until
dawn, don't we?'

Pete finally looked up at Mercer: looked at him frankly, right in the
eyes.

'With the greatest respect, John, I think you're seeing what you want
to see.'

Immediately, Mercer turned his back and walked over to the curtains.
Pete stared at the empty space for a moment, then closed his eyes.

I knew what he was thinking. The killer had changed so many aspects
of his MO that it made no sense to presume he wouldn't kill the girl
before dawn. Mercer was simply hoping. It was what the team had been
concerned about in the canteen. What would it do to him if we couldn't
save these people? This case, this killer. Mercer was making assumptions
based on what he wanted to be true. Maybe what he needed to be.

Earlier, Pete had made the decision to stick by his boss and friend.
Now I could tell he was seriously doubting the wisdom of that. Greg
was keeping quiet. Mercer clearly wasn't about to acquiesce. Instead, he
began to pace back and forth, as though using the momentum to generate energy.

'Sir, I—'

'Noted.' Mercer stopped pacing, and glared at him. 'It's all been noted.
All of it, all day. Noted.'

The air chilled instantly. Pete looked stung by Mercer's outburst.

'It's actually my decision,' he reminded us. 'I'm in charge here, and I know what I'm doing. I'm not broken yet, you know. But if that's what you think, what else should we do, Pete? Tell me. Two hours ago our killer was in the woods. Where else should we begin?'

Pete closed his eyes.

'All right, John,' he said quietly. 'Search team?'

'Search team, yes,' Mercer said. *Praise the Lord*. 'Check to see if the helicopter will fly. Wake up Search and Rescue and get some dogs out there. Get bodies physically into the woods.'

'It's a huge—'

'A huge area, of course, so start from where Banks was picked up. Mark will see what he can get from the interviews. If Banks can remember something specific, it'll narrow the parameters.' He turned to me. 'You've interviewed victims before?'

I nodded.

'First interview, just get as much as you can: confirmation of what he's told us so far, information about Jodie, anything about the woods. Ease him into remembering more, but don't give up too easily.'

'I know what I'm doing.'

It must have sounded snappy, because Mercer frowned. Everyone was rebelling against him. He ran his fingers through his hair.

'All right. You and Pete, get going. Pete, keep in touch. Be safe.'

'Yes, John.'

We left the room, and I followed Pete out to the entrance. He walked briskly, not saying anything but occasionally shaking his head, and I had to move quickly to keep up. He paused when we got to Reception, and turned to look at me.

'What are you going to do?' I said.

'I'm going to go to the woods and organise the search team. What else is there?' He sighed and shook his head one last time.

'Look after him.'

I nodded, slightly uncertainly. He stared at me for a second, then nodded in return. The glass doors slid open behind him, and he huddled up and headed outside, into the snow.

Scott

In the dream, Scott was in his old bedroom. The one he'd been in during his second year at university.

Of the six bedrooms in the house, it was the smallest by far. He'd moved in with five friends he'd met in first year; the two who'd found the property took the large rooms downstairs, and he'd agreed to go in this box room to save argument among the others. It was only twice the width of the single bed and slightly less than twice the length, but he didn't have much stuff, and he quite liked the idea of existing in such a small space. It streamlined you as a person: kept you focused. His few possessions fitted in easily enough – CDs, videos and random objects, all on the bookcase by the window – while most of the materials he needed for his degree could be stored in the studio space the department allocated to him.

It was the year he'd met Jodie, and in the dream she was there too. They were sitting side-by-side on the bed, pillows propped against the wall to form a backrest, drinking vodka and Coke and watching a film on his worn-out video-recorder. Flickering light from the screen was casting odd shadows around the walls.

It was an old, damp room. The smell from the food they ate up here, the smoke from the cigarettes … it hung in the air for days before settling into the wallpaper and bed sheets, getting under the skin of the room.

Nevertheless, he was glad to be back here. These had been happy times. Even though it was only a dream, every time he touched his new girlfriend he felt a thrill of excitement. The air seemed to glisten with possibility.

Scott drifted up slightly out of sleep, but not enough for it to leave him. They were curious, these dreams, so vivid and detailed that they felt real, but even in the thick of them he knew they weren't. They were strange, swirling concoctions of memory and imagination, images and instincts, and he found it hard to discern exactly what was what.

There was comfort in them, but he knew there were also dangers here. It was as though he was standing on the edge of some more terrible memory, and his mind had to keep distracting him from it. As he sank back into the dream, the bedroom solidified around him again, and it

128

felt precarious: the walls, the curtains – all a paper-thin defence. It might occlude the threat from view, but it wouldn't keep it out for ever. Sooner or later, the real memories would find him, and all this would fall apart.

'Let me see.'

Suddenly, it was daytime, with bright light coming through the pale curtains, and Jodie was sitting on the edge of the bed. There was a pile of canvases at the far end. She was leaning over, reaching out for them.

He sat up quickly. 'Whoa. Hang on.'

He wanted to sort them first, make sure she only saw the ones he thought were best. He'd told her they were all rubbish, but in reality there were a couple that he thought might be all right – although he would wait to see her reaction before he admitted it.

It was no use protesting, anyway. Jodie was forceful. Already, she understood him too well.

'Ah-ah.' She slapped his hand away. 'I know your game, lad. Just let me see.'

He settled back reluctantly, and watched as she worked through his paintings. She spent more time on each piece than was necessary simply to be polite, even the really bad ones, and she asked questions and listened to his answers.

'I am quite proud of this one,' he said, when she reached the best.

'You should be. You should be proud of all of them. You're really talented.'

'No.'

She slapped his leg this time. 'Yes, you are.'

He gave up. Jodie was major computers, minor business studies, and by her own admission she didn't have a creative bone in her body. The paintings were pleasant enough, but he knew that if she'd been a fine-art student she would be far more critical – even snobby. Talent wasn't strictly the issue: any monkey could learn to paint. But what was the harm? He could take the compliments and enjoy them for what they were. He liked it that she said things like that. He wanted to impress her, and—

—the sun was blocked out. A shadow had passed over the room.

The devil, Scott thought, although he didn't know what that meant. He heard a throaty rattling to his left and turned slowly to face it.

Something else was in the room, sitting beside him on the bed. Its face was so close he could smell the heat rising off it, but he couldn't see it. There was just the impression of red and black skin, of an elongated snout like a goat's.

The face tilted quickly from side to side like a metronome, blurring the features even further.

You like my artwork and you support me.

Scott turned back to warn Jodie – but stopped abruptly, confused. The old student bedroom had disappeared. He was sitting in their front room, the one they lived in now, on the left-hand side of the settee.

Impossibly, he was staring at himself.

The second him was standing in the centre of the room, his face half hidden by the camera he was holding.

'Say "Cheese".'

'Cheese!'

He looked to his right in time to see Jodie illuminated by a flash at the other end of the settee. She was curled up like a cat, her legs tucked beneath her, giving the camera a huge grin.

Another flash.

The him with the camera frowned at the screen on the back.

'This one's better. See what you think.'

Suddenly, Jodie and the other him were gone, and Scott heard the rattle again. It was coming from the kitchen, behind him and to the left. He stood up quickly and backed into the middle of the room.

Round the doorframe, he could see the tumble-dryer, the washing-machine. He stepped to the right and could see more: the fridge, the edge of a cupboard . . .

A set of fingers curled slowly round the doorframe. Then another set, further up. The devil. A second later, a black and red face leaned slowly out into view, and then the thing rushed out at him.

'Let me see!'

They were in the bedroom. He was standing behind Jodie, reaching round her and holding his hands over her eyes. She kept pulling half-heart-edly at his wrists. Outside, he could see the weather was cold; the air hard and still. He started to shiver, and turned his attention back to Jodie.

'I love you.'

He took his hands away.

'Happy Birthday.'

The painting was on the bed, positioned on the pillows so that it rested against the headboard.

Starting with the photograph he'd taken of Jodie on the settee, he'd applied the same iterative process he'd been using recently in his work: painting, scanning, reducing the picture quality, painting again. The final painting on the bed, from about halfway through the process, was both Jodie and not Jodie. It was square blocks of colour – browns and pinks and beiges – painted onto a canvas that was about seventy blocks high by forty wide. If you blurred your eyes, you could see her. Sort of. He had worked very hard, and he was proud of it.

She put her hands to her mouth for a second, then turned and hugged him.

'I love it,' she said. 'It's perfect.'

He held her tightly, looking over her shoulder at the painting. She was telling him how wonderful it was, how much she loved him, thanking him for all the effort he'd put in ... She could say what she wanted, but he knew. He'd seen the disappointment in her eyes, and then the way it was swiftly hidden.

I fucked up. I should have given her the first painting I did. He still could, but it wouldn't be the same. You could always do different things for someone; they told you, and you changed it. The trick was getting it right first time.

I just wanted to give you something different, he thought. *Any idiot can paint. I wanted to do something that nobody else would do for you. Something that was me. I wanted—*

Over her shoulder, Scott saw the devil. It was crawling awkwardly out from underneath the bed, steam rising off its face.

'Jodie—'

But she was holding him too tight, like a backpack tied round his front. She wouldn't let him go. He couldn't move.

The devil rose to full height, its joints clicking and cracking and popping, then walked across to them. Panic fluttered inside him. Somewhere, a baby was crying. He frowned.

'Shhhh.'

Bang!

His head was gone from the shoulders up, replaced by white, hissing static, a cloud of nausea.

Inexplicably, he was on his face on the carpet, back in the front room. The painting was leaned against the far wall, behind the dining table, where it had been for the ten months since her birthday.

'We must put that up,' one of them would say, and yet for some reason neither of them ever had. He fixed his attention on it now, blurring his eyes so that she came into focus. Jodie.

I love your brown hair.

As he stared at it, blocks of colour began fading away. He blinked, willing them to return, but instead even more began to disappear.

The smoothness of your skin.

Her hair vanished.

Small squares of white were appearing everywhere, the pink and beige shades of her skin melting out of existence.

I love the feel of your neck on my lips.

It was nearly all gone. Three more squares. Two.

Scott didn't see the last blocks fade: there was simply a moment when he realised he was staring at a blank white canvas, abandoned against a wall.

A moment when he realised he'd lost her.

4 DECEMBER   **2.00 A.M.**
5 HOURS, 20 MINUTES UNTIL DAWN

Mark

Each floor of the hospital seemed to inhabit its own shade of the spectrum. The reception area and waiting room downstairs had been pale blue. Here, one floor up, everything was either washed-out green or turquoise. Whoever had designed the building had used a colour-scheme with all the vibrancy sucked out of the palette. It was all very 'hospital', I thought. If you woke up here confused, the pastel shades alone would convince you that you were sick.

Because of the nature of our enquiry, Scott Banks had been given his own room in the east wing. It was small, with enough space around a single bed to fit a trolley of equipment on one side and a chair for me on the other. It was also very dark. The blinds were drawn and the lights had been dimmed. It felt appropriate that the bandaged figure on the bed had a covering of shadow to rest under.

He was sleeping, his slow and steady breathing interrupted by an intermittent hitch in his throat: a wheeze and a click. The only other sound in the room was from the equipment: the quietly comforting beep of his pulse, registered by a quivering green line on a machine by the bed. He was on a drip: IV fluids were keeping his temperature steady and administering morphine to take the teeth out of the pain he'd feel when awake.

The entire right side of his head was padded with gauze to form a football of bandages; his left cheek was patterned with butterfly plasters. White blankets on the bed were pulled up to his chin.

Another wheeze and click, his chest rising and lowering almost imperceptibly.

I found I was synchronising my own breathing with his, allowing it to calm me down. It had been tense downstairs after Pete left, and I'd been glad when Li returned. He'd brought me up here about ten minutes ago, a journey that took in a cramped, noisy elevator and then what felt like endless corridors filled with movement and activity. Wherever I'd walked, I was exactly where somebody else needed to be. More practised, Li had moved through the throng with ease, while I floundered behind, catching the instructions he called back to me.

'... sleeping at the moment. And that's all I ask; that you let him sleep when he needs to. He has to rest ...'

And so on.

I'd nodded, although he couldn't have seen me, and wondered what the fuck he thought I was going to do. Jab his patient with a pen, presumably.

When we arrived at the room, the security guard had already been in place. He was tall and solid, dressed in a pale brown uniform. Li introduced me, but I showed him my badge anyway and made sure he understood the deal. Hospital personnel and myself aside, nobody was to be allowed in to see Scott Banks.

Now I was sitting quietly with his file on my lap, attempting to formulate an interview strategy. But the quiet and the dark were soothing, and it was difficult to think. I felt the tension and the bustle of the day lifting from me, the length and exhaustion settling in, and I had to keep mentally slapping myself back on course.

Confidence comes from knowledge.

What did I know here? The closest parallel I could think of was Daniel Roseneil. He had also been tortured, but physical pain was only a part of it. Roseneil was a man who had been forced to abandon someone he loved. Even though that decision was tempered by the context, the responsibility for it had been too overwhelming for him to bear, and so he had let go of the memory – thrown it where it couldn't be found. It was likely that Scott would be the same.

He wants to help but he's afraid to remember.

I pictured it as a door in his head. His mind would have shut the trauma away on the other side. But he could still see the door itself and he'd be getting certain impressions of what lay behind it. His girlfriend was behind it, and she was in danger, so part of him wanted to open the door and help her. But another part of him knew what else was shut away there and wouldn't let him go near. My job was to help him reconcile the two. I had to keep the scared part comforted and distracted while I led the other across to the door and helped him open it.

To do so, I would have to disregard the argument we'd had downstairs. Thinking with my head, I was sure Pete was right. Scott's girlfriend was probably dead and the killer gone. Inside this room, though, there were going to be two simple truths that I would stick to no matter what: Jodie was alive; and we were going to find her. Those were the ground rules.

Then there was the method.

When it comes down to it, all interviews are actually very similar. I remembered interrogating an old man we were fairly sure had abducted a child from a playground, and when I sat down with him I knew straight away that he was our guy. He was eaten up with self-disgust, and a part of him clearly wanted to confess and get what he'd done out in the open; but at that time he couldn't bring himself to admit it. So all we got was lies and evasions. He wasn't there, he was somewhere else; he never saw her. He would never hurt a little girl.

But the truth existed in the straight chronology of his memory, and so I took him along it, step by step. Where were you at twelve? Then where did you go? Visualise it – walk through the day in your head. The old man did, and every so often he'd bump up against one of his lies and have to blur the detail. At that point, he suddenly couldn't remember quite as well, and so we'd back off for a bit and talk about something else. Then we'd press a little more. He wasn't going anywhere and he knew it, which allowed the truth to come out in degrees. Yes, he was there at the playground, but he didn't do anything, didn't see the little girl. Ten minutes later we'd got to, well, maybe he did see her. Then, yes, she went for a walk with him but she was fine – he left her by the trees and someone else must have hurt her afterwards. And so on. Step by step, he gave it up. He knew we had him, but it was too difficult for him to run straight there and say, 'I did it.' At the end of the interview, he actually looked grateful.

This was a different situation, but the same principle applied. Scott's experiences formed a wound. I would have to press carefully around the edges to see which parts were tender, slowly getting him used to the pressure. We would work gently, approaching the truth with patience.

Or as much patience as the time limit allowed.

I looked up from the rise and fall of his chest to his face. The part of it I could see, anyway. It was two o'clock in the morning; about seven hours until dawn. Regardless of my promise to Doctor Li, if Scott Banks didn't wake up soon I might end up having to jab him with a pen after all.

In the meantime, I adjusted the file slightly, leaned back in the chair and closed my eyes.

'Hello?'

I jerked awake. Scott's file hit the floor and the papers spread out in a fan. Shit. I leaned down to gather them back together, looking up at the bed at the same time. Scott was watching me. My brain told me that in order to salvage my self-respect I would have to pretend I hadn't been asleep, but I decided that was hopeless.

How fucking professional do you look right now?

'I'm sorry.' I spoke quietly, as though he was still asleep. 'It's been a long day.'

'That's okay.'

He kept his voice down, too. Perhaps it was the room: the hospital forcing us into a conversation full of whispers.

'You looked like you were having a nightmare,' he said.

'I was. I'm sorry.'

The dream was already fading, but I knew it had been about Lise. I couldn't remember what. Had it been the same as that morning? The only impression I had left was the sound of the sea, rushing and breaking. The same feeling of despair; it was like starvation, but inside the heart.

'I keep having nightmares, too,' Scott said. 'I can't remember them properly. Everything's confused.'

'I think that's to be expected. Do you know where you are?'

He nodded carefully. 'But you're not a doctor. Are you here to protect me?'

'Like in the movies?' I could have smiled – some guard I'd be right now – but it wouldn't hurt for Scott to know he was safe. 'I suppose I am, sort of. My name's Mark Nelson. I'm a detective. Basically, I'm here to keep you company, chat for a bit. See if we can shed some light on what's happened to you this evening.'

135

He considered this for a moment, and then began an attempt at pulling himself up into a sitting position. The trolley by the bedside moved with him, the bag on the drip beginning to rock gently.

I felt a flush of panic. 'Careful you don't knock that.'

'I'm fine.'

There was a hard edge to his voice, like he was suffering and finding it hard to take, but determined to keep going. The covers fell away slightly, revealing a slim, athletic body. There were bruises like black and purple stains on his skin. I kept my wince inside: bruises don't appear that quickly unless you've been hit very hard. I saw more bandages as well, covering what must have been numerous cuts. The tube leading from his arm to the trolley was tied tightly to him with swathes of white cloth.

'Your doctor would kill us both if he saw you doing that,' I said. 'He seems a pretty tough guy.'

'He didn't want me to speak to you.'

'No.'

'But I have to.'

I nodded, noting the language: 'have to', not 'want to'.

'I need to tape record our conversations.' I gestured at the equipment I'd brought. 'Is that okay?'

'Yes.'

'If at any point you want to stop' – I spread my hands – 'that's fine. We take a break, pick it up again later on. Basically, I'll be back and forth for the duration. We'll see how we get on.'

'I don't know how much help I'm going to be.' He frowned. 'My head keeps going ... in circles.'

'Well, we'll just take things easy to start with,' I said. 'I want you to stay as calm and relaxed as possible. You may not remember properly at the moment, but I know you're very worried about your girlfriend.'

Immediately: 'Jodie.'

'I know you're worried about her. And that might make you feel panicky. As much as possible, I want you to try not to worry. The guy in charge is the best there is at this sort of thing. So we'll do the worrying for you.'

'But she's still there. In the woods.'

'We know.' I tried to be as reassuring and decisive as possible. 'And we're going to find her. There's a search team in the woods. Jodie's going to be fine.'

His expression settled down a little. 'Do you promise?'

'I promise.'

Change the subject.

'What I want to do first is get as much information from you as possible. Some of it might help us find Jodie, but we'd be talking about all this anyway, because you've been the victim of a crime. This conversation is about you. Okay?'

He nodded uncertainly. I weighed it up and decided to keep moving the conversation away from Jodie. Steer it onto safer ground for now. I put his file on the floor and gave him my full attention.

'Let's start with your flat. You were working at home today?'

'Not really working.'

'What were you doing?'

'I've got the week off. I was doing some things on the computer. Photo-art stuff.'

'Oh, right. You're an artist?'

'No.' He looked sad for a moment. 'Not really. But I was messing around with that today. Then I went and did some weights in our spare room.'

Our spare room. So he lived with Jodie. No great surprise, but still an important detail. And it raised the question again. This couple had a base, but rather than holding them there like all the others the 50/50 Killer had taken them into the woods instead. Why had he done that?

'What time was this?' I said.

'About three, maybe.'

Scott ran through what he remembered. The delivery was slightly fragmented, but I took that to be a symptom of both the painkillers he was on and the overall confusion he was suffering. The important thing was that the basic details matched what he'd told the first officer on the scene, and then the doctors here. It was a good indication that what he *could* recall was at least coming out right.

When he'd nearly finished exercising, he'd heard a noise, he said, and emerged from his weights room expecting to find Jodie home from work early. The television had been on, but the front room was empty. He'd walked across.

'And I had time to think "What?" and then he came at me.'

The man hiding in the kitchen had leaped out from the side. Scott had been attacked and subdued – hit hard, before having something pressed into his face. That was all he could remember from the flat.

The more he talked, the more frustrated he became – increasingly angry, to the point where he seemed almost disgusted with himself. I recognised the emotion, and as he finished, if his hands hadn't been bandaged up like boxing gloves, I thought he might have punched himself on the thigh in anger. It was something I'd done myself over the past six months, when the feelings got too much for me. Sometimes you had to let them out.

'I was so stupid,' he said. 'So useless.'

'No, you weren't.'

I tried to put myself in his situation. He obviously kept himself in good shape, yet all that time spent working out had proved meaningless when it actually mattered. If he'd been able to defend himself everything would have turned out differently. By failing, it felt like he'd condemned them both to what followed.

It was an area of self-recrimination that I wanted to keep him away from for now.

'I lift weights a bit, too,' I said. 'You know how it feels after a big workout – you can barely lift your arms. The man who did this to you has done it before, and he's smart. He waited until you were exhausted and less capable of fighting back, and he distracted you so he could get the upper hand. It would have happened the same to anyone.'

But he kept shaking his head.

All too much, I thought. Move on.

'Let's talk about the man in the devil mask.'

I picked up the file again, mainly so I had something to do with my hands.

'I know it's difficult,' I said, 'but I want you to separate him off in your head. I don't want to know about the things he did, but I am interested in anything you can tell me about him. Imagine him just standing in a street. What do you see him wearing?'

The look of frustration on Scott's face remained, but he seemed to relax a little. He thought about the question carefully.

'I'm not sure about his clothes,' he said. 'He had trainers on. They were white, scuffed. Blue bits round the lace holes, I think. Dark, anyway. The rest of his clothes were black, I think. Like he had overalls on.'

He spoke quietly, his expression settling. It was going to be a night of peaks and troughs, I realised. Every time he flinched, I would need to back off a little.

After talking about his clothes, we moved on to a more general physical description. By the time Scott had confirmed the previous accounts we had of the killer – short brown hair, quite tall, strong build – he seemed to have calmed down enough to move on to something more specific.

'Do you remember how you got to the woods?' I said.

'We were in a van.'

'You and Jodie?'

He nodded.

'She was tied up in the back already. I felt so awful. I think we stopped on the way, maybe once or twice, I don't remember.'

'What happened then?'

'There was something, but ... I think he got out, but I'm not sure.'

He frowned, looking annoyed with himself again.

Move on.

'Okay. Then he took you to the woods?'

'When we all got out, he put a bag over my head. There was nothing I could do.'

I nodded. Wherever I moved the conversation, the guilt he was feeling kept surfacing in one form or another. He was veering between I should have done this and I couldn't do anything.

I decided to leap forward in time. 'So you had a bag on your head on the way into the woods, but what about on the way out? Can you remember that?'

Immediately, he shook his head.

'Can you remember how long you were running before you reached the road?'

'No. A while.'

'Like a few minutes or more like an hour?'

'I can't remember. More like an hour.'

I glanced at the pulse monitor on the machine by the bed. His heart rate was increasing. Time to retreat slightly.

'Never mind,' I said. 'Do you remember the man being there at that point? Was he chasing you?'

'Chasing ... ?' Scott frowned. 'No.'

I could see the question ticking away inside. Obviously, it led to others. If he wasn't being chased, why not? How had he got away? After a moment, his subconscious warned him to back off and not test this ground with any real weight.

'I'm sorry.' He shook his head firmly. 'Everything in the woods is just ... flashes. Dark and cold. Snow. I was running most of the time. It's all a mess until I reached the road.'

'Okay.'

'I do remember talking to myself. In the woods, before I got to the road. I told myself over and over that it was going to be okay.'

'That's understandable,' I said. 'In that kind of situation, your subconscious can sometimes take over. It helps to get you through it.'

That's when it happened. Something – either a memory or a fragment of my dream – appeared in my head. It was a voice in my head, clearer and more distinct than my thoughts.

Swim, it said. *Swim as hard as you can.*

I shook my head.

'That's all I remember,' Scott said. 'It's like you just said – like someone else took charge and told me to take a back seat. I don't know where I was or what I was doing.'

'Don't worry.' I leaned forwards, shook my head again. The voice had gone, but it felt like something was crawling in there. 'If you can't remember that, we'll … we'll leave it for now.'

Pull yourself together. But it wasn't as easy as that. My heart was beating too quickly. The voice had brought a flash of panic with it. Suddenly, I couldn't think properly.

Scott and I were staring at each other. He was waiting for me.

'Okay,' I said. 'Okay. Let's talk about Jodie for a moment. How would you describe her? What's she like as a person?'

He started to answer, but then stopped. His expression became blank for a moment, and I understood immediately that I'd slipped up. Moved too quickly. Before I had a chance to reverse away from the subject, his face crumpled and he began to cry.

I sat there for a second, thinking, You fucking idiot, over and over again.

'It's okay,' I said.

But it wasn't. It might not have been a direct question about the ordeal itself, but it didn't need to be. The fact that he was here meant he'd probably abandoned Jodie in the woods. He might not remember doing it, but thinking about her in any depth would still bring up those feelings of weakness, betrayal and guilt. What's she like? His feelings about her were a straight route into the heart of his evening. His mind would probably rather run over hot coals than think about that, and if my mind had been properly here in the room where it belonged, I'd have realised that.

'It's okay,' I repeated.

But the blinds had come down. He was crying quietly to himself. I sighed inwardly, annoyed at myself. What the fuck was wrong with me? Maybe it was for the best. Maybe it was time for both of us to take a break.

He wasn't listening, but I said it again anyway as I stood up: the same lie I'd started the interview with. The despair I was feeling seemed to cancel out the conviction I was aiming for.

I said, 'We're going to find her.'

Eileen

Eileen was upstairs in John's study, reclining in the comfortable leather chair he occupied for at least an hour most evenings. Since he couldn't be here, it seemed a shame to let it go to waste. When John used to get up early, she'd often rolled across and slept on his side of the bed to feel closer to him in his absence. This was much the same, although her emotions were somewhat different.

The study was where her husband did most of his work at home. There were two bookcases side-by-side along the wall, and a desk opposite where he kept his computer. Behind it, the wall was adorned with framed certificates, newspaper reports and photographs: clippings that spanned his entire career. The room was illuminated by a single standing lamp, the light from it pale and soft.

Across from her the curtains were open, and her reflection stared back from beyond the window: a gentle, almost ghostly blur. It was holding the phone against the side of its face.

In her ear, the ringing continued, her frustration growing with every infuriating burst of sound.

Pick it up, she demanded.

Their home number was programmed into John's mobile. She visualised him looking at the display, knowing it was her and debating whether to take the call. The frustration was joined by anger.

Answer me.

She watched her reflection pick up the glass of wine and take another sip.

'Hi, there,' he said.

Thank God. Now that he had answered, her fear relaxed slightly. The anger remained. She put the glass down on the table beside her, perhaps a little loudly.

'You took your time.'

'I'm sorry. I had to move out into the corridor. I *am* at work.'

John had never liked talking on the phone, and he was uncomfortable with other people's silences. So she let one pan out for a moment to see what he did. It was gratifyingly awkward, and then he said: 'It's late for you to still be up.'

'Yes, isn't it?'

There was a clock on the far wall – coming up on twenty past two in the morning. It was a long time since Eileen had looked at a clock and seen that.

When she was younger, it had been more common. She'd made a habit of staying up as late as possible, and rising early on, because there was simply so much to do. On your death bed, you weren't going to look back on your life and wish you'd spent more of it sleeping. John had always been like that as well. There was the same drive to him, and it was partly what had attracted her to him in the first place. For a long time, there had been an ease and rhythm to their relationship, and it had helped to persuade her they were well-matched, equal partners. That it was all okay.

Strange to think that now – given how much she hated his dedication to work – but true.

As they'd grown older together, of course, things had changed. While Eileen's day had dwindled at both ends, John's had become even longer. He would come to bed hours after her, and then she'd wake to find his side empty again in the morning. It hadn't seemed to matter at the time, but John's breakdown had forced her to reconsider that. When he came out of hospital, the fact he was suddenly in her bed every evening brought home to her all the times when he hadn't been. It began to feel as though she'd been dutifully keeping it warm for him the whole time: waiting patiently, while he put her to one side and chased goals of his own. Goals which, in the end, had jeopardised them both. Those days should have been long behind them.

'It *is* late,' he repeated. 'I thought you'd be in bed by now.'

'That's why you didn't call? You didn't think I'd be waiting up to hear from you?'

Panicking? Scared out of my ... fucking *mind*?

'I don't know. I'm sorry.'

'You know you're supposed to ring me.'

'There just hasn't been a chance.'

Eileen felt her jaw clench, recognising the tone in her husband's voice. Imagining him there. He was looking off to one side, she thought, running his hand through his hair, already distracted from this conversation and concentrating on something else. On all the other things that were apparently more important to him than she was.

'It's really busy here,' he said. 'Non-stop. You know how it can be.'

'I remember exactly how it can be.'

She was simmering. The emotion was fresh but familiar. It had got to a point during his recovery when she was as angry with John as she would have been if he'd had an affair. In a way, he had – though with his work, not another woman. But Eileen had seethed quietly and put those feelings to one side, for no other reason than that he was her husband and this was her life. Whatever mistakes had been made, they could fix them together. All she really asked was that he didn't repeat them, or at least that he didn't put himself in a position where they might repeat themselves. Yes, she recalled perfectly how it could be. It seemed to be her husband who was blanking the risk he was taking.

Another sip of wine.

'Are you okay?' he said. 'You sound like you've been drinking.'

'I have been drinking. I still am drinking.'

He paused. 'It's two thirty in the morning.'

'So I should be in bed?'

'No. I just mean it's late to be drinking.'

'I suppose it is.'

Eileen's sister had said exactly that when they'd spoken on the phone earlier, just before midnight. She shouldn't be drowning her sorrows this late. 'Why not, though?' Eileen had replied. She was sick of taking responsibility for all the shoulds. John *should* be here with her – there was one – but he wasn't. Why did it always fall to her to do the responsible thing? She needed to do something to keep calm.

Up at two thirty, she realised. Nearly a bottle of wine down. It really was like being young again. All she needed now was John beside her to share the experience.

'Are you going to bed soon?' he asked.

'I don't know. When will you be home?'

'It's all go here, so I'm not sure. One of those cases where if we don't move on it quickly, we'll lose it, and …'

'Where are you?'

'Where? I'm at the hospital. We're interviewing someone. He's injured and he's receiving treatment here.'

'Yes, I know what a hospital is for. Rutlands, I guess? Is that where you are?'

'Rutlands, yes.'

Eileen nodded to herself. Rutlands was the hospital she'd taken him to when he broke down at Andrew Dyson's funeral. The place held unhappy memories; she'd spent that first night there, and then been back to visit on each of the four days he'd been in before being released. She associated the long corridors of the psychiatric unit with the feeling that her world was broken beyond repair.

Briefly, she wondered how John felt, being back in the place, and she felt concern for him beneath the anger. Just as quickly, she suppressed it. The choice to be back there was his. It affected her, too, and he shouldn't be doing this to her. That was the bottom line. Eileen's sister had said she owed it to herself to be harder, and that was true: it was time for the scales of their commitment to tilt back towards level, and after everything he'd put her through John really ought to have known that. 'Do you want me to come and get you?' her sister had asked, concerned, and Eileen had smiled because she knew Debra would be here in a heartbeat if she asked her to, no matter how much it put her out. 'No, thank you,' she'd said. 'It's something I need to sort out. It needs dealing with.'

Eileen said it firmly now: 'I want you to come home. To me.'

There was a moment of silence on the other end of the line.

'I can't do that right now.'

'Well, that's what I want.'

Too quick and snappy, she told herself, too petulant. She fought to regain her composure, and then repeated herself: 'I hear what you're saying, John, but this is what I want you to do. Please come home.'

'I can't. I wish I could, but it's my job.'

She almost laughed. 'A man's gotta do?'

'What?'

'Nothing.'

She sipped the wine, and then put it down hard again as something occurred to her.

'Tell me this isn't about Andrew?' In the window opposite, her reflection leaned forwards suddenly. 'Oh God, John. Tell me you're not after that man again?'

'No,' he said. 'It's nothing to do with that.'

Was the drink making her paranoid? Whatever the reason, she wasn't sure she believed him.

'Promise me,' she said.

'I promise. We're following up on a home invasion. It's very nasty, but it's nothing to do with that.'

The panic settled a little, but not totally.

'If it's "very nasty" you should leave it for someone else.'

'Well, it's certainly been a long day. But I'm fine.'

'*But I'm not!*' she wanted to scream at him. '*It's not about you.*'

Instead, she kept quiet. The truth was that she could shout and rage and cry, and perhaps if she did he'd relent and come home. But that wouldn't achieve anything, not really. If she had to *make* him come back, it wasn't worth it.

The truth, despite what she'd said to Debra, was that this call had taken Eileen two hours to work up to. Instead of picking up the phone *just yet*, she'd kept telling herself that he'd be home soon, or if he wasn't that he would call. I'll give him ten minutes, she'd thought; I'll give him until one o'clock; then half past. In reality, she'd been dreading this conversation. Not because he might choose his job over her – he'd already done that, after all – but because of the way she knew he'd do it: by acting as though he was simply a normal man doing a normal job; by treating her like she was an over-protective wife, nagging him and interfering.

It was always going to come down to this. Could she throw the truth in his face and spell it out for him? Confront her husband with his own weakness, the way he was making her feel, and force him to acknowledge it? Concern and anger brought the words as far as her lips, but then love held them back. The resulting frustration and confusion seemed close to tearing her apart inside.

'I'll be home as soon as I can.'

'Here's what's going to happen, John. You come home as soon as you can. That's what I want. But in the meantime, you phone me. Every two hours.'

'Phone you?'

She was aware even as she said it that there was something almost childish about the request. Call me. Check in. But to hell with that; it was the least he could do, wasn't it? A compromise. A small gesture he could make for her, even if he refused to do everything that he should.

'Every two hours. To let me know you're okay.'

'I'll try, but—'

Before he could say anything else, Eileen hung up.

For a moment, the silence in the room was stunning. Trembling slightly, she stared at her reflection in the window, emptying her head of thought. Perhaps it wasn't wise to do so. There was a hard knot of emotion in her throat – a combination of anger and hurt, fear and love – and experience had taught her that throwing a cover over it would do nothing to resolve the problem. You could hide those feelings; you could wash them down with alcohol. But sooner or later you had to untangle them and straighten out the threads.

Tonight, her mind wasn't going to be nimble enough to pick at her feelings; attempting to do so would probably only make everything worse. There was no point working herself up any more than she already had. Morning, a clear head ... Her hand shook as she finished the remaining wine with a single swallow.

It's going to be okay. He'll be okay, and so will you.

Then she stood up and made her way downstairs.

Drinking more probably wasn't wise, either, but she could live with that. Just another glass – or however many she wanted, in fact – and then she'd go to bed, taking the phone with her. God help him if he didn't call. Just see. In the meantime, she needed to calm down. She needed medicine to settle her thoughts.

They had a lot of wine. Over the years, they'd amassed a respectable cellar, bringing out the finer bottles on special days or for occasional dinner parties, and then picking out additions from the places they visited on quiet holidays. As Eileen opened the door in the kitchen that led to the cellar, she knew that out of the forty or fifty bottles down there, she could probably remember the when and where of buying at least half of them. There was comfort in that. In some ways, the wine was a record of their history together as a couple. It seemed appropriate that, tonight she should find some consolation there.

4 DECEMBER   **2.30 A.M.**
4 HOURS, 50 MINUTES UNTIL DAWN

Mark

Decompression.

Two-thirty in the morning and, once again, I was negotiating the hospital's corridors. More precisely, I was trying to reverse the series of rights and lefts I'd stored away in my head and find the lift to the ground floor and failing miserably. The place was a maze. What I actually felt most like doing was lying down on a gurney and going to sleep. Either that or kicking one around the corridor until the fucking thing fell apart.

I found a crowded lift that was heading down, squeezed inside and breathed deeply as the doors slid shut.

I was pissed off with myself, but I was calming down: I understood vhat had happened with Scott. My job was to build rapport and empathise with how he felt – get into his head a little. I'd done that; I'd just done it too well. And I'd got bitten as a result.

Somewhere deep down, even more than usual, Lise was on my mind. Partly it was the day itself: my first day as a detective. But it was more than that; it was this investigation, too. When I'd watched the interview with Daniel Roseneil earlier, I'd not blamed him for not remembering. And how could I? When I looked at Scott, when I saw the survivor left behind, I was in danger of seeing myself.

I had to guard against that. Because while I was in the room I had to convince myself that Jodie was still alive, though deep down I knew she probably wasn't. If I allowed too much empathy, too many thoughts of Lise ... I had to guard against it. Not only for Scott's sake, but for mine.

So: decompression. I treated the lift as an airlock, imagining those feelings being left behind at the level above. I'd pick some of them up on my way back to the next interview.

Ground floor.

I stepped out with the throng, turned right, and then reversed and turned left instead.

Following Doctor Li's instructions, I found Greg and Mercer secreted away in an old locker room at the back of the hospital. This end of the building was being cleared out and renovated, and many of the corridors were closed off: blocked by bleary polythene sheets smeared with dust. The overhead lights were flickering slightly, buzzing a little bit more. Almost immediately, they started to hurt my head.

The locker room we'd been given was half ripped out. Old, six-foot lockers had been pulled away from the walls and stacked in sad piles at the far end. The strip-lights above were as harsh as crime-scene lamps.

Mercer was sitting in the middle on an old plastic chair. He looked like something that had been discarded with the rest of the room's contents. The light hollowed out his eyes and bleached his skin white, bringing out the imperfections of age and making him seem even older than he was. He was staring into space, a blank expression on his face. I found it impossible to tell whether he was concentrating very hard on something or thinking of nothing at all.

Greg, however, had definitely been busy. An impressive amount of computer equipment had been unloaded from the van and set up on three long tables. There was a laptop on each, a printer that would double as a fax, and lots of recording equipment. The power came from a coil of

extension cable running out of the room and down the corridor. There
were no sockets at the base of the walls here, just old blue pipes that
looked strong enough to stand on.

The laptop in the centre was logged into the virtual briefing room. To
the left, the screen was showing a live video feed that was mostly darkness; the screen to the right, which Greg was working at, was filled with
programming script. From his expression, it was giving him difficulty.

'Interview number one,' I said, placing my recording equipment on
the desk beside him.

'Thanks.'

'How's it going?'

He nodded at the screen. 'Trying to get Pete on now. He's at the woods
but I'm having trouble getting a link-up. Fucking computers.'

'Well, let me run through what I've got.'

While Greg focused his attention on the connection, I gave them both
a summary of the interview with Scott: the attack at his home; the van
ride; the bag over his head on the walk through the woods. Greg made a
token effort at listening but was clearly preoccupied, while Mercer stared
at me the whole time, not even blinking. It was unnerving. I wasn't sure
if what I was saying was sinking in or was just light bouncing off his
windows.

When I paused, uncertain whether to continue, he blinked and
prompted me: 'What about his girlfriend?'

'He said she was in the van when the killer abducted him. If he's right
about the times, she was probably abducted from work.'

Mercer nodded. 'From the rental agreement for their flat, she works
for SafeSide Insurance. We need to wake up someone there; see what's
what.'

'Okay.'

'Because she might not have been at work today,' he said. 'Bear in
mind, she spent yesterday at Simpson's house.'

'Of course, yeah.'

I'd forgotten about that, or put it out of my mind, at least.

Mercer held something out to me. A passport photograph.

'From his wallet.'

I studied it carefully.

'Well, it matches the description we had from Simpson's neighbour.'

The girl in the photograph had brown hair and a slightly lopsided,
appealing smile. Her expression said: I hate having my photograph
taken. She wasn't beautiful, but there was certainly something about

her. Character, maybe. The photograph was only one still frame, but it seemed to have captured something of her personality.

I imagined Scott waiting outside the booth, chatting to her through the curtain as the lights flashed. Maybe whispering stuff to make her smile. And then clipping off a spare picture for his wallet. Showing it to people. *This is Jodie. Isn't she gorgeous?*

If you looked in my wallet, you'd find a similar picture of Lise.

'It's scanned and loaded,' Mercer said. 'Jodie McNeice. This is the girl whose life we have about five hours left to save.'

It was a loaded comment. Greg and I didn't reply.

I was distracted, though, still thinking about Kevin Simpson. Although I knew it was the case, I didn't want it to be true that Jodie had been having an affair. From the interview, it was obvious how much Scott loved her. He'd kept this photo of her in his wallet as a reminder of their life together, and Jodie looked too happy in it to have been cheating on him. But I suppose everybody looks happy when there's a camera pointed at them; it's what people do. I thought back to the joyous portrait of the Roseneils on their wedding day. It was wrong to accept that kind of thing at face value. Beneath the smiles and the cheery anecdotes that people are prepared to share, there are always faultlines and cracks. Secrets. People only let you see what they want you to.

'I'll have someone get a copy to Yvonne Gregory, too,' I said. 'See if she can positively ID her from Simpson's house.'

'Good.' Mercer rubbed some life into his cheeks – a man coming out of a light sleep – then stood up and began pacing. 'Good. What else from the interview? What can Banks tell us about where he was held?'

'Not much at the moment. He's very confused. Tired, upset. He doesn't remember a lot about what happened. It hurts him to try.'

Mercer ran his hand through his hair.

'Because of the torture?'

'It's partly that. But there's more blocked out than the injuries. When he was talking about Jodie at the end, he became quite distressed. That was when I decided to break the interview for a while.'

'He doesn't remember escaping out of the woods?'

'Not really, no. Those memories are especially sensitive for him. If he remembers running through the woods, he's moving closer to remembering what happened just before that.'

'That's what we want, though, isn't it?' Mercer sounded surprised. 'I know it's not pleasant, but if he can remember some landmark from the woods, it's going to help us find his girlfriend.'

I shook my head. Mercer had a point, but Scott was a victim, too. I remembered him crying, the shutters coming down. Pushing him and getting a result would be bad enough. In all likelihood, pushing him wouldn't even achieve that.

'He needs to be treated carefully,' I said. 'If we move too fast we might lose him altogether.'

'Yes, but if we move too slowly we certainly *will* lose her.'

We probably already have.

'I'll do what I can.'

Mercer nodded, as though I'd agreed with him.

'I know it's unpleasant,' he said, 'and probably the last thing he needs, but it's necessary. You also need to ask him about Kevin Simpson. See if he knows who he is, or what his connection to Jodie is, beyond the obvious.'

I nodded slowly. The way Scott was wired at the moment, if he suspected that Jodie had been having an affair on top of everything else, I didn't know what his reaction would be. I imagined it would be very bad. But I couldn't object any further without taking on the core of Mercer's argument – that Jodie was still alive. Saving her was all that mattered to him right now.

Greg took advantage of the break in conversation and coughed quietly. I looked across and saw that the third laptop was working.

'We're off to the woods,' he said.

One of the ways I'd prepared for this job was to read as much as I could about the city in advance. I bought a notepad, a guide book, several pamphlets with useful local information, and I studied maps until I could see the layout of the city when I closed my eyes. The woods ran for about ten miles along the top of the city, spreading north. If you walked straight into them from the ring road, you had about four miles of hills and trees to negotiate before you hit the mountains.

Forty square miles of old land: designated as a nature reserve, although nowhere near as friendly and welcoming as the title might imply. The woods were thick, even impenetrable in places. A couple of nature walks curled through the edge, close to town, but none went more than a mile or so in.

Some places on earth you go to escape into the quiet: to feel relaxed and get away from everything. But there are others that are dangerous for those exact same reasons, and the woods north of our city were generally felt to be the latter type of quiet place. There were people there who were attracted to the isolation for their own reasons: homeless people with nowhere else to go; criminals with private business to conduct. There were even rumours that, closer to the mountains, you'd find separatists, living in small bunches. Nobody a defenceless, civilised person would want to meet while out walking. It would be like heading a long way into a zoo and then realising there weren't any bars on the cages.

Not an easy place to search at noon on a sunny day. At two thirty in the morning, in weather like this, it was going to be more or less impossible.

Live on the video feed, Pete looked like he was in the Arctic. The collar of his coat was turned up, his shoulders were hunched, and his cheeks and forehead converged as he squinted against the snow, as though he'd been grimacing and the wind had changed. In all my life, I'd never seen anyone look so cold and miserable.

Greg had moved to a different screen, where he was cropping an image of what looked like a map. Mercer sat down at the desk in front of the webcam. I stood between and behind.

'Hi, Pete,' Mercer said. 'You've got Greg here, too. And that's Mark you can see in the background.'

He grunted. 'Right.'

'How are things going?'

Pete's expression said that might be the stupidest question he'd ever heard.

'Slow,' he said. 'And cold.'

'Progress?'

Pete looked around. 'Well, I'm standing where our Mr Banks ran out onto the road. We're setting up the cordon at the moment. One man every hundred metres or at bends in the road, in order to keep a line of sight. If anyone comes out of the woods, we'll see them.'

'Good,' Mercer said. 'Have they found the van yet?'

'We've got the van,' Pete said. 'Half a mile from here. Parked and covered in snow.'

'Excellent.'

Despite his obvious tiredness, I thought Mercer seemed a little brighter. The fact the van had remained at the scene supported his theory that the killer had, too.

'Get the bomb squad to check it before forensics go in.'

'Yes, John.'

'In the meantime, let's have a look at the search area. Greg, how are we doing?'

Greg leaned back in his chair. He looked a little dissatisfied with th
results of his labours.

'Best I can do.' He turned the laptop so we could see. 'Not great.'

A white line curled across the base of the monitor, which I guessed wa
meant to represent the ring road at the northern edge of the city. Eacl
of the men forming the cordon along it was attached to the department'
satellite tracking system; they appeared as small yellow circles spreading
out from the centre. Every few seconds, the screen updated and the
moved further apart.

A cluster in the middle of the screen was marked as Pete's position, an
also where Scott had come out of the woods. A cluster further to the lef
was where the van had been found.

Above this, the bulk of the screen showed a rough map of the wood
– light and dark patches of green separated by occasional bright line
representing the known paths. The main path led directly up from th
cluster where the van had been abandoned, went north for a couple o
miles and then curved round to the right, turning slowly until it came
back south to the ring road. In effect, it formed a large, lower-case n
resting on the ring road. The van had been found at the base of the lef
leg; Scott had emerged slightly to the right of this.

Above all this, the curling blue thread of a stream cut across, forming
a lopsided smile towards the top of the screen. It didn't quite touch the
bridge of the n.

Greg moved the mouse pointer over the screen.

'A lot of this is just woodland, and the paths probably aren't as clear a
this.' The pointer touched several small white outlines dotted around th
screen. 'These are old stone buildings. Broken-down structures.'

Pete had been looking at all this, his expression growing more dubiou
with every word.

'That's fantastic, Greg,' he said. 'We'll take this in with us, shall we? Fil
it in while we fucking go?'

Greg held his hands up. 'Don't shoot the messenger.'

'Well, no, it looks really pretty onscreen. But from where I'm standing
those trees back there are just a long, black, fucking wall. So I'd like a
bit more guidance, please, before I start sending good officers into the
middle of that.'

Mercer had been peering intently at the screen. Now he reached across
and took the mouse from Greg. The pointer moved to the cluster o
yellow circles by Carl Farmer's van.

'This is what's obvious to me,' he said. 'Banks and his girlfriend were taken into the woods here. Along this path.'

He moved his hand and the cursor traced the white line up the monitor – the left leg of the n.

'Judging from where Banks came out of the woods, I think at some point they must have gone into this area here.'

He moved the mouse pointer across, circling it between the legs of the n.

I nodded to myself. It was guesswork, but it was educated guesswork. Scott had run from wherever he'd been kept prisoner and emerged out of dense, difficult woodland between two paths. If he hadn't been in that area already, he would have had to cross one of those paths to get there. Surely, if he'd been running through undergrowth and had stumbled across an easier route, he would have shifted onto that instead.

It was only an assumption, of course. Given his disorientation, Scott might have blundered across a path without realising it. And even if the killer was still holding Jodie alive somewhere in there, he might well have moved her, taken her deeper into the woods. But it was a good call, simply because it wasn't possible to search forty square miles of dense woodland in the time we had left. Even cut down by the pathways, it was ridiculous. But by designating a more limited search area, Mercer had turned an impossible task into something that felt more manageable. We had a place to start.

'Okay.' Pete sighed. 'Let's say you're right. That's what? About eight square miles?'

'If that. You've got warm bodies?'

'I've got bodies, not warm ones. Thirty officers, apart from the ones in the cordon – nowhere near enough. We've got volunteers from Search and Rescue here, too. Ten civilians, three dogs.'

'Have the dogs picked up anything?'

'Not yet. The handlers have got them here and by the van. But the dogs are trained to find people who are lost, not track down where they've come from. And the snow's not helping. There are no marks on the ground, and the scent trail's buried.'

Mercer looked unimpressed by this. 'What about the helicopter?'

'Against their better judgment, it's in the air and on its way.'

'That's something. We need it to feed back any heat traces it finds; each and every one needs to be checked. In the meantime, there are all those structures to be looked at.'

Pete grimaced, perhaps at the prospect of the task ahead, but more likely at the use of the word 'we'. If Mercer noticed it, he ignored it:

'Chances are he'd be holding her indoors. He wouldn't want to be outside in weather like this.'

'No,' Pete agreed, 'he wouldn't. But that doesn't mean he isn't. He could be anywhere.'

He could be on the other side of the city by now.

'Well, we have to limit the search somehow, don't we?' Mercer said patiently. 'Otherwise it's impossible. So we'll assume he's inside one of these buildings. And also check out heat traces as they come up. Unfortunately, it's all we've got to go on for now.'

For a second, snow falling around him, Pete simply stared out of the screen. Then: 'So we haven't got anything from Banks so far?'

'Not yet,' Mercer said. 'He seems to be blanking a lot out.'

I sank a little inside, annoyed at myself for not recognising the way the conversation had been steered. Pete was dismayed, even borderline antagonistic, about the scale of what needed to be done out there; and I was reluctant to press Scott. Mercer had turned two problems against each other, probably figuring that any objections I had wouldn't cut much ice with a man standing out in the snow facing a difficult, lengthy search. And of course he was right.

'Well, I appreciate that,' Pete said. 'But we're assuming his girlfriend's life is at stake here. Anything he can tell us is going to help. Even if it's just remembering being inside somewhere.'

Mercer turned to look at me. I glanced at the map and then looked at Pete's grim face on the screen, snow falling in the background. My objections suddenly seemed trivial, and I didn't have the energy to argue.

'Okay.' I sighed quietly. 'I'll talk to him.'

4 DECEMBER   **2.50 A.M.**
4 HOURS, 30 MINUTES UNTIL DAWN

Scott

As the night went on, the tone of Scott's dreams had begun to shift. His sleeping mind seemed to be at war with itself. Something had happened to him. Part of his subconscious was insisting that it be brought out and examined, while another part was attempting, increasingly ineffectively, to bury and hide it. On the surface the dreams were comforting, but increasingly he could feel poison seeping up from below the surface.

Happier thoughts and memories were a house made of tissue, the foundations resting in a pool of black ink. Gradually, everything was darkening.

In this dream, the phone had woken him, and for the duration of the call his mind remained tangled in the last sticky threads of sleep. On the other end of the line, Jodie was crying. When she spoke, her voice was shaky and weak. She told him what was wrong. She told him what she'd done.

He was sitting upright on the edge of the bed, listening. As he did, he was twisting the cord with one hand: tangling the coils around his fingers. He stopped and reached out, moving the yellow curtains aside, eyes flinching against the early-morning sun. Six twenty. Already, it looked warm. It was going to be a hot day in the office.

'I don't know what to say,' Jodie told him.

That should have been his line, shouldn't it? It was absurd to feel so unaffected. He'd always been the patient one in the relationship – the one who remained calm, the one who reacted with understanding – but this was ridiculous. Jodie might as well have been sleeping in the bed behind him, rather than a hundred miles away, phoning to tell him what should have been the most horrible thing he could imagine.

He said, 'I don't know, either.'

Cars were heading past. The world outside seemed oblivious. He let go of the curtain and the bedroom settled back into a more comfortable darkness.

'I've been up all night trying to think of something to say.'

'It didn't work, did it?'

She deserved that, but straight away he felt the urge to apologise for being so sharp. Don't. For once, he needed to suppress that side of himself.

'I guess not. I was rehearsing this, trying to make it into something coherent. I guess I've fucked that up like I fuck everything up.'

Normally, when she wandered into this kind of self-recrimination, he wanted to reassure her. But that would be out of place. He wasn't going to turn this round and give comfort to her, as though she was the one who'd been hurt.

'You've not slept at all?' he said.

'No, I've been up all night. Being sick, mostly.'

He didn't laugh.

She told him again, 'I don't know what to say.'

'Well, you said that already.'

'But I don't know what else there is.'

There's nothing, he thought. You just have to keep saying that, because for now it sums up everything perfectly. I don't know what to say.

For the rest of the conversation, they circled each other. Jodie asked whether their relationship was over; Scott told her he needed time to think. In reality, though, he needed time to feel. He was surprised at himself for taking it so well. Generally, he was quite an insecure person, but for some reason this didn't feel like the end of the world. She'd fucked her business partner? It wasn't so bad. Only the sensation that he'd been hollowed out deep inside convinced him that, some time soon, he was going to collapse inwards and start caring very much.

I am emotionally concussed.

Nothing could be worked out over the phone. But even so ...

'I'll call you after work,' he said.

'Do you promise?'

It was ridiculous: she sounded so wounded and upset, as though he'd done something wrong. Half of him wanted to reach across all that distance and slap her as hard as he could. The other half wanted to hold her and tell her it was okay. Ridiculously, there was something about the battle between those two sides that almost thrilled him.

'I promise,' he said. 'I just need to think about things.'

That produced a new burst of desperation: 'Do you love me?'

'I've got to go.'

The telephone clicked down, cutting off the sound of her crying.

Scott sat there for a few moments, feeling the silence crawl all over him. The air was pressurised: it was like being underwater. He could hear the cars outside, people's voices, but he was numb to it. He was an empty house. The light was hitting windows while nobody looked out; the wind was hitting the walls, the walls not feeling it.

On the bedside table, the clock said 6:34 in bright red figures.

He heard a noise behind him. A breathing sound.

Scott turned around very slowly, the bed creaking underneath him.

The thing was standing in the doorway, its shoulders rising and falling quite heavily, as though it had been forced to run a long way to find him. It was holding something in its hand.

When he saw that, Scott tried to move – but he couldn't. His forearms were held pressed against his thighs, held tightly in place by bonds he couldn't see.

Panic.

'Number Eighty,' the thing said. Its voice sounded more normal than it had in the earlier dreams. "'You chose me.' What does that mean?'

What did it mean? Scott started to tell it that he didn't know. If it was about Jodie ... it was wrong. She hadn't chosen him at all, quite the opposite. But then an image pressed itself into his head. Jodie, sitting on the bed in her hotel room, her head in her hands. Crying.

'She didn't have to phone me,' he said. 'She could have pretended it never happened. She never even had to tell me.'

The devil inclined its head.

'And what did you do next?'

'I'm not well,' he told the answerphone at work. The tape was whirring slowly around in the empty office. His boss was never in until at least nine, sometimes didn't come in at all.

'I've been up half the night. I think I've eaten something dodgy. I feel dreadful.'

He said a few more things, none of them particularly convincing, and put the phone down.

Then he threw the glass of water on the bedside table against the far wall. It shattered, blew apart, and immediately he regretted it. The floorboards whispered as he swept up the broken glass, and the bin downstairs gave a few dusty rattles as it accepted the debris.

He collected his keys, his wallet and his coat, and headed out of the door.

'You went to see her, didn't you?'

The devil was crouching in front of him. Scott's sleeping mind accepted this; on one level he understood what was happening. These memories of Jodie's affair were two years old, but the devil existed in more recent memories, and the two were connected. They had spoken about this event. And when the memories shared moments, the narrative had a chance to cross. The poison could seep up.

He nodded.

Her hotel bedroom was much bigger than he'd imagined it would be. Normally, he liked hotels. There was something reassuring about the narrowness of the corridors, the soft lighting, the cave-like ambience of the rooms. But there was nothing comforting about those things now. He kept imagining Jodie and Kevin together.

She met him in the corridor and they walked to her room without saying much. She flicked on the light.

There was a cabinet along one wall, supporting a small television and a tray of tea and coffee-making equipment. No discarded sachets or dirty cups, he noticed, but she would definitely have made a drink. He wondered whether room service had cleared away one used cup or two.

The double bed was against the opposite wall, a lamp at either side of the headboard. A double-seater settee and two chairs circled a low table at the far end of the room.

'Coffee?' she said.

He nodded, but she was making it anyway.

'This kettle takes ages to boil.'

He watched her fidgeting; she didn't seem able to stand still or relax. A long minute of silence later, steam ribboned up from the kettle's spout. She passed him the mug of coffee, holding it gingerly by the rim and base so that he could take the handle.

'Thanks,' he said.

'That's okay.'

'Are you surprised I came down?'

'I'm pleased.'

'Right.'

'Please don't ...' As she said it, the words ran out of air, and she had to try again. 'Please don't leave me.'

'We need to talk about that.'

'Please don't leave me. I don't know what I'll do if you do.'

He sipped his coffee.

'I'll do anything,' she said. 'I really will. I'd do anything to be able to take it back, and I wish I could, but I can't. All I can do is say sorry. I was so drunk. It was such a huge mistake.'

He put the cup down on the floor.

She said, 'I hate myself for it more than you ever could.'

'I don't hate you, Jodie.'

'You should.'

Self-pity again, all but begging for reassurance in return. Instead, he spread his hands and tried to talk plainly.

'We need to figure out where we go from here.'

'Okay.'

'I want things to work out,' he said. 'But the truth is, I really don't know how they're going to. I've felt weird all day. Weird, and so, so hurt. It's not sunk in yet.'

'I'll quit if I have to.' She said it too quickly. 'If that's what you want, I'll do it. I'll do it right now.'

He looked at her. She'd made it sound so easy, so simple, but she'd

158

been a partner in this business from the beginning; there had been three years of hard work before it started taking off. There should have been more conflict on her face, but instead she looked utterly committed.

She would choose him. If he wanted her to, she would walk away from everything else. To save their relationship. He continued to stare, not knowing what to say in reply.

On the one hand, there was no way he could ask her to do that. But he knew they couldn't be together if she was still working with Kevin, still seeing him every day. There was no middle ground between the two.

So he didn't say anything. After a moment, she nodded.

Over the next two years, Scott remembered that gesture and used it to justify what happened. That one nod gave him the ability to lie to himself. It hadn't been his decision.

He hadn't asked her to give up her life.

She did it willingly, of her own accord.

You chose me . . .

Suddenly, he was somewhere else: some horrible place where the images were shorter and sharper. It was the dark, stone building, and the devil was leaning over him, holding the screwdriver in one hand. Steam was rising off it.

The devil pressed the red-hot blade down on his shoulder. Scott tried to flinch away, but he couldn't move. Everything was numb for a moment . . . but then he felt the pain reverberate through his collar bone, all the way down to his ribs.

He began to scream, his mouth open, his head whipping from side to side. The noises he was making he couldn't even identify.

But the devil kept the blade pressed down hard. Scott could hear his skin sizzling. He could smell himself burning.

Was it possible to pass out within a dream?

As the thing took the screwdriver away and moved it down to the inside of his thigh, he discovered that it wasn't.

Mark

After Pete had signed out and headed off to co-ordinate the search, I logged onto the virtual briefing room and flagged down my door-to-door team. Annoyingly, all three of them looked as though they could keep going for days, and I felt momentarily inadequate. I was so tired I could hardly keep my thoughts in a straight line. But then, they were coding interviews in a nice warm office with access to as much coffee as they could physically drink.

I went through what I needed them to do. Wake Yvonne Gregory up – politely – and take round the picture of Jodie McNeice for identification, then get hold of someone at Jodie's work and see if they could confirm where she'd been for the last few days. There would be more to do later, I said, probably vaguely. It was two onerous tasks with the threat of more to follow, but they appeared to soak it up. I envied them their energy. However much I dressed it up, it couldn't be entirely down to caffeine.

On the way up to Scott's room, the tiredness hit me properly. I was walking down corridors and my vision was prowling ahead of me, occasionally getting distracted and lost. At the same time, I was doing my best to leave most of my thoughts behind. When I stopped, everything around me seemed to keep moving for a second. I was drunk on my own exhaustion.

'Excuse me, Officer.'

'Sorry.'

It wasn't so bad downstairs. On the lower level, people were moving about in small numbers, carrying cardboard files or pushing trolleys and cleaning-carts. But one floor up nobody was fucking around. There were lives to be saved, and everything was all very urgent and practised. I had to minimise myself as much as possible and keep out of the way, and the task was a little beyond me. I felt unsteady in my body and in my mind, and I needed to get some calm and resolve together before I talked to Scott.

Two minutes later, feeling pretty much the same, I was there.

I'd forgotten how quiet and still the room was. The soft light lent it a feeling of peace, underlined by the soporific constant of Scott's pulse on the machine by his bed. He was still propped up where I'd left him, his head tilted away to face the slatted blinds on the window. He looked comfortable, though, and for a moment I thought he might be asleep. But then he turned to look at me.

'It's you.' Almost immediately, he turned back to the window. 'I thought it would be the doctor again.'

I closed the door gently.

'Do you want the doctor? I can get one if you like. Believe me, there are hundreds of them out there.'

'No. I was hoping it would be you. I'm sorry about before.'

'There's nothing to be sorry about.'

I sat down in the chair by the bed, my legs trembling slightly, and switched on the recording equipment.

'What time is it?'

'Just after three,' I said.

'You've not found her yet?'

'Not yet, no,' I said. The questions were interesting. Was he aware on some level about the dawn deadline? 'But we will. Officers are searching for her in the woods right now. There are a number of places we think she might be being held.'

Having been out of the room for a while, I'd forgotten the horror of Scott's appearance. Even hidden behind the bandages and gauze, his injuries were painful to look at.

'But it's a large area to cover,' I said, 'so we really need any help you can give us. Difficult as it is, we need you to remember as much as you can about what happened to you.'

Perhaps it was a trick of the light or my memory, as well, but I thought the shadows in his face were deeper than before, and the hurt there more settled, more internal. He looked haunted, as though the memories he was avoiding had been left for dead in the woods, and now their ghosts were beginning to solidify in the half-lit dusk of the room. He was so crushed down by sadness that the physical pain seemed barely to register.

Finally, he turned to look at me, too tired to be embarrassed by his misery. But he didn't shake his head or make excuses.

'I have remembered something. It's strange.'

'What?'

'In the van. Do you remember I thought we stopped a couple of times on the way?'

'Sure.'

'Well, this is strange, but I think there was a child in the van with us.'

I couldn't hide my surprise. 'A child?'

'I mean a baby,' he said, as though that made it sound more normal. 'The guy in the devil mask, he kept whispering to someone in the passenger seat. Like, reassuring them? And I remember hearing a baby crying. And then, after one of the stops, I didn't hear it any more.'

I looked at him for a moment, weighing it up. It wasn't that I didn't believe him, exactly, but I had to consider the trauma he'd been through, the medication he was on. His mind might be trying to make sense of something entirely different by visualising it in a certain way.

Or else it might be true. In which case, he was right: it was strange. I filed it away for discussion downstairs.

'Can you remember anything the man said?'

'Not really. Not then, anyway.'

I paused. 'At some other time?'

'Yeah.' He nodded slowly. 'Actually, I think he was talking to me *a lot*. But it's like waking up with a bad hangover. You know you spoke to someone, but what you talked about is blank. Like we had a big conversation, but I can't remember what it was about.'

He thought hard for a moment, then shook his head. But he didn't seem distressed, only confused, and I got the impression that some part of him wanted me to keep asking questions.

'This man,' I said carefully, 'he follows people for a long time. He learns things about them. And what he finds out, he uses that information against them.'

'I don't understand. What does that mean?'

'You know that he's hurt you. The thing is, the way he hurts people isn't just physical. He'll have been saying things to upset you. He might have told you bad stuff about Jodie, for example.'

Scott looked at me.

'Does that mean anything to you?' I said.

But he seemed to have gone far away.

'Scott?'

He said very quietly: 'Kevin.'

I tried to hide any recognition of the name.

'Is that something you remember?'

'I think so. He was talking to me about Kevin.'

'Who's Kevin?'

He started to answer, but then stopped and turned away.

Be careful, I told myself. *Don't lead him anywhere. Let him tell it in his own time.*

162

He stared at the window for a long time. I sat as patiently as I could, listening to the gentle beep of the machine and wondering whether he was searching for words or memories, or simply gathering the resolve to talk to me at all.

Finally, he said, 'Jodie had an affair.'

'Okay.'

'Not an affair. A one-night stand.'

'When was this?'

'A couple of years ago. Kevin was a friend of hers from university. When they left, they set up this company together, built it from nothing. It was starting to do quite well, and this one time, they were away on business for a night. Staying in a hotel.'

He took a deep breath, and then went through the facts quickly, as though they were the last few reps in an exercise session.

'She got drunk. Ended up fucking him. Called me the next day and told me. And I know it doesn't make any sense, but I think the man in the devil mask was talking to me about that.'

I sat back.

It wasn't at all what I'd been expecting, and it took me a moment to put it into context. He was telling me not only that Jodie had started CCL with Kevin Simpson and had a brief affair with him *two years* ago, but that the 50/50 Killer had known about this. Even though it was possible he'd been following the couple for that long, it seemed unimaginable. But we hadn't heard from him in two years, had we? And, like Mercer said, he'd been planning something in that time.

'What happened after that night?' I said.

'We talked about it, about stuff. Splitting up. But it was just a drunken mistake. I didn't want to break up with her over it.'

I remembered what we'd talked about downstairs: that Jodie worked for an insurance firm now.

'She left the company?'

'It was her decision – I didn't ask her to.' He looked frustrated. 'I didn't stop her, either, but staying on there, our relationship wouldn't have worked. She'd poured so much of her energy into it that she ended up seeing more of him than she did of me, and I wouldn't have been able to carry on like that. I guess she knew that. So she chose me.'

'Okay.'

And then what? I wondered.

What Scott was talking about had happened two years ago. Had Jodie been carrying on an affair with Simpson the whole time? And had the 50/50 Killer talked to him about that as well? Surely, he must have done.

But Scott was becoming distressed.

'She chose me,' he repeated.

I thought his use of words was telling: 'She chose me.' He was fumbling in the direction of what had happened, and if he found it he wasn't going to like what he held in his hands.

'It's okay,' I told him. 'Like I said before, the man who did this to you, he was talking about that to hurt you. Do you understand? He was using it to upset you.'

'Is that "the game"?'

I looked at him, considering what to say. He seemed desperate for an answer, but the truth might be too much for him.

'What do you remember about that?'

'I just remember those words. He said something about a game. He said I'd thank him for it in the end.' The half of his face that was visible suddenly looked determined. 'Tell me.'

I stared at him. His expression didn't change. Part of me was sure I should back off at this point, but the truth was we needed information and I'd said I'd press him as much as I could. If he was willing to ask, I should be willing to answer.

'The "game",' I said quietly, 'is that he targets couples. One of the couple has to die at dawn, and it's always up to one of them to decide which it will be. He picks one, and then uses emotional and physical torture to force them to betray their partner. That's what the game is.'

It sounded harsh and bleak, but there was no safe way of explaining it. 'Tell me,' he'd said. There it was. I leaned back.

On the surface, the determination remained, but something else was creeping in. Memories surfacing, perhaps, or the implications of what I'd told him. The determination disappeared. Ever so slowly, panic began to take its place.

'So I betrayed her?'

'We don't know that.'

'That's what it means—'

'Whatever happened,' I interrupted gently, 'there was nothing you could have done.'

He swallowed. His voice trembled slightly: 'Why?'

I leaned forwards.

'Why does he do this?' Scott demanded.

That was the question.

And it's always the question, isn't it? I'd asked it myself enough times in the last six months, and I'd always been left with the same inadequate handful of answers. Why did she drown? Because of the events that took us to the beach. Because of the physics of the waves. Because of the biology of a body in the water. Those are the only reasons. I wanted something deeper than that, but the truth is, the world doesn't care about what seems important to me.

Why did the 50/50 Killer do this to people? He did it to destroy the love between them, to make them turn their backs on each other. He was a wolf of space, whatever that might mean. A devil. But all of that only raised more questions. When you ask 'Why?' the answer is the sum of a hundred different reasons, none of them satisfactory on its own, none of them satisfactory together. Like me, Scott didn't want those answers. He was asking 'Why?' on a level where answers don't even exist.

'We don't know,' I admitted. 'All we can do is interpret the facts and make theories. When we catch him, perhaps then we'll be able to ask him why he does it. But what's important right now is that we stop him before he hurts Jodie.'

Any more than he already has.

The panicked look hadn't left Scott's face, but at least the emotion hadn't overtaken him yet.

I reached into the file I'd brought, picked out the photograph of Carl Farmer and passed it to Scott. He took it from me and looked it over, his face growing still. His hand started shaking.

He asked, 'Is this him?'

'I was hoping you could tell me.'

He concentrated, staring at the photograph intently.

'I've seen him before. I know I have. He's been to the house. A few months ago. He checked our meter.'

'Okay.'

I thought: yes. That was two IDs we had now, from two independent sources. However unlikely it might seem, the 50/50 Killer really had allowed us to see his face.

'But I don't know if it's the man in the woods.' He passed the picture back to me. 'All I remember is that he looked like the Devil. Not just because of the mask. The man in my head ... he wasn't even a man.'

He turned to face the blinds, and I allowed his comment to hang in the air. Daniel Roseneil had said something very similar: *He was the Devil.*

He wasn't, of course. There was no such thing as the Devil. There were just malformed people who had grown up twisted. But even though I knew that, I wasn't so sure that Daniel and Scott were entirely wrong. In our unsatisfactory world of cause and effect, where the answers never satisfy, maybe it was as true as it could be.

'Stone walls,' Scott said quietly.

He was still turned away from me, still facing the window. Despite myself, I felt a flutter of excitement.

'Stone walls?'

'The place I was in, it had stone walls.' He swallowed. 'I remember that. It was narrow, cramped. The walls were close to my shoulders.'

'Okay, Scott. That's good.'

So he'd been held inside one of the buildings in the woods. That limited the scope of the search a little – there were several, according to the map, but it wasn't impossible. Perhaps we had a chance of finding Jodie alive before dawn after all.

'Can you remember anything else about it?'

'I remember the stone walls. He was crouching in front of me, talking to me.'

Scott kept nodding very slightly, over and over. Something was hurting him, but he was enduring it for as long as he could.

'He was whispering to me in the dark. Right up close. I was so frightened.'

I'd got everything I needed from this second interview, and my gut instinct was to back off – move Scott away from wherever his memory was leading him. But actually, that wouldn't be fair. It was too one-way. If he was prepared to talk, I had to be prepared to listen.

'Was it pitch black?' I asked.

'No. There was some light.'

'A fire?'

'Yes. I think so. He used it to—'

Without warning, the memory arrived. He stopped nodding, stopped talking, and became utterly still. Then he raised one hand slowly to his face. I fought an urge to do the same.

'It's okay, Scott,' I said. 'It's okay.'

'There were stone walls.'

'Thank you. You've done well.'

'Old stone walls.'

He didn't start crying this time, but he kept his hand up over his injured eye. I'd done this to him; I'd caused this. So I felt I should stay, and do anything I could to help him cope with the memory he'd just

166

uncovered. But I was going to have to leave him for a while. I needed to get this information downstairs and let Pete know where his search teams should be looking.

'I'll be back as soon as I can, Scott.'

I felt guilty as I stood, picking up the recording equipment and making my way to the door. As I reached it, I turned back.

'Thank you,' I said again.

But he showed no signs that he'd heard me. He was facing towards the window, his hand still half touching the bandages on his face.

---

4 DECEMBER   **3.20 A.M.**
4 HOURS UNTIL DAWN

Charlie

The war had begun.

Charlie huddled, shivering, at the back of his shelter. It wasn't from the cold. There were nerves as well; nerves which were making his body shake. Sweet threads of excitement were firing in his stomach, and his heart was trembling. The Moment was coming.

The sky would crack and there would be ...

He frowned in the dark. Well, there would definitely be heat, and he guessed there would probably be light, too. Beyond that, maybe he should have some faith. Maybe wait and see. Until it happened, he had the fire, and that was giving off enough heat and light for now.

'You need to make a big fire,' the devil had told him. 'You make a big fire, and then they can't see you.'

Two days ago, it had shown him how. He'd come back to this camp and found the devil sitting cross-legged in the centre of the small clearing, conjuring up kindling. There had already been a large pile of dry wood beside it, which the devil had slowly added to. *Can you see it appearing?* Charlie couldn't at first, and it had deflated him to think that perhaps he wasn't worthy after all. The devil had been disappointed, too, but also reassuring, encouraging him to stare at the pile and concentrate. Eventually, narrowing his eyes, he had seen it grow. The elation had been like nothing else he'd ever felt.

The devil had approved.

'When this is over,' it had promised, 'I'll teach you how to do that yourself. And not just with wood.'

Charlie's shelter was set back among the trees, and the fire from that magic wood was burning about ten metres away, in the centre of the small clearing. It was a dancing crown of flame, large enough to fit the brow of a giant. The sky threw down snow; the fire repaid it with smoke and curls of ash, floating up on immense waves of heat. Despite the weather, it remained bright and hot: a circle of tethered Hell, raging defiantly against the heavens. The wood charred and glowed. Occasionally, a log collapsed, and a plume of burning dust flowered in the air. Even this far away, the heat was rolling off it. His cheeks felt swollen and his body was damp with sweat.

He swapped the knife to his other hand and rubbed his hand down his leg. Then swapped it back and took a good grip on the handle. He needed to keep himself on form. Needed to be ready.

It was a good fire – but then, it had to be.

'You're one of my soldiers now,' the devil had explained. 'You know what that means? It means when the angels fly overhead, they look down at you and all they see is fire.'

The angels were flying now. There was no going back.

'So you need fire to hide yourself.'

He'd been hearing them in the sky for the last hour, and if there'd ever been any doubt about the devil's words and promises, it had disappeared completely. The angels were terrifying. They roared through the air, the noise like a hundred heavy swords whirling round. Down below them, the trees quivered and shook with fear. Charlie held himself still in the midst of it. In the distance, lights were flashing down from the sky. The whole time, he kept calm.

The Moment was coming, and he needed to be steady when it arrived.

It had started about a week ago.

Until then, Charlie's life had been fairly regimented. The council paid for him to stay in the Home on the Hill, which meant bed and board and three square meals and everything. Unlike some of the other residents, he was allowed to stay or go more or less as he pleased. The nurses were concerned about the man who spoke to him in his head, but it was a long time since he'd told Charlie to do anything wrong. More often than not, he found the things the man said to him upsetting, and when it got very bad he took the nurses' advice and went to bed and ignored everybody. The man shut up after a while. Charlie was happy to socialise, and the nurses didn't mind him going into Town, or for a walk, or whatever he wanted. Sign out, sign in. But he didn't like Town. The man told him people there were different and didn't like him. He preferred the isolation of walking in the woods. It was quieter here. There was nobody around, and that made him happy.

But last week, walking a little deeper than usual, he'd realised he wasn't alone. He'd been moving casually along the trail, glancing here and there, when suddenly the hairs on the back of his neck had stood up. Something was different. The man in his head told him to stop walking, and so he had.

For a moment, all he'd been able to hear was birdsong. Then the breeze had picked up, making the tops of the trees rustle together: a sound like a waterfall. And then, off to his right, a stick had cracked.

Look over there, the man had told him, and so he had.

The devil had been about thirty or forty metres away, walking down a path that ran nearly parallel to the main trail. Charlie couldn't see much of its body, which seemed to be almost totally black, but he could see its head very clearly because the red skin stood out against the evergreen leaves and the browns of the tree trunks. He began to shiver.

The devil had walked on, apparently oblivious of Charlie, but then just before disappearing out of sight, it had paused. It hadn't looked at him; all it had done was cock its head slightly, as though listening to some internal radar; but he'd known full well it was sensing him. It didn't seem to care. A couple of seconds later, it had been on its way again, vanishing into the undergrowth.

Follow it, the man had told him urgently.

No. Charlie had shaken his head. He didn't want to.

Follow it!

Charlie had stood there for a minute, frightened, upset, but also intrigued. Part of him didn't want the devil to get away so that he never saw it again. The man in his head seemed to know that, and so he beamed streams of words into that part of Charlie's brain and made it grow, until it became too much to ignore.

His body had started moving without his consent. He was cutting through the undergrowth between the paths and, as always, everything felt a lot easier and simpler now he wasn't holding himself back.

But the devil was gone. He hadn't found it that day.

When he returned to the Home, the man had cautioned him not to say anything to anyone, not even his friend Jack, and that worried Charlie. It was a long time since he'd heard the man sound so hushed and serious. He was miserable and couldn't sleep very well, and when he did the man spoke to him in his dreams, reassuring and convincing him.

The next day, Charlie woke up full of purpose. He went back to the woods and walked around in the same area. He broke sticks deliberately under his boots. He coughed loudly and muttered to himself. Eventually, he cupped his hands around his mouth and called to the devil: 'Please come out. I want to talk to you about everything.'

Eventually, the devil had shown itself.

It stepped out of the undergrowth beside the track and stood in front of Charlie, plain as the cold sunlight streaming down between the trees. Its body was black and baggy, its face hideous. The skin was rubbery and pink, as if the top layer had been scorched away in a fire. Small horns protruded from its head at the top, almost lost in the shaggy mop of lank black hair.

I've been looking for you, the man in his head told Charlie. *Tell it.*

As he deliberated, unable to find the words, the devil just stood there, plain as day. The birds still singing. The trees still rustling. Charlie felt a thrill rising within him: a sense of joy. It built up and up, starting in his stomach and billowing up into his chest and then his throat.

Tell it! the man ordered again. And this time he did.

But the devil turned and walked away. Later, it told him that it had been weighing him up from the beginning, deciding whether he was worthy. He'd had to come back a couple more times before it decided that he was.

Voices.

Not close, he thought, but not too far away, either.

It was difficult to judge distances tonight. Sound, like the flames in the fire, seemed chaotic – fractured and thrown about. In Charlie's mind there were noises everywhere. The devil had told him what would happen, and what would be happening all around the world. Places were burning. Cities were erupting into violence; buildings being reduced to rubble. Smoke was filling the sky. People were screaming and shouting, gunshots cracking the icy air. The war had begun in every single household, town and country, and the woods were only one small part of that big international process. With one key difference. The devil was here, deep in the woods, and his enemies were coming for him. Even as the planet was engulfed by the flames of battle, the war might be won or lost right here.

You're a soldier now, the man reminded him, and so he was.

The angels had flown overhead and seen the fire he had made. Soon they would send men in to investigate – to check if the heat was from flames or from the hellfire of the devil's army – and because the burning circle was so large, the devil had explained, Charlie would be hidden from them at first. The shelter in the undergrowth would keep him secret until it was time to engage the enemy.

It wouldn't be long now.

He swapped the knife between hands, wiping his palm again.

The nerves were still there, of course, but the man kept telling him it was a good thing. They were engaged in important business, after all, and nerves would help keep them both alert and ready.

And you have the knife.

That was true. Like any good soldier, he had received his weapons and his supplies. First, the devil had raised up firewood to fuel the decoy. Then it had revealed the shelter it had constructed for him, among the trees. Finally, it had given him this knife.

Charlie looked at it, careful not to allow the metal to glint in the firelight. The blade was long and thin: a centimetre across at its widest point, where it met the handle, and then tapering to a cruel point a hand's length away. The edge was very sharp, and somehow, despite being so slim, the knife felt solid. There was no give in it.

'A good knife,' the devil had said when it handed it to him. 'It will serve you well.'

Charlie nodded. He knew it was a good weapon. The devil had told him it was one it had carried itself. It had killed one of the devil's enemies and still bore the rust of that man's blood. Because of this, it had magical properties.

The voices were getting closer.

Charlie took a better grip on the knife. And – a secret hidden among the trees – he kept very still, waiting.

4 DECEMBER   **3.30 A.M.**
3 HOURS, 50 MINUTES UNTIL DAWN

Mark

Back in our makeshift office downstairs, it was obvious that something had gone wrong. There had been escalating tension between Greg and Mercer all day, and the atmosphere told me that things either had come to a head in my absence or would do shortly. The team was fraying.

Lost in their respective thoughts, neither paid me much attention as I summarised the second interview with Scott. Greg concentrated on uploading the data files. Mercer sat to one side, staring into space, occasionally nodding to indicate I should continue. I told him about the stone walls and the fire, the brief affair between Jodie and Kevin Simpson.

'Your door-to-door team reported in before you got back,' he said. 'Simpson's neighbour has identified Jodie McNeice from the photograph. It was definitely her at his house.'

My heart sank a little, even though I'd known it already. The affair had continued, then. I remembered the killer talking to Simpson on the recording. *How do you think she's feeling now? Is she pleased she's home? Or does she wish she was still here with you?*

'She set up CCL with Simpson,' I said. 'As far as Scott knows, their relationship was one night, two years ago. She left and she hasn't seen Simpson since.'

You think you love her. Don't you.

'So he doesn't know about the current affair?' Mercer asked.

'I think on some level he probably does know. It seems like the kind of thing the killer would have used against him. But if so, he doesn't remember.'

Mercer looked up at me. His eyes were bloodshot from tiredness and there was something about him that seemed to be slowing down.

'He does remember a baby, though,' I said.

Mercer blinked. 'A baby?'

'Yeah.' I explained what Scott had told me. 'But I don't know whether we should take that literally or not.'

He stared at me for a moment. There was emptiness in his expression. Whereas earlier on, he'd looked as if he was taking every fact as it came – slotting each one neatly into place – now it was more as though they were piling up on him. He looked in danger of collapse.

Greg was in the mood to be confrontational. 'Why would he have a baby with him?'

'Forget about that for now.' Mercer looked down at the floor, speaking slowly. 'I need to think about it. Get the information to Pete.'

'Yes, sir.'

Feeling uncomfortable, I sat down and began forming the data into an alert message to send to the comms van at the woods. While I waited for receipt, I scanned through the report from my door-to-door team. It was brief but comprehensive. They'd talked to SafeSide Insurance. Apparently,

Jodie had disappeared in her lunch-hour – gone off and not come back. Her boss said she'd also been absent from work the day before, reportedly with a migraine. But obviously that had been a lie. She'd taken the day off to spend it with Kevin Simpson.

Greg nudged me, catching my attention. When I looked up at him, he nodded almost imperceptibly towards Mercer. I glanced across.

My gaze rested on him, held fast.

He'd barely moved since last speaking to me. He was sitting there, eyes closed, slowly rubbing the bridge of his nose. Gently, back and forth. If not for that, he might have been asleep. Even as it was, he looked like he was in a trance.

'Are you okay, sir?'

He raised his eyebrows, but kept rubbing his nose. 'Could you get me some coffee, Mark?'

Greg nudged me again as I stood up, and I almost shook his arm away.

'Of course,' I said.

The nearest drinks machine turned out to be the one in reception. It served black coffee at boiling point in thin, plastic cups. Carrying three back together proved traumatic. I spilled hot liquid over myself before I'd even left the foyer, shocking my hands, and then twice more along the corridor. It began to feel like everything was against me. I swore, resisting the urge to throw the cups against the wall.

Back in the locker room, I put them down and rubbed my mildly burned hands on my trousers. Things seemed to have improved a little. Mercer was active and awake, if bleary-eyed, and he and Greg were sitting at the left-hand computer. Onscreen, Simon had joined us from his van at Scott and Jodie's flat.

'The whole woods in this weather?' he said, his eyebrow arched. He looked and sounded as fresh as he had when he'd greeted me at Kevin Simpson's house that morning. 'My word.'

Mercer was in no mood for dissent, however subtle: 'What have you got for us there?'

'We're well under way. I'll talk you through the shots we've taken. Have you got the file open, Greg?'

'Will have in a moment.'

Simon had already filed an initial report on what his SOCOs had found at Scott's flat so far. Greg clicked through to find the photographs and video footage for us to refer to as we went.

The first picture he pulled up showed the exterior of the building. It looked like a capital H that had been pushed onto its back in the snow.

'Six flats,' Simon said, 'two on each floor. Banks and his girlfriend live in the one on the bottom left. Access is via the door in the middle, and then to each flat by central corridors and stairwell.'

'So no lofts or attics for him to hide in?' Mercer said.

'None of that, no. But plenty of evidence that he's been up to his other tricks. Bear with me.'

Simon started working on the computer at his end. A second later, a number of the thumbnail picture files on the main screen were highlighted. Greg opened each in turn, laying them out side by side.

Photographs of unscrewed plug sockets, their fronts lying discarded on the carpet. Light fittings ripped from the ceiling. Drawers removed. Boxes toppled.

'He's always tidied up after himself before,' Greg said.

It was the exact opposite of what had been found at previous crime scenes. First, he had allowed us to see his face. And now this.

'He doesn't feel the need to take care any more,' Mercer said. 'He's not bothered about being caught.'

There it was again. Despite his exhaustion, Mercer always seemed to be just a couple of steps too far ahead for us to make sense of his thoughts. Hiding his own identity was no longer important to the killer. And now, apparently, he didn't even care about getting caught.

It was a step beyond what Greg was prepared to accept.

'Well, no, that doesn't follow. He already had the girl in the van by then, so it's more likely he didn't have time. He was probably planning to come back later and finish off then.'

Mercer shook his head, gesturing with one hand. It was all so plain and obvious to him.

'No. Think of the phone call he made to Simpson's employers. The mask he left us at Carl Farmer's house. This is a dialogue we're involved in here—'

'He's changed his MO—'

'Don't interrupt me!'

But Greg was unimpressed and made no attempt to hide it. He closed his eyes and kept talking over his boss.

'—*he's changed his MO*, and the fact is we don't know what he's doing.'

'I know—'

'But I'm sure that "being caught" is *not* part of his fucking plan.'

'I know what he's doing!' Mercer banged his fist down on the desk and then pointed at the onscreen map. 'He's there in the woods waiting for us. This whole thing ... We're involved in his game. Can't you see that? He's giving us until *dawn* to save this girl's life.'

The silence rang in the office. He glared at us, then leaned heavily back in his chair, closing his eyes. He looked like a man under caution who'd been manipulated into blurting out a confession. He shook his head. I could tell he was annoyed with himself for losing his temper.

Greg and I looked at each other. Greg was pale, but his cheeks were mottled with anger of his own. Mercer's outburst had obviously unsettled him.

It had unsettled me, too. The implication appeared to be that the 50/50 Killer had changed his MO for the sole reason of involving us. He wasn't simply taunting us: it was the whole point. In Mercer's head, he had made this all about himself. The 50/50 Killer had caught our attention with Kevin Simpson, and now he was waiting patiently in the woods to see whether the famous Detective Sergeant John Mercer could find him by dawn and save a girl's life. That was why it didn't matter about hiding any more. It was one final game, with Jodie McNeice's life deciding the winner.

And it was bullshit, surely. Looking at him, I felt a mixture of concern and embarrassment. Nothing in his theory contradicted the facts, but there was hardly enough to support it. It was all too easy to remember what Pete had said before he'd left the hospital. The likelihood was that Jodie was dead. It was simply that Mercer needed her to be alive so that he could save her and beat this man.

That desperate need, barely even hidden now, felt like a far better explanation for his theory than that it was true.

He sighed and leaned forwards again. 'It doesn't matter, anyway. What else have we got?'

'Ah.' Simon was as cheerful as ever. 'The delights of the living room.'

It seemed strange to carry on after the outburst, but Greg shook his head and turned back to the laptop. He minimised the photographs of the killer's discarded equipment and opened the next file.

It was a shot taken from the lounge doorway. Nearest the camera, there was a glass dining table with a computer on it, and then, further away, a settee facing a television in the corner by the window. The television was switched on. Halfway along the wall to the right, a door led away into what looked like a kitchen. A solid metal chair lay on its side in the centre of the room, and there was smashed glass on the floor.

'Okay,' Mercer said. 'We've got signs that Banks was attacked in the living room, which fits in with what he remembers so far.'

'Not seen a baby around, have you, Simon?' Greg said sarcastically.

Simon's expression changed slowly. He looked confused for the first time that day. 'Why do you ask that?'

'Because Banks remembers the killer having a baby with him, of course.' Greg frowned. 'Why? You haven't, have you?'

'No, no.' Simon pursed one side of his mouth, full of thought. 'We haven't. It's interesting, though. Hunter was on the news earlier. He's been on all day, in fact. His team have an abducted baby. Not personally, of course.'

For a moment, there was only the hum of the computer equipment, interrupted by a *clank* in the locker room's old plumbing.

I glanced over at Mercer. He was looking at the floor: the same reaction, in fact, as when I'd told him what Scott had said about the baby. He didn't seem surprised. A second later, I put it together.

He knew.

Hunter was the man who should, by rights, have been in charge of the 50/50 case; now he was investigating an abducted baby. Mercer had known that, and when I'd told him what Scott had said, alarm bells had gone off. He wasn't going to allow the investigation to slip away from him.

I looked at Greg. He'd seen it, too. The expression on his face was one of disbelief.

Simon was oblivious of all this.

'It's probably unconnected,' he said. 'It's something to do with custody problems, so they're looking for the father. I was only half listening. I was mostly just being amused by the delightful Mr Hunter playing to the cameras.'

Mercer rubbed his face slowly. 'Right. It won't be connected. I'll look it up in a moment.'

'Shouldn't we do that now?'

'In a minute.' Mercer glared at Greg, then turned back to the screen. 'What else have you got for us?'

Simon paused, picking up on the atmosphere.

'Well, there's a computer in the living room,' he said. 'You might have seen it in the last picture. Switched on. Very pretty screensaver running.'

'Don't touch it, please.'

'Nobody has, Greg. I know how territorial you are.'

'Are you happy to travel, Greg? Check out any emails, files, key-logging software.'

'Gladly.'

'Wait, I'm still here,' Simon reminded us. 'Before you all run off, you'll want to see the last file, the one at the bottom.'

Greg minimised the open picture and clicked on the file Simon had indicated.

The photograph had been taken in the bedroom, the cameraman standing at the foot of the bed, facing the headboard. On the cream wall there was one of the 50/50 Killer's spider webs. It was large, ugly and – like the design we'd found at Simpson's house – appeared to have been drawn in thick black marker. Each line was about the width of a fingertip. Each had been slashed with a short cross-stroke.

Mercer leaned across to see.

'Greg, would you open up one of the photographs taken at Farmer's house?'

He began to click through.

Earlier on, standing in Farmer's front room, we'd identified the web the killer had drawn on Kevin Simpson's wall, and then assumed that the others sketched there were draft versions of the same design. But when Greg opened up the photograph and placed the images side-by-side on the screen for comparison, it took only a moment to find it.

'There.'

One of the sketches on the wall had been left at Simpson's house; a second at Scott and Jodie's. Two out of perhaps thirty.

Mercer looked fascinated. He pointed at the photograph of Carl Farmer's wall.

'Some of the designs are obviously very similar,' he said. 'You know what we're seeing here? I almost got it while we were there but I lost the thread. These are his notes.'

Greg frowned. 'What does that mean?'

'The laptop was in the corner of the room,' he said quietly. 'I can imagine him working there. He watched video clips, listened to things he'd recorded. And all the time he was standing there, making notes on the wall.'

'The spider webs are supposed to represent the victims?'

'In a way. He studies people for a long time, and these are the connections he's worked out between them. Then he cuts each strand, one by one.'

Mercer tapped the screen, singling out individual broken threads.

'He's using what he learns to make them sacrifice their partner and save their own lives. But the whole web is what he's after. In his mind, the victim he's really after is the relationship itself.'

I tilted my head slightly to look at the designs. For a moment I saw nothing, but then it came into focus. I still didn't understand, exactly, but I *saw* them. In front of my eyes, the spider webs became ragged, ruined things: the intricate connections of a relationship, cut and torn and destroyed, left hanging on the wall in the same way that the bodies of the victims were discarded underneath.

Notes.

I tried to picture the world through the killer's eyes. It was impossible. I couldn't imagine the mental filter that turned information about people into these awful, ugly things. And yet that filter existed. For all their horror, the spider webs were not arbitrary. It was clear that each had been carefully thought out and planned. Earlier drafts had not been quite right, which meant that, random as they might seem to us, the killer had found fault in them and changed tiny details, gradually perfecting the designs.

I looked at Greg, who was also staring at the screen. He knew Mercer was right, but seemed reluctant to admit it because of everything else and was doing his best to look blank.

'Okay,' he said. 'Can we check Hunter's case now, please?'

Mercer didn't say anything. He moved back to his own laptop and began working through the log-ins.

While it loaded, I turned my attention back to the web left at Scott's flat, glancing here and there, taking in the smears and checks the killer had made. He'd been symbolically breaking the strands holding Scott and Jodie together as a unit. There were ten, twelve, maybe fifteen. Each represented a break: a lie, perhaps, or a harsh truth. This was love, spelled out mechanically. A series of illusory strands and ties that could be un-picked one by one, until the relationship fell apart and died. The body of it bent slowly backwards, a single vertebra snapping at a time.

One of those smears, positioned carefully in the web by some logic I couldn't fathom, represented the affair between Jodie and Kevin Simpson. I found myself wondering which it might be, or whether it even mattered.

Suddenly, Mercer sighed.

'Fucking hell,' Greg muttered.

Mercer had one elbow on the desk, eyes closed, the tips of his fingers massaging his forehead. There was a desperation to the movement, as though he was telling himself: Keep it together; keep it together.

The screen had opened up on the main information page for Hunter's investigation. *'James Reardon'*, it said at the top. To the right of the name, in the corner of the screen, there was a picture of Reardon, of the runaway father Hunter's team were seeking.

Carl Farmer.

Pete

In the dark of the woods, the torches formed cones of light with sharp, defined edges. They cut across the pitted midriffs of trees and found millions of crystals glistening in the solid coating of snow on the uneven ground.

It was freezing cold. Every time Pete breathed out, he felt a painful humming in his otherwise numb lips. His breath steamed, and he imagined it solidifying into a balloon of ice, then cracking in the air. Further in front, more snow was flashing down, a blur of movement in the bobbing torch lights. Even through his coat, he felt it all over him: a series of constant, soft touches.

'Watch your footing,' he told the officer behind him.

'Yes, sir.'

There was barely disguised sarcasm in the officer's voice. Pete let it go for the moment. The situation meant that a certain amount of annoyance was understandable, even when walking on the paths. Now, they were working their way through a tangle of undergrowth and down a gentle but awkward slope in the land. It wasn't easy and it wasn't pleasant. But still, it had to be done.

'I don't want you falling on me, is all,' he said dryly.

The officer said nothing.

Despite himself, Pete was irritated. He needed them more alert than this; he needed more concentration. The fire was visible through the trees, probably about a hundred metres down, where the slope levelled out. The light from it was broken into fragments and the trees in between seemed to swell and waver as the flames shifted. A big fire. That made him nervous.

He had thirty men in total. Six of them he'd left at the vans to co-ordinate the search teams and the helicopter. That gave him six teams of four officers, with a search-and-rescue volunteer familiar with the land joining each. The dogs had found nothing, but the volunteers insisted on staying and helping anyway, which Pete considered put his officers' bitching into some kind of perspective. When the report had come through about the fire, the volunteer had brought them as close along the main path as they could get, and then Pete had told him to wait there, leaving an officer with him for protection.

The fire was too big. It implied more than one person, and he wasn't going to risk a civilian walking into something and getting hurt. Of course, the downside to that was he had only two officers with him. And those two didn't seem able to keep their minds on the fucking job.

The slope gradually evened out. For the most part, Pete kept the torch pointed at the ground, checking his footing. Occasionally, he lifted the beam and scanned the trees in front and to either side.

Nothing.

'There's nobody here,' one of the officers said.

'Who lit that fire, then?' Pete said. 'Did it spontaneously fucking combust?'

'No. But all this activity, they'll be long gone.'

'We'll see.'

He shook his head. For Christ's sake! It wasn't like he was under any illusions himself. The chances of finding this girl, Jodie, alive were ridiculously slim, and the search became more difficult and complicated with every sweep the helicopter made. Word had come through on the radio that Banks had been held in a stone building, so all those needed to be searched whether the helicopter picked up a heat trace or not. But it kept feeding back information on heat sources away from the recognised structures. All of those needed to be investigated, too, because the killer might have moved into the undergrowth.

His team had done two so far, both of them torches in the faces of derelicts sleeping rough, both so frozen they couldn't do anything except look bewildered and frightened. John would have wanted him to drag them out on the off-chance – but then, John wanted a lot of things. Pete had to work with the resources he had at ground level, and there simply wasn't the manpower to start rounding everyone up over a fucking pipe-dream.

It was depressing work, unlikely to yield positive results, but normally he would put such thoughts out of his mind, get his head down and plough through it. And he was trying, but it wasn't only the weather or the likelihood of success that was bothering him tonight. There was

John to think about, too. Pete had never been good at staying angry, and since the last broadcast he'd let the irritation go and concern had grown in its place. Over the years they'd become more than colleagues; they were friends, so John's attitude bothered him. He really did think this was possible, and it was obvious he had far too much riding on the outcome. When the girl was eventually found dead, Pete would go home, sleep badly and then come back the next day and start on the next case. John, though ... He was in serious danger of unravelling completely.

And so every unhelpful comment made him want to bite the heads off the officers with him. The job was what it was. They needed to take it on the chin, not keep reminding him how difficult it was. Every complaint just brought his concerns into sharper focus, and for the purposes of the search he needed to distance himself from those kind of thoughts.

In a normal situation, he might have attempted to explain a little of this – but then, in a normal situation, he wouldn't have to. Everyone was working hard; everyone was stressed. He needed to bear that in mind, if nothing else.

'Both of you, take care,' he said.

'Yes, sir. If anyone's here, I'm going to ask if I can sit down for a bit and warm up. That okay?'

Pete managed a wry smile in the dark. 'Sounds good to me.'

He led them towards the fire, raising his torch to shoulder height and aiming the beam around the trees.

'Police,' he shouted. 'If anyone's here, make your presence known at once.'

He got the response he was anticipating: none at all, apart from the crackle of the fire. It had clearly been lit for quite some time: there was an enormous amount of burned wood and ashes at the edges, while in the centre there was still a heaped pile burning beneath large, strong flames. The heat coming off it was intense. When he looked away, green flashes were scarred on his retinas.

It was possible that the fire had been abandoned some time ago, he thought. Certainly, the snow didn't seem to be touching it. But that meant it must have been soaked in something – paraffin, maybe – and it all seemed too much effort for one person. A man on his own surely wouldn't have set so much kindling burning at once. Perhaps there had been a few people here, conducting business they didn't want the police to know about.

Pete shone the torch at the edges of the fire. The snow all round it was undisturbed. He tried further out in all directions, but still there was nothing.

'No footprints. Whoever was here left long enough ago for their tracks to have been covered.'

'First sweep of the helicopter, they'll have been off.'

Pete nodded. They would probably have assumed the police were looking for them. But wherever they'd gone, the helicopter would pick them up: either that, or they'd try for the road and run into the officers cordoned there.

Still, there was nothing here, was there? He kicked the snow at his feet. No debris. He wouldn't have been surprised by needles or bottles or old food, or *something*, at least, and it seemed unlikely they'd have tidied up before leaving. The snow couldn't have covered everything.

He aimed the torch into the tree line, moving it slowly round in a full circle, listening carefully. It was utterly silent here, and that in itself struck him as—

Something there.

He moved the torch back and found it.

'What is *that*?' one of the officers said.

All three angled beams of light into the trees. At first, Pete wasn't sure what he was seeing. It looked like a triangular hole in the ground of the slope – a cave-mouth – except the angles were too symmetrical for that.

'A tent,' he realised.

The torch-light went all the way to the back; there was nobody in there.

Pete lowered the torch to the entrance, saw the new footprints and swirls in the snow. Followed them round with the beam, just as the shrieking man exploded out of the trees beside him.

He understood the danger a half-second before it hit him, swinging the torch at his attacker. Too late, though – something thudded against the top of his arm. It didn't feel like much but suddenly his hand was empty and useless. 'Fuck.' Thud, thud – he was turning, trying to fight the man off, but he couldn't lift his arm properly to defend himself. The woods were whirling around him. And then – *thud!* – the blow on his shoulder was too sharp, too *wrong*. Nothing like the hard impact of a punch, and suddenly he was on his knees from it.

'Down!'

Everybody was shouting. Pete caught the scent of pepper-spray in the air, and glanced up to see his attacker falling away backwards into the snow. Both the other officers were immediately on him: shouting, pinning his arm. A baton came down and the man screamed again. The light caught something falling out of his hand.

A knife.

Pete touched his shoulder. His glove came away wet.

'Fuck,' he said to himself.

He eased himself down into a sitting position. Not the worst thing in the world, to be stabbed in the upper arm. Not great, but not terrible. But the last blow bothered him. Down onto his shoulder, near his collarbone. That wasn't good.

'Sir?'

'Get that helicopter back here,' he managed. 'Have it do something fucking useful.'

At least now, maybe he could go home. There were stars filling his vision. Pete closed his eyes and lay back.

There wasn't a lot of pain. And he was reasonably sure he wasn't going to die. So the last thing he thought about was what happened to Andrew Dyson, not in relation to himself but in terms of what this, right here and now, was going to do to John.

And then there was the presence crouching beside him. The officer's hand on his chest, and the clamour of his panicked voice on the radio. And then nothing.

---

4 DECEMBER   **4.10 A.M.**
3 HOURS, 10 MINUTES UNTIL DAWN

Mark

After Simon had logged off, Greg and Mercer had a predictable, yet remarkably calm, argument about how to proceed.

Greg was adamant that we should contact Hunter and merge the teams, and I thought he was right. We were looking for the same man, after all, and the investigation into the abducted baby had a large number of officers attached to it, many of whom could be sent to the woods to help with the search there.

Mercer, of course, disagreed. He argued that it would complicate matters. Any benefit gained from the additional men would be outweighed by the loss of time involved, because Hunter wasn't going to give up his resources without a thorough understanding of the situation. There was an urgent operation under way and it needed to keep moving forwards.

Of course, the real argument occurred in all the things that were left unsaid. They both knew that if Mercer contacted Hunter the case would be taken away from him. Any 'urgency' in the search of the woods was based on his assumptions rather than the facts. And we all knew that he'd kept quiet when I mentioned the baby, presumably intending to check that himself while hoping there was no connection. His need to catch the 50/50 Killer had taken him into the realm of professional misconduct, and this was undoubtedly the final moment at which we might step back from joining him.

But Greg didn't mention any of that. The argument was kept on a practical and functional level, where ultimately it was Mercer's decision.

'We're wasting more time here,' he said.

Greg was simmering, but he held himself in check and gave up. 'Do you need me for anything else before I head out?'

Mercer shook his head.

'Okay, then.'

Greg gave me a look as he walked over to the door. I didn't know what it meant at the time: whether it was the equivalent of Pete's 'Look after him', or something else. Later, I would understand that it was a look of reassurance: an *It'll be okay*. I should have thought more on the fact that he'd given up the argument too easily, but I was tired and stressed, and I put it down to the effects of Mercer's earlier outburst.

When he was gone, Mercer returned to his familiar pose: eyes closed, fingers massaging his forehead. It was as though this action was his way of recharging himself. Or maybe absolving himself from thought for a time.

'Coffee, sir?'

He didn't say anything, but raised his eyebrows. I figured that was as close to a yes as I was going to get.

Five minutes later, I was back with two coffees, and Mercer was back from the dead: elbows on the desk, hands clasped in front of him, staring intently at the screen.

'Thanks.'

He took the coffee and gestured absently to the monitor in the middle.

'Sit down. I've printed you a copy.'

I picked up the sheets of paper. It was the summary of Hunter's investigation, headed with the name James Reardon and the familiar picture of the man we knew as Carl Farmer.

184

I sipped my coffee and started to read through the details.

The first thing that struck me was the sheer amount of information about Reardon. Birthdate, family history, employment record. This was almost certainly not a fake identity. Here, finally, was the man behind the nests.

Reardon was thirty-one years old, and in his brief time on the planet he'd notched up a number of offences and upset a lot of people. A very bright child, he'd become increasingly distracted and disruptive as he grew older. As an adult, he had two charges against him for affray, three for drunk and disorderly, one for assault, several minor drug issues. And so on. The impression the report gave was of a big guy who turned into a nasty drunk – who lost control when he lost control – although the past few years had seen his offences become concentrated in a different area.

Amanda Reardon, his estranged wife, now went by her original surname of Taylor. There was a photograph of her in the file: thin blonde hair, pale skin. She was younger than Reardon but looked older, and most of that was in her eyes: she seemed tired all the way down to her soul. Like she was constantly on guard and unable to sleep much.

Their relationship had been on and off for several years. It was a dull and dispiriting tale of break-ups and reconciliations, punctuated by accusations of James Reardon being dangerous, volatile, unreliable – all retracted when the couple got back together again. A familiar story. I thought it was sad the way that certain people stuck with partners who were so clearly wrong for them, as though they believed they'd never find anything better. You invest and you cling.

Their second daughter, Karli, had been born just over a year and a half ago, and she seemed to be the turning point.

The document contained a brief summary of the initial custody battle that followed their separation. Amanda Taylor was awarded residence, but Reardon challenged it for both children, claiming that she was an unfit mother. He wasn't his own best advocate. On one occasion he was alleged to have attacked the car she was in, shattering the windscreen with a hammer, and then assaulting her by the roadside. A restraining order had been hard fought and repeatedly broken. There was more besides, but the end result was that James Reardon had recently been refused all access to his children in the short term. Amanda Taylor had patiently played the game, and she had won.

Hunter's current investigation related to James Reardon's abduction of his daughter Karli yesterday morning. The summary gave the details. Amanda Taylor's boyfriend, Colin Barnes, had taken Karli to the park in her pushchair around nine, and a man followed and then assaulted him. Barnes had identified Reardon as his attacker. Reardon had run off taking his little girl with him, and subsequently vanished. Appeals for him to come forward had been met with silence.

I looked at the photograph, and was struck once again by how hard he looked: how blank. It was easy to imagine those eyes staring out of the holes in a mask, illuminated by a flicker of fire. Easy to believe this was the man who had tortured Scott and who would, if she was still alive, be torturing Jodie right now.

Easy – but could we be sure?

The first thing I realised was that the timings fitted, and that Reardon's connection to the case was independently corroborated. The killer had left Kevin Simpson's house after eight o'clock. The baby had been abducted around nine by James Reardon. Megan Cook had seen Reardon entering the Carl Farmer address at eleven. That was two independent witnesses, but we also had a third. Scott had identified Reardon as the man who came round to read their meter.

There was a triangulation of guilt there. Individually, there might be other explanations for the witness testimony, but together they seemed unshakeable.

I glanced up at Mercer, who was lost in the document. Despite everything, I realised he had been right so far. We had the killer's face; we had the killer's real name and identity. Maybe there still wasn't enough to justify the theory this was a direct challenge to us, but then, I didn't have another theory to offer in its place. What was Reardon doing? What had he been planning and what was he now carrying out?

I turned back to the summary.

Reardon's age and temperament fitted the profile: intelligent but anti-social; volatile in his youth, more controlled and calculating as the years had gone by. My gut feeling was that we'd also find a certain symmetry between the ups and downs of his relationship with his wife and the 50/50 crimes. But that was—

'Have you read about his parents?' Mercer said.

'Not yet.'

'They died in a car crash six years ago. They left Reardon their house and a reasonably large sum of money. He sold the house; used the cash to rent a place. Since then, he's only worked sporadically, here and there.'

I nodded. Another box; another tick.

My excitement was growing. The more I read, the more clicked into place.

The most telling detail in the summary was in connection with Reardon's custody battle. I felt my breath catching as I saw it. Towards the end of the legal battle, after his last access visit, their daughter had been returned to Amanda Taylor with a new teddy bear as a present. Suspicious, Taylor had opened the toy up and discovered a listening device secreted within the foam.

Reardon denied planting it, but admitted that he was desperate – concerned about the company his ex-girlfriend was keeping and the effect it might have on their children. The case had made the news: only a small item, but the clipping had been scanned and included in the file. Reardon had declined to give a full interview, but had spoken briefly to the reporter.

'Nobody understands how much a father loves his child,' he said. 'That woman doesn't know what love is.'

I looked across at Mercer and he was almost glowing. I caught sight of how I imagined the old John Mercer: the man who'd solved all of those high-profile cases, who could look through the files and single out the key details that would break them.

At that moment, all the weariness of the day's work and conflicts appeared to have lifted from him. He was fresh again. For the first time that day, I thought he seemed capable of seeing all this through. And I got the impression that, maybe for the first time, he felt it, too. There was a visible energy about him. It gave me a small thrill to see it.

All day long, I realised, I'd been fighting against a feeling of disappointment. Rightly or wrongly, this wasn't only about a good job for me; it was more than that. I was here at least partly because I wanted to do something as a validation of Lise's belief in me: something that would have made her proud. And yet it had felt as though I'd achieved no more in that regard than if I'd got a job filing paper in an office. But right there, right then, I was finally seeing the man I'd come here to work for.

'We're going to get him,' he told me.

I nodded; I believed him.

And I suppose it was inevitable that, right then, with a single beep from the computer in front of us, it all began to fall apart.

Eileen

Eileen was having the dream again: the one she'd had the Friday before and then spoken to John about over breakfast. The one in which he left her.

I hope you're not planning to run away.

In real life he'd told her he was too tired to run, but in the dream he'd clearly found the energy from somewhere. Clothes were missing from the wardrobes, books from the shelves, paintings from the walls. She drifted from room to room and saw her possessions sagging into the spaces he'd left. A home which had been comfortably full of two people's possessions was reduced to a house half emptied, and the items still here looked awkward and out of place as a result. When two people's lives came together and grew, you couldn't simply rip one away and expect the remainder to stand unsupported, as it had before. It didn't work that way. Things had been carefully balanced, which meant they would fall.

At first, the noise brought her out of the dream slowly. While the events in her head were still vivid and real, she became aware of the bed at her back and the covers over her body.

The alarm was going off.

That didn't seem right. She lifted her head off the pillow, peering around the bedroom with bleary eyes.

The curtains were black, the dressing table clouded in shadow. She checked the display. Only half past four, and the numbers weren't flashing.

The phone in the study.

It all came back to her then – John working late; the fear and the anger; the promise she'd extracted from him to phone her every two hours. What had happened? It had been her intention to stay awake to see if he called, but she remembered lying down on the bed, resting, and that had obviously been that. Idiot, she thought.

At least he's phoned.

She swung her legs over the side of the bed and got rather unsteadily to her feet. The wine was swirling the remains of the dream around in her head, and tilting the world. It was hard to negotiate the hallway in the darkness, with everything turning slowly, and on the way she banged into the wall and, from there, the banister, and then missed the door to the study, flat-palming the cold wall just past it. Three or four desperate seconds to find the light switch. The same again while she winced and rubbed her eyes against the harsh pain of the light.

The whole time, the phone kept ringing.

'Hello?'

'Eileen?'

A man's voice, but not John's.

'Yes,' she said. 'Who is this?'

'It's Geoff Hunter,' he said. 'I'm sorry for calling you so late. I wouldn't normally disturb you.'

Hunter. An image of John's noxious colleague rose in her head, and she frowned. Of course he wouldn't normally disturb her, so what the hell did he want now? And why wasn't this John?

She froze. Something had happened to him.

Panic rose inside her, concern and love for her husband immediately replacing the anger she'd felt at his neglect of her, the risk he was taking at their expense. If he was hurt, if anything had happened ... But if something had, it wouldn't be Hunter phoning her. One of his team would do that. And so it must be about—

'James Reardon,' she remembered. 'You've found him?'

'Not yet.'

'Then what do you want?'

'It's your husband.'

There was an unpleasant note of triumph in his voice. Eileen closed her eyes and felt herself falling away. She didn't know exactly what was coming next, but she had an idea.

Hunter said, 'There's something I think you deserve to know.'

---

4 DECEMBER   **4.40 A.M.**
2 HOURS, 40 MINUTES UNTIL DAWN

Mark

Detective Inspector Alan White was Mercer's direct superior, but was slightly younger than him. It happens that way sometimes. In any organisation, there comes a point when you stop rising automatically up the ranks and have to push to move ahead. Mercer could have done that, I was sure, but he was happy enough to stay where he was, whereas White had involved himself more in politics and pulled himself higher up the ladder. From brief mentions in Mercer's book, there seemed to be good history and mutual respect between them, but right now that history was doing little to stop White looking incredibly pissed off. Perhaps it tempered the anger with a hint of sadness and regret, but that certainly wasn't going to prevent him doing his job.

I'd been aware of Mercer reporting to White that afternoon as I read through the 50/50 file, but this was the first time I'd actually seen him. He had black, receding hair, and a face with a strange sort of muscular pudge to it. His dark brown eyes were intimidating even through a computer screen and over a distance of miles. They could probably have scorched off skin in person.

'John,' he repeated, 'I want to know what's going on. This morning, you picked up a home invasion. All day you've been talking to me about a home invasion.'

'That's the case we've been working on, Alan—'

'No, cut the shit, John. I look at the file now, and I see a home invasion with a lot of activity we both know I should have been informed about. And why am I looking at the file? Because I've just had Geoff Hunter shouting down the phone at me. So I repeat – *again* – what the fuck is going on?'

Mercer stared back at him. For a moment, there was only steel in his face, but then the glimmer of a smile appeared.

He understood this was it now, the end, and he also knew exactly what had happened. He'd trusted someone, and he'd been betrayed. So Geoff Hunter had been on the phone to White. Earlier on, when Greg had left the locker room, I'd noticed he'd given up too easily, and now we both understood why. Finally losing patience, he'd taken the decision to go over Mercer's head. In many ways, I found I couldn't blame him.

'I was about to contact you both,' Mercer said.

'Is that right?'

'Yes.' He picked his words slowly and carefully. 'There was some doubt at the beginning of the case, but now it seems clear. The man we're looking for is the man responsible for Andrew's death. Among others.'

Some doubt at the beginning of the case. There was irony in that, of course, because it was Greg who'd queried the link at first. Mercer was staring down at his keyboard, with the same thin, humourless smile.

'We've talked about this, haven't we, John?' White said. 'You know my feelings. It was always going to be Geoff's case from now on. So that's bad enough. Compounding matters, I understand you've actually uncovered a link with Geoff's current operation. That's right?'

Mercer nodded once. 'That's correct.'

'Do you have any idea how difficult that makes this?'

'We've only just read the file summary now—'

'John—'

Mercer spread his hands: 'The connection is a new development.'

'John, please.' White shook his head and looked away. He looked as if he was rolling something around his mouth and not enjoying the taste all that much.

Mercer just waited.

'Right,' White said. 'Geoff's on his way to the ring road now, since that's where most of the men are. He'll be taking over. Until he's evaluated the situation, he's ordered the search teams out of the woods.'

Mercer looked up, frantic. 'But Alan—'

'No buts, John. It's the middle of the fucking night and there's a blizzard. What were you thinking?'

'Ordered', I noted. Past tense. White had already made the decision to replace Mercer before he made this call. Mercer sensed it, too. He was beginning to panic.

'We're at a key point in this, Alan. We're so, so close. A girl could die if we lose hold of this now.'

'You're far too close,' White said, 'and it's clouding your judgment. I've skimmed the file and what you're doing is madness. You're risking more of your men in there – you do realise that?'

'Alan—'

'We both know Geoff is perfectly competent. He will look at this case and he will take it forward in the most appropriate manner.'

'Damn it, Alan, we have to save her!'

There was a pause. White just looked at him, his expression wavering between contempt and pity. As with Mercer's previous outburst, I felt embarrassed on his behalf. Five minutes ago he had been bright and positive. Now he was collapsing, and it was painful to watch. We had all been worried about what the case meant to him, and what failure today might do. I was seeing that happen.

'I wish you could see yourself,' White said quietly.

'I'm fine.'

'I'll be the judge of that. No, you're not fine; you're falling apart. I'm telling you to go home. And out of respect for our history, that's all I'm telling you right now. But we'll be talking a lot more about this when you've slept.'

Mercer took a deep breath. Then released it slowly.

'Am I understood?' White said.

'Yes, Alan.'

'Put your man on.'

When Mercer didn't move, I activated the webcam on my own monitor and clicked the onscreen view so that White would receive the feed.

'Detective Nelson,' I said.

'I assume you heard all that?'

'Yes, sir.'

'I need you to prepare a report for Detective Sergeant Hunter.'

'Okay.'

He went through it. Hunter wanted a summary of the day's events: what had happened; what we knew so far; what our current situation was. The facts, White emphasised.

I listened, nodding in all the right places, and every second it felt like I was betraying Mercer. I wanted to do something – make some rebellious gesture of support – but that wouldn't accomplish anything. I was paid to do whatever job got handed down to me, and I forced myself to keep that in mind. Even so, below the surface the guilt and frustration were building. All the men, out of the woods.

When I disconnected, the locker room was very quiet. The soft hum of the computer equipment gave the silence an ominous feel: the atmosphere was charged, as though the air couldn't stand it any more and the next time there was a noise it would start screaming.

I looked at Mercer.

In the last few hours, I'd become used to him sitting a certain way: elbows on his knees or on the desk, his head in his hands, looking as though he was either concentrating very hard on something or allowing himself to drift and rest. Now that it was over, he was simply leaning back in the chair, hands resting casually on his thighs. The acceptance in his face revealed a number of emotions. Anger, certainly. But also, thought, a sense of relief.

He reminded me of my father. When I was a child and his business had failed, he'd sat me down to explain about it. I'd felt awkward, because I was young and it was the first time I'd seen my father look vulnerable. He'd always been a rock, and it was terrible to see him stained by failure, and the worst thing was him knowing I was seeing it. Mercer had that same combination of age, fragility and sadness.

In my father's case, it had been reined in by a lifetime's understanding that whatever life dealt you, however hard it might be, you took it and kept going. Mercer just looked beaten, and that was immeasurably worse.

'I'm sorry, sir,' I said. 'I wanted you to see it through.'

He stared at me for a moment, as though weighing me up. Considering me. Seeing through me, almost. Then, he leaned forwards, and seemed about to speak.

Before he could, a sharp noise broke the silence, jarring us both. Mercer patted at himself. His mobile was ringing.

'Shit.'

He took it out of his pocket, looked at the display, and then paused, debating the call. I waited, but he just let it ring. The caller wasn't giving up. Thirty seconds later, Mercer used his fingernail to turn the phone off at the top, cutting the call dead, and then put it down on the desk by all his papers.

'My wife.' He closed his eyes.

'You don't want to talk to her?' I said.

'Not right now, no. I'll be home soon.'

I looked at my watch. 'It's late for her still to be up. Or else it's early.'

'She worries about me. But everyone worries about me, don't they?'

I thought about that. It reminded me, along with the impression I'd just had, that I hadn't replied to my parents after that text earlier on. They were worried about me, too, even though they didn't need to be. I knew how annoying it could be.

'People—'

It felt stupid, because he wasn't going to see it this way, not at the moment.

'People care,' I said.

'No, people worry. And you know what? I worry about myself sometimes. I'm the one who has to deal with it. People seem to forget that. But it's been two years, and I have to do something. I can't just sit at home for ever. Nobody seems to remember that, either. Well' – he glanced up at the screen – 'almost nobody.'

I started to reply, but then stopped. 'Almost nobody', he'd said. The words struck me as odd, and a second later something occurred to me: *He's been planning this for two years*, Mercer had said.

It was two years since we'd heard from the 50/50 Killer, and it was also two years since Mercer's breakdown. And he thought there was a connection. Staring over at him, I realised that had been at least part of the basis for his approach to the case. He thought that the two-year break had less to do with planning, more to do with the killer's desire to let the policeman in charge of the investigation recover and return to the fray.

Could he possibly be right? Unlikely as it might have seemed earlier on, now that it was just the two of us here the idea had a curious power.

'I know what everybody's been saying,' Mercer said. 'It's been obviou all day. Tiptoeing around me. They think it's all about Andrew. That can't cope with the pressure. That I'm too close to it. That I'm just goin to ... I don't know, fall over or something.'

He opened his eyes and looked straight at me.

'Do you know what I need, Mark?'

'No, sir.'

'Not even what I need, but what I want? What I want – more tha anything – is not to feel like a *fucking invalid*.'

I stared at him.

'And faith,' he said. 'That's what I've wanted. A bit of faith. Two year ago, everyone might have disagreed or might not have understood, bu they wouldn't have doubted me. But all day it's like I've been on proba tion and nobody trusts me any more. Do they honestly think I'd still b here now if I didn't think I had to be?'

'I don't know, sir.'

'Just a bit of faith.' He shook his head. 'My team to back me u like they used to. Instead, I've been on my own with this all day, whil everyone *worries*. And now ... Well, we're done, aren't we?'

'I don't know.'

'Yes. We're done.'

He put his elbows on the desk, rested his head in his hands. 'And I'n glad.'

We sat in silence. He didn't move, didn't do anything. I couldn't eve see him breathing he was so still. I wanted to excuse myself quietly an walk out of the room. Instead:

'Sir?'

There was no reply.

'Are you okay, sir?'

Nothing.

The computer in front of me beeped once, the screen coming to lif and I turned my attention to that instead. The search team at the woods requesting a connection. I clicked them through, assuming it would b Pete again, or maybe Hunter.

Rather than either of them, however, I found myself faced by an offic I'd never seen. He looked nervous and kept glancing off camera, unsur whether the connection was working.

'Detective Nelson,' I prompted.

He stared out of the screen, and I saw in his eyes that it was more tha nerves. Something was wrong.

'Sir, we've got a situation here.'

'What's happened?'

'I don't know. We've only got radio contact with the officers in the woods. I was just told to get through to you. There's been some kind of accident.'

Out of the corner of my eye, I saw Mercer slowly look up at his screen.

'Officer,' I said, 'please calm down. Tell us what you know.'

'It's Detective Dwyer, sir. He's been attacked.'

Oh, shit. 'Please clarify that.'

Mercer stood up too quickly, like a drunk who'd been asleep at a bar. His chair clattered on the floor behind him, and he began struggling to get his arms into his coat. His face was grim and determined.

I turned back to the screen: 'Clarify, officer.'

'Stabbed, sir. In the woods.'

'Get me a car,' Mercer told me.

'What's his situation?'

'I don't know,' the officer said. 'I've just had radio through from Detective Dwyer's group. They've had to bring the helicopter for him.'

I felt a swirl of air as Mercer moved past.

'Get me a fucking car,' he said.

Then he was out of the door, calling back to me from the corridor. 'Have it meet me out front.'

PART FOUR

I would like to thank all my colleagues at the department for their help and support throughout the time I have worked there, and also in my absence. In particular, I extend my thanks to the various members of my team who have, over the years, taught me everything I know about humility, humanity and care in this difficult job: everything we have achieved is always due in part, and mostly entirely, to your professionalism and expertise. It would have been impossible to write this book without you.

One person more than any other has supported me, trusted me and stuck by me – in spite of endless provocation – over the years. You forgive me, you understand my faults, and you teach me everything I need to know about the qualities mentioned above in terms of my real life.

Most importantly, you allow me to forget who I am at work and to be the human being underneath. And so this book is dedicated to you, Eileen, with affection and love.

From *Damage Done*, by John Mercer

Jodie

An average song, Jodie thought, lasts about four minutes.

She had longer ones saved on her player, and a few that were shorter, but four minutes probably wasn't a bad average to work with. In theory, then, it should be possible for her to count the songs she listened to and keep track of how much time had passed. Fifteen songs would equal one hour.

Of course, she didn't know what time it had been when she'd first put the headphones on. That was a problem. Regardless, it was something she could do to keep herself occupied. She kept count as she went along.

It was at seventy-four when the iRiver beeped once to warn her that the battery was low. Panic had rippled through her: it was bad enough being handcuffed alone in the dark, in the freezing cold, without having to deal with the quiet as well.

The machine finally gave up the ghost in the middle of song number ninety-two. It beeped one last time, and then went quiet.

Her ears were ringing a little. Every time she breathed in, the mucus in her nose rolled and clicked; the pool of it in the back of her throat was making her queasy, and her nostrils were sore and numb.

Do the maths.

Probably about six hours since the man had opened the door – from when she'd known he was looking at her, talking to her, and it had taken all her effort not to open her eyes, or scream, or do *something*. But she refused to acknowledge him; wouldn't even listen. After the door had shut, she'd kept her eyes closed. A small part of her mind had been telling her he was in there with her, squatting down right in front, close enough to touch. Just waiting.

A few minutes later, the longest few minutes her pulse had ever known, she'd dared to open one of her eyes, just a slit, and of course she was alone.

Six hours since that. She didn't know whether it seemed longer or shorter. It had been more like time out: a period when she'd stepped away from her life so that she didn't have to deal with what was happening. A period of safety.

It was stupid, but as time had passed and the man hadn't returned, Jodie had come to think of the music as a talisman: it had put a shield up round her, like a spell.

Borrowed time.

Now the player had died, she was no longer safe.

Jodie shuffled against the rock.

Six hours. Was it nearly morning, then? It seemed a little lighter outside, but perhaps it was her imagination. Or the fire. She could see the light from it in the outline of the door, and in the splayed, wavering fingers reaching into the storeroom along the stone walls.

Her back hurt a great deal at the top, on either side of her spine, as if someone had been pressing their thumbs in hard near her shoulderblades. She stretched out her legs. The right threatened to cramp as she moved, and she had to work it carefully: coaxing it first back under her, and then slowly out again, back and forth, until she could straighten it properly without pain.

She rubbed her thighs but could only feel dull pressure; they seemed as cold and dead as meat in a freezer. The backs of her hands, too, right between the finger and thumb. As best she could, she rubbed each hand in turn with the palm of the other. It burned.

It was very quiet outside.

Jodie stood up as much as she could. The world tipped slightly. Her vision starred over; her shoulder hit the wall.

Steady, said the voice in her head.

She forced herself to breathe slowly, and started to move forwards again: a few shuffling steps to reach the door. Small hope that the man in the devil mask had unbolted it and left, but it was always possible. Maybe she would open the door and there'd be a film crew. Her friends and family applauding.

A gentle push on the door; it didn't move. The small hope collapsed instantly. It had been larger than she'd allowed herself to think. But she was still locked inside.

Keep thinking.

The gap at the edge of the door. Nervously, she crouched down a little further and pressed her eye to the hole. Half expecting a needle to be pushed through from the other side.

Still night.

And the man hadn't left. He was lying beside the fire, about ten metres from the storehouse. The great pile of burning wood had decreased, and most of the ground beneath the metal was covered in black and white ash. It was a landscape of dust and ruin, a small pile of blackening wood at the centre. The man lay on the side nearest her, stretched out on a blanket, his back to her, legs slightly curled.

Was he sleeping?

It looked for all the world as if he was.

She took in every other detail she could. It had stopped snowing now. She could see his footprints patterning the ground. They led off mainly in the direction she'd seen him come from earlier, when he'd returned to the fire to heat the screwdriver. Scott must be over there somewhere.

His body, anyway.

Be strong.

But how could she be? She was locked in here, at the mercy of a psychopath who'd tortured her boyfriend, and now appeared to be sleeping calmly by the campfire. How could he do that? Was he exhausted from what he'd done to Scott? She couldn't bear it. She backed away from the door and sat down on the pile of rocks that had been her seat through the night.

Be strong.

No, she told the voice. All that was over. She couldn't break the door down. Even if she could, he would wake up, and then he'd heat bits of metal and start on her. And whatever happened, he would wake up eventually.

Think. You're not done yet.

She looked at the door in despair, watching the firelight flickering round the edge. And she thought: how am I not done? What am I supposed to do to stop this from happening?

For that, the voice had no answer.

4 DECEMBER   **5.00 A.M.**
2 HOURS, 20 MINUTES UNTIL DAWN

Mark

The officer who'd phoned in from the woods was called Bates. He was very young and he looked tired, half frozen and panicked, so I stayed as patient as I could and tried to reassure him that everything was okay. He needed to find out exactly what had happened and keep me informed, I said. He nodded and then didn't do anything.

'That means *now*.'

He didn't nod that time, but at least he ran off to see if there was any news.

I stood up and paced. This had turned into a shit-storm beyond all expectations. Before the report on Pete, Mercer was in trouble but at least he'd been about to head home. Things were out of our hands. Now, I had no doubt, he was heading out to the woods. God only knew what he thought he could achieve. Probably he wasn't thinking much of anything. Another member of his team had been injured, possibly killed, so it would be fear and guilt driving him on.

But mainly I was worried about Pete, and I felt isolated and powerless stuck here at the hospital. Then it occurred to me that I was stuck in a *hospital*, and there was at least something I could do. I ran out of the locker room, down to the main desk, and told them we had an officer injured, possibly seriously, and that he'd be here shortly.

When I got back to the locker room, Bates was on camera again. 'They've brought him out, sir,' he told me. 'He's in the air – they're taking him to the hospital now.'

'They're expecting him. Are we any clearer on what happened? On his injuries?'

'He was stabbed three or four times. In the shoulder and arm.'

Jesus. 'They got the guy who did it?'

'Yes, sir. A guy living rough in the woods. Looks like they walked into his camp and he got edgy.'

'Young or old?'

'Old, I reckon.'

So not Farmer or Reardon, or whatever the fuck he wanted to call himself. At least Pete was out of there and on his way. Stabbed in the shoulder and arm, though – no wonder Bates looked frightened. Christ. Whatever the pressures we'd been under here, sitting safely in the hospital had made it too easy to forget the dangerous environment the search teams had been working in.

'Have you been in tonight?' I said. 'The woods?'

'No, sir. Glad to say, I'm manning the communications here. I wouldn't go in there for love or money.'

I was about to tell him that he wouldn't need to now, not the way the investigation had turned, but then I remembered Mercer.

'Is Hunter there yet?'

'No, sir.'

'Hang on.'

I loaded the map of the woods on another screen. The updates were still working. Yellow circles representing the search teams were bunched in clusters at various points in the woods.

The screen blinked once, and all of them moved a little closer to the road.

Earlier on, Pete had been doubtful about the mechanics of the search, and that doubt appeared to have been vindicated. None of the teams had got very far before being recalled. On screen, the true difficulty was less obvious than it must have been when you were out there, faced with the woods and the snow, but it was still clear enough. It had always been an impossible task.

So you think he's just there, then? Waiting for us?

It had seemed ridiculous when Pete said it. Why would the 50/50 Killer want to be caught? And yet I couldn't help thinking that he must have known how hard it was going to be, and that if he really was waiting for us there, it wasn't as foolish as it might have seemed. Wouldn't he have expected us to be hampered by the terrain? To lose time – even men – in the type of encounter Pete had been involved in?

I rubbed my face.

Reardon could have kept Scott and Jodie at their flat. He could have taken them anywhere. Why the woods?

There had to be a reason for the deviation in his MO. For taking them out into the wilds; for allowing us to discover his real face and, from there, his real name. He had given himself to us and then begun playing out his game in one of the most inaccessible places he could have chosen. From what he'd given us, we would find him eventually. But we wouldn't find him before dawn.

The screen blinked again and everyone moved a fraction closer to the road.

He's still being careful … It's what he's being careful about *that's changed.*

Careful to escape us until dawn. To see if we could find him before then and save Jodie McNeice's life.

Earlier on, the idea had seemed outlandish. But if not that, *why these woods*? Why let Scott go? I was aware of a sinking sensation inside myself. Something was wrong.

'I'll be back in a minute.'

'Yes, sir.'

I didn't want to talk to Officer Bates any more. I minimised the window, leaving the connection open, and sat there breathing slowly, trying to get a grip on myself.

There was nothing I could do. It was out of my hands.

I repeated that to myself. I didn't believe it.

I was meant to be preparing a summary for Hunter – the facts of the day – but instead I was staring at the map. The screen updated: everyone moved a little further away from her. From Jodie and Reardon.

We're going to find her.

All tiredness had left me now. In fact, my heart felt wired to the mains. It was pounding hard, the way it did whenever I thought about Lise and what had happened that day; the same racing, sinking feeling I got whenever I relived the event in my head, building inexorably towards the loss of her, the absence.

Jodie's going to be fine.

I promise.

I found myself reaching out to the desk, picking up the photograph of Jodie that we'd taken from Scott's wallet.

It reminded me. We only take photographs of the happy times; so in themselves they tell us nothing. Scott carried this around without knowing Jodie was having an affair. I wondered what secrets lay hidden behind the picture taken on the Roseneils' wedding day. I wondered what secrets Lise might have kept from me.

Still staring at the photograph of Jodie, I thought about Lise. In the canteen, Greg had guessed I didn't have a girl to drag cross-country with me, but in reality nothing could have been further from the truth. The fact was that she'd been with me every minute of that journey, just as she had every other day for the last six months. She'd surfaced in one form or another throughout the day. After my first interview with Scott, I'd been worried I was empathising with him too much. In reality, it was inevitable.

I closed my eyes.

The image that came to me was of Daniel Roseneil. His bruised, downturned face as he gave that faltering testimony; the peaks of horror emerging from the mist of his memory. After watching that, I'd told myself that I didn't blame him for not remembering. I'd been thinking about how often we tell someone we can't live without them, that we'd die for them, that we'd do anything. About how rarely we're called on those promises. When it came to the victims left behind, I didn't blame any of them for allowing themselves to forget. Of course I didn't.

I opened my eyes, looking at the photograph of Jodie again.

Scott was different from Daniel in one way, wasn't he? Different from me, too.

My hand twitched, as though it was about to do something of its own accord.

Scott hadn't lost her. Not yet.

All Mercer had wanted was a bit of faith; I realised, too late, that I'd found some. *Jodie is alive in those woods.* The panic intensified. The screen blinked, the circles almost all at the road now, and it grew ever stronger.

This time I let my hand go where it wanted. My fingers found the edge of the desk, and I used it to push my chair back, stood up too quickly. I might be about to get myself into trouble, but I didn't want to think about that. Didn't want to stand here and do nothing. Not again.

Perhaps it wasn't too late.

For the first time all day, I knew exactly what I had to do.

4 DECEMBER   **5.05 A.M.**
2 HOURS, 15 MINUTES UNTIL DAWN

Scott

'You're not here,' Scott said. 'I know what you are and where you're from. You were never here.'

In the dream, he was back in his front room, sitting on the settee, feeling the comfortable, familiar sturdiness of it supporting him. There was a large clock on the opposite wall – that shouldn't be there. The minute hand was ticking round, but it was going too quickly. He could literally see it moving.

Six o'clock.

One minute past six.

Two minutes.

The man in the devil mask – only a man, a man in a mask – was squatting in front of him, leaning his elbows on Scott's knees. He had never been here in the flat with him. The man was a memory from that other place, from the stone building, where he had hurt him so badly. As the night passed, he seemed able to invade every thought and memory Scott had.

Five minutes past six.

The weight on his legs was familiar, as were the things the man kept saying. His dreaming mind was dressing the memories of the stone building in thinner and thinner cloth.

204

'I'm not here?' the man said, and then glanced left and right, before looking back. 'Tell me where we are.'

'In my front room.'

'At home?'

'Yes.'

'Where you live with Jodie?'

Scott didn't say anything, because it occurred to him: Jodie ... where was she? It was twenty past six. She should have been back from work by now. He looked to his right and saw that the living-room window was open, the curtains wavering slightly. A second later, a very cold breeze touched him, and he began to shiver uncontrollably.

Jodie wasn't here at the moment, and he told himself not to think about it. She was simply in another part of the flat.

'It's all right.' The man noticed his confusion. 'She's in the room next door, isn't she?'

He thought about it and nodded slowly. Yes, that was right. Jodie had gone to lie down. She'd come back from work looking so sad that he'd immediately asked her what was wrong. Nothing, she'd said, dropping her handbag on the chair and then collapsing next to him. He'd tried to coax it out of her. Bad day? Want to talk about it? She hadn't, and they'd just sat there for a while.

'She's asleep,' he said.

The man in the devil mask inclined his head. 'You had an argument.'

'No.'

'You did, but you don't realise it.'

Scott shook his head – but actually he wasn't sure. Perhaps the man was right. All he could remember was that they'd been sitting there and, as happened so often, he hadn't been able to make the right gesture or say the right thing. Maybe he'd felt so frustrated and powerless that, rather than just not saying the right thing, he'd ended up saying the wrong one instead.

It happened too much. But she was so unhappy! And it frustrated him that there seemed to be nothing he could do. Her moods were immune from him. She came home unhappy; he could do nothing. The next day, the same; and the next. Every day rhymed with the last.

'It's all right,' the man reassured him. 'It's what happens.'

'No.'

The curtains wavered again. The pressure on his knees increased as the man leaned forwards conspiratorially.

'Why is she through there, then?' he said.

'She's had a bad day.'

'She's unhappy. Do you know why?'

Scott shook his head. He wished he did. If he knew what was wrong he could do something to change it and try to make her happy again. He would do anything, if only he knew that it would help.

'Do you want me to tell you?' the man said.

'Yes.'

'Do you remember when we talked about her fucking Kevin Simpson in that dirty little hotel?'

'Yes.'

'It hurt when it happened. But you're over that now, aren't you?'

He nodded slowly.

In the time afterwards, it had felt as though there would never be a single minute when he wouldn't think about it, never mind a day or a week, but eventually that minute had come. And then the day, and then the week. Now he hardly thought about it at all.

'Don't you think that she's over it, too?' the man said.

Scott just looked at him.

'You felt hurt. Now that's faded. And it's the same for her. When it happened, she felt so guilty that she was prepared to give up everything she'd worked for just to save her relationship with you. And because the guilt has faded, she regrets that decision.'

Scott shook his head. 'No.'

The man said, 'Whether you like it or not, she no longer feels guilty. She doesn't hate herself. All that's gone. But the choice she made. She gave something up for you and she has to live with that every day.'

'No.'

'She does.' The man nodded. 'She works at a job she hates and then she comes home to you and your stupid paintings. There's no guilt any more, only loss. And she's started resenting you for that.'

'It was her choice. I didn't force her.'

'She doesn't love you, Scott. She's not worthy of your love in return.'

He started to cry again. 'She does still love me.'

'I know what she thinks better than you do.'

Scott looked down and saw that the man was holding something. Not the hot screwdriver this time, not the knife. It was just a single sheet of paper. But for some reason he found that even more terrifying, and he pushed himself back against the settee.

The world blurred slightly; the room grew darker and colder, and his shivering intensified. The man was little more than a black shape in the shadowy air, light from some unidentifiable source flickering across his red mask.

He put the piece of paper close to Scott's hands and shook it gently. *Take this.* For a moment Scott didn't. The cold had robbed him of dexterity, and the fingers of one hand looked twisted and wrong. But the man pressed it into his other hand and, involuntarily, he gripped it.

Scott turned his face to the ceiling and prayed to God to make this stop, but everything above him was lost in darkness.

'You think she just had a bad day at work,' the man said. 'But that's not what really happened.'

'Yes, it is.' He started crying. 'That's all it is.'

'Read that, then,' the man told him. 'Here.'

The man picked a torch up off the floor, switched it on and moved it round, holding it close to Scott's ear so that the light shone back, forming a ring on the page like the stain from a coffee cup. Halos of beige and brown spread out. The man tilted the torch and the circle became an ellipse.

'Read it.'

Scott closed his eye and shook his head. But for some reason the words started coming to him anyway.

```
I think maybe I'd like to see you. I do feel
bad about it, because I'll have to lie to Scott,
but I think it might do me good.
```

How could this be happening? But then he realised he was dreaming. It didn't matter what he did, how tightly he shut his eye. The words were on the page and the page had already been read.

```
Can you get the day off tomorrow? Though, having
said that, I'm sure one of your hundred skivvies
will hold the fort for you!
```

He opened his eye. Yes, he thought, Jodie and Kevin. He remembered now.

```
I could call in sick and come round. Would that
be okay?
```

The man peered round the edge of the paper. 'She was fucking Kevin Simpson again.'

'I don't believe you.'

He flicked the light to Scott's face and then to the page again. Directing him. There was something on the back of the paper, Scott noticed. Curling black script, handwriting. He wasn't meant to see that.

'This is how much she loves you,' the man said. 'You put up with her, suffer for her, worry about her, and she goes and fucks somebody else.'

But Scott was distracted: he was trying to make out what was written on the back of the page. It was all in reverse, but he caught one word here, another there.

The man seemed to realise this, and he took the torch away.

'Your relationship means nothing,' he said.

'No.'

'She cheated on you. You're stupid to think you love her.'

'She would have told me!' Scott was sobbing. He wouldn't believe it. 'She would have told me.'

And just like that, the man in the devil mask was gone.

Scott looked around.

The front room had become lighter again. The clock was gone. Everything seemed normal. But the silence: it was heavy and full. It was as if something had disappeared and taken the volume with it, but soon it would return, louder and more violent than before.

Get out.

For a moment, a spell had been cast on him. His hands wouldn't move; his legs wouldn't. Then he was on his feet, stumbling towards the corridor, his mind insistent as it reasserted control. All that was over; it was done with. There was no man. Not any more. No hot screwdrivers or hammers or knives. He was safe at home with Jodie—

The bedroom. He leaned against the doorframe and looked at her. She was lying facing away from him on the far side of the bed, her legs curled up, her chest rising and falling gently as she slept. *She would have told me.* Light from the hall rested on the floor and the corner of the bed, but it didn't quite reach her. The room was so quiet and peaceful that it formed a knot in his throat. For some reason, even though she was right there, he knew she was unreachable. Gone from him.

'I love you,' he said.

There was no response, just the same steady breathing. He walked over to join her. The bed creaked with his weight, then he swung his legs up and moved across to lie behind her, his chest against her back. He put his arm round her and pressed his wet face into her hair. She didn't wake up.

'No matter what you've done,' he whispered, 'I love you.'

And in her sleep, she reached up and took hold of his hand.

DECEMBER   **5.10 A.M.**

HOURS, 10 MINUTES UNTIL DAWN

Mark

Everything was more straightforward; the clear sense of purpose I felt had removed almost all the pressure and tension that had been growing in me throughout the day. Even making my way through the hospital corridors was simpler than before. It seemed less busy, easier to negotiate. Maybe was because this time I put myself in the middle of the corridor and walked. People could move around me. We all had similar business to conduct here on some level, after all.

When I arrived at Scott's room, I nodded to the security guard, and then walked in, closing the door behind me. Scott was asleep, although nowhere near as peacefully as before. He was lying on his side, his face contorted in an uncomfortable frown.

Dreaming. Probably nothing good.

I walked across, touched his shoulder—

'Wha—?'

—and he jerked awake, frightened and confused. I left my hand there for a second, and gave him what I hoped was a reassuring look.

'It's okay, Scott. It's only me.'

I moved away and took my seat on the chair. He breathed heavily, then rolled onto his back and took a moment to compose himself. Finally, with some effort, he levered himself up into a sitting position.

'Bad dream?' I said.

He ignored me. 'Have you found her?'

'No.' I avoided the false assurances I'd given him earlier on. As things stood, it wasn't a case of 'Not yet.'

I said, 'We're having some problems with that.'

'Problems.'

'It's a difficult area to search. A lot of ground to cover. And in this weather, in the dark, it's proving difficult.'

Immediately, he looked nervous.

I pressed on anyway. 'So we're going to need your help. We're going to need you to tell us a bit more than you have done until now.'

'But I've told you everything I remember.'

'I know you have.' Be patient with him. 'And you've done well. B
we need to go a little further.'

He shook his head at the prospect. I stared at him impassively. In o
last conversation, we'd talked about the game the killer played, and he
asked me: *So I betrayed Jodie?* There was no definite answer I could gi
to that, not even now, but deep down Scott knew the truth. And he
had a couple of hours alone to dwell on it. His mind was telling hi
to keep his back to what happened, and now here I was, threatening
make him turn round.

'If we don't find Jodie soon,' I said, 'there's a good chance we wor
find her at all.'

'But I don't know. I can't remember.'

I was sympathetic, but there was almost a petulance to him.

'What else did the man talk to you about?'

'I don't know.'

I just looked at him, letting him know that he wasn't getting off t
hook that easily. It was in his face that he could remember somethin
Even if he couldn't, he was going to have to try.

The tension in the silence steadily increased, but I was implacable.
the end, I forced him to break it.

'All I know is, we talked about Jodie.'

'That's not all you know. I appreciate it's hard, Scott.'

He started to cry. 'I don't know.'

My instinct was to back off, but that was no good. I kept looking
him – the same implacable expression as before – and settled back
the chair, trying to dilute my expression with some compassion, son
understanding.

'I know what you're thinking,' I said. 'I know what you're afraid of.

He shook his head and looked away.

'You're scared that you left her to die,' I said, 'and you don't thir
you'll be able to forgive yourself for that, or else you think people w
judge you for it. I understand more than you think. But Scott, look
the window. It's not dawn yet.'

I leaned forwards.

'She's still alive. Whatever you think you've done, it's not too late
take it back. I envy you that.'

He sniffed, shook his head again. 'You don't understand.'

'What did you talk about?'

Nothing. He was trembling.

I sighed to myself. I had no idea whether what I was going to say next would make the slightest bit of difference, but it was all I had left.

Empathy.

'Listen for a minute.' I checked my watch. 'It won't take long, and I think we've still got some time. I want to tell you something.'

We were on holiday, camping. This beach campsite. We went swimming. Just messing about, really, but we drifted out of our depth, and didn't realise the current was so strong. We called for help, but there wasn't anybody on the beach. So we just had to swim for it. And basically, I made it to shore and she didn't. There was nothing anyone could have done.

That was what I'd told the rest of the team earlier on in the canteen. But in its own way, this was my version of the photograph of Jodie that Scott kept in his wallet. It was a snapshot of an event in my life. One I kept close at hand; one I was prepared to share with people. And like that passport photo, it was only a small part of the whole story. The real truth is always between the lines. It's hidden inside what you don't say.

We were on holiday, camping. This beach campsite.

My memories of the evening were disjointed, as though what happened later had reached back and smashed a hammer onto the time leading up to it, leaving me only fragments to sort through. The tension of tent poles: I remember feeding them awkwardly through the tight canvas loops, curving them into position, the tent stretching itself into shape. Lise wafting away mosquitoes as we hammered pegs into the packed, sandy ground. Her bikini bottom was tangled slightly at the back.

We went swimming. Just messing about, really, but we drifted out of our depth, and didn't realise the current was so strong.

It was me that noticed first. I wasn't a confident swimmer and the sea was slightly rougher than I was comfortable with, so I felt the need to put my toes down on the seafloor every so often. And at one point I tried and went under. When I came back up, I was shocked, coughing.

Panicking.

'It's all right,' Lise said. 'Just swim back to shore.'

But I was floundering, and I accidentally kicked her in the stomach; I still remember the soft-hard impact. She told me, 'Calm down,' but I wasn't listening, just clawing for the shore, instinct taking over and telling me I needed to get myself safe above and beyond anything else.

Swim, I thought. Swim as hard as you can.

I noticed how rough the water was this far from shore: choppy on th
surface, full of motion underneath around my chest and legs. I swar
hard, for what felt a long time, and when I stopped for a moment I sav
that I was further from the beach than when I'd started.

Lise had been swimming, too; we were still very close to each othe
at that point. I looked at her and saw my own panic reflected back a
me. That was what did it. I'd never seen her look scared before; she wa
normally so calm, so together.

'Scream,' she told me seriously.

We called for help, but there wasn't anybody on the beach.

I'd never shouted for help in my life and it sounded ridiculous an
wrong, but I screamed. I screamed as loud as I could, over and ove
Above the noise of the waves I could hear her doing the same.

I was half shouting, half swimming when a wave punched me on th
back, knocking me under. My lungs filled with water, and I was cough
ing and choking as I came up, my eyes stinging. The world around m
was just a blur, a smear. Lise was further away, a misty smudge of colou
In my head, curtains of dark water were pulling themselves round he
Taking her from me.

So we just had to swim for it.

I started out again, thrashing as hard as I could, blind except for flashe
of the sky. But I was panicking too much to control myself, and the se
kept pushing me under. I understood very clearly that I was going t
die, and I'd never felt frightened on such a primal level before. Fightin
against the waves, I was tensing my arms so hard that the muscles starte
to spasm. Mentally, I was absent: just an animal with death in sigh
struggling desperately to escape. I wasn't thinking about Lise. At tha
moment, all that mattered was myself.

And basically, I made it to shore and she didn't.

It was a minute, if that, before I staggered up the beach. I was onl
wearing shorts, but I might as well have been swimming fully clothed. M
arms and legs felt waterlogged: heavy and tired. Immediately, I collapse
to my knees on the sand and then forward onto my elbows, coughin
out water, then heaving in air. When I could breathe, I forced myself t
my feet and turned to scan the sea. Calling out for her.

There was nothing anyone could have done.

The funeral. Friends, colleagues; my parents and hers. The sea neve
surrendered Lise's body, so all these people were standing round a patc
of land that could never genuinely be called a grave. Her mother's scar
was blowing softly to one side in the breeze. She told me:

'There was nothing you could have done, Mark.'

I'd started crying when she said that, but I'd accepted it anyway, and at single sentence lay at the heart of the picture I kept to show people. ust as someone seeing the photograph of Jodie would smile and say mething complimentary, so the people listening to me would nod and e sympathetic. There wasn't anything anyone could have done, so it was d, but everything was right with the world. They wouldn't look for the uth below the surface.

But I couldn't hand Scott that picture. If I wanted to know his secrets, had to be prepared to show mine.

was standing on the beach,' I said. 'And I was looking for her, trying see her. Screaming her name. And suddenly, there she was.'

I'd spotted her out in the water, about fifty metres from shore. By heer blind luck, I'd escaped the current, while Lise had made hardly any rogress at all.

'She was shouting something, but I couldn't hear it. I don't know if he could even see me. Maybe she was just screaming.'

I could see her, though. I could see the terror and panic and pain on er face.

Scott had turned back to look at me. He'd stopped crying as well, lthough the part of his face that was visible was red and swollen, gleam- ng in the light. I wasn't naïve enough to think that telling him this story as going to flick a switch and make everything okay, but at least he was oking at me. Listening to me. At least I'd got him back for as long as could keep him.

'I went back into the water,' I said, 'but only up to my knees. I was aving to her, shouting that she'd be okay, that she just needed to keep wimming. But the sea was so choppy. One minute she was there and hen the next she just wasn't.'

I remembered the last I'd seen of her: a black Y bobbing in the waves. fter that, it was only the waves, and I was screaming, 'You'll be okay' o nothing.

'You didn't go back in?' Scott said.

'I wanted to,' I said. 'I started to. But I didn't dare. I was too scared to o back into the water. And so my fiancée drowned.'

Scott stared at me, shocked. I could hear him breathing.

I smiled as best I could.

'I know deep down there was nothing I could have done. I could ave gone back in, and then I'd probably have drowned too. She was a stronger swimmer than I was. But I still blame myself for what I didn't do. I could have tried to save her, but I didn't because I was too afraid of dying myself. Do you understand?'

He nodded slowly.

'And in a way, that's the game,' I said. 'That's all the killer is, that's all he does. He stacks it so that there's too much to cope with, too much to deal with, until your only option is to walk away. Anybody would do the same. But I can't imagine what she was thinking when she died. I can't bear to.'

When I said that, Scott looked so desperate, so helpless, that I wanted to take it all back. But we were in the thick of it now; it would be harder to retreat than to push through to the other side.

He said, 'I abandoned her.'

I nodded.

'You probably did. But right now you're in the same position I was in when I was standing on that beach. Your girlfriend is still alive, Scott.'

One of the ground rules for the interview. This time, I actually believed it.

'So you've got one up on me. In your own way, you can still go back in there and save her. If you don't, you'll live with it, and everybody will understand. But please, don't make the same mistake that I did. You won't be able to live with yourself. Do you understand what I'm saying?'

His voice was sad as he whispered again: 'I abandoned her.'

I leaned forwards, clasping my hands together. If this was going to happen, it would happen now.

'What do you remember?'

The question hung in the air for a moment, and the only sound was the soft beeping of Scott's pulse on the machine by the bed. It was calm now.

'He showed me something. A piece of paper.'

'In the woods? You were in an old stone building, and he was talking to you for a long time. Is that when he showed you this piece of paper?'

'I think so.'

'Did you read it?'

'I didn't want to. He made me.'

'What was it?'

'It was an email.' He took a deep breath. 'She was having an affair with Kevin Simpson. Her ex-business partner. It was something about that.'

'Okay.'

He shook his head. 'You knew that, didn't you?'

'No. We knew she'd spent some time at Simpson's house. I didn't want to tell you before. The man who abducted you did the same thing to Kevin Simpson. He was murdered yesterday morning.'

'Good.'

I didn't reply.

Scott didn't say anything, either. His face had grown curiously blank, but it seemed hard to maintain and was threatening to collapse into something else. Anger? Grief? Self-pity? I couldn't tell.

Keep it moving.

'So he showed you this email,' I said. 'What happened next?'

'I told him I gave up,' he said. 'Just like that. "I give up." I kept saying it over and over again so that he'd understand and stop hurting me.'

I nodded. 'And then?'

'He ... let me go.' Scott sniffed. 'Oh, God, he let me go. As easy as that. I left her.'

I was willing him on, but I forced myself to keep calm.

'He untied you? How did you know which way to go?'

'No.' Scott frowned. 'He walked with me for a while. Just a few minutes, I think. We crossed a river, crossed a path. All the time he was talking to me, telling me he'd take care of everything, that I'd made the right decision. He even told me I could come back if I changed my mind. Then we stopped and he pointed into the trees. He told me what direction to head in.'

We crossed a river, crossed a path.

I wanted to run downstairs as fast as I could. The search teams had been looking in the wrong area. The river was north of the top bar of the 'n' and the camp was just a few minutes from there.

He looked at me with something close to desperation: 'And ... so I ran.'

I gave him a gentle smile, then walked over, sat on the edge of the bed and put my hand on his shoulder.

'Thank you,' I said. 'You've done everything you can. The next time I come up here will be to tell you we've found Jodie and we've got the man who did this to you.'

He started crying again. But he nodded.

I gave his shoulder a careful squeeze, then stood up and walked across to the door. As I opened it, I turned to look back. Light from the hall rested on the floor and the corner of the bed, but it didn't quite reach him.

'Officer.'

He looked suddenly quite peaceful, despite his tears.

'Whatever happens, thank you.'

'I'll be back soon, Scott.'

I went out into the corridor, closing the door softly behind me. The and only then, I started to run.

4 DECEMBER
1 HOUR, 50 MINUTES UNTIL DAWN

5.30 A.M

Eileen

She tried phoning John one last time.

Her finger trembled as she pressed [redial], and her entire hand shoo as she held the receiver to her ear. One last time. Since he'd switched h phone off, she'd repeatedly tried calling him, convinced that this time h would answer. But on each occasion, there was just—

Beep, beep, beep

Eileen threw the receiver across the study. It cracked open on the wa and clattered to the floor in two neat pieces, the circuit board leaning ou on stubby wires. She couldn't even break a phone properly.

She slumped down, and the chair rolled back on its wheels until nudged the wall behind.

The second bottle of wine was on the table in front of her. She somehow managed to get two-thirds of the way down before abandor ing it and going to bed. The empty glass was covered with last night misty fingerprints. Even so, as late as it was, the idea of pouring out th remainder was appealing. Except it was no longer even too late to b drinking; now it was too early. And two hours of sleep was never goin to be enough to cancel out the debt in her head. The proof of that wa lying broken against the far wall. Such an explosion of frustration wa totally unlike her. The alcohol had mixed with her emotions, goading he into stupid, thoughtless action.

Why have you done this to me, John?

Had she really asked so much of him? They were supposed to be partnership – that was what she'd dedicated her life to over the years. S when he'd collapsed her world had collapsed with him and she'd neve felt so afraid, not ever. The idea that it could happen again, that he woul even risk putting her through that …

Had she asked so much?

And yet he couldn't even phone her. One simple thing, set against everything she'd given him, and he couldn't even do that.

Eileen's thoughts were like a car travelling through fog. All she could do was let the emotions guide her. She was sad and she was angry, but more than anything she was hurt. Deeply hurt.

This was her husband who had done this to her. After all the love and support and the pain, after asking so little in return, he'd just … put her aside for something more important to him, something which could destroy both of them. He'd lied to her, devalued her, given her nothing back. He didn't seem to care how he made her feel.

He doesn't care about you at all.

Eileen could feel her face tensing. She realised she was sitting in his chair, staring at the curtains opposite with an expression of bitter hatred.

After the phone call from Hunter, she'd stood there aimlessly for a time, before dialling John's mobile. It had rung and rung – and then cut dead. Eileen had stared at the handset in disbelief for a second, then tried again. There had just been that undulating beep. He had turned it off.

He *knew*.

After that, she'd spent a few minutes walking purposefully from room to room, switching on all the lights in the house.

'I think you should know,' Hunter had said, 'what case your husband is working on.'

A click of the switch had illuminated each room, but already she'd been moving on to the next. Each room, a slap: we have an emergency here; everyone wake up.

'He's after the man who killed Andrew Dyson.'

She'd done her best to keep any surprise out of her voice and fill it instead with indifference: 'Oh?'

As she'd gone through the house, bringing it quickly to life, a feeling of panic had been trailing close behind, spurring her on.

'He's made a huge mistake in keeping quiet about that, and not just with you. He's been removed from the case.'

'Well, I'm sure you're pleased about that, Detective Hunter.'

Even keeping moving, she'd found her throat was tight, her breath thin, as though her heart had become a fist which was pushing its way slowly upwards. There was nothing she could do to stop it bursting out, only delay the inevitable.

217

'He'll be home with you shortly, anyway. Where he belongs.'

By the time she had finished illuminating the house – standing there in the bright, cold kitchen, unsure what to do next – the fear had lodged in her windpipe. He'd lied to her. How could he? She had stood in the kitchen, remembering the last words she'd said to Hunter before cutting him off.

'And that's what you woke me up to tell me? You actually imagine I didn't know that already? You underestimate John and you underestimate me. Do us all a favour, and stop wasting our time.'

Had she managed to inject the correct amount of venom and derision into her voice? Probably not. She was sure Hunter could tell how upset and angry she was, so the denial would only have made it worse. But he was insignificant to her: one of those men who, incapable of raising themselves up, were forced to push others down instead and take whatever pleasure they could from that. Deep inside, those men always knew exactly how pathetic they were. So let him have his triumph. Ultimately it was at John's expense, anyway, and although her defence of her husband had come instinctively at the time, it had been as much about her as about him. She no longer cared how he might feel.

He cut you off.

And right then the panic had hit her. It hadn't knocked her over and she didn't fall, but nevertheless it was too much. She'd taken slow, deep breaths, trying to calm herself. And she'd stayed like that, deliberately thinking of nothing, for a long time, until she realised that her fingers were digging hard into her arms, and that she needed to do something.

So: back upstairs, each step a mountain. All the time, she'd been telling herself: It was a mistake. He didn't mean to cancel the call, didn't mean to turn off his mobile.

He wouldn't do that to me.

Back in the study, she'd picked up the phone again.

And again.

Until now, finally, it was broken.

Eileen walked over to the computer and looked at the wall behind it. At the display John had made.

He'd tacked up fifty, maybe sixty, sheets of paper to form a collage of different colours, shapes and sizes. There were printouts from old files, invariably the ones containing the single detail that had finally unlocked the investigation for him. Press clippings and articles. His framed certificates. Pictures of the team.

All of it together formed a snapshot of his state of mind. John used it to focus his ideas and draw inspiration from, but to Eileen, if she blurred her eyes, it gave her an insight into his state of mind. These were the things that occupied him and filled his thoughts.

And where was she in all this? Where did his wife fit in?

The answer was that she didn't, not on the wall. John had kept the two sides of his life separate, and so instead of Eileen becoming lost among his work there were two pictures on the desk by the computer. The first was a reprint of the photograph downstairs, the one from their wedding day. The second picture, beside it, was simply of her and had been taken more recently. I loved you then, he seemed to be saying; time has passed, and I still love you now.

She blinked away tears – *No, don't* – and looked back at the wall.

The newest sheets had been added to the right-hand side of the display. Here she found a small photograph of Andrew Dyson, the man her husband had lost and whose murder had been the tipping point for him. Beside it, John had put up the eulogy he'd been preparing to read at Andrew's funeral, at the moment when everything finally tumbled down.

> *I fall asleep in the full and certain hope*
> *That my slumber shall not be broken;*
> *And that though I be all-forgetting,*
> *Yet shall I not be all-forgotten,*
> *But continue that life in the thoughts and deeds*
> *Of those I loved.*
>
> **EPITAPH OF SAMUEL BUTLER**

Eileen read it again, concentrating on the last three lines.

I won't be forgotten. I will continue my life in the thoughts and deeds of those I loved.

They were words that John had taken to heart. She had seen the sorrow he still carried with him over what had happened. And his work was so important to him; the tension and frustration his incapacity had caused him over the last two years had been obvious. She'd seen it there while he was recovering, in the listless way he'd moved about the house. Even at the beginning, when she could pretend to herself that he'd never return to work in any capacity, she'd known he was already sensing the bars that had appeared. The barrier between John's nature and his broken ability. And this terrible man beyond them, who had done that to Andrew, and to him.

For the last two years, those bars had cast a shadow of sadness on him and after a time it was only Eileen's fear that had kept them in place. Because she loved him, she had relented, lifting them and allowing him beyond, on the promise that he didn't wander far. And now, that man in sight once again, he had. Had she been so blind as to not realise that it was inevitable? He was her husband; she knew what he did. Long ago she'd loved him for his dedication, his hard work, his commitment to helping people. To saving them.

Now, after his breakdown, those same characteristics filled her with dread. What if it happened again?

Eileen sat down and closed her eyes.

She should have known it would come down to this. In asking what she had of John, she'd been attempting to stop him being the man she had loved for all those years. He'd tried to be that new person for her, but it was impossible for him, and it was that difference – the discrepancy between what they each needed from him now – that was tearing them apart. At that moment, it seemed impassable. She couldn't bear it.

So Eileen sat for a time in his chair, eyes closed, fingers rubbing slowly back and forth along her lower lip, not knowing what to do. It felt like he was a speck on a dark horizon. She was too frightened to keep watching, but what choice had he left her? He had taken her life along with him without her consent.

All right, John, she thought. *If this is what you need ...*

She sat there for a while longer, thinking. And then she got up, walked slowly across to the phone, and began to put the pieces back together.

4 DECEMBER   **5.50 A.M**
1 HOUR, 30 MINUTES UNTIL DAWN

Mark

Thirty minutes after my interview with Scott, I was back in the locker room, listening to the clank of water in the pipes and looking at a piece of Scott's artwork. Greg had been working at the flat and the evidence he'd gathered there had been added to the file – silently, I noted. He hadn't made any effort to contact us here. By now, he would have known the repercussions of his actions, and he would also have seen what was happening at the woods. I wondered what he was thinking.

The middle laptop showed the onscreen map. Most of the circles were clustered together at the comms van, but a small group of four was on the move, a quarter of the way up the screen.

The updates were painful. For seconds on end the display was static and they went nowhere. Then a flicker, and a slight adjustment to their position. Progress was excruciatingly slow, but at least they were moving in the right direction.

In the meantime I looked at the artwork. It showed a face, painted in shades of green and yellow, reduced down to blocks of colour. If you blurred your eyes, it made sense, but if you looked here and there, the overall image vanished. It was beautifully done, but the context made it ominous. The face appeared to be screaming as it fell apart, dissolving into a kind of soup.

'I've got the week off,' I remembered Scott saying. 'I was doing some things on the computer. Photo-art stuff.'

'You're an artist?'

'No.'

But the picture was good, I thought. I didn't understand why he was so reticent about acknowledging an obvious talent. The more I looked, however, the more prominent the pain within it seemed. Most of it was my imagination, but still, it was like a howl of anguish. *Help me!*

The map flickered again, the circles moving painfully slowly.

We were doing our best in that regard.

After running back to our makeshift office, I'd reopened the window to the comms team at the woods and sent through an urgent request for attention. I was worried I was going to get Hunter. I didn't know what the fuck I was going to say if I did. But it was Mercer who answered.

He still looked exhausted, but a combination of adrenalin and the bite of the early-morning air had brought some life to him.

'Just arrived.' He glanced off camera, frustrated. 'Hunter's not here yet, but everyone's back at the van. He really has put the search on hold. Everyone knows he's in charge, too, but nobody's called me on it yet.'

'Right.'

'Pete's okay, though,' he said. 'That's something.'

'I heard. We've been searching in the wrong area, sir.'

That caught his attention. He stared into the camera. 'Tell me.'

'I just talked to Scott again. On his way out of the woods, he remembers crossing a river, not far from where he was held.'

As soon as I started speaking, Mercer's attention drifted off-screen again. I guessed he was looking at the map. I did the same, and we saw it at the same time.

'There.'

A small area north of the river. It was hard to tell from the minimal details on display, but it looked like it was meant to represent a clearing in the trees with a handful of small buildings. I double-clicked on it to access more information. There wasn't much, but the report suggested that it might have once been part of a small farm, the buildings used to house animals.

When I read that, I knew we'd found Jodie.

'How is he?' Mercer said.

'He's okay, I think. Or he will be if we can reach Jodie in time.'

'We will,' Mercer said. 'Get the information into the system. I need to move on this before Hunter gets here.'

'Will anyone there go in with you?'

'Someone will.'

He looked at me for a moment. For the first time that day, I was receiving his complete and undivided attention.

'Thank you, Mark.'

'No problem,' I said. 'Take care.'

But already he was gone.

I minimised the window and set about uploading my last interview with Scott – the last one tonight, anyway. There would have to be more over the next few days, but hopefully in those I'd have the chance to treat him a little more kindly. And by then we'd have found Jodie.

It's out of your hands, I'd thought.

And it really was – but I knew the relief I felt wasn't entirely down to that. Talking to Scott had been like confession, the unburdening of a lie that had stained my soul for too long now, and in the aftermath I felt free of it. A part of me was still aching inside, but at least now I'd removed the weight that had been there: pressing down; adding to the pain. At least now that injury could get some air.

I tried to picture Lise, and I still couldn't, not properly; her expression remained in shadow. But finally I could dare to hope about what might be there. I could imagine she might be smiling.

Every few seconds there was a flicker on the screen, and the circles moved a fraction of a centimetre.

Not even halfway there yet.

I needed a distraction, so I turned to the email exchange that Greg had found on Scott and Jodie's computer.

Because of the connection I felt to Scott, there was something sad and even embarrassing about these private details becoming so public. Intimate thoughts and messages were all just evidence now. They were important. The emails provided a link between Jodie and Kevin Simpson, and also gave an insight into the relationship between Scott and Jodie. Their personal problems were integral to the case.

The relationship was the victim.

I clicked through the emails, scanning the contents one at a time. The first was from Kevin. It was tentative, friendly:

```
Was just wondering how you'd been. Feels weird
that you vanished out of my life so totally. I
understand, but it still feels weird. It's okay
if you don't want to reply or if you can't.
```

Perhaps stupidly, I was pleased by the contents. The message had been sent a little over a month ago, and it had the feel of someone re-establishing contact after a long absence. Of course, it didn't matter whether the affair had been long or short – but even so, I felt better for Scott that it hadn't been continuing for the last two years.

Looking at the dates, there had been a break of over a week before Jodie replied. I imagined her weighing it up in that time: considering whether to email back or to let things remain lying where they'd fallen.

```
I'm okay [she wrote eventually]. Getting along
alright. The usual sort of stuff really, nothing
exciting. Hate work though. How's 'our' business
doing by the way? Ho ho.
```

CCL: the business they'd started together, which Jodie had abandoned in order to salvage her relationship with Scott. The next few emails were mainly about that, and playing catch-up on the things they'd both missed. The business was doing well, Simpson told her:

```
I have sixteen employees now. Can you believe
that? I'm a manager! I'm sure you remember I
can't even manage myself.
```

To her credit, Jodie managed to be as gracious as possible in her replies, even though I was sure it must have stung to hear he was making a success of the company without her. Perhaps she was simply trying to reassure herself.

> I'm proud that you've made such a good go of it
> [she wrote]. Although obviously with me there you'd
> have done even better ...
>
> I never wanted you to go [he replied]. I asked you
> not to, remember? Actually, I think the word is
> 'begged', but let's brush over that.

As the emails went on, Jodie's initial caution seemed to ease, and after bit of skirting around history they both relaxed. Jodie appeared relieved to be able to talk, and the messages became longer and more frequent. The regret she felt about leaving CCL was implicit at first, surfacing gradually as she began talking more about her own life. *Getting along alright* she'd said at first, but in her later messages she took that lie apart.

> I hate my job. All I do is punch figures in
> all day and get paid a tiny amount for the
> privilege. But there's nothing I want to do,
> anyway. Everything feels grey and useless. I'll
> be thirty before long and I've got nothing.

That comment – 'I've got nothing' – stood out, summing up the tone of the later messages. Jodie talked as though she'd given up most of the things in life that were important to her, and now wasn't sure it had been worth it for the few that were left.

I winced for Scott as I read it. Inevitably, over the course of the night, I'd ended up feeling close to him. I had to force myself to remain impartial. I wanted to understand and empathise with Jodie's feelings.

I could imagine how it must have felt for her. The one-night stand with Simpson had been a terrible mistake: one which at the time she would probably have done anything to overcome. Giving up the company must have seemed a small sacrifice to make. But then, time passed. And now, although her mistake was in the past, forgotten and forgiven, she was still paying compensation for it. When you give up something important, every day of your life you don't have it any more. Dissatisfied with her job, her life, I imagined Jodie felt she was being punished, over and over again, for a crime that was gone.

How are things with Scott? [Simpson asked]

He wrote that as a throwaway at the end of an email: one simple question among all the others. But Jodie zeroed straight in on it, as though the other things he'd written were static, used to scramble the real topic of conversation. Maybe that was simply hindsight on my part. When you look back, knowing how things will end, it all begins to look like fate.

He's fine [she said]. He just carries on as normal
all the time. He doesn't really notice. But I
can't talk to him about it and I don't know what
I'd say even if I could. I don't know what's
wrong. I'm just being silly but I don't feel
like I'm anything any more.

You shouldn't say that. Do you love him?

There was a break in the messages then. The frequency had increased to about one a day, but it was nearly a week before Jodie eventually replied:

I think I do still love him. It's just that
I don't love anything else. I'm so bored with
it all. There's nothing in my life. Unless
something changes this is how it's going to be
for ever, and when I think about that I have to
go to bed or something. I can't face the world.
But when I get up again it's still there.

That message had been sent less than a week ago. Simpson's reply had come the same day:

You sound so unhappy, Jodie, and I'm really
sorry. Do you want to meet up some time? Only as
friends, I promise - I'm over all that now. You
could come round and I'll stick a pot of coffee
on and we can talk about stuff. Sometimes it
helps to have a fresh pair of sympathetic ears
to moan at, and I'll honestly try to give you
the best advice I can. I have no agenda.

Reading these, I began to feel a bit strange. I was staring at the screen so intensely that the old locker room around me was almost whiting out. I frowned and leaned back. There were only a couple more emails to read, and the first was from Jodie.

Okay [she wrote]. I think maybe I'd like to see you. I do feel bad about it, because I'll have to lie to Scott, but I think it might do me good. I don't know. Can you get the day off tomorrow? Though, having said that, I'm sure one of your sixteen skivvies will hold the fort for you! I could call in sick and come round. Would that be okay?

And then one final email from Simpson:

I can do that, sure. I'll be up and about first thing, so call round any time. If I don't hear from you I'll expect you, but don't worry if you can't make it. Coffee machine already cleaned out ready! Hope I can help. Take care. Kevin x.

I checked the case file to see if any more had arrived, but that was it.

My frown remained.

There had been a lot of assumptions made over the course of the investigation, and one of them was that Jodie and Kevin had been having an affair. But actually, we had no proof of that; we'd just inferred it from the killer's words on the audio recording, and the fact that Jodie had spent the previous day at Simpson's house.

These emails didn't confirm it. The last one Jodie sent would be incriminating out of context, so I imagined it was the one the 50/50 Killer had chosen to show to Scott, but within the body of the entire exchange it was more harmless than it seemed. For all we knew, their encounter could have been as innocent as the emails implied. Perhaps Jodie had gone round to Kevin's house simply to talk over problems with an old friend who wouldn't need filling in on the background.

I felt a burst of nerves in my chest. There was something important here, but I wasn't sure what. I clicked back through the emails.

Do you want to meet up some time? Kevin had written. *Only as friends, I promise – I'm over all that now.*

And earlier on: *I never wanted you to go ... I think the word is 'begged' but let's brush over that.*

No, I thought, let's not. Why did you beg her not to leave?

The answer presented itself a second later, through the voice of the killer.

You think you love her. Don't you.

For Jodie, I realised, what had happened two years ago was a stupid, drunken mistake, but for Kevin Simpson it had been more. They'd been friends at university, colleagues afterwards, and it wasn't enough. What happened had been exactly what he wanted.

I placed that idea down gently, and with a dark thrill I felt it slotting neatly in. I wasn't yet sure what picture I was building up, but I sat there quietly, allowing my thoughts to roam.

After a moment, I opened up the photograph of the spider web at Simpson's house. If Mercer was right, this was how the killer saw the relationship between Kevin and Jodie; this was his intended 'victim'. But if I was right, there hadn't been a relationship as such, certainly not a mutually accepted one. And that wasn't the only difference from the earlier crimes. There was the nature of the game. Jodie wouldn't have had to suffer to save Kevin Simpson. In fact, she hadn't even known there was a choice to be made.

I'd been assuming the 50/50 Killer used torture to make the person with the choice change their mind: either through the pain of their own suffering or through the guilt and grief from their partner's. But despite the torture here, there had been no back-and-forth; no opportunity for the decision to be changed and the victims to switch. Why? Had the differences in the relationship dictated the differences in the game? I tried to think through the repercussions of that. What was he doing?

In the corner of my eye, I saw the screen flicker: the circles moving, making steady but slow progress. Just over halfway there.

Ignore it.

Impressions and ideas were reeling through my mind. I needed something to settle long enough for me to see it. I stared at the spider web design, rubbing my chin, teetering on the edge of understanding.

Jodie

Careful.

She turned the headphone round between her fingers. Her dexterit
was a bit lacking. There was an intense, numbing coldness in her ski
which would have hampered her even without the handcuffs. But also, i
the relative darkness, she could hardly see what she was doing.

At least she knew what she was doing.

Jodie's pulse was fluttering. Timid excitement kept flaring inside he
and she had to resist the urge to shout, or even laugh out loud.

Ever since she'd thought of it, she couldn't start quickly enough. Th
man outside might wake up at any moment. In fact, she wanted to reac
back in time and throttle herself – curled up listening to music, all te
rified and self-pitying. He could have been asleep for hours. She ha
wasted so much time feeling guilty and frustrated and terrified. But the
was no point in thinking back on it.

The headphone was like a small oval stone. She ran it round betwee
her fingers.

Normally, it would slot into her ear and rest there. The cables forme
a Y, one arm slightly shorter than the other. At the base was the plug tha
went into the iRiver.

She had already detached that, discarding the base unit. Then she ha
knelt down by the pile of slabs at the back of the storeroom, taking th
shorter cable and running it back and forth over the sharpest edge of roc
she could find. Cutting the thin plastic and then the wire inside: weaken
ing it until she could snap off the headphone.

Now, crouching by the door, she had about a metre of cable with on
solid curl of plastic at the end.

She checked through the gap in the door. The man didn't appear t
have moved. He was still lying there, apparently sleeping. Apparently
She couldn't be sure because she couldn't see his face. Perhaps he wa
entranced by the fire, his thoughts lost in the flames. Or maybe waitin
for her to try something like this.

Fuck him, though. One way or the other, she would find out.

Just get on with it, the voice told her.

It sounded a lot more confident now – but then it had every righ
to. When she'd collapsed onto the makeshift seat it had kept reassurin

228

er that she wasn't done yet, telling her to go back over what she knew. ven if she'd convinced herself there was nothing, maybe she was wrong. here could be one small detail she'd not considered. A flaw in his plan, 1 opportunity. Her life would be saved or lost because of it.

Years ago, she'd watched a programme on serial killers. There was one she couldn't remember his name – who kidnapped his victims and held 1em for a long time. As it went on, they became pliant, subservient, illing to do anything to please their captor, even though the end result as always the same. The policeman interviewed on camera had calmly xplained that one of the photographs they'd uncovered showed a victim untied, unrestrained – sitting meekly, with the killer's thumb lodged in 1eir eye socket. And that fucking well wasn't going to be her.

So she'd worked back through it, as much as she could bear.

The waste ground.

The ride in the van.

Walking through the woods.

Slipping; nearly falling.

Being locked in here.

Scott screaming.

At that point she'd paused, convinced that she'd missed something. 1e backtracked a little.

Being locked in here. It was something to do with that. She tried her est to recall every sensation, but all she got was a handful of general 1pressions. The voice had told her to observe everything, and she had. /here was it now she needed it?

She thought it over, frantically trying to recall.

The answer had come to her a second later. Immediately, she'd moved ver to the door, kneeling down on the cold stone and searching along 1e edges. Not interested in the hole in the wood any more, but checking 1t the same side, a little further down.

The answer lay in what she didn't remember.

No padlock, no chain, and yet the door was locked somehow.

There. She hadn't been able to reach into the gap between door and :ame to touch it, but the light from the fire had showed it to her in sil-ouette. A thin black line stretching across. That was the lock.

Jodie's pulse had quickened.

She had squatted there for a moment, picking apart the memory. 1e'd ducked down, working her way awkwardly into the storeroom. /hat else? Gradually, she'd convinced herself of what she'd seen on the ay in.

A loop of rusted metal attached to the stone. An old black hook on the door itself.

The excitement had flared.

Now she took one last look through the spy hole to make sure the man hadn't moved. He was still there: still sleeping. It was now or never.

Carefully ... so carefully ... Jodie put the headphone into the spy hole. The door was thick, but the hole was large enough to take her index finger and she used it to push the head through. When it was clear, she fed the cable through after it. It was slow going. The head caught on the rough outer surface of the door, the cable looping out, but she kept feeding it through, and eventually the tension and weight of it dislodged it. The head clattered slightly, and she winced.

Keep going.

More and more cable.

She kept tight hold of the plug. When the cable was almost all through, she pressed her face against her hand, peering through the spy hole as best she could.

The man was gone.

No!

She stared out in disbelief. There was just the fire, crackling and beginning to die, and the ruffled blanket he'd been lying on. She was too late.

Calm down. Think.

Okay, she told herself. Footprints – she should be able to see his tracks in the snow. There were none coming towards her, so surely he hadn't noticed the cable emerging from the door. If he had, wouldn't he have been over here by now?

A fresh set led off to the left, which was the opposite direction from where Scott had been kept, which was the way out of the woods as well. There were no new tracks heading in that direction. Wherever he'd gone it was deeper.

She listened. Nothing.

He's woken up, walked a little way into the woods.

Slowly, Jodie pulled the cable back through. The headphone was oval, curled, a little like a hook. If it could hang in her ear it could—

The cable stopped coming. She took a deep breath and hoped her memory was good. That it wasn't a bolt across the doorframe. She pulled harder.

For a moment, nothing happened. Then there was a tiny screech of old metal as the hook lifted out of its cradle. She pushed the door, and it opened.

Yes!

She stumbled outside. The open space was a shock, but also a treasure. Her heart was hammering. Now that she had her freedom, she must do anything she could to keep it.

The clearing was smaller than she'd thought, no more than fifteen metres to the tree line at the far edge. The fire was closer as well. Immediately, the heat from it warmed her.

To the right, another old stone building. To the left, the footprints leading off to the tree line. Beyond that, between the trees, there was only darkness. The woods were quiet and peaceful – barely any sound. There was a slight early-morning breeze, though: wafting the flames and icing her skin.

The fire cracked.

Run.

But she couldn't run. Scott might still be alive in that other storeroom, and even if he wasn't, she couldn't bring herself to leave him here. She loved him, and he deserved better. If she could – *now* that she could – she had to look after him.

Jodie walked across to the fire. A lot of it had burned out, but a thatch of wood in the centre was still alight. She rummaged at the edges of the ash, picking up one piece of wood, discarding it. Then another.

This one would do. It was the width of her wrist and about a half-metre long, solid and sharp. The end was blackened, but glowing red in places.

Lighter fluid, she thought.

It was there, shielded from the flames by one of the stone columns. She edged round and picked it up. Half full.

That was when she saw him. She froze.

The man with the devil mask was standing in the trees to the left, about ten metres away. Holding the knife and staring at her. Even through the mask, Jodie could tell he was shocked at seeing her free.

She rose slowly to her feet, the lighter fluid in one hand, the smouldering wood in the other. It was awkward because of the handcuffs; she had to hold them pressed together.

He didn't say anything, but took a hesitant step into the clearing. She took a corresponding step back, moving towards the other stone building.

Run.

No. It was too late for that. She could never outpace him.

And whatever happened, after everything she'd done, she wasn't going to leave Scott.

Mark

I opened up the photograph taken of the wall at Carl Farmer's house
moving the window so that it rested alongside the other picture, the spi
der web at Kevin Simpson's.

The first thing I was drawn to was the poem.

> *In the space between the days*
> *you lost the melancholy shepherd of the stars.*
> *The moon is gone and the wolves of space move in*
> *grow bold*
> *and pick his flock off one by one.*

Earlier on, I'd wondered about his mental landscape, trying to imagin
how he saw the world, and the nature of the mental filter that allowed hin
to transform relationships into those ragged *things*. The poem still hadn'
been identified, so we were assuming for now the 50/50 Killer had writter
it himself. It was one of the few insights we had into his state of mind.

I stared at the words. All around them, the spider webs were painte
on the wall like trophies.

The wolves of space.

There was obviously a religious element to the poem, although it wa
far from an orthodox one. The devil mask, too, I thought: he didn't us
it simply to frighten his victims or obscure his identity; he used it becaus
of what it represented to him. Did he see himself as a demon? As som
cold, calculating force of evil?

He studied the couples for such a long time. He listened and watched
carefully drafting designs. Making plans.

These are his notes.

Picking the flock off, one by one.

When he finally visited them, he was equally clinical. There was th
calm, gentle way he spoke to his victims: reassuring them even as he cu
and burned them. No emotion to it; no immediate pleasure taken fron
the torture and pain. He didn't care about the people. He wasn't attack
ing them so much as the relationship between them, and the method
he used were just the means to an end: a way of getting what he wante
from them.

I stared at the screen.

Getting what he wanted from them.

Many of the drafts – even the final versions of the spider webs – were complete, unbroken. The lines were uncut; there were no checks or smears. But when he was finished with his victims the designs were ruined. So he didn't take the relationship away with him: he left it there hanging, broken, on the wall. What he took away was the difference between the two.

He took love.

I continued to stare at the screen, allowing it to come.

That was the reason behind the choice. The torture was directed at one of the couple to force them to give up the other. Then that partner was tortured physically and emotionally, so that when they were finally – mercifully – killed, they would die in the full knowledge that the person they loved had condemned them to it. Reardon isolated the one he murdered, and ripped apart the relationship in their head. He destroyed any illusion they had of the love they thought they'd possessed, taking it from them.

That was why. Reardon really did think he was some kind of devil. And in his own mind, he was doing the devil's work: erasing love from the world one small bit at a time; turning it bad and taking it inside himself. Collecting it.

There was no need for me to open the audio file again to recall the hideous noise he'd made as Kevin Simpson died below him: that sucking, breathing sound. I'd thought at the time that it was as though he'd been drawing Simpson's soul in through his teeth. Now I was convinced that I'd been closer than I'd realised. In his head, the killer had been capturing the love Simpson had once imagined he felt for Jodie.

Picture her in your head now. Imagine her sleeping peacefully in her boyfriend's arms.

The dark thrill in me had intensified. Why had the game with Kevin Simpson been so one-sided? Because the relationship was one-sided. The only person with anything the killer wanted was Simpson himself. He was the one who loved Jodie, knowing that she didn't feel the same in return. She had used him and walked away. The whole game with the emails was the killer making Simpson understand that: turning his love bad so the killer could harvest it. And he didn't need Jodie there to do that.

I hope you understand now how stupid you were. How little she deserved everything you invested in her.

The killer had spelled this out to him, and then taken his ruined emo‑
tions.

I blew out heavily, leaning back in my chair and rubbing my eyes.
was sure I was right.

On the monitor, the small group of circles had reached the stream
Mercer would be there soon. If his theory was true he'd be meeting
Reardon, the wolf of space, very soon, and I felt a chill run through m
at the prospect. But he had four well-trained officers with him. He knev
what he was doing. Rather than being concerned for him, I forced mysel
to will him on. Get there in time. Save Jodie's life. Stop this man doing
what he does.

Reardon's only a man. He's not really a devil.

I had to keep thinking like that. No matter how the 50/50 Killer sav
himself, in reality he was James Reardon, painfully human, and ther
would be clear and understandable reasons for what he did. Causes and
effects. Never excuses, but explanations.

Keeping that in mind, I minimised the photograph of the spider webs
opened the file on James Reardon and began to go over the details, search
ing for the patterns below the surface.

4 DECEMBER   **6.35 A.M.**
45 MINUTES UNTIL DAWN

Jodie

Just one opportunity, she'd told herself, was all she needed. A single ga
in his plans that she could exploit. The voice had been preparing her fo
it all night, but now that the opportunity had arrived, it had deserted
her, left her in silence.

Jodie had no idea what to do. Her mind was blank.

She backed up towards the closed storeroom. The man in the devi
mask took a few careful steps towards her.

'Get back,' she said.

She squeezed the can of lighter fluid towards him. A string of fue
squirted out into the snow, not quite reaching his feet.

He stopped where he was and held out his hand. 'Give me that.'

She glanced behind her to make sure of her footing, and then stepped
back until she was nearly touching the storeroom door. Now she was here
she was committed. She wouldn't let him get anywhere near Scott again.

The man left his hand out, as though she was bound to reconsider, see sense. Now that he'd got over the shock, she could tell that he was angry. Really angry. These were the first emotions she'd seen from him, and she thought: *Good. Be angry, you fucker.* She hated him. Although she was frightened, she also wanted to hurt him for what he'd done. Kill him if she could. Rip him to pieces.

Come and see what you get.

The threat of the fuel and the burning wood might be enough to keep him away from her, but she couldn't stop him moving – not without tackling him directly.

He circled round slowly, trying to approach her from the far side of the fire. The flames obscured him for a moment, and all she could see was the devil's face, and then he was beyond them, back in sight.

Slow, cautious movements.

He stopped at the edge of the clearing, and she realised he'd cut off her escape route. She could still attempt to run towards town, but now he was even closer. There were miles of wood, and she'd be running with him right on her heels. If there'd ever been a chance of making it before, it was gone.

Keeping her eyes on the man, Jodie reached and pulled the door. Perhaps if Scott was still alive, and she could get him out of there, they might stand a chance of fighting off this man together.

'Why don't you put that down?'

She shook her head.

The man was struggling to control his temper. 'Get back into that room.'

'Fuck you.'

'If you get back in there,' he said, gritting his teeth, 'we can both pretend this never happened.'

The door wouldn't open. She glanced behind her once – there was a bolt sliding across this one – then very quickly back at the man.

In that time, he'd taken a step forward.

The door was locked more securely than hers had been. She could undo it, but not without devoting effort and attention to it, and he clearly wasn't about to allow her that. She'd need both hands, too.

'I'm not going to hurt you,' he said.

Another step.

'This is just a game.'

When he said that, something rose up inside her. *Pay attention*, the voice had told her when Scott was screaming. *Use it when you can.* Each terrible second of it was still with her. The guilt and pain, the frustration and anger. Everything, all of it, it all suddenly erupted to the surface.

'Fuck you!' She found herself almost bent double with the force of it, spitting it at him. She wanted to kill him. 'I heard what you did to him, you fucking sick bastard!'

Her arms were trembling. In front of her, the burning tip of the wood danced around.

'Fuck me?' The man sounded colder now. The mask twitched as his face contorted beneath it. 'What do you know, anyway, you fucking whore? You don't understand why I'm doing this. You don't know what it's like to love a child.'

He took a step closer. She waved the burning wood at him but all it did was scar her vision. He wasn't frightened of her; he was overtaken by anger himself.

'You don't know what love *is*.'

She squirted lighter fluid onto the end of the wood. It burst brightly into life.

'Keep back,' she said.

'Or what?'

He came at her then, his free hand out, the other holding the knife back and down by his side, ready to swing it at her. She half fell, half dodged out of the way. Moving sideways, back towards the fire, squirting the can at him. *Get him with it. Fucking kill him.*

He held his arm up to cover his eyes, but swiped at her surprisingly quickly with the other hand. The knife cut the air in front of her.

'Come here! Fucking bitch.'

She hated him. He was this big, solid thing coming at her. She kept jerking the can: throwing the lighter fluid at him, backing away across the clearing.

But he came straight at her, quick and strong.

The knife was held low again, and he was shouting at her with rage, trying to startle and frighten her, to make her flinch and turn away. That was her first instinct, but she fought it, *remembering how Scott had screamed*, and gripped down on the can as hard as she could.

The lighter fluid arced out at him again – and then he slammed into her, knocking her backwards. She hit the ground before she knew what had happened. Her lungs felt knocked out through her chest, and she tried to scream but couldn't. Pain. Panic – the burning wood was pinned between them, scorching her face – and then suddenly the man launched himself aside. The burning wood disappeared with him.

She lay there for perhaps a full second, too shocked by the impact and the burn to move. Then – *Keep going* – she forced herself to roll the opposite way. Centimetres of safety. But the man was staggering across the clearing, moving away from her.

His front was engulfed in flame.

He was smacking himself, patting madly at the cross-stitch of fire burning bright yellow in the early-morning light. But the flames were too much. His sleeves were alight, his mask, his hair. He was screeching. She had done this to him and she was glad. His hair was burning like the head of a candle.

Jodie got to her feet.

Even on fire, the man still had the knife. She had nothing.

He dropped to his knees, pressing himself into the snow, rolling this way and that. The air was full of hiss and sizzle. Smoke rose from him as he put out the flames.

Run.

No.

She walked awkwardly across to the campfire and kicked one of the stone columns. Nothing, so she kicked it again, harder. The man was on his hands and knees, bellowing with anger and pain. One last kick and everything collapsed. A *shriek* of metal; a cloud of ash and dust and bright orange sparks billowing in the air, warming her.

Fuck you, she thought, and picked up one of the stones. It was about the size of a brick. Same sort of weight.

The man struggled to his feet but didn't make it. He fell onto his elbows.

Jodie stumbled across, holding the stone to her chest. This man wasn't going to hurt anyone again. Not her; not Scott. He wasn't going to bring anyone else out into the woods and torture them, and he was going to pay for everything he'd done tonight.

He was going to pay for everything.

She lifted the rock, held it out a little—

'Wait!'

—and brought it down hard on the back of his head. She felt the impact more than heard it: felt the reverberation in her arms, and imagined his brain jolting loose inside the cracked skull. Immediately, he was flat in the snow: limp and empty and gone. There was no blood.

Do it again. Make sure.

'Stop!'

Who was talking? she wondered. Suddenly there were hands on he pulling her away.

She fought them, turning and lashing out.

'Get off me!'

But they were too strong; someone wrapped their arms around her i a bear hug and lifted her up. The brick fell away into the snow.

'It's okay,' someone said. 'It's okay. It's the police.'

She kept kicking as she was hoisted back across the clearing, whippin her head from side to side. Through her tears, she saw a man in a hug black coat crouching beside the man on the ground, and then she wa swung round to face the other way. There were more men across th clearing.

Policemen. One of them was approaching with a large blanket.

Calm down.

The man holding her put her down gently, and took the blanket from the other policeman. She was still shaking, but she allowed him to drap it over her shoulders and pull it round her. Then she turned and co lapsed against him.

He held her, and said quiet soothing things to her that she didn properly hear.

The man over by the body said, 'It's him.'

The policeman held her even tighter. If it wasn't for him, Jodie though she'd be on the floor now. But at the same time she was shivering wit adrenalin.

'Scott!' She remembered suddenly, moving away from him slightly.

'It's okay.' He released her and looked down into her face. 'Scott safe. He's at the hospital. He helped us find you.'

Jodie was confused. At the hospital? How was he at the hospital? Tha didn't make any sense. Why would the man have let him go? She looke over at the storeroom on the far edge of the clearing. For the first time she noticed that something had been drawn on it. Some kind of ... spi der's web, it looked like.

'But ...'

'It's okay,' the man said again. 'We'll explain everything later. Th main thing is, you're safe now.'

Jodie looked up at him. He was old and solid, and she'd never seer a man look so tired. Harrowed, almost. For a strange second, it was a though he'd been here with her for every single minute of the night Beneath the exhaustion, his expression was almost fatherly. There wa something else there, too. He looked relieved, but not just that. H looked *peaceful*. She simply fell back against him. It was easier for now. He hugged her gently, and whispered: 'We found you.'

Mark

Panic.

Before I'd even properly collected my ideas and thoughts together, I opened the connection to the search team at the woods and sent out an alarm. All I knew for sure was that I needed to speak to someone urgently. There was that feeling again, that something was wrong; only now it was a hundred times stronger and focused entirely differently.

I waited.

The locker room was unbearably hot and claustrophobic. It probably always had been, but this was the first time it had also felt threatening. The artificial lights were buzzing, and the heavy *clank* of the pipes kept jolting me. I thought of all the people working in the hospital and how far away they were. I was on my own here, down long, empty corridors blocked off by sheets of dirty polythene. I kept glancing over my shoulder, checking the corners, the doorway.

It took a minute for Officer Bates to arrive at the camera. He looked tired, but also flushed and excited, and he spoke before I could say anything:

'Sir, they've found her.'

I acknowledged that on one level, brushed it aside on another.

'Is Hunter there?'

'He's gone back to the department. He's not happy.'

'Listen to me very carefully. You need to get the men there moving. I need you to re-establish the cordon along the road.'

He frowned, maybe thinking I'd misunderstood him.

'But they've got him. Detective Sergeant Mercer radioed in from the woods. The girl's there and they've got the kidnapper. Why do we need the cordon?'

'Because I'm telling you to.' I checked the map. 'Do it now. East and west, as far as they can go. I'll take responsibility. They need to make sure that *nobody else* comes out of those woods. Do that now, and then come back.'

'Yes, sir.'

And stop calling me, sir. But he was already gone, probably spurred into action by the edge in my voice.

It was strange: I felt panicked inside, but on the surface I was calm and practical. My mind had taken charge for the moment.

Think things through, it told me. Breathe deeply.

Swim as hard as you can.

And don't turn your back on the fucking door.

At least they'd found her – that was something. If nothing else, Scott and Jodie would both survive the night, and that was surely the most important thing. And they probably had got their man. There wasn't necessarily anything to worry about.

But it wouldn't hurt to set up the cordon anyway. Until it was all over, I was adamant that nobody else should be allowed to leave those woods. Nobody. Actually, I wasn't calm at all; I was trembling. I felt like there was a massive hole growing in my chest. There *was* something to worry about. Call it a leap straight from A to D. Mercer would understand.

I glanced at the doorway.

Fuck this.

The best way to deal with fear is to face it straight off, get it out of the way. Bates would be busy sorting out the cordon for a moment, so I went over to the door, circling it before stepping out into the corridor.

Nobody around. The lights were still flickering, humming like wasps against the ceiling. The corridor kept blinking.

You're over-reacting. There was no reason to think I was in danger, and Scott had the security guard outside his room.

On camera, Bates had returned. 'They're on their way out.'

'Okay.'

What else?

'We've got everything under control out here.' Bates looked at me curiously. 'Are you okay, sir?'

'I'm fine.'

But I wasn't fine.

The far monitor showed the case file on Reardon. I'd been reading through, looking for clues and explanations, and my attention had been caught by one small detail. Meaningless in itself, perhaps, but it stopped me in my tracks. During the most recent custody dispute, the court had accepted that Reardon planted the listening device in his child's teddy bear, and when I'd first read that it had seemed like a validation of his guilt.

But Reardon denied doing it.

I'd pondered that for a moment. If he had done it, would he bother denying it? Was there any point in that – anything to be gained? It was ill likely, I told myself, that he was responsible. But the thought remained. What if it was someone else?

And if not Reardon, then who?

We knew the 50/50 Killer used surveillance equipment to research his targets, often over a long period of time. Was it possible one of his devices had been found and falsely attributed to Reardon?

We knew he destroyed relationships. Until now, he'd always targeted couples, but that didn't mean he couldn't have broadened his range.

'Nobody understands how much a father loves his child,' Reardon had said.

I'd reopened the photographs of the wall where the 50/50 Killer had made his notes. So many of the designs were similar that it had made sense to think of them as drafts. But then I remembered what he'd told Kevin Simpson in the audio recording: 'If it's any consolation, she and Scott are one of my couples.'

One of my couples.

At that moment, the screen beeped once: a new report arriving in the main file. The air hummed as I clicked through to it.

It was a forensics report from the woods. The van had eventually been checked and declared safe, and Simon and his team had been granted access. This was their first report, and in the centre of the screen there was a photograph of what they'd found. Painted inside the van, a third spider web. That made three in total.

One for Jodie and Kevin. A second for Jodie and Scott.

The third for James Reardon and his child?

I turned back to the camera at the woods.

After his wife had called earlier, Mercer had left his mobile phone on the desk in front of me. I picked it up and switched it on.

'I need to talk to Mercer,' I said. 'Urgently. Get me a patch-through number to someone on the search team.'

Jodie

Scott was alive!

And warm in the hospital, Jodie thought ruefully. As she walk
through the woods, wrapped in a safety blanket, she felt colder than s
remembered being all night. But the knowledge that he was alive w
warming her just as much as the blanket.

The policeman – John, his name was – had said they could wait
the fire in the woods and be lifted out by helicopter, but she'd shak
her head. She had to get out of this place, not least because of *him*. Th
man just lying there. After what he'd done to Scott, Jodie was glad she
killed him, but she couldn't look at him any longer.

She knew it had a lot to do with the way her body was shivering a
trembling. Shock. It was also because she was warming up. Over th
course of the night, the cold had seeped into her skin, numbing her, un
there was so little feeling in her body that the sensation wasn't even pa
any more. Now she was thawing: passing back up into the stage of bei
frozen. The hurt and discomfort were returning.

But you're alive, she told herself. And Scott is too. No matter wha
you're both safe now. Stop worrying. Stop feeling guilty for what you'
done. You're both alive.

Her heart didn't feel like it could handle the elation that came with tho
thoughts. She felt fragile as a bird. So she kept the thoughts out of her hea
and concentrated on walking. Each footstep, packing down the snow, ga
the sound of someone leaning back in a leather chair. It was comfortin
She was leaving this terrible place, one foot in front of the other.

The officer ahead was shining a torch around to all sides, but it w
hardly necessary any more; the rising sun had brought the woods to sti
grey life around them. In the trees, birds were singing. It was early mor
ing, a new day.

Behind her, John was close enough to talk. Jodie found him an im
mensely reassuring presence. He kept saying things that she only ha
heard, but which nevertheless calmed her. Perhaps it was stupid, but sh
couldn't help imagining that the voice she'd been hearing all night ha
been his: full of kindness, comfort and quiet encouragment. *You will g
through this. Hang on, keep yourself together. I will find you.* And he ha
When he'd embraced her, she'd somehow understood that he'd bee

242

searching for her all night. In his face, she saw a man who'd been tried and tested, but who had refused to stop or give up. Now, finally, he seemed at peace with himself.

Behind her, Jodie heard an electronic crackle. She jumped.

'Mercer.'

She glanced back and realised John was speaking into the headset he was wearing. *It's okay.* The three of them kept walking.

'Mark,' she heard him say, 'calm down. He's dead. Jodie is safe; she's here with me now. We're on our way out.'

Whereas his words had washed over her before, for some reason she found herself listening to this conversation more carefully.

He paused, then said: 'No, it's definitely him. What makes—'

More silence. One foot in front of the other, they kept going. She was filled with an irrational fear. Something was wrong. They were going to make her go back to that place, when she needed to keep moving. She needed to get to Scott and tell him how sorry she was for everything ...

'We've got three independent witnesses. Whatever you're thinking, there's no—'

The officer leading the way looked back, and then stopped. Jodie's instinct to keep going was so strong that she almost bumped into him. She forced herself to stop as well, ignoring the feeling of alarm it produced. *Run!* John was a little behind them, standing still, staring at the ground, listening.

Another crackle, this time from the officer in front of her. He raised his hand to his ear, his head slightly to one side.

'Westmoreland,' he said. 'Go.'

She turned back to John. He gave her a brief smile, but his expression betrayed him. As Jodie watched, his face suddenly drained of emotion.

'Christ,' he said, closing his eyes and scratching his forehead. 'And there was another one back at his camp, as well. On the door.'

They were talking about that horrible drawing, Jodie realised. Similar to the one she'd seen painted on the inside of the van that had brought them here.

She fought the urge to start running.

Scott. I need to see Scott.

'Sir,' Westmoreland called, 'this is important. From the men at the scene.'

John touched his earpiece. 'Mark, I'll call you back.'

He walked quickly up to them. Westmoreland still had his head on the side, listening carefully, nodding.

'They've found a note, sir. In the other building.'

'Have them read it.'

'Read it to me, please.'

Westmoreland was silent again, listening.

'"Dear Detective Sergeant Mercer,"' he began.

4 DECEMBER   6.51 A.M

29 MINUTES UNTIL DAWN

Mark

I kept searching through the files. There was *something* I was missin
There had to be, because I was sure I was right. The killer had been pla
ing a third game with James Reardon. He had made Reardon wait o
there in the woods and hold Jodie captive until dawn. It wasn't tortu
but it was a sacrifice he had to make in exchange for his child's life. T
50/50 Killer might not have been able to collect love from either of the
but Reardon would still fulfil a useful purpose in the game as a whole.

But what Mercer said was also true: three independent witnesses p
Reardon in the frame. Amanda Taylor's boyfriend, Colin Barnes, h
identified Reardon as the man who'd assaulted him and abducted Ka
Megan Cook had seen him enter the house rented by Carl Farmer; a
Scott thought he recognised him from a utility visit a month or so bac
They couldn't all be lying. Together they created a web of their own, a
Reardon was inescapably trapped at the centre. So I must have miss
something.

I opened the transcript of the interview with Megan. If the killer h
been following Reardon for a long time, he could easily have used
photograph when setting up the van licensing and the Carl Farmer ne
One of the things he would have made Reardon do would be to deliv
the mask that morning and implicate himself further.

I scanned through the file.

There.

'Did you see him arrive?' I'd asked Megan.

'Yeah. I was on the phone by the front window.'

She hadn't told me who she was talking to. But I'd asked her how lo
Reardon had been inside the house.

'I was only on the phone for a minute, and I saw him come out, so
can't have been long.'

244

Only a minute. Could it have been him, the real killer? Cold-calling
er for some reason, any reason: a ploy to get her over to the window
r the moment when James Reardon appeared at the house? The only
ghting of the 50/50 Killer, engineered to lead us in the direction of a
lse suspect. So that he could wait for us there, challenge us as Mercer
lieved, without ever being in any real danger of getting caught?

That still left Scott and Colin Barnes's testimony though. Admittedly,
cott was in pieces at the moment, so perhaps his memory couldn't en-
rely be trusted, but Barnes had been adamant: James Reardon had at-
cked him and abducted Karli. And that didn't make sense, because my
eory depended on the 50/50 Killer taking the baby and blackmailing
eardon.

So either Colin Barnes was mistaken or else he was lying.

I opened the file on Karli Reardon's abduction. My heart was beating
ercely.

The transcript of Barnes's statement loaded. As it did, I considered one
ossible explanation. Maybe Barnes hadn't actually *seen* his attacker at
l, and because of the history with Reardon had just made an assump-
on. A sensible one, perhaps, but not necessarily—

The file opened and I stopped thinking altogether.

There it was on the screen. I stared for a moment, unable to make
nse of what I was seeing.

Something had ... It couldn't be right. That ...

My world dropped away.

And somewhere, far away in the hospital, an alarm began to sound.

DECEMBER   6.52 A.M.
8 MINUTES UNTIL DAWN

cott

here was no flat any more. No comfortable settee to sit on. No Jodie,
sleep in another room. His dreams had given up all pretence of dress-
ıg his memories in brighter clothes; the artifice had been stripped away.
Tow, as Scott slept, he was simply *there* again: back in the stone outhouse
ı the woods, perched on that awkward seat, cramped and tortured, with
ıe man in the devil mask squatting down in front of him.

'You're blind to the truth.' The man held the torch under the chin of
ıe mask, illuminating it. 'You don't love her. Not any more.'

245

It's a game, Scott reminded himself. The man was the devil, whic meant he had lied. Jodie hadn't cheated on him. In fact, none of t things the man had told him were true. Not necessarily.

But the evidence had been right there in front of him, hadn't it? An it was true that Jodie was unhappy, so it wasn't such a stretch to imagi her cheating on him again. He did that now: pictured it in his hea Turned the image round. Jodie and Kevin. Kevin and Jodie. It mac sense.

The man's voice became kinder, more soothing. 'She certainly doesn love you.'

Scott shook his head.

He thought back on everything the man had talked to him about t night. The painting Jodie hadn't wanted; the one-night stand with Kev Simpson; the general unhappiness that had permeated both their live but especially hers, for so long now. He pictured her pacing the house, though he'd put her in a cage. Going back and forth to the job she hate Every morning when they woke up, it felt like a bit more of her had die Living with him, all her lights were slowly going out, one by one.

When had he last seen her smile? He couldn't remember. And Sco loved her so much that it broke his heart he couldn't show her how mud she mattered to him, how important she was. Or that he could say an do those things, but they weren't enough.

He would do anything to make things right again.

'Tell me you hate her,' the man repeated. 'The game will be over the All this pain will end.'

He would do anything at all.

And maybe now, even if she never knew it, he could.

'No.'

The man in the devil mask looked at him, implacable.

'No?'

Scott was trembling with the cold. His skin felt dead. And there w so much pain. Perhaps because of that, he was almost delirious. It wasn about thinking. He felt his spirit lifting, and he said it again.

'No. I love her.'

The man settled back on his heels, tilting his head slightly. Throug the mask, there was the slightest hint of defeat.

'All right, then.'

And then Scott was standing outside the stone building. The man ha cut the rope tying his arms to his thighs but had left him cuffed. H legs were weak, his back bowed – half broken from the cramp. The man stripped the clothes off him and threw them into the empty storeroom.

'We'll leave these here as well.'

He was talking about the pages in his hand. He laid them carefully on top of Scott's clothes, showing him each in turn.

Five Hundred Reasons Why I Love You.

Scott felt immense sorrow when he saw that. He wished more than anything that he'd been able to finish it. He hoped she would understand.

Two hundred and seventy-four reasons said: I realise everything's not perfect, least of all me, but I'm still trying because I so desperately don't want to lose you.

He started crying. 'Can I see her?'

'No.'

'Please. Please can I see her again?'

The email next, except he turned that over and left it with the small black handwriting facing up. Scott caught sight of the top line – '*Dear Detective Sergeant Mercer*' – and then the man closed the door. There was a screech of metal as he pulled the bolt across.

'Why?' Scott sobbed. 'Why are you doing this?'

The man didn't answer. Instead, he walked across to the fire and selected a burning log. Then he held the screwdriver up and pointed deeper into the woods.

'We're going this way.'

He didn't know where the man led him; it was too dark to see much, and he kept tripping. But the man used the burning wood to force him on: pushing it into his bare back, producing jabs of agony. Scott was terrified, frantic. He knew what was going to happen; the images came into his head without reason but with absolute conviction. The man was going to make him lie face down on the frozen woodland ground, and then he was going to take out his knife and put it through Scott's throat, carve it out. He could imagine his screams, suddenly reduced to gargles of panic; his blood fanning across the snow.

How would it feel, to die? To disappear from the world?

Scott pleaded with the man, but he said nothing.

They walked for about ten minutes and then the man told him to stop. He pointed the screwdriver at the base of a tree.

'Sit there.'

Scott collapsed against it, his bare legs splayed out in the snow in front of him. The cold burned them, but he was so frightened that he didn't care.

The man bound him to the tree with two sets of rope. One round his body, holding his arms in place. The other in his mouth, forcing his tongue back and holding his head up. When he'd finished, he stood in front where Scott had no option but to see him.

'You asked me why.'

The man crouched down in front of Scott and pulled the mask up over his face, resting it on the top of his head. He was only a man, Scott realised again. Apart from an awful blankness, there was nothing unusual about his face. He could have been anyone.

'I am a spirit in this shell.' The man's words had a rehearsed air to them. 'I feel nothing because I am separate from it. When I am done, this body will fall and I will float apart from it.'

He leaned over, reaching out, allowing the flames on the wood to lick at the screwdriver. He turned it round, this way and that.

Please no. Please don't hurt me any more.

'When this body falls apart, I will return in another shell to continue my collection. And another.'

As the man took the screwdriver out of the flame, Scott's panic intensified – but then he stared, horrified, as the man lifted the screwdriver to his own face instead. He put the spike of it into his eye and held it there. Something sizzled and crumpled, and the man turned the handle slowly, side to side, smoke curling up his forehead. When he spoke next, his voice was neutral and impassive, and Scott believed every single word of it.

'Eventually,' the man said calmly, 'I will be allowed to take my collection home to my true father.'

Scott woke up and opened his eye. It was difficult. Either the lid was enormously heavy or else the muscles that worked it were too numb for his nerves to find.

So cold. He was so cold. His body was trembling and shaking, but there was no sensation accompanying the movement. He was just aware it was happening. When he had first been sat down here, the cold had burned him. Now it was as though his body belonged to someone else.

It must be nearly morning. The sky was slowly coming to life, and far above him in the trees, birds were beginning to sing. But everything was very distant; there was no feeling in his body, only a small core of heat left and he could feel that dwindling. He was dying from the outside in.

He didn't feel panic any more. Even all the impossible pain had dimmed, while the adrenalin simply sat in his veins, sluggish and frozen. His heart could barely raise the energy to beat.

At least he could close his eye, and it was grateful for the reprieve, falling back into place. There was a breeze against his skin, but it might have been hot, cold – he couldn't tell. It didn't matter.

Scott allowed himself to drift. The world seemed reluctant to fade away, but in the end it couldn't cling to him and he fell back into sleep. The dreams returned, solidifying around him, only these were more like proper dreams. They were made-up, fantasies.

In one, Jodie was standing behind him, reaching round to knot his tie.

He smiled. He still loved her, despite everything. She was so perfect for him.

Jodie said: 'You don't have to go. Not if you don't want to.'

And then he was on a beach he'd never seen before. He was sitting on the sand, watching the waves, listening to the sound of them swelling in and breaking on the shore. It was a gentle, rushing noise, repeated over and over.

In his dream, Jodie was there, too: sitting quietly next to him, the wind rolling her hair. It was sunny, and it felt wonderful. There wasn't any cold, not any more. Jodie looked at him and smiled, and when she leaned her head against him he reached over and took her hand.

Even this was slowly fading. He closed his eyes and listened as the noise of the sea grew dimmer.

And as Scott died, it told him very gently: *Shhhhh*.

4 DECEMBER   **6.58 A.M.**
22 MINUTES UNTIL DAWN

Mark

Was it wrong, what I was thinking?

As I ran along the hospital corridors, yelling at people to move, I wasn't frightened. Even though I was unarmed. Even though I knew now, from the photograph I'd seen of Colin Barnes, that the man I'd spent all night talking to had never been the real Scott Banks at all.

I wasn't scared. In fact, my main concern was that I was going to be too late, and I knew from the alarm that I probably already was.

Was it wrong? Aware of all the other people the 50/50 Killer had mu[r]dered, part of me believes I should have been thinking of them – or [at] least of my job. I'd like to think I was bravely, selflessly doing my dut[y], that I was running upstairs to stop this man before he got away and hu[rt] someone else.

Into the lift.

Foot tapping: come on, come on.

Ting. Out through the doors and running again.

'Get out of the way!'

The truth is I wasn't charging along the corridors because of my job, [or] because of concern for his past or future victims. Instead, I was thinki[ng] about my last conversation with him – with Scott, or Carl Farmer, [or] Colin Barnes. I was remembering his expression when I told him abo[ut] Lise; the way he'd thanked me on my way out. I was thinking that h[e] was the wolf of space, pulling relationships to pieces and draining th[e] world of love.

Most of all, I was hearing that sound again in my head. Not the noi[se] from the audio recording this time, but the sound of his slow breathi[ng] as I made my confession, as he listened to me describing her death, an[d] explaining how I felt I'd betrayed her. As he added her to his harvest.

He was only a man – I knew that deep down. Just as I knew that th[e] fourth spider web Mercer had found at the woods couldn't really repr[e]sent me and Lise. How could it? He'd left all of those before he even m[et] me. It was impossible.

But, regardless, that was why I ran so hard. Because if I didn't tak[e] him down now, I was sure I would lose a part of myself for ever.

There was a crowd around the entrance to his room – nurses, doctor[s,] orderlies – all looking anxious, panicked. The sight of me bearing dow[n] on them probably didn't help.

No security guard, I noticed.

'Police.'

They moved out of the way, clearing to either side of the door.

'We don't know what happened,' an orderly said.

'One of the nurses found him like that.'

I stepped through them. 'Move away, please.'

I was desperate for a confrontation, but it wasn't going to make m[e] careless. I kept my distance from the doorway and took in what I coul[d] of the room.

Just inside, a woman in a nurse's uniform was crouched over someo[ne]

ing on the floor. The security guard. Where was Barnes? The bed was empty, the covers pulled roughly aside. The window was open, the blinds that had been closed all night now raised halfway. A breeze was slowly freezing the air, and the plastic rattled against the glass.

I moved in, checked quickly around. There was nobody else in the room, nowhere for anybody to hide. He was gone.

I put my hand on the nurse's shoulder, crouched beside her.

'I found him like this,' she said.

'Okay.'

It was obvious from the tone of her voice that she'd already checked him for signs of life and found none. She sounded lost.

'Would you go outside?' I said, as gently as I could. 'I'd like you to wait in the corridor and make sure that nobody else comes in here. That's very important.'

She nodded slowly and stood up. There was blood on her hands; she rubbed them absently on her uniform as she walked to the door.

Immediately, I went over to the window, shivering as I reached it. There was blood on the sill and the glass; blood on the pull cord for the blinds. Careful not to touch anything, I looked outside. We were at the back of the building, only one floor up – it was possible that he had jumped. But the stones in the wall were uneven, so he could have climbed down, his fingers and toes clawed into the gaps in the brick.

There was no sign of anyone in the car-park below.

I went back to the security guard.

His head was swollen and broken, and his arm rested at a painfully wrong angle. I found that the casual brutality of what had been done to him was somehow even more shocking than the calculated burning of Kevin Simpson. It takes a surprising amount of effort to beat someone to death, and Barnes had made absolutely sure of the job. The guard had been kicked and stamped on repeatedly. There were streaks of blood on his face, a pool of it underneath his head, stains round the neck of his brown uniform. Muddy swirls all around and at the base of the wall.

Bare footprints of blood.

The bed. At the base, stained bandages were scattered. The covers were thrown aside, but there was no blood on the sheets, just an indent where Scott had lain for the night. Not Scott, of course, but Colin Barnes – if that was even his real name.

I pictured him calling out, and the guard opening the door, coming in, bending over the bed to listen. Barnes punching him hard on the side of the head, then calmly pulling the covers back, getting up to finish the

job. My mind constructed a whirlwind of activity. A flurry of violenc
swift, hard blows; blood spattering. I felt the starry thud of a bare he
stamping into an eye socket.

When the guard was dead, Barnes had climbed out of the windov
Now he was gone. I'd lost him.

I wanted to scream.

The chair I'd sat on was knocked over on the far side of the room, b
I was standing where it had been before. The place where I'd spent th
night talking to this man, listening as he manipulated me.

Behind me, the blinds rattled against the window.

I wanted to collapse on the floor. I'd spent so long in here talking
Scott. I'd told him about Lise. And yet all the time it was really *him*.

He would have wanted to be somewhere he could watch what w
happening and keep track of how we were doing.

There were stone walls.

Somewhere he could direct us to see what he wanted, to make us g
where he wanted.

We crossed a river, crossed a path.

The whole time there'd been enough there for us to catch him if w
put it together right. All day his picture had been there in the file. Whi
he was up here, hiding behind fake trauma, parcelling out enough info
mation for us to find Jodie by dawn if we didn't make the right conne
tions in time to discover the truth.

Why?

The question re-occurred to me now. He'd asked me it himself earli
on – curious, I guessed, as to whether we understood him. But why ha
he done this? He'd used Reardon as a distraction, but there was noth
ing there to satisfy his pathology. He'd taken Kevin Simpson, but h
wouldn't be there at dawn to collect anything from Jodie. It didn't mak
sense. He'd risked being caught, and he'd helped us to find her in tim
all apparently for nothing. Why was he challenging us at all?

And where was the real Scott Banks?

Move.

I stepped out into the corridor.

'I'm calling for assistance. Until they arrive, *nobody* goes in that roon
Understand?'

The nurse nodded again. I set off.

The fourth spider web couldn't represent me: Colin Barnes wasn't psy
chic. A fourth spider web, left at the scene in the woods, meant a fourt
ruined relationship, and this was the main prize for him. It would be on

he'd had time to study, one he could cut and destroy. Someone had to know they had been betrayed, so they could be killed and that poisoned love taken from them. A choice had to have—

He was never challenging *us*.

'Oh fuck.'

I felt a buzzing in my pocket – Mercer's phone ringing. The display showed the patch-through number from the search team in the woods.

He was only ever challenging Mercer.

Even as I answered it, I was already running.

4 DECEMBER   **7.10 A.M.**
10 MINUTES UNTIL DAWN

The 50/50 Killer

Preparation.

The devil knew the address and the route off by heart. Two days earlier, it had driven these streets repeatedly to commit them to memory and get used to the timings. When the journey was ingrained, it had taken the vehicle back to the hospital, and parked in the long-stay car-park at the rear of the building. The car was an old, unlicensed hatchback, bought with cash and stored off-road. After locking it and making sure nobody was watching, the devil had left the clothes and items it would require inside, and taped the keys to the underside of the chassis, ready for when it needed them.

The first stop was only three minutes away.

It was one of several rented properties the devil kept: a small, cheap, sub-ground-floor studio flat in the bad area close to the hospital. It had proved ideal for this task, and not only because of its location. Most of the other flats in the block were unoccupied; the ones that weren't, there were babies crying there all the time anyway.

The devil parked the car and went down the front path and outside steps that led to the front door. It was very quiet. Had the baby died? It hoped not. The devil had buried the keys in the flowerpot by the steps, and it exhumed them now. The front door shuddered in its frame and the early morning light fell into the room.

The baby was in the pen bought for it, lying on its back. Sleeping.

The devil picked it up; the child stirred, made a noise.

'Shhh. It's okay. Don't cry.'

Karli Reardon grizzled a little more as she was carried across the room, but didn't start crying properly until they were out in the cold, where she started fighting with surprising strength. The devil supposed this must count as a rude awakening, although to it the temperature had always been irrelevant. Because of what it was, hot and cold didn't affect it the way they did normal human beings.

'Shhh. You'll be fine.'

It jigged the baby in its arms and reproduced the soothing noises it had heard other people make.

Still she wouldn't stop crying.

It strapped her into the baby-chair fitted in the car, then climbed into the driver's seat and smiled across at her. The devil was good at smiling. When that didn't work, it pulled a funny face, but Karli Reardon didn't look like she found the face very funny. The devil quickly became bored, started the engine and set off.

Halfway there, it reached across and opened the glove-compartment, retrieving the mask.

The final destination was less than five minutes away.

It had started at a funeral: the one they held for the murdered detective.

Out of curiosity, and with a dark thrill, the devil had made itself present, surreptitiously, at the back of the chapel. Even before it arrived, there had been a sense within it that something important was about to happen. It hadn't known what, not even whether it would be good or bad, but when John Mercer stood up to deliver the eulogy, the devil realised immediately that the moment had arrived.

It had watched, first spellbound and then frightened, as Mercer unravelled. The other people might have witnessed a breakdown, but the devil recognised it for what it was; it only had to listen to Mercer's words and see the way his eyes were picking out monsters from the audience to know that here was an opposite number. An adversary. The man could sense evil. Any second, their eyes would meet and John Mercer would simply *know*.

Only the actions of the detective's wife and colleagues had saved it from being caught that day. It was frightening. The path had always been clear and straightforward up to that point: there had never been any suspicion there might be someone put on this earth to stand in its way. And now here he was: an adversary. An opposite number.

The way forward had finally been revealed following a day of intense meditation, from which the devil emerged with fresh purpose.

The first thing to do was to find out as much as possible about this enemy.

In the initial stages of his recovery, Eileen Mercer spent a lot of time by her husband's bedside in the hospital, and their house stood empty. When they both returned home, she nursed him. The detective spent his days swaddled in a dressing-gown, reading, watching television, apparently lacking the energy even to walk between rooms.

Neither of them had any inclination to go up into the attic; people rarely do. But if they had, they would have found the devil there, bathed in pale blue light. It saw and heard everything.

Fate had clearly brought John Mercer into its trajectory to be faced and dealt with, but it was initially unsure what the next step on that path should be. It was only when Mercer returned to work against his wife's wishes, leaving his empty promises behind him, that the form the game would take became apparent. It always did. It was a found object, like a fossil, and all the devil's studies ever did was blow the sand away to reveal the structure. To honour his promise, would John Mercer be prepared to deny his purpose in the world? If he did, the devil would have removed an opponent. If he chose his job over his professions of love, the harvest would be rich.

The game was to be a genuine confrontation between the two: a test. But there was comfort to be had in that. At different stages in our life's work, the devil knew, we encounter guardians who must be overcome, and this clearly was one of those moments. To counter fear, it prayed to its father daily, and allowed the game to take shape.

During its studies, other targets came to its attention, and it formed new identities, becoming different people in pursuit of them. As it learned of James Reardon, the devil became Carl Farmer, then Colin Barnes, who initiated a relationship with the mother of Reardon's child. Scott Banks and Jodie McNeice, in contrast, had been one of its couples for nearly three years. But when Kevin Simpson re-established contact with Jodie, the devil had known it was a sign. All the pieces slowly fell into place and, as they did, the fear became a distant memory. It was engaged in truly majestic work.

But in the end, both of those games were only appetisers: components in a larger whole. The real game was always against John Mercer. Either his nemesis would abandon the fight, or else his wife's love would be ripped apart and taken down as penance. Either way, the test would have been passed. Perhaps then, finally, the devil would be allowed to go home.

Whatever happened to the mortal body, what the devil had achieved here would be beautiful. It would leave behind itself a cathedral of death. A chapel cast in flesh and blood, into which the true father could raise itself up, and caper and dance.

There were lights on throughout the house when it arrived, and for a moment it wondered if it had miscalculated: the timing had always been tight. But something told it there was another explanation. If Eileen Mercer was still up, perhaps waiting for her husband, it would need to take care, but nothing was really changed.

The devil parked the car and took the baby out, hoisting her into its arms. She was still crying, so it whispered more platitudes, gently shaking the keys to the house.

It walked up the drive to the front door, and was inside within five seconds. The downstairs hallway was dark, but the doors off it were open, the rooms beyond brightly lit.

It stood still, listening. The house was silent, apart from the baby crying, pushing herself tightly against its chest. Beneath that, it could feel its own heartbeat, slow and regular.

'Shhh.'

Upstairs, a phone began to ring. That would be the police.

The devil headed to the stairs and ascended.

4 DECEMBER
DAWN

7.20 A.M.

Mark

The sky was dark blue overhead, lightening as it stretched down, hazy and yellow to the east. A few stars were still visible, forming fractured constellations. In front of me as I drove, there was a huge shred of cloud. Illuminated by the slowly rising sun, it formed a purple thumbprint pressed into the heavens.

Twenty past seven.

Get out of the way.

I knew vaguely where I was going, but mostly I was trusting the van's GPS. It couldn't quite keep up with me. Lights pulsing, siren blaring, I was driving as fast as the roads would allow. Cars up ahead leaned in to the pavements to let me past, but even this early the traffic was heavy and

kept having to veer to the other side of the road: work my way danger-
usly between lanes, half blinded by oncoming headlights.

Come on, come on.

The streets had been cleared of snow, but were frozen and scattered
with grit. Bursts of crackled dialogue came through the police radio;
sometimes I pressed the mic and responded while keeping an eye on the
road. The reports told me that officers had arrived at the hospital and the
scene was under control. Nobody was answering the phone at Mercer's
house. Armed officers were en route, but—

'I'm nearly there,' I said.

The call at the hospital had been from Mercer, running through the
woods. He gave frantic, garbled instructions to call people, get them
moving. I'd worked most of it out by then, but he told me about the
letter they'd found in the storeroom Scott had been kept in. The one
addressed to him.

The larger game that had been played here.

Dear Detective Sergeant Mercer.

In my head, I could still hear the crunch of undergrowth as he ran, his
breath catching. I could feel his panic.

If you've found this note you've made your choice.

Now I was on my way to his house, driving like the devil, chasing the
evil. Mercer would be out of the woods soon and on his way, but however quickly he got there, and whatever the dispatcher told me, I knew I
was going to be first on the scene.

Eileen …

I turned into the street, slowing down, driving carefully. The house
was marked on the GPS screen with a red circle, three down. A large,
detached property. Square windows, all of them lit up bright yellow. A
big garden sloped upwards in tiers to the front, a path up the middle
to the front door. Driveway down the side. All of it thick with snow,
slightly pink in the early-morning light. An old car was parked outside.
I pulled up, blocking it in.

'Detective Nelson,' I told the dispatcher. 'I'm on scene. I'm going
in.'

The cold hit me hard as I got out, but I was shivering anyway: fear and
adrenalin. I calmed myself as I'd been taught: breathing slowly through
my nose; rolling the saliva around in my mouth. There were armed
officers on their way, but in the meantime I had to make do with the
standard kit stored in the van. I gathered it up. Pepper spray in my right
hand, side-handled baton in my left. It seemed ludicrously insufficient.

Sirens in the distance. Still some way off.

The car parked in front of me *ticked* in the freezing air. I touched
bonnet. Warm. He was here.

Despite my urge to get inside, Andrew Dyson was on my mind, a
forced myself to look at the house and take in the scene before I did
thing. Down the driveway, the snow was undisturbed. The path thro
the garden wasn't: a trail of blurred footsteps led to the front door, wl
was slightly ajar, the only spot of darkness.

Then I saw it. I froze. One of the upstairs windows was cracked; t
was a smear of blood on the glass. The sight spurred me on before I co
even process it.

Move.

I went up through the garden quickly, checking the angles. There v
no footprints in the snow around the path, lots of space between me
the hedges. I kept my eye on the driveway to the right in case he c
out the side.

Halfway up the path, I heard it: a baby crying.

The hairs on my neck stood up, and I stopped in my tracks, about
metres away from the house.

Karli Reardon.

I gripped the handle of the baton so that the main length of it
tended down my left forearm, and positioned it slightly in front of
curling my arm protectively. Rested my right wrist over my left, keep
the pepper spray near to me. Deep breaths.

The baby sounded close, just inside, in fact. The crying came fi
slightly beyond the front door, from an area of shadow I couldn't
into.

'Come out!'

The darkness shifted slightly and he stepped out where I could
him.

Barnes. He was holding Karli Reardon tightly against him. In
other hand, he had a knife.

My heart felt like it was punching me in the throat.

'Police!' I shouted. 'Stay where you are.'

Instead, he stepped out of the porch and onto the path where I co
see him. He was wearing jeans and the devil mask, nothing else. All
bandages had been ripped off, and I could now see the full extent of
madness: the terrible injuries he'd inflicted on himself in order to
us. Cuts and burns all over his torso; mottled purple bruises; the bro
fingers of the hand curled under the baby. Li had said the soles of his

had been burned, too, but he walked as though he felt no pain at all.

In the pale dawn light, he looked like a corpse, animated in spite of itself. He was stained all over with blood. His knife hand was covered. I wanted to look up at the window again, a terrible despair threatening to overwhelm me. *Stay focused.*

He took another step towards me.

I stood my ground. 'Put her down, Barnes.'

The mask was a repulsive thing – red skin and matted black hair – but I reminded myself that it was only a mask. This was a man. He might be capable of controlling the pain he must be suffering, but the pepper spray would bring him down. It would close his lungs to the bare minimum for survival; shut his eyes. He'd be on the floor where I wanted him. Christ, I wanted to. But he knew there was no way I could use it while he was holding the baby.

'Put her down and stay where you are.'

He reached up with his knife-hand and pulled the mask over his head, discarding it. Staring at the ruins underneath, I didn't even see it land in the snow behind him. His real face was a hundred times worse. The left-hand side looked torn apart, the stitches embedded in tight, swollen skin. His eye was missing: just a mass of sore tissue, with more stitches poking out like thick, bristly hairs. He had disfigured himself beyond comprehension. The man I'd interviewed in the hospital, all his wounds now revealed and out in the open.

Beneath the injuries, his expression was full of barely controlled rage. Hate. I struggled to return it as he snarled at me.

'Throw your weapons down and get out of my way.'

The sirens were much closer.

I shook my head. 'That's not going to happen, Colin, and you know it.'

'That's not my name.'

The baby was fighting against him, pushing back with her small hands. He held the knife to her face. Panic cut through my anger.

'Don't—'

'Get out of my way then.'

I hesitated. It was an impossible situation. There was no way I could let him walk away from this, none at all, but I couldn't tackle him, either. And judging by his expression he was quite prepared to carry out his threat. He could hear the sirens, too, and he had no intention of being here when they arrived. If I was determined to stop him, he had nothing to lose. One more death meant little.

Come on. Think! This is what you do.

'Reardon did what you wanted,' I said. 'You can't hurt his daught[er] now. It would be breaking the rules.'

'We're past dawn. All the games are over. You have three seconds.'

'Don't do this, Colin.'

'Two seconds.'

He touched the knife to Karli's cheek again. 'One.'

'Okay.'

I relaxed my position and threw the pepper spray and baton off to on[e] side. But I didn't move. Every second needed to be spun out for as lon[g] as possible while I tried to think of a way to turn this round.

'Now get out of the way.'

Reluctantly, I stepped off the path. 'You don't want to talk to me an[y] more?'

'We're finished.' He moved closer, edging towards me. 'I got mo[re] than I ever wanted from you.'

The reference to Lise made my fists clench. But before I could sa[y] anything—

Lights: flashing over us. Red and blue, sweeping across, casting pulsin[g] shadows on the suddenly shifting house behind him. I kept very still. H[e] stared over my shoulder for a moment, then looked back at me, his fa[ce] full of anger. He pressed the knife into the crease of Karli's neck.

'It's too late, Colin,' I said. 'You can't get away.'

'Shhhh,' he whispered to Karli, not taking his eye off me.

Behind me, I heard car doors opening. Quick voices.

'Police!'

The sound of elbows smacking down on bonnets. The crackle [of] radios. Footfalls. I didn't need to turn round, and I didn't dare. It wa[s] the sound of the armed unit assembling: spreading out, taking up posi[i]tion. I couldn't see them, but I was immediately conscious of all the gun[s] that were pointing at us. Barnes, a cop-killer.

I held one arm up, my hand trembling, and shouted: 'Detective Ma[rk] Nelson. Stay where you are!'

If there was a clear shot, I half wished they'd take it, but I knew it wa[s] too much of a risk. He'd have time to use the knife. Even if they coul[d] get him, I didn't want to think what would happen after that first sho[t] had been fired: the volleys that might explode in its wake, with me an[d] Karli in the firing line.

Barnes was cradling the baby, nuzzling his head close to hers. He spok[e] quietly to her, his breath misting the air. 'Shhhh, now.'

'You can't get away, Colin. Why don't you put her down?'

'Shhhh.'

I glanced up at the brightly lit window above us, the blood there, and it sent a spike into my heart.

'You've got everything you wanted.'

'This is Detective Mark Nelson.' Barnes spoke softly to the screaming baby, but his eye remained on me. He wanted me to see this happen. 'Do you see him there? He should care about you but he doesn't.'

'You've got everything you wanted, Colin. What will this achieve?'

Barnes blanked me. The expression on his face was settled. He'd made up his mind what he was going to do, and he was preparing himself. The anger had disappeared and there was something even more horrible in its place. Anticipation.

'They'll blow you apart, don't you understand?' I said.

'I don't care about that. I can take my harvest home with me.'

Christ.

The chill rippled through me again. Karli was twisting against him, but he held her strongly, clenching her with his broken hand. The police lights striped the contortions of her face.

He whispered, 'Mark should have been protecting you, but he decided it was worth you dying just to stop me leaving.'

'Barnes, you're—'

'Shhhh,' he repeated. 'I know how bad it must feel.'

'You're—'

'But this is what Mark always does. Do you see that?'

You're deluded. Of course he was. But in his head this all made perfect sense. He couldn't get away, but he could steal one last thing to take with him. It didn't matter that it was all based on an absurd pathology: to him it was real, so he was going to do this. There was nothing I could do to stop him. I looked from Karli's face to his, and my heart fell away as he closed his eye. A smile flickered at his lips.

'Colin—'

—For the briefest of moments, it was as though I was somewhere else. Just a flash, but it hummed in my head, sensations spreading through me. *The sound of the sea roared in my ears, and I clawed at the surface, but it dissolved beneath my arms. I was drowning and everything was blurred, but suddenly I caught smeared sight of the beach, a lifetime away in front of me, and as I went under I knew that he was there on the shore! Thank God! Oh God, he was okay.*

—and then I was looking at Barnes again. Even as I saw his arm tense,

preparing to pull the knife across, to cut Karli's throat, I just stare
Everything else around me faded out.

You can do this.

'Colin,' I said, 'I think you've made a mistake.'

'Shhh.' His voice was so quiet I could barely hear it. 'It's coming.'

'You're in more trouble than you realise. Can you feel it inside you?

He didn't move his arm. It stayed tense and ready, a second away fro
moving. But he opened his eye and looked at me.

'I can feel it, too,' I said.

'Can you?'

'Not Karli.'

I forced myself to look at his bruised chest and watched the way it ro
and fell as he breathed. I tried to look hypnotised by it. And I smiled,
though what I was saying actually meant something. Empathy.

'I gave you something in the hospital,' I said.

He nodded. 'And I'm taking it with me.'

I shook my head, still smiling. 'You made a mistake, though. You too
that into you, thinking that she hated me when she died, that she realise
I didn't love her enough to save her. It's not true.'

He stared at me. His expression hardened – almost imperceptibly, b
it was there. Somehow I managed to stop my hand shaking as I gesture
at his chest.

'You know what she was thinking when she died, Colin?' I said. 'Y
know what you've got inside you? Because I do. She was thinking ho
much she loved me.'

'No, she wasn't.'

His smile slowly disappeared. There was something else in his eye no
Was it the beginning of panic? He was thinking through the consequenc
of what I'd said, and I allowed myself to imagine it with him. It wou
be like a sliver of light slowly appearing in his chest. It had been lo
amongst the darkness there, but now that I'd brought it to his attentic
it was beginning to grow. Now that he was aware of it, even if he didn
entirely believe me, I was betting he wouldn't be able to ignore it.

I nodded. 'She saw me on the beach and she was glad that I was sat
She didn't want me to go back in after her.'

'No.'

But he could feel it. I saw it on his face. It was beginning to hurt hir
to work its way through him, like shrapnel shifting inside.

Had his arm relaxed slightly? I thought so. The knife had moved
little way from Karli's throat. His hand was trembling.

Press the fucker.

'I'm sorry, Colin, but it's true. That's what you've got inside you now. 's something you didn't take account of, isn't it?'

His face had grown pale. He'd always been so painstaking, planning verything so carefully. So meticulous. Even the possibility that he'd ade a mistake was too much for him. It spoiled everything.

'The flipside of the sacrifice,' I said. 'That Lise didn't want me to die or her.'

His hand moved slowly down, until the knife hung at his side. I fought he urge to go straight at him. Instead, I glanced at his chest. He was reathing quickly and heavily, and I needed to drive it home.

'I wonder how many more like that you've got in there?'

His chest stopped moving. A second later, the knife fell to the ground, reating a whisper in the snow. He let out a faint noise. A moan.

I held my hand up again and shouted as loud as I could, 'Don't shoot. *Hold your fire!*'

I stared at Barnes for a moment. He was still looking right at me, but is face was blank, almost catatonic, as though his mind had shut itself own to escape from the horror he realised was there inside him. He eeded to poison love before he took it from someone; the idea that he'd ngested something pure was unbearable.

Karli was fighting against him, and he didn't seem to have the strength o hold her, so I stepped forwards carefully, and I took her from him.

His hand, empty now, fluttered uncertainly in the air. Then it went to is chest and he began to claw almost delicately at himself. Fresh blood rom his injuries rolled down. Then, without warning, his legs went and e joined his knife on the ground, curling slowly into a foetal position, ugging himself.

I stepped back, holding Karli tightly and looking down at her with omething approaching disbelief. She was alive. Barnes was down. I eemed to be okay, too, although I only realised now how badly my eart was hammering. Christ, I was shaking.

Footsteps behind me, pounding up the path, the garden.

I looked up at the window, the cracked glass and the smears of blood. ;ileen.

'No!'

Mercer came plunging past me.

'*What have you done to her?*'

I caught sight of his face, full of desperation and fear and hatred, and efore I could do anything he was on Barnes, half kneeling, half falling,

his big hands grabbing at his head, his throat, pounding him, then g
ping.

'*What have you done?*'

I put Karli Reardon down and grabbed Mercer, but he shrugged
off: almost knocked me over, as though I was nothing to him. In g
and loss, he'd found the strength he'd appeared to lack all day, and
seemed enormous now: the physical embodiment of every emotion
side him, solid and unstoppable as a bear.

'Stop him!'

But the other officers had approached, forming a tentative h
circle round the front of the house. Their guns were all pointed towa
the ground, double-handed grips. None of them made a move towa
Mercer. They just stood and watched.

He had Barnes by the neck and was pulling him up, slamming h
down again. Still shouting, screaming, his entire body tensed in conc
tration on hurting the man. Barnes was as lifeless as a doll: he went wh
he was slammed, his head loose on his neck.

I grabbed Mercer again, under one arm and up, getting him in a h
nelson, and I pulled back as hard as I could. He was like a boulder, d
weight. *Smack, smack.* Then there were other hands on him, the offic
around me finally coming to my aid. I stepped back and let them. It to
four to drag Mercer up and away, Barnes almost coming with him fo
moment, and then they were strong-arming him down the path.

For a moment, he continued screaming at them to let him go, but
words broke-down into incoherent sobs. I watched as he collapsed un
the weight of them, and he simply knelt there in the snow, turned av
from us, his hands covering his face.

I looked down at Barnes. He wasn't moving, and there was blood
over his face, his head. The snow beneath him was covered in smud
of crimson. I didn't know whether that was from Mercer's attack or
earlier injuries. I picked Karli up again. As I did so, the head of the arm
unit came and stood beside me, looking down at Barnes.

He blew out, then nodded to himself. 'Mercer saved your life the
The bastard was going for you next.' He stared at me for a second, so
were clear. 'Just like he did for Andy.'

I looked back at him. 'You stupid fuck.'

He shrugged. I passed him the baby, and he took her and wall
off down the path. After I'd glared at his back for a few more secon
I crouched beside Barnes and felt for a pulse. Then I felt some mo
Fucking hell.

A few metres away from me, Mercer was still on his knees. His sobs had disintegrated into nothing. I stared at him. Even with the circumstances as they were, he would surely go down for this.

Dear Detective Sergeant Mercer. If you've found this note, you've made your choice.

He'd made that choice all right, over and over again: his job over his wife. And now, too late, he'd done the opposite. I felt immense sorrow for him. Sympathy.

Our job is to support him.

I glanced up at the quiet, still house, at the blood on the window. Steeling myself. The first thing I could do to support him was go in there.

'Make sure he doesn't get in the house,' I called.

The officers just looked at me. But I guess we could all see that John Mercer wasn't going anywhere for now.

I stood up, taking a deep breath and thinking: deniability.

The knife lay close to Barnes's body.

I reached down and, for what it was worth, I moved it closer.

4 DECEMBER   7.30 A.M.
TEN MINUTES PAST DAWN

Eileen

Miles away, on the other side of the city, Eileen slept.

The dream was the same one she'd been having earlier, before she was woken by Hunter's phone call. In it, she drifted around the house, noting all the absences, the clothes missing from the wardrobe, the books from the shelves.

Days ago, when she'd talked to John about it, she'd been concerned about him abandoning her – taking his things and leaving her on her own. Now, however, she understood what the dream had been telling her. The missing items didn't belong to John; they were hers, and they always had been. Over the days to come, depending on how things went, the dream might well become reality. For now, as a start, she had simply abstracted herself. After she'd fixed the phone, Eileen had called Debra, and, as she'd expected, her sister hadn't hesitated to pick her up.

The dream drifted her into John's study; and at this point she frowned in her sleep. There was something different in here; something about the dream wasn't right. The room was impossibly frozen in the middle of a flurry of invisible violence. John's papers had been torn off the wall and they hung in the air. Eileen stood in the middle of it all, looking in wonder at the pages suspended around her.

Crack.

She turned to the window and saw the starring and blood there. It was as though somebody had punched the glass in rage, injuring himself in the process. A second later, the blood smeared itself across the pane.

Perhaps it was John: driven to anger upon realising what he'd lost. But that didn't feel right, either.

Her sleeping mind took her over to the computer desk. The note was where she had left it, and she looked down at it – then flinched as a mixture of blood and saliva appeared in the centre, spat there in disgust. John would never have done that. The unspoken logic of the dream told her that someone else was responsible, but she didn't know who.

Eileen picked it up carefully.

The blood was unnerving, but it didn't matter. It was only a dream, and she could remember exactly what the note said, because she'd deliberated over the words for so long. She settled a little. In her sleep, she looked at the piece of paper and read what her husband would read when he eventually returned home.

All right, John. If this is what you need, I hope you're happy.

But you've lied to me and you've let me down. You couldn't ring me when I asked you. You couldn't even tell me the truth. I can't describe how awful you've made me feel, but the worst of it is that I still love you and, because of that, I understand. It's what's most important to you, and so you have to do it. But understand that I can't be here any more while you do it. And maybe not after.

I'm safe and well. My sister is coming to pick me up. Please don't contact me. I'll be in touch in my own time.

Love, always, E x x

Asleep in her sister's spare room, Eileen rolled over and stretched her arm out across the empty side of the bed. And finally, she dreamed of nothing at all.

EPILOGUE

The service was due to start at two o'clock, and I made sure I didn't arrive early. I didn't want to sit inside the main chapel. For one thing, there would probably be a lot of people attending, and I had no wish to take a seat from someone who had more right to be there than I did. For another, I'd been in two minds about attending at all. Given what had happened, I'd thought I might feel strange and out of place.

But there were things I was curious about, and in the end I'd bought a smart black suit and practically pulled myself out of the flat. Five to two found me parking up on a stretch of gravel across the road from the church. Christmas was only a few days away, but the weather had been calm since the events of two weeks before. It hadn't snowed again since. Today, the air was cold and hard; the sky a crisp, clear blue. As I crossed the road, the tarmac glittered, even now retaining a sparkle of frost from the night just gone.

I walked up the driveway by myself, the envelope in my hand. I hadn't been sure about bringing that, either. I'd picked it up on the way out, but I didn't know yet what I would do with it. Perhaps I would just carry it away again at the end of the service.

There was a bitter breeze. It pressed ice against my face, and rolled my tie across my jacket.

At the top of the drive, by the church, a line of black cars was parked. The procession had already arrived, the coffin been taken in. Groups of people, young and old, were gathering around the entrance, following the family and close friends who had gone inside. Others waited on the grass verges nearby, finishing cigarettes. Nobody was talking. Everyone seemed hunched around their thoughts and feelings, as though protecting them from the cold.

A peaked stone archway led into the porch area of the church, with chapels to either side. The doorway to the left, the chapel where the service was taking place, was full of people, the one to the right less so.

267

I moved that way. A video screen had been set up at the far end, so t[l]
the overflow could watch the service from there.

I sat down in a pew at the back, by myself.

'Jesus said, "I am the resurrection and the life. Those who believe in [m]
even though they die, will live. And everyone who lives and believes [in]
me will never die."'

The minister paused, pushing his glasses up his nose. Behind him, [the]
choir, wearing plain white sheets, looked like candles, squat and unlit

'We are here today to mourn the passing of Scott Andrew Banks.'

Even through the video feed, I could hear people crying quietly. Sc[ott]
had been found shortly after dawn that day, tied to a tree half a mile fr[om]
the clearing. The only time I'd seen him, beyond the fractured, ble[ak]
painting on his computer, was in the autopsy report. From that, I kn[ew]
he'd been wounded in exactly the same way as the man I'd interview[ed]
in the hospital; Barnes, or whatever his real name was, had created a m[ir-]
ror image of Scott's suffering on his own body. Scott had been left to [die]
slowly from exposure, but we'd probably never know exactly what ha[p-]
pened between them that night.

On the screen we could see the minister and the first two rows of [the]
congregation. I thought I could pick out Jodie on the right-hand side [of]
the front. It was strange that I'd yet to meet her. I saw her briefly th[at]
night in the department, but I didn't speak to her and the investigati[on]
had been taken out of our hands the next morning. Hunter's man h[ad]
interviewed her a few days later, and I'd read the transcript. That w[as]
when the questions had started to occur to me. What interested me m[ore]
was what *wasn't* there. It reminded me of the photograph Scott had ke[pt]
in his wallet. The way we see only what people are prepared to show [us.]

'Death is always tragic,' the minister said. 'The absence of a loved o[ne]
is something most of us have experienced, and each of us knows that t[he]
loss is cataclysmic. In Scott's case, a vibrant and talented young man w[as]
taken from us before his time, which makes the loss even harder to be[ar.]
He leaves behind him a mother, Teri, a father, Michael, and his girlfrie[nd,]
Jodie. In a few moments we will all sing a hymn together, and then Jo[die]
will speak to us about Scott and share some of her memories with us.'

I looked down at the envelope in my hands, still undecided abo[ut]
whether or not I should give it to her. Jodie and Scott's computer w[as]
impounded at the department, but the hard drive had been itemised a[nd]
the document in the envelope hadn't been included in the list of files t[he]
IT team had found. Clearly, though, Scott had written it, which mea[nt]

that Barnes must have deleted it when he abducted him. But he had taken it to use as notes in the woods, to refer to as he tried to turn Scott against Jodie.

Five Hundred Reasons Why I Love You.

Barnes had left it, along with the note to Mercer, in the old storeroom. A few pages at the end either hadn't printed or had gone missing, because the list stopped at Number 274. But still, it was something. On impulse, I'd made a copy. I shouldn't have, but I thought that Scott might have wanted Jodie to have one. After reading her interview transcript, I wasn't so sure. There were things I needed to talk to her about first.

'Although our loved ones are taken from us, we must, in our grief, try to remember one thing. They have sailed over the horizon, but a horizon is simply a matter of what we currently see. One day we, too, will make that journey, and we will see them again. This we trust and believe, through Jesus Christ, our Lord.'

Amen.

I settled back. In my everyday life, no matter how much I might want to on an emotional level, I could never justify believing in any of the comforts of religion. An afterlife, a purpose to it all, a god looking down on us with any sense of benevolence – to me, it was all just wishful thinking. People who had left us no longer existed, except in our hearts and memories. There was no eternal reward or punishment. No divine plan.

But I'd found in the past that funerals allowed me some time off from that hard intellectual position. For half an hour, I'd be able to take some comfort. I'd be able to imagine that people did go on and that, when they were taken from us, it was either because it was their time or because someone or something had stolen them away: a theft God had watched and taken count of. For half an hour, I could fool myself that the question 'why' had an answer that made at least a subtle kind of sense.

Today, though, I didn't feel that way.

When I thought back to what had happened at Mercer's house, I knew it hadn't been any kind of message from beyond the grave. Quite the opposite, in fact. There was nobody to receive a message from. Lise remained lost at sea, and wherever her body was, she wasn't thinking anything any more. She wasn't hating me or loving me. She was simply gone.

What did it matter what she had thought of me during those brief moments in the sea? I'd never know what had gone through her mind, and whatever I chose to believe wouldn't change anything. Because I missed her so much, I was driven to imagine the expression on her face *right now*, as if she was still here. I wanted to hear the things she might say. But there was no reality to any of it beyond the one I imposed; the one I made up for myself. The only real afterlife people have is in the minds of those they leave behind.

I could choose to base that on one awful, unknowable moment at the end or, instead, I could think of all the years leading up to that. If I chose the latter, there was no doubt about what I'd see on her face or the things I'd hear her say.

From now on, I'd decided, I would choose to picture her smiling.

And I'd imagine that, when she talked to me, she'd be whispering it in my ear and telling me the truth.

There was nothing you could have done.

After the service, Jodie walked out of the church, squinting against the bright daylight. The whole sky was grey-white, but light shone through, from behind, and everywhere she looked the world was sparkling. It was freezing, though. The steam from her breath billowed in the air, and, along with the sudden cold on her cheeks, it reminded her too much of the night it had happened.

Keep it together.

But she was still trembling. A couple of times during the reading, she'd had to stop and take a sip of water. Her hand had been visibly shaking then, and now it was even worse. Her throat was tight, her stomach … The whole core of her was tensed and constricted. She recognised the sensation. It was a mixture of panic and despair, and it was rising inexorably towards the surface. But she refused to allow herself to cry; she simply couldn't do that. Mustn't. If she did, people would comfort her and she would break down properly, perhaps even irretrievably.

Except she wouldn't, of course, and that was the problem. She was feeling pain and grief and guilt that were impossible to bear, and yet she continued to do so. Each second led to the next, and the whole time something inside was burning, impossible to soothe, as if her soul had fallen asleep too close to a fire. If anyone touched her, if she thought too deeply about what had happened, it would wake up and begin screaming.

Because nobody here knew the truth.

But if it hurt her – if it was difficult – that was good. She deserved this, and she couldn't shy away from it. Funerals were supposed to be an important, cathartic part of the grieving process: you could let it all out, and everybody would join you; all of you attempting to avert your eyes from the tragedy and instead celebrate the life leading up to it. It was supposed to be a chance a say goodbye; a chance to say: we loved you. No matter how much she wanted to hide, to disappear, it was her duty to be at the centre of that. She owed it not only to Scott, but to the people attending. In many ways, she represented the heart of the tragedy, and so she had a role to perform. People needed her. It wasn't their fault that in reality she had no right to be the focus of the pain, that she had caused it all.

You can't think that way. It's stupid.

It wasn't, though. The guilt she felt was righteous in its intensity. But she couldn't share any of it and she had no right to collapse under it; no right to accept sympathy or comfort.

Jodie took a deep breath, and began moving between groups of people. Circulating; letting people know she was okay, and checking that they were, too. She shook hands and embraced their mutual friends, Scott's family and colleagues. 'Thank you so much for coming.' Over and over again, she heard the same things from different people. 'We're so sorry for your loss,' they said. 'Just let me know if I can do anything.' It was almost unbearable, but she forced herself to nod: to play the role that was expected of her. There were gentle smiles as brief memories were shared. People told her how lovely her tribute had been, and she had to fight back the urge to turn and run. Yes, how much she had loved him. None of them knew about how she'd betrayed him, or about how false her words had seemed to her. All of them except the handful at the end, when she had started to unravel: 'I miss him so much. I wish he could be here so I could explain.' And even those words – people wouldn't have understood what lay behind them.

It built up inside, person after person. Jodie could feel herself faltering, struggling. She couldn't cry. Couldn't allow herself to be as devastated as she felt. The knowledge that the people speaking to her would mistake it for grief only made it worse. But she couldn't take it. She would have to escape from this soon, before she drowned in her sorrow, her shame.

I'm sorry, she thought.

There was a man standing slightly away from everybody else, leaning against a tree, watching her patiently. Jodie glanced at him, then away, unnerved by the way he was staring at her. It was like he'd caught her out. Who was he? There was something familiar about him, so she looked back. He was about her age, tall, wearing a black suit and holding an envelope in his hand. She placed him a second later: she'd seen him that night at the police station.

A detective. Her heart skipped slightly.

Now that they'd made eye contact, he smiled at her, but even though it was friendly, she looked away quickly. It was Mark something; she recognised him now. He was the one who'd interviewed the man in the hospital, the one John had spoken to on the phone, when she'd still thought Scott was alive. The euphoria then was in stark contrast to the despair she had felt ever since. Now she was beginning to panic, too.

You're going to have to talk to him.

Okay. Jodie gathered herself together, trying to keep calm, and walked over to where he was standing. The breeze blew a strand of hair across her face, and she brushed it back behind her ear.

'Hello,' she said, squinting against the light. 'Thank you for coming.'

'I wanted to come,' Mark said. 'I didn't know whether I should ... but anyway, I wanted to. How are you holding up?'

'Oh. Well, you know ...'

She faltered; it was such a direct and personal question for someone to ask, especially someone who didn't know her. But at the same time there was something honest about it. She smiled without humour.

'Not that well.'

'I understand,' he said. 'We were taken off the investigation, but I did read the interview. For what it's worth, I'm sorry about what happened to you.'

'Thank you.'

But she noticed again the way he'd worded it, offering sympathy not only for her loss but for the entire situation: 'what happened to you'.

The panic was stronger now. Did he know?

'How's John?' she said.

Mark looked off down the driveway, considering that. There didn't look to be an easy answer to the question, but she knew a lot had happened that she wasn't aware of. She hadn't seen John since that night, but the officer who'd taken her statement had alluded to the trouble he was in. There were hints of a larger picture, but not enough for her to see it.

'He's all right,' Mark said finally. 'He's not with the department at the moment, and there are investigations pending. But it could have been a lot worse.'

'If you see him, tell him I said thank you.'

'I will.'

Neither of them spoke for a moment, but Jodie didn't feel able to move away. On some level, she didn't want to.

The silence prompted her. 'What about the man?'

Mark was still looking down the driveway: 'He died.'

She'd been told already, at the interview – and she realised that Mark would surely have known. It was as though the truth was being gently coaxed out of her without her consent. Her heart was beating too quickly. But she didn't move away.

Mark said, 'We still don't know who he really was, but I guess in many ways it doesn't matter. We know what he did to people, the choices he forced them to make.'

She was trembling again, but she tried to keep her voice calm.

'Right.'

Mark looked at her.

'The impossible choices,' he said.

For a moment, the panic threatened to overwhelm her. He knew. Jodie stared at him, and he stared back. She was frozen. But there was a sympathy in his face which was entirely different from the comfort offered by the other people here. It was genuine, and it was full of understanding. Despite herself, Jodie felt relief. She wanted to fall into that look, collapse and rest for a while. Instead, she felt her face crumple, and she began to cry.

'It's okay,' he said.

She hadn't meant to lie in the interview; it had been more about what she didn't say than what she did, and the omission had been natural. When she'd told the policeman who interviewed her that the man had locked her in the storeroom, that was true. And when he'd asked what happened next, she'd told him that after a while she'd heard Scott begin screaming, and that was also true. He hadn't asked what had happened in between.

When she'd been locked in the storeroom, the voice had told her not to think about certain things, to put them out of her head; and that really was all she'd done. At the time, what mattered had been getting out of there alive, and some things – her guilt and shame – weren't going to help her. The voice's advice had been practical and reassuring. *Don't think about that.* She had to get out of the situation, and she had to do everything she could to make sure they were both okay. But ultimately, that *she* was okay.

So she had discarded the emotions and feelings that would hinder her in that. Very deliberately, she had tried not to think about what happened when the man in the devil mask had come back to the storeroom. About the choice she'd had to make. And about how quickly the voice had made the decision on her behalf.

Scott. The voice had told her to remember the pain he was in, to use it when it came down to it, and she had. But now those screams filled her thoughts. The voice had told her to forget about the choice to save her own life, and now, below the surface, she could think of little else.

I'm so sorry.

Mark put his hand on her shoulder while she cried.

'It's okay,' he repeated softly. 'That way I see it, that kind of thing is nobody else's business. The people involved have to live with the consequences. It's not for anybody else to judge.'

Jodie was looking at the ground. But she nodded.

After a moment, Mark gave her shoulder a slight squeeze, then took his hand away. 'Here.'

He was holding something out to her. Jodie expected to see the envelope he'd been holding, but instead he was offering her a small card. She took it. A business card. It had his name and departmental telephone number on it. The implication was clear.

'Thank you,' she said.

'If you ever want to talk,' he said, 'you know where to find me.'

'Thank you.'

'It's okay.' He stepped back, ready to leave. 'Take care of yourself, Jodie.'

She noticed that he was now holding the envelope tightly against his stomach. Guarding it, almost.

'What's that?' Jodie asked.

He smiled at her gently.

'Something for another day,' he said.